I0584957

Thomas Sergeant Perry

English Literature in the Eighteenth Century

Thomas Sergeant Perry

English Literature in the Eighteenth Century

ISBN/EAN: 9783337737726

Printed in Europe, USA, Canada, Australia, Japan

Cover: Foto ©Andreas Hilbeck / pixelio.de

More available books at **www.hansebooks.com**

ENGLISH LITERATURE

IN

THE EIGHTEENTH CENTURY

BY

THOMAS SERGEANT PERRY

NEW YORK

HARPER & BROTHERS, FRANKLIN SQUARE

1883

TO

JOHN FISKE

WHOSE FRIENDSHIP AND EXAMPLE HAVE CONTINUALLY ENCOURAGED ME

I AFFECTIONATELY DEDICATE THIS BOOK

PREFACE.

THIS volume contains the substance of a course of lectures delivered in Cambridge, and repeated in part in Philadelphia, during the winter of 1881–82. This statement will, it is hoped, incline the reader to overlook the direct appeals to his memory and attention, which may be permissible to one reading aloud to a friendly audience, although less pardonable in the formality of print.

In preparing this book for the press I have endeavored to make the references to the works of other writers as full and as exact as possible, but I would once more explicitly acknowledge my indebtedness to Mr. J. A. Symonds, whose volumes on Italian literature have been of constant service; to Mr. Leslie Stephen, whose " History of English Thought in the Eighteenth Century " is a thorough exposition of many subjects barely mentioned by me; to Mr. Karl Hillebrand's profound " German Thought," and to Mr. Alexandre Beljame's " Le Public et les Hommes de Lettres." This last-mentioned book I have made use of continually, especially in the pages on the periodicals that preceded the *Tatler*, on Pope, and on Addison. Mr. Beljame's thoroughness and precision make his volume of inestimable value to the student of the first half of the last century, and I am the more desirous of insisting in this place upon my obligations to him because his suggestiveness is so manifold that continual reference to his pages would have been monotonous. The literary histories of Hettner, Biedermann, Julian Schmidt, and Koberstein have been frequently consulted, and seldom in vain.

It will be noticed that this book is by no means a complete history of the literature of the last century: many important authors, like Prior and Smollett, have but a word given them; Fielding receives no full discussion; and many other writers are not even mentioned. My aim, however, has been rather to supplement the histories by pointing out, so far as I could, the more evident laws that govern literature. I have accordingly tried to show the principles that went to the formation of the literature of the last century, and also the causes of its overthrow. Many will doubtless be unwilling to subscribe to the belief that letters are controlled by laws. Mrs. Oliphant, a writer who deserves and receives the respect of all her many readers, affirms, in her admirable "Literary History of England in the End of the Eighteenth and the Beginning of the Nineteenth Century" (i. 7 and 8), that "every singer is a new miracle—created if nothing else is created—no growth developed out of precedent poets, but something sprung from an impulse which is not reducible to law." If this statement is correct, literature forms a singular exception to what has seemed a universal rule. When we consider Mrs. Oliphant's delightful novels we find them occupying a normal position in the development of fiction, with their exact drawing of life and avoidance of direct

moral teaching. Mrs. Oliphant acknowledges the existence in society of " a slow progression, which, however
faint, however deferred, yet gradually goes on, leaving
one generation always a trifle better than that which
preceded it, with some scrap of new possession, some
right assured, some small inheritance gained. From
age to age the advance may be small, yet it is appreci-
able. . . . New modifications and conditions arise, the
public sense is awakened, or it is cultivated, or at all
events it is changed. . . . The reforms from which we
hoped most, the advances for which we struggled most
strenuously, do not produce all the good we expected ;
but we cannot, nor would we, undo them. In everything there is a current onward, perhaps downward, but
never back. . . . The principle indeed changes from
time to time. It comes to a climax. . . . All is not absolute good or advantage to the human race; but yet
the race is stepping onward, it discovers new powers, it
learns new ameliorations, and if it also makes proof of
novel sufferings and dangers, it finds new defences and
medicines for them. . . . It is in fact a real progress
through a thousand drawbacks, and every age leaves
some foundation upon which the next can build." This
lucid description of the gradual progress of society might,
it seems to me, apply perfectly to, literature, but this,
and its application to art, Mrs. Oliphant denies, because
we have not advanced upon Shakspere, Bacon, Chaucer,
and Fra Angelico. This is, in brief, her reason for
limiting the extent to which law may be affirmed to
exist. According to her, and to a very current opinion
which she represents, literature and art are outside of
law.

Yet if we are unwilling to regard art and literature as miraculous, may we not be justified in supposing that there is some confusion in thus limiting the rules that govern the human mind in its other relations? Does it follow from the proposition that literature is governed by law that there should be a regular gradation of genius? that Dryden's plays should be superior to Shakspere's, and Dean Milman's to both? If these expectations are disappointed, is the law of progress at fault? I think not. Those who agree with Mrs. Oliphant in finding progress in political history certainly cannot find, let us say, in the arguments uttered a few years ago in Congress in favor of what was called the Force Law, an advance upon the position that was taken in Parliament, nearly two and a half centuries ago, against Charles I.; yet no one will deny the general advance in personal freedom throughout the civilized world since that day, and that in this country liberty is not a mere oratorical catch-word. The great literary glory of the reign of Elizabeth was but one expression of the same fervor that inspired Drake and Raleigh; and in our own time, when literature appears to languish, Mrs. Oliphant's own novels are expressing the same wider interest in the people that in politics makes itself felt as the spread of democracy. The construction of an arrears-of-rent bill is less dramatic than was the attempt to arrest the five members of the House of Commons, just as Marlowe's "Dr. Faustus" is more thrilling than any novel of the realists, but one is as much governed by law as the other, is equally the result of antecedent causes. To ask nothing but heroics of literature would be like demanding

nothing but the expression of devotion in painting.
May we not hope that the present interest in reality
and distrust of literary conventions may in time help
the production of masterpieces? George Eliot's novels,
for example, show us how far the province of literature
has been enlarged, how great has been the addition to
the material of writers, if the phrase may be allowed,
within a century. There is no need of fearing that
heroism is extinct, and it is not impossible that literature may yet flash into a brilliancy for which long years
spent in studying real life shall have prepared writers
and readers. At any rate, a genius, in the future as in
the past and the present, is bound by the necessity of
building on the foundations that society is laying every
day. Every apparently insignificant action of ours contributes its mite to the sum of circumstances which inspire the writer, whose vision may be dim or inaccurate,
but who can see only what exists or may exist, and is
limited by experience whether this be treated literally
or be modified by the imagination. No writer can escape this limitation any more than he can imagine a
sixth sense. If these statements are accurate, and a
general, although not uniform, progress is acknowledged
to exist in society, literature may also be said to be
under the sway of law, or, rather, to move in accordance
with law. We shall not expect every later writer to be
greater than Shakspere, any more than we shall expect
a greater enthusiasm for high truths in the birthplace
of Daisy Miller than in the Athens of Pericles. Yet it
may well be that, although the vivid genius is absent,
there is a general widening of human interest and sym-
pathies, which will be more apparent when it is crystal-

lized by some great writer than it is now, when, as Cottle sang of climbing Malvern Hills,

> " It needs the evidence of close deduction
> To know that ever I shall reach the top."

Before closing, I wish to express my gratitude to the trustees and the officials of the Boston Public Library for their unfailing kindness.

My hearty thanks are also due to my friend, Mr. George Pellew, for many valuable suggestions and for much assistance in correcting proofs.

CONTENTS.

CHAPTER I.

CHAPTER II.

CHAPTER III.

CHAPTER IV.

CHAPTER V.

CHAPTER VI.

CHAPTER VII.

CHAPTER VIII.

CHAPTER IX.

ENGLISH LITERATURE

IN

THE EIGHTEENTH CENTURY.

———

CHAPTER I.

I. WHATEVER the period that may be chosen as the starting-point in the study of literature, and especially of modern literature, it is necessary to go back to find out the origin of the theories and the formulas then existing, to see what influences were at work, and to learn the general current of the thought of the time. Even if these lectures began with Chaucer, it is obvious that we should have to study Chaucer's indebtedness to Italian models and to mediæval literature before we could fully comprehend his precise position; and in beginning with the writers of the Restoration period, while we shall have to study briefly those authors who went before as well as some of those who lived in other countries, we have as a sort of excuse for choosing this as a starting-point that with these writers what we feel to be modern literature begins.

Of course, this is not a scientific division. By no stretch of language can Shakspere or Ben Jonson be numbered among ancient authors: all that I mean is

1

this, that Addison and Pope are the first writers of whom we feel that they are, so to speak, our fellow-citizens rather than remote beings whom we admire for their intellectual gifts. As Vernon Lee puts it, in speaking of the Italian writers of the last century: "It is in dealing with them that we first find that we have to do no longer with our remote ancestors living in castellated houses, travelling on horseback, fighting in the streets, and carousing at banquets, but with the grandfathers of our grandfathers, steady, formal, hypocritical people, paying visits in coaches, going to operas, giving dinner-parties, and litigating and slandering rather than assassinating and poisoning." *

This feeling is due to many causes. The fact that civilization was then firmly settled gave a different tone to literature. Earlier, the joyous pride in the possession of national life, which was strongly felt in the time of Elizabeth, on account of the awakening of that age to the consciousness of new powers; the great discoveries in physical science; the opening of unknown lands; the revelation of the beauties of classical literature; the unaccustomed religious freedom — all these things inspired the writers of what we call the Elizabethan period with a sort of primal fire and energy which make them seem remote from our cooler, critical days.

They appeared even more remote to our ancestors at the time of Queen Anne. Then the pride of national life had faded into political rancor, and the early enthusiasm for science had been succeeded by a period of patient research and examination of detail. The Royal Society was founded in 1662, and it had formed a nucleus for the reception and dissemination of new discoveries. What had been widespread superstitions gave way before new

---

* "Studies of the Eighteenth Century in Italy," p. 10.

truths : astrology, for instance, lost its hold on the teachers of the people ; witchcraft ceased to be believed in. The world was freed from a dead weight of idle terrors. Bacon's influence, too, helped to turn the current of men's thoughts to material progress, so that what we feel to be the underlying principles of modern civilization began to be fixed towards the end of the seventeenth century. Admiration for intellectual greatness does not produce this feeling of kinship so surely as does agreement in looking at practical questions, and our full comprehension of the past, and our consequent sympathy with it, begin practically with the generation to which Dryden belonged. All before then seems to belong to the imagination ; he and his contemporaries appear to be the first to fall within the range of our observation. Then, too, not only is the sequence of thought unbroken since that time—for, it must be distinctly borne in mind, this sequence cannot be broken—but we have abundant material from which to study its advance ; and the whole intellectual life of the present century is the direct outcome of what was hoped or feared, taught or denounced, in the last century. It is time that we cease to repeat one of its faults, and learn to treat our predecessors with the respect they deserve.

This is particularly our duty now when we boast our ability to enjoy all varieties of literary work, when we have a kind word for every man who has any claim to greatness. Of one thing we may be sure, that this universal taste accompanies meagre performance in the way of creation. Now, for instance, when the English drama is entirely a thing of the past, the taste of the reading public is exceedingly catholic ; but if at the present time real plays were written which interested us, our feelings would be enlisted in behalf of any older dramatist who seemed to support our theory of how plays should be

written, and against those who did not. At the time of
the Restoration, Shakspere's fame had greatly diminish-
ed ; yet there was considerable interest in the drama, and
the qualities that were most admired were very different from those of the Elizabethan era : the zeal which
animated the playwrights after 1660, their eagerness for
correctness, rendered them only more sensitive to what
seemed to them to be Shakspere's roughness. Moreover, to take the dramatic literature alone, the original
native vigor had gone out, giving place, as we shall see
more at length hereafter, to a form of dramatic composition which substituted a very artificial mode of composition for the wild luxuriousness of the great play-writers.
The time had become a critical one : people had begun to
study methods and workmanship, to make comparisons
between different theories, and to let observation replace
inspiration. This, too, is another point of resemblance between that time and our own.

II. Another reason why this period seems closely connected with the present is, that it was then that English prose began to be written—a prose which we can
understand without difficulty, which, except that it is
much more intelligible, is practically the prose of the present day. This may be better illustrated by a few examples than it can be described in many pages. Thus, to
study some of the earlier prose * in Hobbes's "Leviathan "
(1651), we find this method of writing (p. 170) : "And as
to Rebellion in particular against Monarchy ; one of the
most frequent causes of it, is the Reading of the books of
Policy, and Histories of the ancient Greeks, and Romans ;
from which, young men, and all others that are unprovided

---

* Nathanael Ingelo's " Bentivoglio and Urania," 1650, is exceptionally
well written.

of the Antidote of solid Reason, receiving a strong and delightful impression of the great exploits of war, atchieved by the Conductors of their Armies, receive withal a pleasing Idea of all they have done besides ; and imagine their great prosperity not to have proceeded from the æmulation of particular men, but from the vertue of their popular form of government : not considering the frequent Seditions, and Civil wars, produced by the imperfection of their Policy. From the reading, I say, of such books, men have undertaken to kill their Kings, because the Greek and Latin writers, in their books and discourses of Policy, make it lawful and laudable, for any man so to do ; provided before he do it, he call him Tyrant. For they say not *Regicide*, that is, killing of a king, but *Tyrannicide*, that is, killing of a Tyrant, is lawfull. From the same books, they that live under a Monarch conceive an opinion, that the Subjects in a Popular Common-wealth enjoy Liberty; but that in a Monarchy they are all slaves. I say they that live under a Monarchy conceive such an opinion ; not they that live under a Popular Government: for they find no such matter. In summe, I cannot imagine how anything can be more prejudicial to a Monarchy, than the allowing of such things to be publiquely read, without present applying of such correctives of discreet Masters, as are fit to take away their Venome : Which Venome I will not doubt to compare to the biting of a mad Dog, which is a disease the Physicians call *Hydrophobia*, or fear of Water. For as he that is so bitten, has a continual torment of thirst, and yet abhorreth water ; and is in such an estate, as if the poyson endeavoured to convert him into a Dog : So when a Monarchy is once bitten to the quick, by those Democratical writers, that continually snarle at that estate ; it wanteth nothing more than a strong Monarch, which nevertheless, out of a certain *Ty-*

rannophobia, or fear of being strongly governed, when they have him, they abhorre."

Another example may be taken from Burton's "Anatomy of Melancholy" (1621) : "Chess-play is a good and witty exercise of the mind for some kind of men, and fit for such melancholy, Rhasis holds, as are idle, and have extravagant, impertinent thoughts, or troubled with cares, nothing better to distract their mind, and alter their meditations : invented (some say) by the general of an army in a famine, to keep soldiers from mutiny : but if it proceed from overmuch study, in such a case it may do more harm than good ; it is a game too troublesome for some men's brains, too full of anxiety, all out as bad as study ; besides it is a testy, choleric game, and very offensive to him that loseth the mate. William the Conqueror, in his younger years, playing at chess with a Prince of France (Dauphiné was not annexed to that crown in those days), losing a mate, knocked the chess-board about his pate, which was a cause afterward of much enmity between them."

Perhaps more characteristic is this: "He that shall but see that geometrical tower of Garezenda at Bologna in Italy, the steeple and clock at Strasburg, will admire the effects of art, or that engine of Archimedes, to remove the earth itself, if he had but a place to fasten his instrument : Archimedis Cochlea, and rare devices to corrivate waters, musical instruments, and tri-syllable echoes, again, again, and again repeated, with myriads of such. What vast tomes are extant in law, physic, and divinity, for profit, pleasure, practice, speculation, in verse or prose, etc. ! their names alone are the subject of whole volumes, we have thousands of authors of all sorts, many great libraries full well furnished like so many dishes of meat, served out for several palates ; and he is a very block that is affected with none of them."

, There is no need of many such instances to prove the general rule that English prose is a modern acquirement. Even Milton, with his wonderful ear for rhythm, was often as clumsy as the others when he undertook to write prose, which was the work, as he said, of his left hand. For instance ("The Reason of Church Government Urged Against Prelaty," lib. i. chap. i.) : "To come within the narrowness of Household Government, observation will shew us many deep Counsellors of State and Judges do demean themselves incorruptly in the settled course of affairs, and many worthy Preachers upright in their Lives, powerful in their Audience ; but look upon either of these Men where they are left to their own disciplining at home, and you shall soon perceive, for all their single knowledge and uprightness, how deficient they are in the regulating of their own Family ; not only in what may concern the virtuous and decent composure of their minds in their several places, but that which is of a lower and easier performance, the right possessing of the outward Vessel, their Body, in Health or Sickness, Rest or Labour, Diet or Abstinence, whereby to render it more pliant to the Soul, and useful to the Common-wealth: when if men were but as good to discipline themselves, as some are to tutor their Horses and Hawks, it could not be so gross in most households."

These extracts are not intended to throw doubts on Hobbes's humor, Burton's learning, or Milton's eloquence ; and I pass over Bacon's simplicity, Hooker's fine harmonies, and Jeremy Taylor's poetical prose, contenting myself with showing that before the Restoration there was no practical, every-day prose. Milton, when, as he said, he wished "to soar a little," had a magnificent abundance of words at his command, and at times he broke out into a rich poetical prose. But when he had to write some plain description, his prose lumbered as clumsily as a heavy cart

over rough paving-stones.   The same man who could write
such lines as

> " From morn
> To noon he fell, from noon to dewy eve,
> A summer's day; and with the setting sun
> Dropt from the zenith like a falling star,"

seemed when he was writing prose to have lost all knowledge of syntax, and all appreciation of the balance of a
sentence.   The trouble was that the writers before Dryden would weigh down their prose with numberless paren-
theses, side-remarks, and let their sentences involve themselves inextricably.   Only when their prose took on a
poetical form could they command it.   Of Bunyan, on
the other hand, who knew nothing of the classicisms which
so often embarrassed his more learned contemporaries,
but who was the master of a true colloquial style, I shall
speak later.   That this awkward form of writing should
have lasted long, need not be wondered at.   In the first
place, there was no great reading public that should demand clearness.   Milton's pamphlets were read by scholars
who probably thought that in reading English instead of
Latin they were making sufficient sacrifice to indolence ;
and the practice of writing awkward Latin made them tolerant of clumsy English.   Then, what we see of the present
condition of the German language may serve to show us
that it is only by a great deal of attrition that a simple
style is produced.   We never open a German book without noticing the artificial construction and shapeless form
of the German sentence, both of which are sure to disappear in time as the language is more used.   If we read
Plattdeutsch, we find perfectly simple constructions ; and
so, in the books that were read by the populace in the
middle of the seventeenth century, we find a style which
is readily intelligible to us nowadays.   It was pedantry

that injured the English style then, just as it does the German now. Howell's "Letters," to be sure (1618–1650), were written in an easy, graceful manner ; but then he not only could boast that he was able to pray in a separate language for every day of the week and in seven on Sunday, but he also was familiar with foreign literatures, and doubtless copied Balzac, the famous letter-writer who had really nothing to say, and so devoted himself to saying that very well.

What produced the change in writing English prose we may take to have been, as Mr. Saintsbury has said in his life of Dryden, in the "English Men of Letters" series, "the influences of the pulpit, of political discussion, of miscellaneous writing—partly fictitious, partly discursive—and, lastly, of literary criticism." All of these things, we may notice, were different varieties of the one great cause, practice. When only scholars read, the theatre supplied the literary pabulum of the great majority of the people ; the Puritans read the Bible, and but little else— and the "Pilgrim's Progress" shows how the populace had made the phraseology of the Bible their own ; but as political matters became of more general interest, the pamphlets adapted themselves to the wants of readers.

There can, too, be but little doubt that those who were accustomed to listening rather than to reading acquired a tolerance for spoken words which those who are mainly accustomed to reading do not enjoy. As Dr. Johnson said when he snatched the book from some one who began to read aloud to him, we can read much more easily with our eyes than with our ears : and so doubtless we have lost to some extent the possibility of comprehending at once the long sentences of plays which our ancestors grasped at once. This may to some extent explain, what is otherwise not very clear, why ignorant audiences enjoyed, for instance, Shakspere's and Ben Jonson's plays, which we

prefer to read by ourselves ; how these comparatively ignorant people were able to listen intelligently to long decla-
mations. This, however, is but a digression.

The extent to which theology was studied we can hardly imagine at present ; and the hot discussions that raged
on all sorts of ecclesiastical questions were far from having
a civilizing effect on literature.

III. With the Restoration, however, there came new
influences. Questions of politics, as I have said, presented
themselves for settlement, and the long-winded style soon
ceased to find readers.

It is customary to explain the change in literature by
ascribing the various modifications to what is called the
French influence which entered the country with the return of Charles II. There is a great deal of truth in the
statement, but not enough to give a complete explanation
of the striking differences between the literature of the
Elizabethan era and what we may vaguely call that of
Queen Anne. And, if the statement were precise, it would
still be necessary to explain what is meant by the French
influence. Taken vaguely, the French influence in literature lay in the direction of correctness, especially in the
way of correctness as compared with the work of rough,
untutored genius. Yet the tendency towards precision and
the observance of rules was more widespread than might be
imagined by those who think they wholly account for it
by calling it French. We may ask, meanwhile, how did
the French happen to be interested in it ? and, also, by
whom were their rules imposed upon the English ?

We are all familiar with the enormous influence of the
Renaissance on modern society. The light came from antiquity that expelled the dull gloom of the dark ages,
and the world seemed young again. The fall of Con-
stantinople in 1453 sent a number of Greeks to seek new

homes in Europe, where they should be secure from Mahometan tyranny. Already, too, in Italy scholars had begun to take their shattered relations to the past. While the rest of Europe was still in darkness, more than a glimmering of light had begun to dawn in that peninsula. There were scholars already there who had made the best of such advantages as they had, and were eager for more. The invention of the printing-press, the first of the great mechanical inventions, in 1450, suddenly brought copies of the ancient authors to hungry readers, and literature began anew. The mediæval literature, it must be remembered, was considerable in amount ; but it had grown artificial and unfruitful when these finer models were rediscovered. It is impossible at this time to describe the growth of literature in the different countries of Europe. There is opportunity for the mention of but a few of the important facts connected with the way in which literature developed itself. In the first place, we should bear in mind the extent to which the European knowledge of antiquity is, in the main, a knowledge of Rome, and of Greece through Rome. Roman literature was for the most part an awkward copy of Greek originals : its early native development was crowded out of existence by the superior Hellenic culture. The rude mythology of Latium gave way before the Greek gods and goddesses with all their legendary history ; the humbler Latin deities surviving only in the simple faith of the rustics. The Greek arts found new patrons in Italy, and almost all Roman literature was made to follow Greek models. Horace's odes, Terence's plays, Vergil's free use of Homer, sufficiently illustrate this. Now, when the classical literature was discovered anew, Greek and Roman writers were not so clearly distinguished as they have been in later times. They were classical writers, and that was enough.

What we notice in modern Europe is this, that it was much more commonly the Roman than the Grecian writers who served as models. Thus the modern drama of Italy, France, and England began with copying Seneca in tragedy, and Plautus and Terence in comedy. The pastorals of the same countries, which were long a favorite method of writing, were imitations of Vergil and Calpurnius rather than of the Greek originals.*

In a hasty sketch of the work of centuries, only somewhat general statements can be made ; and, without going into further particulars or noting the few exceptions, it may be enough to say that modern literature was built up on a tradition of a tradition. At first, the effect of the Renaissance was almost entirely a stimulating one. The long-winded romances, the dull allegories, the artificial poetry of mediæval literature were driven out—in fact, they were already dead, as was mediæval art,† and in their place came the inspiring forces of wit, grace, eloquence, and taste. In remoter countries, as Spain and England, the ef-

---

* Symonds, "Renaissance in Italy," v. 132, note, says : "The more we study Italian literature in the sixteenth century, the more we are compelled to acknowledge that humanism and all its consequences were a revival of Latin culture, only slightly tinctured with the simpler and purer influences of the Greeks."

Sidney said of *Gorboduc,* in his "Defense of Poesy," that it was "full of stately speeches and well-sounding phrases, climbing to the height of Seneca his style, and as full of notable morality, which it doth most delightfully teach and so obtain the very end of Poesy."

Scaliger, "Poetices," vi. 6, says: "Seneca quem nullo Græcorum majestate inferiorem existimo, cultu vero ac nitore etiam Euripide majorem. Inventiones sane illorum sunt : at majestas carminis, sonus, spiritus ipsius."

"Malherbe . . . n'estimoit point du tout les Grecs. . . . Pour les Latins, ceux qu'il aimoit le plus étoit Stace, et, apres lui, Sénèque le Tragique."—Racan, "Vie de Malherbe."

† *Vide* Renan, "Mélanges d'Histoire et de Voyages," p. 209 et seq.

fect appeared later, but it came, if anything, with greater results than in France and Italy ; and, with the new learning,
came a natural desire to do their work well : to settle the
laws which were to rule literary production.

It will always be found that a period of great creative
fervor is followed by one of careful workmanship. The
Elizabethan drama was in many ways devoid of art. In
Marlowe there are magnificent bits of exaggeration; in
Shakspere there are false notes — although nowadays, as
was the case in Pope's time, reference to them is dangerous :

> " One tragic sentence if I dare deride,
>
>   *   *   *   *   *
>
> How will our fathers rise up in a rage,
> And swear all shame is lost in George's age !"

and it is easy to see how the same quality existed in the
later writers until we come to Davenant, in whom, as we
shall see, forced fury became a sort of parody of the really grand style. Even in Ben Jonson we see the contrast
of artistic workmanship ; and his cool precision found many
admirers and imitators.

Then, too, with the complications of politics and the
fervor of religious dissensions, the theatre became the resort of courtiers alone, and lost its authority as a place for
the expression of national feeling. With the rise of Puritanism English life was severed into two distinct branches.
One clung to literature, the other to religion, and it is perhaps only in our own days that the two currents are again
uniting.

As soon as literature became the property of the ruling
classes, it of course lost its national spirit and acquired
a sort of cosmopolitan polish. Nowhere had literature become so much the possession of the aristocracy as in
France, where the court was the sole patron of literary

fame. What it was there in the seventeenth century may be seen in Taine's essay on Racine; and the literature of France was built up almost entirely on that of Rome. The French, for instance, cared very little for Homer until this century, as may be readily shown.

In the revival of letters, the French naturally found the acquisition of Latin infinitely easier than that of Greek,[*] and, moreover, Vergil's fame had lived throughout the dark ages—mainly, to be sure, from the poet's reputation as a magician; the other great writers were almost forgotten. In the sixteenth century, Julius Cæsar Scaliger, in his "Poetices," lib. v. (1561), lavished every sort of praise on Vergil, and had no good words for Homer. With what judgment he did this may be gathered from the way in which he went astray in some of his comments. In the sixth book of the "Æneid," 667, Vergil placed a certain Musæus at the head of a band of poets—a Musæus whose name alone has come down to us. Scaliger[†] imagined that he meant the author of "Hero and Leander"[‡]—the poem which was paraphrased rather than translated by Marlowe and Chapman, begun, that is, by Marlowe and finished by

---

[*] As to the way in which the Catholic Church threw its weight on the side of Latin as against Greek literature, see Nisard, "Littérature Française," i. 431, and Mark Pattison's "Casaubon," p. 113.

[†] This was the general opinion. "When Aldus Manutius conceived his great idea of issuing Greek literature from the Venetian press, he put forth 'Hero and Leander' first of all in 1498, with a preface that ran as follows: 'I was desirous that Musæus, the most ancient poet, should form a prelude to Aristotle and the other sages who will shortly be imprinted at my hands.'"—Symonds, "Greek Poets," ii. 348 [Am. ed.].

See also Waller's poem, "On the King's Escape." Addison, *Spectator*, No. 62, expresses his doubts on account of the conceits in the poem. Criticism, like everything else, is a plant of slow growth.

[‡] About 1540 appeared in Spanish Boscan's blank-verse translation of "Hero and Leander;" in 1541, Marot's French version.

Chapman, and published among Marlowe's works. Chapman, too, thought that the original poem was by the older Musæus, as we see by the last line :

"They [Hero and Leander] were the first that ever poet sung."

The Greek poem was apparently written by the grammarian Musæus in the fifth century of the Christian era. Scaliger, having fallen into this error, went on to prove that the author of the "Hero and Leander" was in every way superior to Homer, saying, "If Musæus had written what Homer wrote, we may conclude that he would have done much better :" * "Arbitror enim si Musæus ea quæ Homerus scripsit, scripsisset, longè melius eum scripturum judicemus."

For more than two centuries Scaliger's opinion of the superiority of Vergil remained the opinion of the French nation. There were, to be sure, men who knew how to admire both : La Fontaine, Racine, Boileau, and others ; but, in general, the French agreed with Voltaire in putting Homer below Tasso.† Voltaire said ("Essai sur les Mœurs," chap. cxxi.) : "As for the 'Iliad,' let every reader ask himself what his judgment would be if he were to read that poem and Tasso for the first time without knowing the names of the authors or when the poems were written, and deciding only from the pleasure

---

* "Poetices," v. 215 et seq. : "Musæi hiatus rari, et lectis utitur verbis."

See further *de Homero et Vergilio :* "Loquax Achilles in concione minas perfert deteriores, flet etiam apud matrem, atque hic est, a quo virum fortissimum Hectorem interfectum credi vult ? Nihil putidius Hectoris morte." "Homeri epitheta sæpè frigida, aut puerilia, aut locis inepta."

Ronsard seems to have been one of the earliest of Greek-reading Frenchmen. One of his sonnets begins,

"Je veux lire en trois jours l'Iliade d'Homère,
    Et pour ce, Corydon, ferme bien l'huis sur moi."

† *Vide* Sainte-Beuve, "Causeries du Lundi," xii. 78 et seq.

that each gave him. Would he not in every respect give the preference to Tasso? Would he not find in the Italian poet more control, interest, variety, precision, grace, and that delicacy which sets off the sublime? In a few centuries all comparison between them will be impossible."

Need we wonder that Goethe said ("Eckermann," Feb. 24, 1830) : "It took the French some time to appreciate the great merit of Homer : there was required for this nothing less than a complete revolution in their civilization"?

The French in the age of Louis XIV. had acquired a civilization that was in many ways superior to that of all the rest of Europe, and, while England was led to follow the literary methods of France by causes that were entirely national, the great reputation of the Augustan age of French literature naturally inspired imitation. And, to repeat, French literature, like that of Italy, was especially a copy of the Roman literature, which, as I have said, was itself a copy of that of Greece. Just as a light that is reflected into a dark corner by a series of mirrors loses something with every additional mirror,* so did the inspiration of Greek literature, through Rome and France, shine with feeble glow in what is sometimes called the Augustan age of English letters. Greek literature was original ; and what is best in all literature is the most natural form of expression—a form that grows from the soil. We shall see later how the revival of the natural forces in English and French, and their appearance in German literature, coincided with renewed study of the Greek.

This digression, however, must not make us lose sight of the question now before us, which is the amount and

---

* Dr. Johnson said ("Boswell," vii. 188 : April 29, 1778): "Modern writers are the moons of literature ; they shine with reflected light—with light borrowed from the ancients."

nature of the French influence. We are always too ready to think that we have explained a difficulty if we are able to give it a name, and in the present case the explanation of the change in English literature might be left where it is without further discussion. Yet a more careful examination will make it clear that the subject, which is obscure at the best, needs more light. Fully to understand the relation of the writers of this period to their predecessors and to their foreign rivals, we must bear in mind the complex sequences of the Renaissance. When all the majesty of antiquity broke upon Europe, there seemed to be but one feeling possible : that of unrestrained admiration before its great glory. Writers—and the writers do but represent the reading public—fairly prostrated themselves before the past. They turned away from their own literature to welcome the newly discovered one. The first thing to be done was to study the writings of Greece and Rome, and everywhere, in Italy, in France, in England, we find the effort was made to remodel the vernacular after the classic languages. Boccaccio, Mr. Symonds tells us, "sought to give the fulness and sonority of Latin to the periods of Italian prose. He had the Ciceronian cadence and the labyrinthine sentences of Livy in view."* And Boccaccio's prose became the model copied by later writers when it was finally settled that Latin was not to be the literary language of Italy.

In France we find Ronsard complaining of the meagreness of his native tongue, while at the same time he denounces those who avoided the difficulty by writing in Latin. He, too, was abused for introducing classicisms into the French language. Yet how could he rest satisfied with the comparatively meagre vocabulary and

---

* "Renaissance in Italy," iv. 133 ; v. 246 et seq.

homely construction of his time when he turned his attention to the imitations of the classics? These strangers
demanded more ceremony. They were translated freely
into the leading modern languages. Sébilet, in his "Poétique" (1548), says: "Pourtant t'avertis-je que la version
ou traduction est aujourd'hui le plus fréquent et mieux
reçu des estimés poëtes et des doctes lecteurs."* In the
same year Sébilet published a metrical translation of the
"Iphigenia in Aulis" of Euripides. In 1549 also appeared Du Bellay's "Défense et Illustration de la Langue
Françoise." He urged very strongly the intelligent imitation of the ancients, with a just criticism of translation,
saying that Demosthenes, Homer, Cicero, and Vergil do
not sound so well in French as in their original tongue.
In a translation, "il vous semblera passer de l'ardente
montagne d'Ætne sur le froid sommet de Caucase. Et
ce que je dy des langues latine et grecque se doit reci-
proquement dire de tous les vulgaires." What he urged
was the intelligent imitation of Greek and Latin, not mere
slavish copying. Baïf translated from the Greek; and in
this little band we find the most enthusiastic welcome
given to the Renaissance.

In England there was very similar enthusiasm. Gascoigne's translation, through the Italian, of the "Jocasta"
of Euripides (1566), is a familiar instance, and we see the
same Græco-Latin revival that found its French equivalent in the ardor of the Pleiad. In England and Spain
there was for a time a sort of compromise: to take the
former country alone, Shakspere stands at the junction
of two great streams which may represent respectively
the Middle Ages and classical antiquity. In France the
wars of the League interrupted the normal growth of lite-

---

* Quoted in Egger's "L'Hellénisme en France," i. 260.

rature, and when peace again prevailed it was the new, arid
correctness of Malherbe that defined the narrow channels
in which French literature was to run for two centuries.
Malherbe met with fierce opposition: Mademoiselle de
Gournay, for instance, Montaigne's adopted daughter, exposed his incompleteness; but the times were favorable,
and his commonplace aversion to extravagance, whether
mediæval or in imitation of the classics, won the day.
After all, the classicism of the Pleiad could scarcely hope
to live: it was as remote from the popular affection as
was the wearing of togas or the observance of the Pana-
thenaic festival. Then, too, Malherbe touched the chord
of patriotism, and in denouncing mediævalism he struck
what was to be the prevailing note of European civilization for a long time. The nation that did that most effec-
tually was sure to take the lead. France did this by being
the first country to give to the world a new literature,
which was distinctly neither mediæval nor a mere tracing
over of the classics. It stepped, almost at one stride, from
the Græco-Latin period to its own version of classicism,
while in England we see two very decided movements
flourishing side by side, both of which finally succumbed
before the French influence. The most important of these
was the dramatic, which need not be described here, with
its close relation to the popular life; the other, the tone
of the court, with its pedantic imitation of Italian poetry.
With the first study of the classics came the attempt to
employ classical constructions, while euphuism was an
effort to develop the language in a modern fashion. Lyly,
as has been clearly shown in an admirable paper by Mr.
Friedrich Landmann,* imitated an old Spanish writer,

---

* "Der Euphuismus, sein Wesen, seine Quelle, seine Geschichte." Gies-
sen: 1881; and "New Shakspere Society's Transactions," 1880-2, No.
XIII. p. 241.

Guevara, who may be called the founder of what is known as Euphuism.* The general groping for new light introduced a thousand other affectations. Sidney's "Arcadia," for example, abounds in imitations of the Spanish pastoral romances ; and perhaps even more marked was the influence of Sylvester's translation of "Du Bartas," 1598. Dryden, it will be remembered, wrote, in his dedication of the "Spanish Friar," 1691: "I thought inimitable Spenser a mean poet in comparison of Sylvester's 'Du Bartas,' and was rapt into an ecstasy when I read these lines:

> ' Now when the winter's keener breath began
> To crystallize the Baltic ocean,
> To glaze the lakes, to bridle up the floods,
> And periwig with snow † the baldpate woods.'

I am much deceived if this be not abominable fustian." Yet Dryden was not the only one who admired this abominable fustian. Space is lacking for a description of all

---

* It is interesting to observe that euphuism still makes an occasional appearance in English prose, as alliteration does in English verse, and abundant instances of both are to be found in the writings of Swinburne. Lyly, for instance, wrote many such sentences as this: " Gentleman, as you may suspect me of idlenesse in giving eare to your talke, so may you convince me of lightnesse in answering such toyes: certes, as you have made mine eares glow at the rehearsall of your love, so have you galled my heart with the remembraunce of your folly." Swinburne says: " The buoyant beauty of surrounding verse, the 'innumerable laughter'; the profound murmur of its many measures, the fervent flow of stanzas now like the ripples and now like the gulfs of the sea," etc. ("Essays," p. 255). Lyly might have written this line: " Neither by defect of form nor by any default of force" (ib. p. 108).

For conceits outdoing even Lyly, see Pater, " Studies in the History of the Renaissance," *passim*.

† Sylvester says " wool." Cf. this phrase of Du Bartas, " monts enfarinés d'une neige éternelle." But see Sainte-Beuve, "Poésie du XVI. Siècle," p. 68.

the affectations of the writers at the time of Elizabeth.
Gongorism in Spain, and Marinism in Italy, show how
widespread was the confusion which the new cultivation
wrought in the language. Can we be surprised that Malherbe carried the reaction against conceits as far as he did,
when we read such passages as these from " Du Bartas "?
The world, he tells us, would have remained in a state of
confusion, if the divine Word

> " N'eût comme siringué dedans ces membres morts
>   Je ne sais quel esprit qui meut tout ce grand corps."

or this, expressive of a galloping horse ?

> " Le champ plat bat, abat, détrappe, grappe, attrappe
>   Le vent qui va devant—"

Other examples of his lawlessness may be found : " Il
gagne du dauphin la ba-branlante échine;" " Sur pé-pétil-
lant;" " La peur, à qui ba-bat incessamment la flanc."
These may be compared with such gems as the following
in English from A. Fraunce's translation of Tasso's " Lam-
entations of Amyntas," 1587 :

> " I'le quench theyr thirst by my hartbloud,
> Blynde boy's, proud gyrle's thirst : and glut their eyes with aboundant
> Streams of purpled gore of tootoo wretched Amyntas."

Malherbe killed these affectations with one blow; in
England they died a lingering death. In France, Malherbe was followed by Corneille, Racine, and Boileau, who
flourished under a strong government that embodied the
most complete reaction against extravagance of every sort.
License in literature was as impossible as political freedom, and the completeness with which France adopted
the idea of submission to authority made its brilliant civilization the model for the rest of Europe. England, on
the contrary, was ruled by divided counsels. The great

dramatists held their position by reason of their close relation with the people. Yet the court followed the prevailing fashions of Spain and Italy.

IV. Let us take, for instance, those whom Dr. Johnson called the metaphysical poets, as if metaphysics were synonymous with obscurity. According to him, " They were wholly employed on something unexpected and surprising. . . . Their courtship was void of fondness, and their lamentation of sorrow. Their wish was only to say what they hoped had never been said before." Yet, he acknowledged, " great labor, directed by great ability, is never wholly lost; if they frequently threw away their wit upon false conceits, they likewise sometimes struck out unexpected truth; if their conceits were far-fetched, they were often worth the carriage. . . . If their greatness seldom elevates, their acuteness often surprises; if the imagination is not always gratified, at least the powers of reflection and comparison are employed ; and in the mass of materials which ingenious absurdity has thrown together, genuine and useful knowledge may be sometimes found buried, perhaps, in grossness of expression, but useful to those who know their value ; and such as, when they are expanded to perspicuity and polished to elegance, may give lustre to works which have more propriety, though less copiousness, of sentiment." Donne and Cowley were the chief offenders whom Dr. Johnson brings into court. Donne was borne in 1573, nine years after Shakspere, and he died in 1631, so that it is impossible to charge him with being the product of a degenerate age. Dr. Johnson quotes many examples of his poetry to show that the characteristics of his school were " enormous and disgusting hyperboles," " unexpected and unnatural thoughts," " violent and unnatural fictions," " slight and trifling sentiments." He quotes from Donne :

> "Though God be our true glass through which we see
> All, since the being of all things is he,
> Yet are the trunks, which do to us derive
> Things in proportion fit, by perspective
> Deeds of good men ; for by their living here,
> Virtues, indeed remote, seem to be near."

and asks, "Who but Donne would have thought that a good man is a telescope?" Yet naturally, in writing the life of Cowley, he had most to say about the form which the fault took in that writer. Now, to understand Donne's position, it is essential to remember that the poetry of the time of Elizabeth was of two kinds, that of the stage and that of the court. That of the stage was the expression of the national feeling ; that of the court was the expression of but a small number of cultivated people familiar with Spanish and Italian literatures, who were already affected by the euphuism which Lyly's "Euphues" (1580) introduced into England by those foreign sources. An example of it may be found in Shakspere's "Love's Labour's Lost," where are these lines (I. i. 163) :

> " Our court, you know, is haunted
> With a refined traveller of Spain :
> A man in all the world's new fashion planted,
> That hath a mint of phrases in his brain ;
> One whom the music of his own vain tongue
> Doth ravish like enchanting harmony ;"

and later in the play the King of Navarre and his lords forswear

> " Taffeta phrases, silken terms precise,
> Three-piled hyperboles, spruce affectation,
> Figures pedantical ;"

and determine to woo henceforth

> " In russet yeas and honest kersey noes."

Sidney's "Sonnets" (1591) show the same tendency to

making a display of wit, and Donne carries the tendency very far. The affectations that marked the metaphysical school then were not mere inventions of a later time ; they were not a reaction against the vigor of the play-writers : they were rather one of the forms in which the renewed intellectual excitement of the Renaissance found expression. The fantastic poetry was coincident in time with the glory of the English stage, and some of the poets, who when they wrote for the court racked heaven and earth for all sorts of conceits, wrote plays which are models of dignity and vigor : Beaumont is an instance. In fact, it is impossible to overlook a certain resemblance between the literary school of the court at the time of Elizabeth and the neo-romantic æstheticism of the present day. The language and emotions of Bunthorne, for instance, may represent for us something which will enable us to understand how euphuism and its results struck our ancestors.

When the stage was in its prime, the metaphysical school was less prominent : the poems were read, but they do not to our mind stand as representatives of that period. Yet their influence remained ; and when the stage lost its glory, and the popular impulse that inspired it took the form of Puritanic zeal, the literature of the court remained true to its old principles of literary affectation, and Cowley (1618–1667) preserved very closely the traditions of the school of Donne. It is easy to turn Cowley into ridicule. Dr. Johnson, as I have said, collected a number of ludicrous bits from his poems. For example :

> " All armed in brass, the richest dress of war
> (A dismal glorious sight !), he shone afar.
> The sun himself started with sudden fright,
> To see his beams return so dismal bright ;"

and this :

"His bloody eyes he hurls round, his sharp paws
  Tear up the ground ; then runs he wild about,
  Lashing his angry tail and roaring out.
  Beasts creep into their dens, and tremble there ;
  Trees, though no wind is stirring, shake with fear ;
  Silence and horror fill the place around ;
  Echo itself dares scarce repeat the sound ;"

or this ode to the Muse :

"Go, the rich chariot instantly prepare ;
  The queen, my muse, will take the air :
  Unruly Fancy with strong Judgment trace ;
  Put in nimble-footed Wit,
  Smooth-paced Eloquence join with it ;
  Sound Memory with young Invention place ;
  Harness all the winged race :
  Let the postilion Nature mount, and let
  The coachman Art be set ;
  And let the airy footmen, running all beside,
  Make a long row of goodly pride,
  Figures, Conceits, Raptures, and Sentences,
  In a well-worded dress ;
  And innocent Loves, and pleasant Truths, and rueful Lies,
  In all their gaudy liveries.
  Mount, glorious queen ! thy travelling throne,
  And bid it to put on," etc.

It is not hard to imagine the emotions with which Dr. Johnson must have read these lines. Yet Cowley was better than his faults. His poem on the death of Hervey contains some fine passages :

"Say, for you saw us, ye immortal lights,
  How oft unwearied have we spent the nights,
  Till the Ledæan stars, so fam'd for love,
    Wonder'd at us from above !
  We spent them not in toys, in lusts, or wine ;
    But search of deep philosophy,
    Wit, eloquence, and poetry,
  Arts which I loved, for they, my friend, were thine."

While Cowley, after all, did service to the mechanism of literature by his ingenuity, even if, as Dryden said, " he could never forgive any conceit which came in his way, but swept, like a drag-net, great and small," it was Waller who more especially struck out the path which was to be followed for about two hundred years ; and to do that is what falls to the lot of but few writers. That Waller should have been the man to do it, is a thought that may arouse the hopes of the most diffident. To us he is simply the author of " Go, Lovely Rose," and the lines " On a Girdle ;" his other poems rest untouched on the shelf. Dryden said of him : " The excellence and dignity of rhyme were never fully known till Mr. Waller taught it ; he first made writing easily an art, first showed us to conclude the sense, most commonly, in distichs, which in the verse of those before him runs on for so many lines together that the reader is out of breath to overtake it." That is to say, Waller was the first English poet to use the couplet. He began with it in a poem written about 1623 (he was born in 1605, and died in 1687) in a poem, " Of the Danger his Majesty [being Prince] Escaped in the Road at St. Andero "—

> " These mighty peers placed in the gilded barge,
> Proud with the burden of so brave a charge,
> With painted oars the youths began to sweep
> Neptune's smooth face, and cleave the yielding deep;
> Which soon becomes the seat of sudden war
> Between the wind and tide that fiercely jar.
> As when a sort of lusty shepherds try
> Their force at football, care of victory
> Makes them salute so rudely breast to breast,
> That their encounter seems too rough for jest;
> They ply their feet, and still the restless ball,
> Tossed to and fro is urged by them all.
> So fares the doubtful barge 'twixt tide and winds
> And like effect of their contention finds."

The sea gets rougher, however,

> " And now no hope of grace
> Among them shines, save in the Prince's face;
>
> *　　　*　　　*　　　*　　　*
>
> The gentle vessel (wont with state and pride
> On the smooth back of silver Thames to ride)—"

It will be noticed that boats sail on the " smooth face " of Neptune and on the " smooth back " of rivers—

> " Wanders astonished on the angry main.
>
> *　　　*　　　*　　　*　　　*
>
> The pale Iberians had expired with fear,
> But that their wonder did divert their care,
> To see the Prince with danger moved no more
> Than with the pleasures of their court before;
> Godlike his courage seemed, whom nor delight
> Could soften, nor the face of death affright.
> Next to the power of making tempests cease,
> Was in that storm to have so calm a peace."

Certainly the outlook was bad for poetry when lines such as these should set a fashion. They were the model which all the writers who hoped for success were gradually obliged to follow. I could find passages in Waller's heroic measure less grotesque than this one, of which the sole merit, it seems to me, is technical correctness ; and as a favorable specimen I would mention his panegyric on Cromwell. Yet the lines just read have been admired in their day, and may, without extreme unfairness, show what it was that gave him for a time the name of the greatest English poet. In his straining for classical illustrations we see very much the same quality that is to be noticed in Cowley. Waller, in order to convince us that a storm was really severe, tells us, " Great Maro could no greater tempest feign ;" and Cowley says that his heart was an Etna, which enclosed Cupid's forge instead of Vulcan's shop. Allusions to the classics were for a long time the common tools of poets. It is in the short pieces, however, that Waller's conceits are most striking, as, for instance, in the one on the head of a stag :

> " O fertile head ! which every year
> Could such a crop of wonder bear !
> The teeming earth did never bring
> So soon, so hard, so huge a thing;
> Which might it never have been cast,
> (Each year's growth added to the last)
> These lofty branches had supplied
> The earth's bold sons' prodigious pride,
> Heaven with these engines had been scaled,
> When mountains heaped on mountains failed."

In general, indeed, we may say that Waller's lyrics are very cold. It was for his management of the heroic couplet especially that he was admired. This measure had long been in use ; it was Chaucer's favorite form, and was derived, doubtless, from the French writers whom he knew and the Italian writers whom he translated. It was employed by numberless later writers, and generally, among the metaphysical school at least, it had become very rough and graceless. Thus Donne wrote ("An Anatomy of the World," in Works, p. 88) :

> "Seas are so deep, that whales being struck to-day,
> Perchance to-morrow scarce at middle way
> Of their wished journey's end, the bottom, die :
> And men, to sound depths, so much line untie,
> As one might justly think that there would rise
> At end thereof one of the antipodes :
> If under all a vault infernal be,
> Which sure is spacious, except that we
> Invent another torment, that there must
> Millions into a strait hot room be thrust,
> Then solidness and roundness have no place." . . .

There is no need of giving other examples of the way English writers let the sense run into any desired number of lines by means of what are called enjambments. Waller was the first English writer who treated the couplet as a unit separate and coherent—as, so to speak, a shapely, well-defined brick as compared with the stone of different sizes that previous artisans made use of.* Before he died he found the couplet universally adopted.

---

* It may be said that Waller accomplished what many were essaying, and that he gave the awkward couplet a new grace. Here are some further examples of its earlier treatment (Peyton's " Glasse of Time," 1620, p. 15):

" We have, great God, that which these never knew,
 Thine own example and the scripture true,
 Thy all divine and holy moral law
 Which these as yet have never heard or saw."

T. May, " The Victorious Reigne of Edward III.," 1635, lib. ii. :

" Nor yet had Edward in his active mind
 The claim and conquest of great France designed,
 Nor looked abroad ; domestic businesse
 Employ'd his early manhood ; the redresse
 Of those distempers which had grown at home
 Too great for any youth to overcome.
 But such a youth as his, had yet detained
 His spirit there." . . .

In the " Obsequies to the Memorie of Mr. Edward King," 1638, the volume in which Milton's " Lycidas " first appeared, thirteen of the elegies were in English. Of the twelve—*i. e.*, excluding the " Lycidas "—seven were in the measure of five feet, three of four feet, the other two of six feet. One of the seven runs thus :

" No, Death ! I'll not examine God's decree,
 Nor question Providence in chiding thee.
 Discreet Religion binds us to admire
 The ways of Providence and not inquire."

See also Joseph Hall's verses, *infra*, and compare Sylvester's " Du Bartas."

What the couplet did was to replace the stanza : it had previously been employed for rather light subjects, and Puttenham, in his "Art of English Poesie" (1589), affirmed that the stanza alone was suitable for serious topics. Indeed, as Mr. Mark Pattison has shown (Introduction to his edition of Pope's "Essay on Man," p. 19), "the stanza in verse is the analogue of the prose sentence as constructed by Hooker, Jeremy Taylor, or Milton. Each of these stately periods carries along with it, over and above its direct predication, all the conditions and exceptions to which the writer wishes to submit that predication, all woven into one structure. There is in each stanza or sentence so much as fills the mind to the utmost strain of its capacity for attention ; and then a pause for reflection and digestion."

Take for an example any stanza from the "Fairy Queen" (IV. 2, xvi., for instance) :

> " As when two warlike brigandines at sea,
>   With murderous weapons arm'd to cruel fight,
> Do meet together on the watery lea,
> They stem each other with so fell despight,
> That with the shock of their own heedless might
> Their wooden ribs are shaken nigh asunder ;
> They which from shore behold the dreadful sight
> Of flashing fire, and hear the ordnance thunder,
> Do greatly stand amaz'd at such unwonted wonder."

Mr. Pattison goes on : "The same process which broke up the composite period of earlier prose into the disjointed modern style of short sentences took place in verse. The stanza gradually gave way before the couplet."*

---

* It is worth while noticing, however, how long it was before the couplet lost its elasticity. At first, it was broken by enjambments ; in Waller's hands it admitted of almost any prolongation of the sentence. Dryden, too, wrote whole paragraphs in this measure. Not until Pope's time did

Denham is another author to whom the later poets (Prior, for instance) expressed their indebtedness for the couplet. A few lines from his "Cooper's Hill" (1643) will show, I think, that he had considerable mastery of versification, in spite of the fact that the sense is continued from verse to verse :

> " So fares the stag ; among the enraged hounds,
> Repels their force, and wounds returns for wounds ;
> And as a hero, whom his baser foes
> In troops surround, now these assails, now those,
> Though prodigal of life, disdains to die
> By common hands ; but if he can descry
> Some nobler foe approach, to him he calls,
> And begs his fate, and then contented falls."

Certainly these lines have something of the smoothness which we have learned to associate with the couplet, and elsewhere in his writings we may find instances of greater mechanical skill. In this very poem, it may be worth while to mention, are these lines, which were the despair of the later poets of the school :

> " O could I flow like thee, and make thy stream
> My great example, as it is my theme !
> Though deep, yet clear ; tho' gentle, yet not dull ;
> Strong without rage, without o'erflowing, full."

Another instance of the decay of the stanza and a proof that the change was not wholly due to French influence— although few will think that any change of the sort has but one cause—is Davenant's "Gondibert" (1650). This is a most tedious poem, which would never be read, even

---

it become the chain, with small links, that held thought firm. We see the same gradual growth in the French heroic verse (of twelve syllables). Du Bartas and Ronsard let the sense run through many couplets ; this was one of Malherbe's main objections to his predecessors. And it was only under Boileau that the couplet finally became a rigid unit.

if it were short, and which has acquired a mock importance by its length, with, however, here and there occasional poetical lines to relieve the reader's weariness. I will quote one or two of these passages, which may also serve to illustrate the form of the stanza :

> " Her mind (scarce to her feeble sex akin)
>   Did as her birth, her right to empire show ;
> Seem'd careless outward when employ'd within ;
>   Her speech, like lovers watch'd, was kind and low."

And these descriptions of the opening day :

> " As day new opening fills the hemisphere,
>   And all at once ; so quickly every street
> Does by an instant opening full appear,
>   When from their dwellings busy dwellers meet.
>
> " From wider gates oppressors sally there ;
>   Here creeps th' afflicted through a narrow door ;
> Groans under wrongs he has not strength to bear,
>   Yet seeks for wealth to injure others more.
>
>   *   *   *   *   *
>
> " Here stooping lab'rers slowly moving are ;
>   Beasts to the rich, whose strength grows rude with ease ;
> And would usurp, did not their rulers' care
>   With toil and tax their furious strength appease."

In the preface to this tolerably unreadable poem—the preface, by the way, was in the form of a letter to Thomas Hobbes, the author of the "Leviathan "—Davenant explains " why I have chosen my interwoven stanza of four, though I am not obliged to excuse the choice ; for numbers in verse must, like distinct kinds of music, be exposed to the uncertain and different taste of several ears. Yet I may declare that I believed it would be more pleasant to the reader, in a work of length, to give this respite or pause between every stanza (having endeavoured that each should contain a period) than to run him out of breath with continued couplets. Nor doth alternate rime by any lowliness of cadence make the sound less heroic, but rather adapt it to a plain and stately composing of music ; and the brevity of the stanza renders it less subtle to the composer, and more easy to the singer, which in *stilo recitativo*, when the story is long, is chiefly requisite. And this was indeed (if I shall not betray vanity in my confession) the reason that prevailed most towards my choice of this stanza, and my division of the main work into cantos, every canto including a sufficient accomplishment of some worthy design or action, for I had so much heat, which you, sir, may call pride, as to presume they might (like the works of Homer ere they were joyned together and made a volume by the Athenian king) be sung at village-feasts ; though not to monarchs after victory, nor to armies before battle. For so (as an inspiration of glory into the one, and of valour into the other) did Homer's spirit, long after his body's rest, wander in music about Greece." Hobbes, by the way, acknowledged this statement by assuring Davenant that "but for the clamour of the multitude, that hide their envy of the present under a reverence of antiquity, I should say further that it would last as long as the Iliad or the Æneid."

When all is said, we find a precedent for the use of this measure in Sir John Davies's "Nosce Teipsum" (1599), although in this older poem the sense runs over from one stanza into a second or third. Wyatt had also employed it in his poem, "The Lover Describeth his being taken with Sight of his Love," as had the Earl of Oxford in 1576, in a poem prefixed to Bedingfield's Cardanus. Dryden made use of it in his stanzas on the "Death of Oliver Cromwell" (1658), and, after also trying the couplet, in his "Annus Mirabilis" (1666). After that time, however, he kept to the couplet, save, of course, in his odes. So that Waller had the satisfaction of living to see the measures that he introduced become the prevailing form.

V. I have to this point tried to give a sketch of the change in the poetical forms, and to show the different steps in this change. The question now suggests itself: Why was the change made? In what way was it possible that the age should be deaf to the majesty of Milton's line and prefer Cowley, Waller, and the playwrights? But when could Milton be a popular poet? Even now, when his place is secured among the greatest of writers, we read him, if we read him at all, at some time from a sense of duty, and then most of us return to him only fitfully, as indeed we do to most great writers. And then, when Milton wrote his finest poems, he was the lonely singer of a fallen cause, and Puritanism meant to his contemporaries a narrow theology, a bigoted view of human life, and the unsoundest political principles. We see that Milton was one of the last of the great poets, and that he was great because, with his magnificent poetical equipment, he represented a great principle of national life; and this has always been part of the inspiration of the greatest poets. Homer is the poet of remote antiquity; Æschylus and Sophocles of Greece in her prime; Vergil, of imperial Rome; Dante, of the Middle Ages; Chaucer, of awakening England; Shakspere of England in a time of vigor and enthusiasm; Milton, of Puritanism; Goethe, of Germany; and—it seems to me—it is their quality as representatives which so much outweighs literary performance of no matter what degree of excellence. Puritanism was inspired by some of the most marked traits of the English character, and Milton brought to its service very complete training. Puritanism flourished and died, though it made a deep mark on both England and America, and left Bunyan's

prose* and Milton's poetry to show how important a part
it had played in English history ; and it showed, too, in
Milton's faults how narrowing it was.

Milton's fame was something which depended a good
deal on politics. After 1688 the Liberals admired him,

---

* It would be interesting to study the gradual growth of Bunyan's fame
in the last two hundred years. The popularity of the " Pilgrim's Progress"
was always acknowledged, but it was frequently spoken of as a book suitable only for the populace. Dr. Young, " Sat." V. iii. 147, speaking of a
newly married couple :

> " With the fourth sun a warm dispute arose
> On Durfey's poesy and Bunyan's prose."

D'Urfey's poetry was notoriously beneath contempt.

John Dunton (for whom *vide infra*), in a talk with the librarian of Harvard College, said, " Nor must I omit amongst these great names [Tillot-
son, Jeremy Taylor, Baxter, Mrs. Katharine Phillips, Mrs. Behn—for Dunton's taste was catholic—and Mrs. Rowe], to mention that of Mr. John Bunyan, who, though a man of very ordinary education, yet was a man of great
natural parts, and as well known for an author throughout England as any
I have mentioned, by the many books he has published, of which the ' Pilgrim's Progress' bears away the bell" (*vide* his " Letters from New England " (Boston, 1867), p. 159).

Swift, in " A Letter to a Young Clergyman:" " I have been better entertained, and more informed, by a few pages in the ' Pilgrim's Progress,'
than by a long discourse on the will and the intellect, and simple or complex ideas."

Sterne, " Tristram Shandy," i. chap. iv. : " My life and opinions . . . will
. . . be no less read than the ' Pilgrim's Progress ' itself."

Vide Knox, " Essays," No. 92 : " Bunyan's ' Pilgrim's Progress ' has
given as much pleasure among the English vulgar as the ' Quixote' of
Cervantes."

Dr. Johnson said it was the only uninspired book, except " Don Quixote,"
which the reader ever wished were longer.

Cowper apologizes for referring to him :

> " I name thee not lest so despised a name,
> Should move a sneer at thy deserved fame."—*Tirocinium.*

It is only in this century, since the Romantic revival, that the prejudice
against its simplicity and mediæval origin has been removed.

and even a hundred years later Johnson, who was a hot Tory, attacked him in his "Lives of the Poets." * Of Milton's influence we shall have occasion to speak later. We can, to be sure, find compliments to him in some of the writings of the time of the Restoration, but most of the authors neglected him, although I fancy that his popularity in this country among people of moderate taste in poetry proves that in England he was read by the survivors of the Puritans. Then, too, his harmonious rhythm inspired, as we shall see, a great deal of tumid blank verse. The real interest of the nation went with its contemporary writers, and in the race for popularity modernness is always tolerably sure to outrun antiquity, and Milton soon appeared like a stranded classic. The edition of 1688, the publication of which was almost a political move, did much to redeem the neglect from which Milton's fame had been suffering.

Even now we are repelled by the tedious theology and the classical form of the "Paradise Lost." How must they have seemed when the modern spirit had the additional charm of novelty?

The Elizabethan poets wrote under the inspiration of a strong feeling. As this decayed, men sought first to make it good by fierce language. Take, for example, these lines from Davenant's "Albovine," as a specimen of the hero's method of courtship:

> " Fill me a bowl with negro's blood, congealed
> Even into livers! Tell her, Hermegild,
> I'll swallow tar to celebrate her health."

Evidently language of this sort contains signs of decay,

---

* The political bias was long-lived. Clough, writing from Oxford, in 1838, says: "It is difficult here even to obtain assent to Milton's greatness as a poet. . . . Were it not for the happy notion that a man's poetry is not at all affected by his opinions, . . . I fear the ' Paradise Lost ' would be utterly unsalable, except for waste paper in the university " (i. 80).

and must soon give place to something different. The courtiers, who could endure declamation of that sort, said that Milton's harmonies sounded like the rumbling of a wheelbarrow ;* they were equally deaf to the charm of the old lyrics, and put into short lines a vast number of feeble sentiments. The songs of the Restoration ask for but little attention. We may find in Waller a few excellent lyrics, as well as such poems as "The Lady who can Sleep when she Pleases," "Of a Tree Cut in Paper ;" in Roscommon, lines "On the Death of a Lady's Dog," † and a "Song on a Young Lady who Sung Finely, and was Afraid of a Cold." Rochester, too, wrote some verses which are marked with some slight ingenuity, but since we are now following mainly the broader streams of literature, we may leave for the present this side-current.

The brief examination that we have given will be sufficient to show us that the outlook for literature after the Restoration was a very dreary one. We have but touched upon the drama, but outside of that we have seen the decadence of the greatest inspiration, the neglect of real genius, and the appearance of a prosaic period. The problem that lay before the writers of that day was a complicated one. Literature, as I have tried to point out, had broken loose from the people, and had to seek support from the court until a public of readers should be found—or, rather, should be made. A proper understanding of the absence of a reading public is necessary for understanding the literature of the last century.

---

* *Vide* Johnson's "Life of J. Philips."

† Yet when shall we find anything new ? Joseph Hall says in his "Satires" (1598):

> "Should Bandel's throstle die without a song ?
> Or Adamantius, my dog, be laid along,
> Down in some ditch without his exequies,
> Or epitaphs, or mournful elegies ?"

CHAPTER II.

I. IT is of the utmost importance that we understand
clearly how few were the readers in the latter half of the
sixteenth century, how small was the public to which
authors could address themselves. The Bible and Bunyan were doubtless widely read; probably Milton's "Paradise Lost" was read by the same people, but this new
literature was far removed from the populace. There was
but little literary interest. Books could not be printed
without a license, and then only by one of the legal print-
ers, and of these there were but twenty—master-printers,
that is ; and in 1666 there were only 140 working-printers.
Moreover, the great fire in London, in that year, destroyed
a large number of books. Again, there are statistics to
illustrate this : between 1666 and (after the fire) June 12,
1680, there were published 3550 books. Of these, 947
treated of theology, the larger number probably being
sermons and pamphlets ; 420 of law, and 153 of medicine,
two fifths thus being special, technical books ; 397 were
educational books, 253 on geography and navigation, including maps. The number of books of all kinds would
then average about 250 a year ; but, deducting reprints,
pamphlets, tracts, sermons, maps, etc., we may estimate the
number, according to Charles Knight,* as less than a hundred a year, and only a few of these belonged to what we

---

* Quoted by Beljame, " Le Public et les Hommes de Lettres."

may call literature. As Dr. Johnson said in his "Life of Milton," "the call for books was not in Milton's age what it is at present. To read was not then a general amusement; neither traders, nor often gentlemen, thought themselves disgraced by ignorance. The women had not then aspired to literature, nor was every house supplied with a closet of knowledge. Those, indeed, who professed learning were not less learned than at any other time; but of that middle race of students who read for pleasure or accomplishment, and who buy the numerous products of modern typography, the number was then comparatively small."

And it was small, probably, in comparison with the numbers of those who were busy readers in the beginning of the century and in the latter half of the previous one. Then every man began to translate from the classic authors, or to rewrite classic stories. Shakspere's "Venus and Adonis" (1593) was but one instance of this. There were Chapman's "Homer" ("Iliad," 1611; "Odyssey," 1615); Marston's "Pygmalion's Image" (1597); Marlowe's "Hero and Leander" (1598), and his "Elegies of Ovid" (1597); Golding's "Metamorphoses" (1565), and Sandys's version of the same (1626). In 1565, Horace's first two Satires were translated by Thomas Colwell; in the next year, two books of the Satires were "Englyshed" by Thomas Drant. A few of the "Odes" in 1621, by John Ashman, and the whole in 1625 by Sir Thomas Hawkins. There was Gavin Douglas's translation of "Vergil," finished in 1513; Surrey's (2d and 4th books), published in 1553;* Phaer's and Twyne's (1558–73); Stanihurst's (1583); Fleming's "Georgics and Bucolics" (1589), in blank verse; and then Dryden's (1697). The list is a long

---

* The first English blank verse, doubtless written in imitation of that of the Italians, Felice Felignei, and Trissino, whose "Italia Liberata" (*vide infra*) appeared in 1548.

one, but the whole number of books published then on all subjects was considerable, and at that time the proportion of poems and books about literature was great. As I have said, this enthusiasm for the classics had a great share in inspiring the writers for the stage, and the drama was something of popular interest. But the great bulk of the English people drew inspiration from the Bible. The classics became the property of the learned alone, while Puritanism grew narrower. We may see its course illustrated by what we know of Milton's life. He was brought up amid all the riches of literature; he studied foreign languages and foreign literatures. His father composed music, and Milton was interested in the art; and he brought to the service of Puritanism the flower of the cultivation which was produced by the Renaissance, and published his greatest works after Puritanism had lost its power. He was a sort of living anachronism. He belonged to one age, which he survived; and he had been trained in an earlier one. His education was unpuritan, and his poem was built on the inspiration of the ancients, yet it appeared in the beginning of what we take to be modern times. Not only had the indirect influence of Puritanism been unfavorable to literature; the Civil Wars and Cromwell's rule had really produced a sort of interregnum of about eighteen years, during which poetry and the drama were neglected and nothing flourished but polemical writing, so that Milton stands out in especial prominence as the sole transmitter of earlier traditions.

Various facts have been collected to prove the general lack of education. Milton's eldest daughter did not know how to write; at least, she put a cross where her signature should be. The spelling of Dryden's wife—a lady of noble family—is a sort of unconscious prophecy of the spelling reform. Booksellers, naturally, did not flourish at this time. In the "Life of the Honourable and Reverend Dr. John North"* (p. 241 et seq.), we find a comparison between the condition of booksellers in 1666 and 1683. At the earlier time, "the shops were spacious and the learned gladly resorted to them, where they seldom failed to meet with agreeable conversation. And the booksellers themselves were knowing and conversible men, with whom, for the sake of bookish knowledge, the greatest Wits were pleased to converse. . . . But now this Emporium is vanished and the Trade contracted into the Hands of two or three Persons, who to make good their Monopoly, ransack, not only the Neighbours of the Trade that are scattered about Town, but all over England, aye, and beyond Sea too, and send abroad their Circulators, and in that Manner get into their hands all that is valuable. The rest of the Trade are content to take their Refuse. . . . And it is wretched to consider what pickpocket work, with Help of the Press, these Demi-booksellers make. They crack their brains to find out selling subjects, and keep hirelings in garrets, on hard meat, to write and correct by the grate ; so puff up an octavo to a sufficient thickness," etc., etc. In these distressing circumstances, editions were small, and the prices paid authors low. There were not more than 1500 copies in each edition of Milton, and 1300 copies were sold in two years, the author receiving £5 down, and five more when 1300 were sold (*vide* Johnson's "Life of Milton"). Doubtless this was a large sale for the time, for, although the poem did not please the court, it evidently found readers elsewhere. And pleasing the court was far from meaning that the writer was rewarded. Butler's "Hudibras" was entirely in the interest of the king and his party, and when the first three cantos ap-

---

* Quoted by Beljame.

peared, at the end of 1662, Lord Buckhurst made it known to the court, and every one was laughing over the story of the Presbyterian justice who endeavored to put down superstition and correct current abuses : the curious mixture of a knight-errant and a pedantic magistrate—a Presbyterian Don Quixote. The king read it, and it became the fashion of the day. Pepys (Dec. 26, 1662) says : "Hither came Mr. Battersby ; and we falling into discourse of a new book of drollery in use, called 'Hudibras,' I would needs go find it out, and met with it at the Temple : cost me 2s. 6d. But when I come to read it, it is so silly an abuse of the Presbyter Knight going to the warrs, that I am ashamed of it ; and by and by meeting at Mr. Townsend's at dinner, I sold it to him for 18d." On the 6th of February, however, he bought it again : "it being certainly some ill-humour to be so against that which all the world cries up to be the example of wit ; for which I am resolved once more to read him and see whether I can find it or no." Another entry, December 10 of the same year, 1663, mentions a visit to a bookseller's, when, by the way, he "could not tell whether to lay out my money for books of pleasure, as plays, which my nature was most earnest in ; but at last" (and this list is certainly curious), "after seeing Chaucer, Dugdale's 'History of Paul's,' Stow's 'London,' Gesner, 'History of Trent,' besides Shakespeare, Jonson and Beaumont's plays, I at last chose Dr. Fuller's 'Worthies,' the 'Cabbala, or Collection of Letters of State, etc., etc.,' and 'Hudibras,' both parts, the book now in greatest fashion for drollery, though I cannot, I confess, see enough where the wit lies." In general, as Pepys shows, the contrary opinion was held. Every one looked on Butler's fortune as made. As Dr. Johnson puts it, "Every eye watched for the golden shower which was to fall upon the author, who certainly

was not without his part in the general expectation."
Nothing came of it. The golden shower was as decep-
tive as a gold-mine, and Butler took up his pen again.
The second part appeared, and Dr. Johnson repeats a story
of how the Duke of Buckingham was told by Wycherley
that Butler deserved well of the royal family, and "that
it was a reproach to the court that a person of his loyalty
and wit should suffer in obscurity and under the wants he
did." The duke was ready with his promises, and offered
to let the poet be introduced to him. While he was waiting to receive the poet, "a brace of ladies" passed by the
open door, and the duke slipped out, and Butler never saw
him. As Colley Cibber said of him,* "Was not his book
always in the pocket of his prince? And what did the
mighty prowess of his knight-errant amount to? Why †—
he died, with the highest esteem of the court—in a garret!"
Cowley was promised by Charles I. and Charles II. the
mastership of the Savoy—an old hospital for the reception of professional beggars—but the sinecure was never
granted him, and he died in neglect.

Writing for the stage was not very satisfactory, although
it was tried by nearly all the writers of the time. Dryden, who probably was paid as much as any one, received,
apparently, about £100 a year, and never more than £100
for any one of his plays. The prologues and epilogues
would bring him, perhaps, five guineas more. For a time
Dryden received from £300 to £400 in return for writing three plays a year—and that is the equivalent of three
times as much at the present time—and he had pensions
from the king, but the reward was scanty and uncertain
for the rest of the dramatic writers. They all had to depend for further support upon such gifts as they might

---

* In his dedication of his "Ximena" to Steele.

† Proctor calls this use of *why* an Americanism.

entice from the rich by complimentary addresses, odes, elegies,* dedications, etc. In a word, there was no *public*. The history of English literature for the next hundred years is an account of the growth of a reading public.

At some other time we shall discuss briefly some of the peculiarities of the stage. Of certain qualities of the poetry mention has been already made, such as the invasion of conceits : the later poets were satisfied with the ingenuity and novelty of the conceits alone ; they looked upon the means as an end, just as, possibly, some of our contemporary verse-writers mistake the use of new and rare epithets as all that is required for poetry. The reaction was in favor of simplicity and correctness. It began, as we saw, in Denham and Waller, who are to some extent the English equivalents of Malherbe, but Dryden was the man who left his mark most distinctly upon the movement, until we come to Pope, who brought it to its highest condition.

II. Possibly the most characteristic form of the poetry of this time is the satirical. There was an absence of strong enthusiasm, and in its place there existed political heat, and, above all, an earnest desire for correctness. The wide-spread licentiousness of the age produced the cynicism which would take pleasure in the study of the faults of mankind rather than in imaginative representations of human excellence. Moreover, the new-born intellectual and scientific interest demanded what was thought to be accuracy. It must be remembered, however, that satire was not absolutely new in English verse. There was George Gascoigne's "Steele Glas," 1576, one of the early poems in blank verse, by the way, from which it may be allowable to quote a few lines (p. 78) :

---

* Dryden received 500 guineas for his elegy, " Eleonora," on the Countess of Abingdon.

" Now these be past, (my priests) yet shall you pray
For common people each in his degree,
That God vouchsafe to grant them all his grace.
When should I now begin to bid my beads ?
Or who shall first be put in common place ?
My wits be weary and my eyes are dim,
I cannot see who best deserves the room.
Stand forth, good Piers, thou plowman by thy name,
Yet so, the sailor saith I do him wrong :
That one contends his pains are without peer,
That other saith that none be like to his ;
Indeed they labour both exceedingly.
But since I see no shipman that can live
Without the plough, and yet I many see
(Which live by land) that never saw the seas :
Therefore, I say, stand forth Piers Plowman first
Thou winnest the room, by very worthyness.

Behold him, priests, and though he stink of sweat,
Disdain him not : for shall I tell you what ?
Such climb to heaven, before the shaven crowns.
But how ? forsooth with true humility.
Not that they hoard their grain when it is cheap,
Nor that they kill the calf to have the milk,
Nor that they set debate between their lords,"

and commit various agrarian outrages.

" I say that sooner some of them
Shall scale the walls which lead us up to heaven
Than corn-fed beasts, whose belly is their God
Although they preach of more perfection."

The priests are also to pray for sailors—

" God them send
More mind of him whenas they come to land—
For toward shipwreck many men can pray."
* * * * * *
But here, methinks, my priests begin to frown,
* * * * * *
And one I hear more saucy than the rest
Which asketh me, when shall our prayers end ?"

To this he answers :

> " When tinkers make no more holes than they found,
> *　　*　　*　　*　　*　　*
> When colliers put no dust into their sacks,
> *　　*　　*　　*　　*　　*
> When smiths shoe horses as they would be shod,
> *　　*　　*　　*　　*　　*
> When brewers put no baggage in their beer.
> *　　*　　*　　*　　*　　*
> When silver sticks not on the teller's fingers,
> And when receivers pay as they receive,
> When all these folk have quite forgotten fraud."

He ends the poem thus :

> " And yet therein I pray you (my good priests)
> Pray still for me, and for my Glass of Steel
> That it (nor I) do any mind offend,
> Because we show all colours in their kind.
> And pray for me that (since my hap is such
> To see men so) I may perceive myself.
> O worthy words to end my worthless verse,
> Pray for me, priests, I pray you pray for me."

But these pensive lines are very different from the usual somewhat brazen rhetoric of the regular satirical poets of England. The first* of these was Joseph Hall (1574–1656), afterwards Bishop of Exeter and of Norwich. At the age of twenty-three, and while he was yet a student at Emmanuel College, Cambridge, the author began the publication of his Satires, the first three books appearing in 1597, the last three in 1598, a little more than twenty years after Gascoigne's " Steele Glas."

" I first adventure," is the way he begins :

---

* The controversy about absolute priority would be sterile. Grosart, in the preface to his edition of Hall's satires, rules out Piers Plowman as a mediæval writer, and mentions, besides Gascoigne, Hake's "Newes out of Powles Church Yard," 1567–69, and Thomas Lodge's "Fig for Momus," 1595. What Hall meant was that he was the first *classical* satirist.

> " I first adventure, with fool-hardy might,
> To tread the steps of perilous despite.
> I first adventure, follow me who list,
> And be the second English satirist.
> *   *   *   *   *   *
> Go, daring muse, on with thy thankless task,
> And do the ugly face of Vice unmask."

And this he did with the vigor he learned from Juvenal and the " Roman ancients "—" Whose words," he says,

> " were short, and darksome was their sense.
> Who reads one line of their harsh poesies,
> Thrice must he take his wind, and breathe him thrice."

Here is an example :

> " Thy grandsire's words savoured of thrifty leeks
> Or manly garlic.
> They naked went, or clad in ruder hide
> Or home-spun russet, void of foreign pride.
> But thou canst sport in garish gauderie,
> To suit a fool's far-fetchéd livery.
> A French head joined to neck Italian :
> The thighs from Germany, the breast from Spain :
> An Englishman in none, a fool in all."

This reminds one of Portia's description of the English lord, "Merchant of Venice," I. i. 79 (1596–7).

He attacks Marlowe, and, in fact, most of his contemporaries :

> " Too popular is tragic poesie,
> Straining his tiptoes for a farthing fee,
> And doth, beside, on rimeless numbers tread :
> Unbid iambics flow from careless head."

He also denounces various social errors :

> " Who ever gives a pair of velvet shoes
> To th' holy rood, or liberally allows
> But a new rope to ring the curfew bell,
> But he desires that his great deed may dwell
> Or graven in the chancel-window glass,
> Or in the lasting tomb of plated brass.

Some stately tomb he builds, Egyptian wise,
Rex regum written on the pyramis :
Whereas great Arthur lives in ruder oak,
That never felt aught but the feller's stroke,
Small honor can be got with gaudy grave,
A rotten name from death it cannot save.
The fairer tomb, the fouler is thy name,
The greater pomp procuring greater shame.
Thy monument make thou thy living deeds,
No other tomb than that true virtue needs !"

Sat. ii. lib. iii.

We cannot linger long over these poems. They were, perhaps, the first attempts in English at adapting ancient poetry to modern times ; a habit which was forgotten, and revived by Rochester in the time of Charles II. It ran through the last century. Hall by no means invented the notion of this sort of satirical writing, although he was a contemporary of the French manipulators of Juvenal, D'Aubigné (1550 – 1630) and Régnier (1573 – 1613) ; he had read but Ariosto's satires and "one base French satire,"* which had inspired him, or helped to

---

* *Vide* the postscript to his satires : " Besides the plain experience thereof in the satires of Ariosto (save which and one base French satire) I could never attain the view of any for my direction." He probably refers to one of the satyr-like French poems of the early part of the sixteenth century, such as adorn " Le Parnasse Satyrique."

The satires of Ariosto and of Alamanni were doubtless Wyatt's model ; thus :

" This [independence] is the cause that I could never yet
Hang on their sleeves that weigh, as thou may'st see,
A chip of chance more than a pound of wit.
This maketh me at home to hunt and hawk ;
And in foul weather at my book to sit ;
In frost and snow, then with my bow to stalk ;
No man doth mark whereso I ride or go,
In lusty leas at liberty I walk ;
And of these news I feel nor weal nor woe." . . .

inspire him, with the notion of modernizing Juvenal. Ariosto's satires are certainly not bitter portrayals of the dark side of life in Italy—for he had a field which would have delighted Juvenal; they lack that writer's tremendous earnestness; they are epistles, and are more like Horace's descriptions of what he saw. That there should have been a similarity of methods among the writers of the Renaissance in modern Europe is not strange in view of the fact that light came to them from but one quarter— namely, from antiquity. Italy was the first to study the classics, and the first to try the experiments which all the rest of civilized Europe tried in turn.

About Hall I will only add that Milton, who had a controversy with him, denounced his "hobbling distick," as he called it, in his " Apology for Smectymnuus;" * that Hall sank into obscurity until Pope's time, who wished that he had modernized him, as he did modernize some of Donne's satires, and that he was much admired by Gray. I think, however, that now those who turn back to him feel as if he was more impressed by a desire to conform to Juvenal than to the facts, and that he would not have been so indignant if the Roman poet had not shown him the way. Donne's satires are very different. He wrote them when but twenty, and they seem to be very genuine expressions of real feeling. Here is one passage:

> " Fool and wretch, wilt thou let Soul be tied
> To men's laws, by which she shall not be tried

---

* " Neither had I read the hobbling distick which he means. For this good hap I had from a careful education to be inured and seasoned betimes with the best and elegantest authors of the learned tongues and thereto brought an ear that could measure a just cadence and scan without articulating; rather nice and humorous in what was tolerable then patient to read every drawling versifier."

> At the last day ?   Oh, will it then serve thee
> To say a Philip or a Gregory,
> A Harry or a Martin taught thee this ?
> Is not this excuse for mere contraries,
> Equally strong ?   Cannot both sides say so ?
> That thou may'st rightly obey Power, her bounds know."

After the Restoration satire naturally had abundance of material.   Marvell denounced the vices of the court, and, as I have said, Butler jeered at the Puritans.   I think that most of us agree with Pepys, and find "Hudibras" tedious, for, as Dr. Johnson said, "Our grandfathers knew the picture from the life ; we judge of the life from the picture," but there are enough clever couplets in Butler to keep his name fresh :

> " The greatest saints and sinners have been made
>   Of proselytes of one another's trade."

> " The subtler all things are
>   They're but to nothing the more near."

> " Those that write in rhyme still make
>   The one verse for the other's sake."

These survive, while "Hudibras" is practically unread. Cleveland (1613–59), too, was never tired of ridiculing the Puritans, whom, for instance, he thus describes:

> " With face and fashion to be known
>   For one of sure election,
>   With eyes all white and many a groan,
>   With neck aside to draw in tone,
>   With harp in's nose, or he is none.
>   See a new teacher of the town,
>   O, the town, the town's new teacher "—

and Cleveland's poems doubtless gave hints to Butler. Butler, too, by no means satirized the Puritans alone : bad poets ; the Royal Society ; critics, of course ; the age of Charles II. ; marriage ; plagiaries — all came in for his clever ridicule in other short poems.   But although many of Butler's lines have become proverbial, and his wit is as epigrammatic as that of Pope, he failed to attain a really high position, because he was unable to see anything but what was contemptible in the Puritans. As Mr. Stopford Brooke says: "Satire should have at least the semblance of truth; yet Butler calls the Puritans cowards." And readers know that perpetual epigrams become in time as wearisome as perpetual punning.

III. Satire, then, was the weapon which, so to speak, ruder craftsmen had been forging, and Dryden was about to polish for the consternation of his foes. In his early days he was a busy writer for the stage, but of the drama, and of his contribution to it, we shall speak at another time. His satirical poems, at least certain parts of them, are what have made him famous and will keep him famous. Had he died at the age of forty, we should have known him as, all things considered, a clever dramatist and an intelligent critic, whose prefaces and brief prose writings were worthy of attention. Davenant had been poet-laureate to Charles I., and was reappointed to the same position by Charles II.; at his death it must have seemed that Butler was the proper man to succeed him, but Dryden was appointed. His first great work was "Absalom and Achitophel," published in November, 1681. And it is with this poem that Dryden first showed how formidable an antagonist he was. Dryden wrote to defend the king. Moreover, he had an opportunity, which he did not neglect, of paying off some of his own personal scores, one, of long standing, being an account with the Duke of Buckingham, who had ridiculed him, with more success than lasting wit, in the "Rehearsal." There were others, too, who came in for incidental notice, yet these debts he paid without any exhibition of the malice that would have taken the sting from his lash.

He describes Shaftesbury thus :

" Of these the false Achitophel was first;
A name to all succeeding ages cursed:
For close designs, and crooked counsels fit;
Sagacious, bold, and turbulent of wit;
Restless, unfix'd in principles and place;
In power unpleased, impatient of disgrace :
A fiery soul, which working out its way,
Fretted the pigmy body to decay,
And o'er-informed the tenement of clay.
A daring pilot in extremity;
Pleased with the danger, when the waves went high
He sought the storms; but for a calm unfit!
Would steer too nigh the sands to boast his wit.
Great wits are sure to madness near allied,
And thin partitions do their bounds divide.
How safe is treason, and how sacred ill,
Where none can sin against the people's will!
Where crowds can wink, and no offence be known,
Since in another's guilt they find their own !
Yet fame deserved no enemy can grudge;
The statesman we abhor, but praise the judge.
In Israel's courts ne'er sat an Abethdin
With more discerning eyes, or hands more clean,
Unbribed, unsought, the wretched to redress;
Swift of despatch, and easy of access.
Oh ! had he been content to serve the crown,
With virtues only proper to the gown;
Or had the rankness of the soil been freed
From cockle that oppressed the noble seed;
David for him his tuneful harp had strung,
And heaven had wanted one immortal song.
But wild ambition loves to slide, not stand,
And fortune's ice prefers, not virtue's land."

Every one will notice the evident truthfulness of this
compact description, and the absence of personal feeling ;
merits which are always rare in controversial writing, and
especially rare at this time. And it is equally impossible

to overlook the unprecedented ease and grace with which the heroic measure is handled. Notice this passage, too, in which Buckingham is described:

> "Some of their chiefs were princes of the land;
>   In the first rank of these did Zimri stand;
>   A man so various that he seemed to be
>   Not one, but all mankind's epitome:
>   Stiff in opinion, always in the wrong;
>   Was everything by starts, and nothing long;
>   But in the course of one revolving moon,
>   Was chymist, fiddler, statesman, and buffoon:
>   Then all for women, painting, rhyming, drinking,
>   Besides ten thousand freaks that died in thinking.
>   Blest madman, that could every hour employ,
>   With something new to wish, or to enjoy:
>   Railing and praising were his usual themes;
>   And both, to show his judgment, in extremes:
>   So over violent, or over civil,
>   That every man with him was God or Devil.
>   In squandering wealth was his peculiar art:
>   Nothing went unrewarded but desert.
>   Beggared by fools, whom still he found too late,
>   He had his jest, and they had his estate.
>   He laughed himself from court; then sought relief
>   By forming parties, but could ne'er be chief:
>   For spite of him, the weight of business fell
>   On Absalom and wise Achitophel;
>   Thus wicked but in will, of means bereft,
>   He left not faction, but of that was left."

Here is the same unexaggerated description, this time of a flimsy character, and it is easy to imagine the force with which the poem must have impressed itself upon its readers. As for the mere sound, the above may be compared with these lines of Rochester's:

> "Well, sir, 'tis granted: I said Dryden's rhymes
>   Were stolen, unequal—nay dull, many times.
>   What foolish patron is there found of his
>   So blindly partial to deny me this?

But that his plays embroidered up and down
With wit and learning, justly pleased the town,
In the same paper I as freely own.
Yet, having this allowed, the heavy mass
That stuffs up his loose volumes must not pass."

Or these from Oldham (1653–83) (from a satire in which
Spenser is dissuading Oldham from poetry) :

" I come, fond Idiot, ere it be too late,
   Kindly to warn thee of thy wretched fate :
Take heed betimes, repent and learn of me
To shun the dang'rous rocks of Poetry :
Had I the choice of Flesh and Blood again,
To act once more in Life's tumultuous scene ;
I'd be a Porter or a Scavenger,
A Groom, or anything but a Poet here :
Hast thou observed some Hawker of the Town,
Cries Matches, Small coal, Brooms, Old shoes and boots,
Socks, Sermons, Ballads, Lies, Gazettes, and Votes ?
So unrecorded to the grave I'd go." . . .

Surely Dryden's superior management of the heroic
verse is evident at once. And it is to be noticed that he
does not confine himself to what Mr. Lowell calls the
"thought coop" of the couplet. The sense runs through
from one line to another. Yet he did this without awk-
wardness. Another quality that he had was that of reasoning in verse, of making statements or arguments as
clear as his own prose—and that is saying a good deal.

This Dryden did without the fierce fury of most of the
satirists, a quality which they copied from Juvenal, just as
they imitated his obscurity and that of Persius. He wrote,
too, with complete self-possession, a sort of lordly superiority to personal pique, as when he speaks of one Samuel
Johnson as Ben-Jochanan :

" A Jew of humble parentage was he,
   By trade a Levite though of low degree :

His pride no higher than the desk aspired,
But for the drudgery of priests was hired
To read and pray in linen ephod brave,
And pick up single shekels from the grave.
Married at last, but finding charge come faster,
He could not live by God, but changed his master,
Inspired by want, was made a factious tool ;
They got a villain, and we lost a fool."

Or his cool reference to Pordage :*

" Lame Mephibosheth, the wizard's son."

In 1681 appeared "The Medal," a satire against sedition; a medal having been struck off to celebrate Shaftesbury's acquittal of the charge of high-treason.

Let us consider for a moment the circumstances in which these poems were read. In the city there were numberless coffee-houses, which were frequented by men of all sorts for the discussion of political, social, and literary news ; but in the country there were but few opportunities of knowing what was going on. The gazettes published only what the licensers of the press allowed, and they naturally did not contain much of the talk of the town. The curiosity of the provinces was allayed, however, by men who made a business of writing news-letters to certain persons of the nobility, clergymen, magistrates, or what not. The writers wandered through the town, picking up scraps of news for their correspondents. Their method may be learned from No. 625 of the *Spectator*, in which a writer says : "In order to make myself useful, I am early in the

---

* Pordage's father had been expelled his charge for insufficiency. One count in the accusation brought against him was this: "That a great dragon came into his chamber with a tail of eight yards long, four great teeth, and did spit fire at him ; and that he contended with him ;" *vide* Scott's "Life of Dryden," chap. v. Apparently it was not thought etiquette to contend with dragons.

antichamber, where I thrust my head into the thick of the press, and catch the news, at the opening of the door, while it is warm. Sometimes I stand by the beefeaters, and take the buzz as it passes by me. At other times I lay my ear close to the wall, and suck in many a valuable whisper, as it runs in a straight line from corner to corner. When I am weary of standing, I repair to one of the neighbouring coffee-houses, . . . and forestall the evening post by two hours. There is a certain gentleman who hath given me the slip. . . . But I have played him a trick. I have purchased a pair of the best coach-horses I could buy for money, and now let him outstrip me if he can." Thus we see that the energy of reporters is not an invention of the nineteenth century.

The poorer people of the country received their information of what was going on in the city from the clergyman, with such comments, words of explanation, warning, and advice as they thought proper ; and, since the clergy belonged to the king's party, they doubtless took every precaution to disseminate what they deemed sound views.

As to the dissenters, they were the great readers of sermons and tracts, and how numerous these were may be gathered from the list at the beginning of this chapter. Preaching was generally forbidden them, and the songs of the time are full of ribald abuse of their conventicles, as their secret reunions were called. They were exposed to severe persecution. Pepys, August 7, 1664, says : "I saw several poor creatures carried by, by constables, for being at a conventicle. They go like lambs, without any resistance. I would to God," he adds, "they would either conform, or be more wise and not be catched." Of their sufferings it is easy to judge from reading any life of Bunyan. Being debarred from preaching, they took to writing, and there are many proofs of their literary activity. By the side of the Pindaric odes, the translations, the ribald plays, the fierce satires of the reign of Charles II., there were appearing a host of religious publications, of which the best known, because the best in every way, was Bunyan's "Pilgrim's Progress,"* which went through eight editions in four years.

Dryden was peculiarly happy in choosing his method of attack. Nowadays, practised readers are weary of fables and allegories ; but these always have a charm for children, and for inexperienced readers, who need this sugaring of the pill, or, as Addison put it (*Spectator*, No. 512) : "This natural pride and ambition of the soul is very much gratified in the reading of a fable ; for in writings of this kind the reader comes in for half of the performance, everything appears to him like a discovery of his own. . . . For this reason the "Absalom and Achitophel" was one of the most popular poems that ever appeared in English." Then a biblical allegory was most fortunate. Dryden stole the very thunder of the Puritans : Zimri, Shimei, Ishbosheth, Jebusites, Barzillai—these names alone would have sanctified any writing.

Not only, however, was it customary to transfer current themes to a biblical setting, as indeed had been done in "Samson Agonistes"—for the translation of the Bible had brought about a change something like that of the Renaissance—but the very names of the poem had been applied

---

* For the origin of this book, see "The Ancient Poem of Guillaume de Guileville, entitled Le Pelerinage de l'Homme, compared with the Pilgrim's Progress of John Bunyan. Edited from Notes collected by the late Mr. Nathaniel Hill. London : Basil Montague Pickering. 1858." It is much to be regretted that the editor did not publish the notes in full. Cf. prefaces of Southey and James Montgomery to their editions of this book, and the interesting but uncritical remarks of George Offor in his reprint, London, 1847.

as they were here. There was, for instance, a play published in 1680, " Absalom's Conspiracy ; or, the Tragedy of Treason," * in which Monmouth had been compared to Absalom.

While in this satire Dryden held his hand, and by his reasonableness disarmed opposition, he was not always gentle with stupidity. In the second part, as it is called, of " Absalom and Achitophel," after many replies from various Whig poets, he reserved some of the writers for his own castigation : as in the line about Pordage, and the celebrated attacks on Settle and Shadwell. Nahum Tate wrote the rest, but Dryden inserted a few most cutting passages. Shadwell he had attacked in " Mac Flecknoe," in October, 1682, and the second part of " Absalom and Achitophel " contained denunciations of both him and Settle. There were sufficient reasons. Shadwell had attacked him in an incredibly coarse way for writing the " Medal." And, although there is much that is unquotable in Dryden's satirical verse, that fault is to be put down to the time in which he lived rather than to his own discredit. He was decorum itself by the side of Shadwell, and, even when he is most violent in his reply, he has an air of good-natured superiority to his foes which must have galled them as much as it may amuse us. His own views on Satire were most reasonable, as he said in his " Essay on Satire "—the preface † to the translation of

---

* Mentioned by Beljame.

† The long prefaces were not, as Swift said of Dryden's, in his lines " On Poetry, a Rhapsody,"

> " Merely writ at first for filling,
> To raise the volume's price a shilling "

(and see also " A Tale of a Tub, " sec. v.), but rather because there was no other means of reaching the public. Then, too, there was the precedent of the French usage. Thus Boileau, in his second preface, ed. 1674 (Vic-

Juvenal and Persius. "How easy it is to call rogue and villain, and that wittily! but how hard to make a man appear a fool, a blockhead, or a knave, without using any of those opprobrious terms! . . . This is the mystery of that noble trade. . . . Neither is it true that this fineness of raillery is offensive; a witty man is tickled while he is hurt in this manner, and a fool feels it not. . . . There is a vast difference between the slovenly butchering of a man, and the fineness of a stroke that separates the head from the body, and leaves it standing in its place. A man may be capable, as Jack Ketch's wife said of his servant, of a plain piece of work, of a bare hanging: but to make a malefactor die sweetly was only belonging to her husband. I wish I could apply it to myself, if the reader would be kind enough to think it belongs to me. The character of Zimri in my 'Absalom' is, in my opinion, worth the whole poem. It is not bloody, but it is ridiculous enough, and he for whom it was intended was too witty to resent it as an injury. . . . I avoided the mention of great crimes, and applied myself to the representing of blind sides and little extravagances, to which, the wittier a man is, he is generally the more obnoxious."

Yet, as he says elsewhere in the same essay: "Good sense and good nature are never separated, though the ignorant world has thought otherwise. Good-nature, by which I mean beneficence and candor, is the product of right reason, which of necessity will give allowance to the failings of others, by considering that there is nothing perfect in mankind." Personal satire will always seem to be the result of ill-nature, and the world will in time become

tor le Duc's ed., p. 28): " J'avois médité une assez longue preface, où, suivant la coutume reçue parmi les écrivains de ce temps, j'espérois rendre un compte fort exact de mes ouvrages, et justifier les libertés que j'ai prises."

indifferent to denunciations, however brilliant, when the inspiring causes have to be found out by remote investigation. We all have our own quarrels in our hands; we are concerned with new forms of folly, and we are cold to Dryden's attacks on forgotten writers like Settle, or Pope's venomous abuse in the "Dunciad." Only those things live that are of universal application. Poetry, it has been said, treats of those qualities that are eternal in man, and the peculiar qualities of Settle and Shadwell are fortunately obsolete. At the end of the last century, Dr. Joseph Warton said that it was an undoubted fact that the "Absalom and Achitophel," which is far from being a virulent satire, was then but little read, and that the "Dunciad" began to be neglected. Yet, while we have grown indifferent to the sum of Dryden's satirical poems, we can never become tired of certain bits in which personality fades away in comparison with the excellence of his wit, as in the lines about Burnet, "Hind and Panther," 2477:

> " Prompt to assail, and careless of defence,
> Invulnerable in his impudence,
> He dares the world, and eager of a name,
> He thrusts about and justles into fame.
>
>   *   *   *   *   *
>
> So fond of loud report that, not to miss
> Of being known (his last and utmost bliss)
> He rather would be known for what he is."

Nothing could be better than the last line, which is all the more intensified by coming at the end of a triplet. When we come to Pope's "Dunciad," we shall see how seldom the later poet gives us the whole character of a man, which Dryden never fails to do.

Of Dryden's other poems I shall speak but briefly; the "Religio Laici," 1681, and the "Hind and the Panther," 1687, were in many ways wonderful poems. Take a few lines of the "Religio Laici," for example, and we shall find Dryden's unfailing dexterity and wit :

> " The unlettered Christian who believes in gross,
> Plods on to heaven, and ne'er is at a loss :
> For the strait gate would be made straiter yet
> Were none admitted there but men of wit."

In the early work he defends Protestantism against atheism and heresy. In the "Hind and the Panther" he writes in defence of the Roman Church, of which he had recently become a member, and the genuineness of his religious fervor has been often questioned. This is a question that falls outside of our present discussion, but it may be worth while to point out some of the inconsistencies with which he has been charged. Certainly, Dryden seemed in earnest when he attacked "the bloody bear, an independent beast," "the buffoon ape" (the atheists), " the bristled Baptist boar," " False Reynard " (the Arians and Socinians), "the insatiate Wolf" (the Presbyterians). Yet it was remembered that he had already written on the other side of the religious controversy. In " Absalom and Achitophel," he had spoken coarsely of the doctrine of transubstantiation. In his "Spanish Friar," 1681, he ridiculed processions, the invocation of saints, and auricular confession. In his "Religio Laici," he attacked the Church of Rome ; in his " Duke of Guise," written in conjunction with Nat Lee, he defended a Catholic prince, and after the death of Charles II., when a Catholic king was on the throne, he wrote the "Hind and the Panther," in which he began by inviting the Church of England to unite with that of Rome, and ended by urging the dissenters to make common cause with Rome against the Church of England.

In politics he showed the same fickleness. In " Amboyna," he tried to stir up the English against the Dutch;, in his "Absalom and Achitophel," and the "Medal," he blamed Shaftesbury for encouraging that war. In literary matters, as about the use of prose or verse in his plays, he was forever wavering. Another charge is brought, that he flattered the Duke and Duchess of Monmouth, who protected him in his need, and then that he abused them in "Absalom and Achitophel," and drew the infamous Duke of Guise, in the play of that name, from the Duke of Monmouth.

Let us remember, however, the almost universal corruption of the time, and in special defence of Dryden the fact that, great poet as he was, he wrote mainly as a journalist, so to speak. In the absence of other ways of reaching the public, his poems were written to order for direct, immediate political effect, and with the same unscrupulousness that is sometimes seen in a corrupt press. This by no means frees his conduct from blame, but it may possibly be in part an explanation.

As I say, I pass over these poems with some celerity, because we now take very little interest in the theological questions which were meat and drink to our ancestors in the seventeenth century, and the poems are in the main dead. They are ingenious pamphlets in verse, and they doubtless set the fashion for the many didactic and theological poems which weighed down the literature of the eighteenth century. They deserve the credit, however, of being about the best of their kind: The "Mac Flecknoe," in which a wretched Irish poet, one Flecknoe, makes over the succession to Shadwell, is short, and will well repay attention. It has the great merit of being the one of the controversial poems of the time that is most nearly readable. The French influence, which Dryden, a thorough Englishman, was helping to introduce, had at least a mollifying influence on this kind of writing. The beginning, familiar as it is, will show this:

"All human things are subject to decay,
And, when fate summons, monarchs must oblige ;
This Flecknoe found, who, like Augustus, young
Was called to empire, and had governed long ;
In prose and verse was owned without dispute,
Through all the realms of Nonsense, absolute.
This aged prince, now flourishing in peace,
And blessed with issue of a large increase,
Worn out with business, did at length debate
To settle the succession of the state ;
And pondering which of all his sons was fit
To reign, and wage immortal war with wit,
Cried, ' 'Tis resolved ! for nature pleads, that he
Should only rule who most resembles me.
Shadwell alone my perfect image bears,
Mature in dulness from his tender years ;
Shadwell alone, of all my sons, is he
Who stands confirmed in full stupidity.
The rest to some faint meaning make pretence,
But Shadwell never deviates into sense.
Some beams of wit on other souls may fall,
Strike through and make a lucid interval ;
But Shadwell's genuine night admits no ray,
His rising fogs prevail upon the day.
Besides, his goodly fabric fills the eye,
And seems designed for thoughtless majesty ;
Thoughtless as monarch oaks, that shade the plain,
And, spread in solemn state, supinely reign.' "

This mock-heroic is sometimes called an imitation of
Boileau's famous poem, "Le Lutrin," which appeared in
1674. In the French poem, certain ecclesiastics are turned
into ridicule, just as is done with the literary adventurer in
the English one. Yet we have Dryden's statement that
the resemblance was accidental.* At any rate, the "Mac-

---

* Some time later, Dryden said in conversation, "If anything of mine
is good, 'tis my ' Mac Flecknoe,' and I value myself the more on it, because
'tis the first piece of ridicule written in heroics." His interlocutor vent-

Flecknoe " has the merit of brevity, and is not dull. The "Religio Laici" is dull, and as to the "Hind and the Panther," I think that there must be few people who can care much for the theological discussions of those two beasts. The long controversy on the Test Acts, the authority of the pope, transubstantiation, etc., are most unfortunately set.

These extracts will serve to show what was the principle which Dryden, by precept and example, fastened on English literature. We will not forget that it was not of his invention, nor yet necessarily what he most admired. He had a warm feeling of reverence for Milton, and it is worthy of note that in 1688 there appeared a new edition of Milton, published by subscription, and that from this time that poet began to receive general admiration. At least, he was no longer overlooked. But in the new and swift advance towards our modern civilization exaggerated weight was laid on the external tokens of this civilization. While England was ready for the change, the French were busy in laying down the laws for its control in literature. Instead of lawlessness, polish; instead of blank verse, rhyme; above all things, elegance. We, who are the living witnesses of a somewhat similar revolution in taste, may readily understand how much more powerful than statute laws are new æsthetic rules. Probably even Nihilists love, or try to love, dados and friezes; and we at once suspect the sincerity of any person who avows a liking for white paint and green blinds. Similar forces were then at work in England to ruin any admiration for the great tragedians. They were looked upon as men of ability,

---

ured to remind the poet of Boileau's "Lutrin," which Dryden said he had read, but had forgotten, and that he had not copied it. In Italian, too, a number of mock-heroics had been written.

who lacked that for·which the modern equivalent is culture. They were void of art, and *art* was the shibboleth
of that age. As Dryden wrote to his "dear friend, Mr.
Congreve, on his comedy called 'The Double Dealer:'"

> "Well, then, the promised hour has come at last,
> The present age of wit obscures the past:
> Strong were our sires, and as they fought they writ,
> Conquering with force of arm, and dint of wit;
> Theirs was the giant race before the flood;
> And thus when Charles returned, our empire stood.
> Like James, he the stubborn soil manured,
> With rules of husbandry the rankness cured;
> Tamed us to manners, when the stage was rude,
> And boisterous English wit with art endued.
> Our age was cultivated thus at length,
> But what we gain'd in skill, we lost in strength.
> Our builders were with want of genius curst;
> The second temple was not like the first,
> Till you, the best Vitruvius, came at length,
> Our beauties equal, but excel our strength."

When we come to speak of the plays, we shall see how
the work of the early writers was regarded and treated.
What was thought in the last century about Dryden's influence on English poetry we may see in Dr. Johnson's
life of that poet. He says: "Every·language of a learned
nation necessarily divides itself into diction scholastic and
popular, grave and familiar, elegant and gross; and from
a nice distinction of these different parts arises a great
part of the beauty of style. . . . There was before the
time of Dryden no poetical diction, no system of words at
once refined from the grossness of domestic use and free
from the harshness of terms appropriated to particular
arts. From those sounds which we hear on small or on
coarse occasions, we do not easily receive strong impressions" (How about Lear's "Pray you, undo this button"?)

" or delightful images ; and words to which we are nearly strangers, whenever they occur, draw that attention on themselves which they should transmit to things. Those happy combinations of words which distinguish poetry from prose had been rarely attempted : we had few elegances or flowers of speech ; the roses had not yet been plucked from the bramble, or different colours had not been joined to enliven one another. . . . The new versification, as it was called, may be considered as owing its establishment to Dryden ; from whose time it is apparent that English poetry had no tendency to relapse to its former savageness."

IV. This has a strange sound to our ears ; savageness, indeed ! We must not forget that the whole aim of this school was the abolition of " eccentricity," of " arbitrariness," as Matthew Arnold calls it,[*] and that although the reaction has died and arbitrariness is again triumphant, this carefulness, the compliance with what the French critics preached as good-sense, once did service.

Its methods are very clearly shown in the translations which Dryden made. And it is curious to notice how every new literary movement inspires its supporters with the desire to make a new translation of the great classics. Something may be said, too, of the changes of public taste with regard to the favorite authors of antiquity, or . of modern times, too, for that matter. We saw in the last chapter the slow growth in France of the admiration of Homer ; in the Elizabethan era Ovid [†] was the favorite

---

[*] " Critical Essays " (Am. ed.), p. 335.

[†] Marot (1495–1544) wrote :

> " Ovidius, maistre Alain Charretier,
> Petrarque aussi, le Roman de la Rose,
> Sont les Messelz, Breviaire, and Psaultier,
> Qu'en ce sainct Temple, on list, en rithme et prose."

poet; with the increase of French influence came renewed respect for Vergil; Pope translated one book of Statius— to be sure, with an apology; Marlowe translated the first book of Lucan at the end of the sixteenth century, and two other translations appeared in 1614 and 1627 respectively. Horace's Satires were translated before the Odes —these last-named were not all done into English, it will be remembered, until 1625, and it is only recently that Catullus has been translated in full. * There is no need of anything like a complete list of the translations of Ovid; the statistics would be tedious. The main point is, that in the Elizabethan age he was a favorite Latin poet, and that his conceits were then thought more highly of than they now are. Horace was greatly admired in the

---

* Proofs of the variations of taste are readily found. As one indication of this relative popularity at the time, take the mottoes to the different numbers of the *Spectator*. We find, from a hurried count, Horace, *Ars Poetica, Epodes*, and *Satires*, 168; *Odes*, 51; Vergil, 124; Ovid, 55; Juvenal, 42; Persius, 10; Martial, 14; Cicero, 26; Lucretius, 5; Terence, 12; Seneca, 3; Lucan, 7; Tacitus, Claudian, and Catullus, 1.

Lovelace translated ten or twelve poems of Catullus, half-a-dozen of Martial's epigrams, and many of those of Ausonius.

"Boileau disait : ' Je puis dire que c'est moi qui ai fait connoitre les satires et les épîtres d'Horace : on ne parlait que de ses odes.' "—Victor Le Duc's "Boileau," p. 7. But Vauquelin de la Fresnaie (*vide infra*) had preceded Boileau by nearly a century with Horatian satires and literary rules.

Percival Stockdale, "Lectures on Truly Eminent English Poets," 1807, vol. i. p. 38: " Your merely great philosophers have always made a most contemptible and ridiculous figure when they have usurped the chair of poetical criticism. Blackmore, 'rumbling rough and fierce,' was the greatest of poets in the opinion of the venerable and illustrious Locke; and Catullus and Parnell were the first favorites of the Muses, in the judgement of David Hume; who was a very great man when he kept within his metaphysical and historical sphere." See, too, vol. ii. p. 652, of his tedious book.

last century ; now we are becoming more sensitive than
were our grandfathers to what we take to be a more purely poetic feeling.　Statius and Lucan scarcely exist for us.

To draw any inferences from the fact that Dryden translated the "Æneid," and Pope Homer, would be a very
dangerous thing, but possibly some of the other instances
are deserving of attention.　Similar alterations of taste
with regard to other things will readily suggest themselves, such as the modern love of the Gothic, and for certain Italian painters ; the cool feeling of us, who are later
born, for the Laocoön and the Apollo Belvedere, in comparison with the admiration they called forth in the last
century.

Every generation, then, has its own way, not only of expressing despairing love, the vanity of all things, and the
mutability of fortune, but it also seeks to render those
great poems that have acquired a somewhat similar immortality into such language as shall at the time seem the
fittest medium of expression.　Thus we see, in every translation, some of the peculiarities of the period in which it
was made.　For example, Chapman says :

> " But when they joined, the dreadful clamour rose
> To such a height, as not the sea, when up the North-spirit blows
> Her raging billows, bellows so against the beaten shore ;
> Nor such a rustling keeps a fire, driven with violent blore
> Through woods that grow against a hill ; nor so the fervent strokes
> Of almost bursting winds resound against a grove of oaks ;
> As did the clamour of these hosts, when both the battles closed."
>
> "Iliad," xiv. 327.

Pope renders the passage as follows :

> " Both armies join : Earth thunders, Ocean roars.
> Not half so loud the bellowing deeps resound,
> When stormy winds disclose the dark profound ;
> Less loud the winds that from the Æolian hall
> Roar through the woods, and make whole forests fall,

> Less loud the woods, when flames in torrents pour,
> Catch the dry mountain and its shades devour."

Other extracts, with appropriate comments, the reader will find in Mr. Matthew Arnold's "Lectures on Translating Homer," reprinted among his "Essays." As Mr. Swinburne well says of Chapman, in the volume devoted to the exposition of that poet's genius, his style "can give us but the pace of a giant for echo of the footfall of a god." We now go back to Chapman with delight, for we are ready to overlook his obvious errors ; but when Pope lived, Chapman's conceits and exaggerations had become insufferable, and a new translation into the language of the day was called for, and this Pope furnished. Pope gives his predecessor credit for the "daring, fiery spirit that animates his translation, which is something like what one might imagine Homer himself would have writ before he arrived at years of discretion," but, he says, Chapman's "expression is involved in fustian." In his own translation, Pope complied with the spirit of his time, and was always clear ; his style, too, was dignified, though with a dignity very unlike Homer's. Homer's eloquence he adorned with countless epigrams, as when Helen appeared on the walls in the third book of the "Iliad :"

> "Before thy presence, father, I appear,
> With conscious shame and reverential fear.
> Ah! had I died, ere to these walls I fled,
> False to my country and my nuptial bed ;
> My brothers, friends, and daughters left behind,
> False to them all, to Paris only kind.
> For this I mourn, till grief or dire disease
> Shall waste the form whose crime it was to please."

This was part of the same spirit that enabled the actors representing Greeks and Romans to appear in high-heeled shoes, coats, and full wigs. Cowper, in his turn, expressed the modern reaction against the epigrammatic couplet, and the reverence for Milton which we shall see growing up throughout the last century; he took Homer out of that, at length, unfashionable suit, and put him into the chains of the Miltonic inversions. Thus, in the answer of Achilles' horses :

> "For not through sloth or tardiness on us
> Aught chargeable, have Ilion's sons thine arms
> Stript from Patroclus' shoulders; but a god,
> Matchless in battle, offspring of bright-haired
> Latona, him contending in the van,
> Slew, for the glory of the chief of Troy."

Cary, Lamb's friend, translated Dante in the same way.

In our own times, which are those of critical examination and experiment, we find Mr. Newman trying the ballad measure, as in this passage :

> "O gentle friend! if thou and I, from this encounter 'scaping,
> Hereafter might forever be from Eld and Death exempted
> As heavenly gods, not I, in sooth, would fight among the foremost,
> Nor liefly thee would I advance to man-ennobling battle.
> Now—sith ten thousand shapes of Death do any-gait pursue us,
> Which never mortal may evade, tho' sly of foot and nimble;
> Onward!" etc.

We have to add Mr. Worsley's translation of the "Odyssey" in the Spenserian stanza; Lord Derby's and Mr. Bryant's into blank verse; Conington's rendering of Vergil, the most polished of authors, in the rough-and-ready measure of "Marmion." One might as well try to whistle a symphony. Then, too, Mr. William Morris, after playing for some time that he was Chaucer, put the "Æneids," as he called the poem, into early English, as thus, when Hector's ghost appears in the second book :

> "Most sorrowful to see he was, and weeping plenteous flood,
> And e'en as torn, behind the car, black with the dust and blood,

His feet all swollen with the thong that pierced them through and
through.

Woe worth the while for what he was! how changed from him we
knew!"

And everywhere we come upon such mock-English as
"why thus wise," etc.

Mr. Arnold recommends translating Homer into English
hexameters, while Mr. Tennyson, again, gives us a specimen in blank verse.

In his discussion of the course to be followed by a translator, Dryden is, as he always is in his prefaces, very interesting. He says : " When I have taken away some of
their expressions, and cut them shorter, it may possibly be
on this consideration that what was beautiful in the Greek
or Latin would not appear so shining in the English ; and
when I have enlarged them, I desire the false critics would
not always think that those thoughts are wholly mine, but
that either they are secretly in the poet, or may be fairly
deduced from him ; or at least, if both these considera-
tions should fail, that my own is of a piece with his, and
that if he were living, and an Englishman, they are such
as he would probably have written. For, after all, a translator is to make his author appear as charming as possibly
he can, provided he maintains his character, and makes
him not unlike himself."* It is really hard to stop quoting, but there is one brief passage which possibly was
newer two hundred years ago than it is now : "Not only
the thoughts, but the style and versification of Virgil and
Ovid are very different ; yet I see, even in our best poets,

---

* The lack of precision in the first translations of foreign books is worthy of note. Anything strange has to have its peculiarities rubbed off
before it interests us. Thus, while now we demand exact rendering of
Homer and Vergil, we accept the Mahabharata very much diluted with
modernisms from the pen of Mr. Edwin Arnold.

who have translated some part of them, that they have confounded their several talents ; and, by endeavouring only at the sweetness and harmony of numbers, have made them both so much alike, that if I did not know the originals, I should never be able to judge by the copies, which was Virgil and which was Ovid." Dryden's *obiter dicta* on matters generally pronounced upon only by scholars are very valuable, for the quality of a man's genius is more important in his judgment of matters of taste than any amount of education. But I resist all temptations to quote lavishly, and pass over to the end of the preface, where Dryden says : " Milton's ' Paradise Lost ' is admirable ; but am I, therefore, bound to maintain, that there are no flats amongst his elevations, when 'tis evident he creeps along sometimes, for above an hundred lines together ? Cannot I admire the height of his invention, and the strength of his invention, without defending his antiquated words, and the perpetual harshness of their sound ? It is as much commendation as a man can bear, to own him excellent ; all beyond is idolatry." This is the place where we rest with regard to Dryden. The modern feeling towards him is certainly not idolatrous.

V. Dryden had no question in his mind as to the form in which the translations should appear : there was but one, and that one he made use of. There is certainly a great charm in his renderings of Chaucer, of whom he speaks at some length. In the older poet's verse Dryden says " there is the rude sweetness of a Scotch tune which is natural and pleasing, though not perfect." I have not space to quote the opening of the " Nun's Priest's Tale," *

---

* The following correspondence explains Dryden's choice :

" DRYDEN TO PEPYS.

" July 14, 1699.

' " *Padron mio,*—I remember last year, when I had the honour of dining

or of "The Cock and the Fox;" but, although the newer
form has a quality which does not belong to Chaucer, it is
yet well worth attention, and I think that even those who
know the originals will read Dryden's versions with delight. And since the bane of the present day is pedantry, and many otherwise worthy persons will avow that
they are led by love of sincerity to condemn any working-
over of Chaucer's material, I would add that even now
there are constantly appearing renderings of Chaucer, and
that in one of the most celebrated we find versions contributed by Wordsworth, Mrs. Browning, R. H. Horne,
etc., whose names are not proverbial for insincerity. The
true test, of course, is the poems themselves, and they are
among the most readable things Dryden ever wrote. In
the course of time the controversial poems will, I think,

---

with you, you were pleased to recommend to me the character of Chaucer's
'Good Parson.' Any desire of yours is a command to me, and accordingly I have put it into my English, with such additions and alterations as I
thought fit.

"Having translated as many fables from Ovid, and as many novels from
Boccace and tales from Chaucer, as will make an indifferent large volume
in folio, I intend them for the press in Michaelmas Term next. In the
mean time, my 'Parson' desires the favour of being known to you, and
promises, if you find any fault in his character, he will reform it. Whenever you please, he shall wait on you, and for the safer conveyance, I will
carry him in my pocket, who am

"My padron's most obedient servant,

"JOHN DRYDEN."

Pepys answered on the same day:

"You truly have obliged me, and, possibly, in saying so, I am more in
earnest than you can readily think, as verily hoping from this your copy
of our 'Good Parson' to fancy some amends made me for the hourly offence I bear with from the sight of so many lewd originals."

Pepys's collection of ballads, left to Magdalen College, Cambridge, was
the main source of Percy's "Reliques;" *vide* his Preface. Pepys was one
of the men whose taste was not merely that of his day.

lose their interest, but the charm of these will never quite disappear. He calls the birds "the painted birds," to be sure, and the nightingale is Philomel. Dryden, in a word, used the language of his time ; and is not that, in some respects, better employment than frantically struggling to use the language of some other time ? Dryden, too, was clear, and that is a merit in these days, when the reader has put before him alliterative obscurity like this :

> "Hollow heaven and the hurricane,
> And hurry of the heavy rain.
>
> "Hurried clouds in the hollow heaven,
> And a heavy rain hard-driven.
>
> "The heavy rain, it hurries amain,
> And heaven and the hurricane.
>
> "Hurrying wind o'er the heaven's hollow,
> And the heavy rain to follow." *

Dryden's odes are well known. His "Song for St. Cecilia's Day" and his "Alexander's Feast" are among the familiar poems of the language ; but there are others less familiar—as, for instance, that on Anne Killigrew, which Dr. Johnson said "is the noblest ode that our language ever·has produced." It was Cowley who revived the composition of odes, which he called "the noblest and highest writing in verse," and Dr. Johnson styled "lax and lawless versification." The odes were further called Pindaric by a flight of the imagination, which was not always to be found in the poems themselves.

The first and finest stanza of the ode on Anne Killigrew runs thus :

> "Thou youngest virgin-daughter of the skies,
> Made in the last promotion of the bless'd ;

---

* "Chimes," D. G. Rossetti's "Ballads and Sonnets," p. 281.

> Whose palms, new-pluck'd from paradise,
> In spreading branches more sublimely rise,
> Rich with immortal green above the rest:
> Whether adopted to some neighb'ring star,
> Thou roll'st above us, in thy wandering race;
>> Or, in procession fix'd and regular,
>> Mov'st with the heaven's majestic pace;
>> Or, called to more superior bliss,
> Thou tread'st, with seraphims, the vast abyss:
> Whatever happy region is thy place,
> Cease thy celestial song a little space;
> Thou wilt have time enough for hymns divine,
>> Since heaven's eternal year is thine.
> Hear then a mortal Muse thy praise rehearse,
>> In no ignoble verse."

Joseph Warton, however, said that "to a cool and candid reader, it appears absolutely unintelligible. Examples of bad writing, of tumid expressions, violent metaphors, far-sought conceits, hyperbolical adulation, unnatural amplifications, interspersed, as usual, with fine lines, might be collected from this applauded ode." And, in fact, in the last stanza we come across a passage that illustrates one of Dryden's faults very clearly:

> "When in mid air the golden trump shall sound,
>> To raise the nations underground:
>> When in the valley of Jehoshaphat,
> The judging God shall close the book of fate;
>> And there the last assizes keep
>> For those who wake and those who sleep:
>> When rattling bones together fly
> From the four corners of the sky."

Indeed, the Day of Judgment seems to have aroused singular notions in Dryden, for elsewhere he speaks of the "drowsy mortals," and says, "When, called in haste, they fumble for their limbs" ("Don Sebastian"). Moreover, it would be hard to name another writer of reputation

who mingles fine lines and bad ones in such confusion as
Dryden continually does.　In the passage I have just read,
the fine-sounding line, which reminds us of the line in Mr.
Fitzgerald's translation of "Omar Khayyam" (2d ed.),
"That we might catch ere closed the book of fate,"* comes
just before the most unpoetic lines of the ode, which then
rises to a finer ending.　It is easy to find many examples of
similar carelessness.　His plays are full of passages that
would have made the fortune of a burlesque.　Thus, in the
"Royal Martyr," Maximin, the tyrant, says to the gods :

> "Keep your rain and sunshine in the skies,
> 　And I'll keep back my flame and sacrifice;
> 　Your trade of Heaven shall soon be at a stand,
> 　And all your goods lie dead upon your hand."

And the same tyrant, when dying, says :

> 　　　　　" And after thee I'll go,
> Revenging still, and following e'en to th' other world my blow,
> And, shoving back this earth on which I sit,
> I'll mount and scatter all the gods I hit."

And how Dryden could mix paltriness with beauty, we
may see in this passage ("Conquest of Granada") :

> 　　　"That busy thing,
> The soul, *is packing up*, and just on wing
> Like parting swallows when they seek the spring."

And often, too, he could be dreary without relief, as when
a dying hero (in "Amboyna") says :

> "Give to my brave
> Employers of the East India Company,

---

* Pope, "Essay on Man," i. 77:
　　　"Heav'n from all creatures hides the book of fate."
Shakspere, "2 Henry IV.," III. i. 45:
　　　"O God! that we might read the book of fate."

The last remembrance of my faithful service;
Tell them I seal that service with my blood;
And, dying, wish to all their factories,
And all the famous merchants of our isle,
That wealth their generous industry deserves."

As Dryden himself said, "A man must not write all he can, but all he ought;" yet very often Dryden was compelled by want to write all he could, and the result was bad. That he should have been ridiculed by some of the writers of his time is not strange, for we will all acknowledge that the contemporaries of a great man are apt to judge him by his failures, while posterity estimates his position by what is best in his work. Everywhere Dryden has given abundant traces of ability. He possessed various qualities—the mastery of versification, and, for that matter, of prose; he reasoned ingeniously; and he had a fine poetic quality that lights up what we nowadays are accustomed to regard as an unpoetic style. His lyrical power, too, must not be forgotten.

These poems lead us to his plays, in which his faults and his merits are most fully shown. Whatever our opinion of his poetic powers may be, there can be no doubt of the important place he fills in any study of English literature. He was the greatest English poet after Milton for at least a century, and he helped, more than any one, to shape the laws which prevailed for that period. We have seen what these were in verse; let us now examine the condition of the stage at the time of the Restoration, and its subsequent development.

CHAPTER III.

I. So far we have seen no very striking instances of any close resemblance between the English and the French styles. Dryden's asperities, as well as his vigor, are very unlike the polish of the French, yet in the imitations of the French thoughtfulness and reason we see a continual effort to model the Englishman after his neighbor across the Channel. In fact, there was hardly any period when the French and English were more unlike than they were just at the time when Dryden lived. In France, after the great civil and religious wars of the sixteenth century, there was a very marked movement towards refinement and social cultivation, and the advance of civilization was very swift. Those who took an interest in literature were quick to respond to their guides, who showed great intelligence in discovering and directing the tastes of the French people. The court, too, was not in hostility to the rest of the country, as was the case in England after the Restoration. There was in France no public outside of fashionable circles,* and these responded quickly to the polish which was

---

* Lotheissen says: "Während des XVII^{ten} Jahrhunderts gibt das Bürgerthum wohl eine Reihe von Gelehrten und gebildeten Männern; es erheben sich aus seinen Reihen die grössten Dichter die Frankreich je besessen; aber diese alle arbeiten nur für Hofkreise, für die Welt des Adels und der hohen Gesellschaft."—"Geschichte der franzözischen Literatur des XVII^{ten} Jahrhunderts," i. 17.

preached and illustrated by the literary leaders. The romances of the time were not mere accumulations of vapid sentiment : they inculcated virtue and refinement ; their heroes were knightly persons—tedious, to be sure, but true to a high ideal. The French tragedians expressed the same civilizing qualities. If it be objected that the Greeks and Romans whom they put upon the stage are really Frenchmen with classical names, that is, after all, a conventionalism which, if once acknowledged to exist, need not trouble us longer. There is a certain amount of pedantry in demanding faithfulness to an ideal when nobody knows with precision what the ideal really is. Then, too, even Greeks and Romans who are like Frenchmen have an advantage over the Greeks and Romans of the English stage after the Restoration, who are like no one that ever lived.

As we have already seen, it was at the end of the sixteenth century and the beginning of the next (1555–1628) that Malherbe in France was really, so far as one man can be said to do anything of the kind, moulding the course which French literature was to follow for two hundred years. His predecessors tried to introduce classical words, phrases, and forms into French. Malherbe, however, though of very moderate ability as a poet, allied himself with those who preferred to aid the development of the French language. This was the democratic side, one may say, if we remember that what we call the people were wholly without influence. Perhaps it would be better to say that this was the modern side. But, while he did this, he threw overboard almost everything else that we are accustomed to regard as essential to poetry ; and, while he insisted on precise versification and exact rhymes, he avoided picturesque language and recommended smooth commonplaces. French literature became correct, but it paid for it by becoming comparatively lifeless. I say *comparatively* lifeless, for, if French tragedy is marked by mannerisms, the comedy at least had a higher life than it had in England.

The correctness, then, of the French was more or less the model set before English writers after the Restoration, yet they seldom attained more than an outside polish. Let us see what it was they did in the drama. Even before the Commonwealth we notice the gradual deterioration of the plays, if indeed Jonson's method may not be looked on as the first step towards artificial composition ; those playwrights whom we call great began to vie with one another in accumulating horrors, although they all had part of the grand style, and knew how to relieve what was terrible by bits of natural beauty and pathos.

II. In preparation for the struggle that was to come, the Puritans early began their attack upon the stage. Even about 1575 they opposed the building of theatres in every way in their power, and they wrote tracts and large volumes against it, but the main attack was made in 1633 in a book called the "Histrio-Mastix," written by William Prynne. Its full title ran thus : "Histrio-Mastix, The Players Scourge ; or, Actors Tragedie, Divided into Two Parts. Wherein it is largely evidenced, by divers Arguments, by the Concurring Authorities and Resolutions of sundry Texts of Scripture, of the whole Primitive Church, both under the Law and the Gospell ; of 55 Synodes and Councils ; of 71 Fathers and Christian Writers before the Year of our Lord 1200 ; of about 150 foraigne and domestique Protestant and Popish Authors, since ; of 40 Heathen Philosophers, Historians, Poets, of many Heathen, many Christian Nations, Repubiliques, Emperors, Princes, Magistrates ; of sundry Apostolicall, Canonicall, Imperiall Constitutions ; and of our own English Statutes, Magistrates, Universities, Writers, Preachers.

That popular Stage-playes (the very Pompes of the Divell which we renounce in Baptisme, if we believe the Fathers) are sinfull, heathenish, lewde, ungodly spectacles, and most pernicious Corruptions ; condemned in all ages, as intolerable Mischiefes to Churches, to Republickes, to the manners, mindes, and soules of men. And that the Profession of Play-poets, of Stage-players ; together with the penning, acting, and frequenting of Stage-plays, are unlawfull, infamous and misbeseeming Christians. All pretences to the contrary are here likewise fully answered ; and the unlawfulness of acting, of beholding Academicall Interludes, briefly discussed ; besides sundry other particulars concerning Dancing, Dicing, Health-Drinking, etc., of which the Table will informe you."

That the work of the literary critic in those days was laborious is shown by this title, as well as by the fact, which I quote at second-hand, that it contains, according to one estimate, one hundred thousand references ;* I have not counted them. It is also said that four thousand texts are quoted against the stage. That it was perilous is shown by Prynne's punishment for his violence. Those who danced or looked on at dancing, he said, assisted at a lewd service of the devil. This was construed as an insult to the queen, who occasionally danced at court masques, and Prynne's sentence ran : "That Master Prynne should be committed to prison during life, pay a fine of £5000 to the king, be

---

* He refers to about one thousand authorities, and there are 1106 pages.

This is his manner (p. 65): "That the stile and subject matter of most is amorous and obscene ; it is as evident as the morning sunne. 1st, by the express and punctual testimony of sundry Fathers. Read but " (sixty-four references) "to whom I adde " (twelve more).

" Peruse, I say, but these several Fathers and councils (whose words, if I should at large transcribe them, would amount unto an ample volume), and you shall find them all concur in this."

expelled Lincoln's Inn, disbarred and disabled ever to exercise the profession of a barrister ; degraded by the University of Oxford of his degree there taken ; and that done, be set in the pillory at Westminster, with a paper on his head declaring the nature of his offence, and have one of his ears there cut off, and at another time be set in the pillory at Cheapside, with a paper as aforesaid, and then have his other ear cut off ; and that a fire shall be made before the said pillory, and the hangman being there ready for that purpose, shall publicly in disgraceful manner cast all the said books which could be produced into the fire to be burnt, as unfit to be seen by any hereafter." *

On the second of September, 1642, the ordinance passed the Lords and Commons, stating that "while these sad causes and set-times of humiliation do continue, stage-plays shall cease and be forborne." This law was evaded in some few instances by the few actors who were found in London ; these acted in obscure taverns, at private houses, etc., but in the main the law was observed.

III. In 1656, Sir William Davenant, of whom mention has been made, ventured to bring forth an entertainment made up of declamation and music "after the manner of the ancients," which was no play, but, in fact, an opera. This was made over into a play and represented in its new form after the Restoration, when its author was Charles

---

* Prynne is said to have recanted, and in 1649 there appeared a thin pamphlet with this title : " Mr. William Prynne his defense of Stage plays ; or, a Retraction of a former book of his called ' Histrio-Mastix.' " In this recantation there is an apology for calling Charles I. Nero, and the queen by worse names, for being interested in plays. Mention is made of the fact that George Buchanan, Barclay, and others wrote for the stage, and it is said that the drama might also teach lessons of virtue.

The genuineness of the pamphlet is, however, open to doubt. No man ever changes his mind after establishing his views by more than seventy-five thousand references.

II.'s poet-laureate, and the manager of one of the two dramatic companies then licensed. The play itself is noteworthy for two or three things outside of its purely literary qualities—these call for no comment. First, it was one of the plays in which women appeared upon the stage. This had happened occasionally before, but now it became the rule, with but few exceptions, that the women's parts should be played by women. Secondly, Davenant introduced in this play something like scene-painting : for the first time an attempt was made, by means of the decoration of the proscenium, to give some scenic effect. In the third place, but less important, was the fact that the music introduced into this play remained, with the singing and dancing, in all the heroic plays ; and fourthly, and finally, it was written in rhymed couplets, after the manner of the French tragedians. That these plays bore much resemblance to the masterpieces of the French stage cannot be affirmed, and even the sound of the lines is very unlike that of the models. Yet it is this resemblance to the eye which is almost the only one between the plays of the two countries. What the English did under the influence of French literature was something different. They were not inspired to any considerable extent by the great plays ; it was rather the long, artificial heroic romances that are responsible for the English heroic drama,* which was really a most mongrel creation. Let us, for example, compare the subjects of the French tragedies with those of Dryden and his fellow-countrymen. The French writers, almost without exception, selected classical subjects, *Cinna, Horace, Britannicus, Iphigeneia, Phœdra, Andromache.* Where do we find such a collection of classical subjects in the English literature of the time ? No : the English playwrights

---

* Yet the French tragedy was not without the same tendency. *Vide* Corneille's " Cid," " Don Sanche," etc.

chose such subjects as the *Indian Queen*, the *Indian Emperor*, the *Maiden Queen*, the *Royal Martyr*, the *Conquest of Granada*, the *Empress of Morocco*. The same inspiration could not have been at work in both countries. The English dramatists found to some extent their plots, and much more their way of drawing characters, in these long romances I have mentioned, very much as the Elizabethan writers took their plots from the early Italian novelists—Bandello, etc.

The English representative of the combination of pastoral and knightly romances is Sidney's "Arcadia" (written in 1580 and 1581, and published in 1590). The pastoral part was due to Italian influence, for it was in Italy that this, like most of the forms of literature that have flourished in Europe, first made its appearance. It was at about the end of the fifteenth century, about 1472, that the earliest of the pastorals was written, the "Orfeo" of Poliziano. This was a combination of tragedy, pastoral, and opera ; a dramatic poem of four hundred and thirty-four lines, and lyrical rather than tragical.* It was quickly followed by a host of rustic comedies, eclogues, etc. One nearly contemporary work which had a great influence on Sidney was Sanazzaro's "Arcadia" (1504). This was in prose and verse, and consisted of twelve prose pieces, each introducing an eclogue ; but, while it referred after a fashion to events in Sanazzaro's life, it lacked all plot. The book is a mere accumulation of pastoral scenery and machinery, not a coherent tale or poem, and we read it now as a collection of charming descriptions, or as a literary curiosity. Here began the custom of giving living persons pastoral names, which ran through all the literatures of Europe, and even survived as late as the beginning of this century.

---

* *Vide* Symonds's "Italian Renaissance," iv. 412.

Pastorals, which soon degenerated into a mere literary form, were at first the poetical representations of a new ideal. As Catholicism lost its hold on the world, and the expectation of a life of happiness beyond the grave grew faint, men looked back to the past as to a period of innocence and flawless happiness. Visions of Paradise, which were as dim as prophecies, seemed to be fragmentary recollections of a distant past; Ovid's "Metamorphoses," Theocritus's "Idylls," and Vergil's "Eclogues" directly favored this idea.* The Golden Age was suddenly put back into the remote time which was supposed to have been a period of pastoral simplicity. This it was which inspired much of the new literature, and in time grew to be the ideal of nature current throughout civilized Europe, which the Italian Arcadians sought to imitate,† and painters and poets had in their mind until Rousseau let in the fresh air with his praise of the Alps in the "Nouvelle Héloïse." Yet, while Rousseau demolished the rococo prettiness of Arcadia, he gave new life to the underlying notion that civilization was degradation, by using all his eloquence to prove that men were born equal and had been happy and virtuous only in a savage state. This was the underlying principle of many socialist schemes.

The notion of a past Golden Age may be said to have died only within a few years, modern scientific discoveries placing it, if anywhere, in the future. The old theory lingers, however, in comparatively recent books. Archbishop Whateley, for instance, in his text-book on Rhetoric, warmly upholds the hypothesis that savages are all degenerate descendants of our original civilization. In the last century there were men who doubted this explanation. Gibbon,

---

* *Vide* Symonds's "Renaissance in Italy," v. 197.
† *Vide* Vernon Lee's "Studies of the Eighteenth Century in Italy."

who was prone to doubt, contested it ; De Maistre, who was inclined to conservatism, eloquently defended it. Even Niebuhr supported the notion.*

We now laugh at Arcadia and its admirers, but we should not forget that it stood, as Mr. Symonds says, for all that was imagined of the Golden Age, combined with refined manners and polite society. It was an aristocratic region, inhabited only by poets, knights, and lovely ladies ; and, now we have learned to look upon it as a feudal territory, we see that the Golden Age of the future must be democratic. Yet, with all its shortcomings, Arcadia kept alive a gracious ideal of honor and sentiment. Surely this merit should not be forgotten. It did good service, for one thing, in refining literature. Mr. Gosse's interesting article in the *Cornhill*, some time in the year 1881, on the matchless Orinda, will well illustrate its most flourishing condition in England, though continual reference to it is to be found in the *Spectator, Rambler*, etc. Sanazzaro in his " Eclogæ Piscatoriæ," I may say incidentally, " hath changed the scene in this kind of poetry from woods and lawns to the barren beach and boundless ocean: introduces sea-calves in the room of kids and lambs, sea-mews for the lark and the linnet, and presents his mistress with oysters instead of fruits and flowers." †   His " Arcadia" found imitators in Spain and Portugal, and in France. The Portuguese imitation, Montemayor's " Diana Enamorada," ‡

---

* *Vide* Tylor's " Primitive Culture," chap. ii.

† Steele, in *Guardian*, No. 28.

‡ In " Don Quixote," the niece said: "Pray, order the ' Diana Enamorada ' . . . to be burned with the rest, for should my uncle be cured of this distemper of chivalry, he may possibly, by reading such books, take it into his head to turn shepherd and wander through the woods and folds, singing and playing on a pipe; and what would be still worse, turn poet, which they say is an incurable and contagious disease." But the book was saved.

contained more plot than the Italian "Arcadia," and was also followed by Sidney. The romances, which also contributed to the formation of the heroic novels, lay at hand ; they were really a part of the inheritance which modern Europe received from the Middle Ages. The first and the most famous of those in prose was the "Amadis of Gaul," written, it is conjectured, by a Portuguese who died in 1403 or 1404, one Lobeira, a busy student of old romances * about Charlemagne and Arthur. This was translated into Spanish about 1500, and from that language into French in 1540. In Spain this novel really established a long line of knightly prose romance. In France it became exceedingly popular, and it was put into English from the French version in 1567. You will remember that "Amadis de Gaule" is one of Don Quixote's books, saved from burning by the priest and the barber. Montaigne, it is curious to note, says, "As to the 'Amadises,' and such kind of stuff, they had not the credit to take me, so much as in my childhood. And I will moreover say (whether boldly or rashly), that this old, heavy soul of mine is now no longer delighted with Ariosto, no, nor with the good fellow Ovid ; his facility and invention, with which I was formerly so ravished, are now of no relish, and I can hardly have the patience to read him " (bk. ii. chap. x.).

In England Sidney's "Arcadia" had no direct followers, with the exception of at least two brief continuations; but in France the romances of this kind became the regular form of the prose fiction of the time. In 1608 appeared the first part of Honoré d'Urfé's "Astræa," translated into

---

* The old French romances doubtless did good service in encouraging the popular enthusiasm for the Crusades, which in their turn gave new material to the romances. *Vide* Palgrave's " History of England and Normandy," iv. 496.

English in 1657; this was succeeded by the heroic romances by Gomberville, Calprenède, and Mlle. de Scudéry. These novels are, in the first place, now absolutely unreadable ; and if their writers had anything to communicate, it could hardly fail to be diluted by the enormous amount of padding which was required to fill up the vast bulk of these colossal stories. Gomberville's " Pharamond," for instance, appeared in French in 1661, and was translated into English a few years later. This translation contains seven hundred and fifty-eight folio pages, with over nine hundred words on each page—say seven hundred thousand words in all. And this is but one of many. In these excessively long-winded stories we find plenty of love-making of a very polite kind, and much fighting. Problems of love - casuistry are continually discussed ; and, more than this, many of them were written about the author's contemporaries, who were turned into Greeks or Romans or Carthaginians; and they went through a travesty of ancient history while talking after the manner of those friends whom the author wished to embalm. Thus Condé appears in one of Mlle. de Scudéry's novels, and others are now interpreted by the curious. Yet for the most part they described simply adventures in cloudland, and are full of gallantry and a sort of chivalrous elegance.

These were admired in France in the first half of the seventeenth century, but by 1660 they began to sink to their proper place in the general estimation. The influence of Boileau and Malherbe was cruelly unfavorable to the natural development of French literature, perhaps, but Boileau's satires put the finishing blow to these romances, which then found their warmest admirers across the Channel. When they were exiled from France, they carried influence from that country into England, as did the *émigrés* into the rest of Europe a century later.

That it takes time for a fashion to spread is as true in literature as it is in millinery, and it is by no means unusual to be able to follow the course of a literary movement as one does that of a northeast storm. To take examples from current history, Dickens is already somewhat old-fashioned in England ; no one there writes stories now about the jollity of Christmas, or of the red-cheeked benevolence which he was fond of describing. When we come across a trace of his mannerism in the work of those who were his contemporaries, we detect a certain antiquity in it ; yet only now is Dickens imitated in France. No one can read Daudet without perceiving how much he owes to Dickens ; and we are surer to find traces of his influence in this country than in England, where the writers have before them many newer models.

In England the classical French stage was first fairly imitated by Addison's "Cato" (1713), which Voltaire called the first *reasonable* play ever written in England ; and yet, while English writers were discussing the laws of the classic stage, and pondering the question of the unities, Milton had, one may almost say, written a Greek play, the "Samson Agonistes" (1671),* which his contem-

---

* It is curious to notice that Milton published his "Comus" in 1634, just after Prynne's "Histrio-Mastix" appeared (1633), with its denunciation of masques. May not his "Samson Agonistes" have been meant as in some sort a contribution to the discussion concerning plays ? He referred in his argument to the question of the unities, and spoke of Greek and Italian models. He distinctly reproved indiscriminate opposition to the stage. "The apostle Paul himself," he says, "thought it not unworthy to insert a verse of Euripides into the text of Holy Scripture; and Parsus, commenting on the Revelation, divides the whole book as a tragedy, into acts, distinguished each by a chorus of heavenly harpings and a song between. Men of highest dignity have labored not a little to be thought able to compose a tragedy." He mentions Dionysius the elder, Augustus Cæsar, Seneca the philosopher. "Gregory Nazianzen, a father

poraries wholly ignored.　After all, they were in a great measure right ; for as a dramatic composition the work is lifeless, and, moreover, as Milton said in his preface, it was not intended for the stage.　Its value to us consists in the intensity of its expression of a state of things which had no pathos to the literary men of his time.　However, we may agree with Voltaire so far as to say that reason had but little place in the composition of the heroic plays. Let us take, for example, this from Lee's "Lucius Junius Brutus."　It is a bit of dialogue between the father, Lucius Junius Brutus, and his son, Titus.

> "*Brutus.* Titus, as I remember,
> You told me you were married.
> 　*Titus.* My lord, I did.
> 　*Brutus.* To Teraminta, Tarquin's natural daughter.
> 　*Titus.* Most true, my lord, to that poor virtuous maid,
> Your Titus, sir, your most unhappy son,
> Is joined for ever.
> 　*Brutus.* No, Titus, not for ever;
> Not but I know the virgin's beautiful,
> For I did oft converse her when I seemed
> Not to converse at all.　Yet more, my son,
> I think her chastely good, most sweetly framed,
> Without the smallest tincture of her father :
> Yet, Titus—Ha! what, man ?　What, all in tears!
> Art thou so soft that only saying *yet*
> Has dashed thee thus ?　Nay, then I'll plunge thee down,
> Down to the bottom of this foolish stream
> Whose brink thus makes thee tremble.　No, my son,
> If thou art mine, thou art not Teraminta's ;
> Or if thou art, I swear thou must not be—
> Thou shalt not be hereafter.

of the Church, thought it not unbecoming the sanctity of his person to write a tragedy, which he entitled 'Christ Suffering.'"　Thus Milton had a word for both sides, and he never objected to being in a minority.　We must remember that he was a child of the Renaissance as well as a Puritan.

Titus.   O the gods !
Forgive me, blood and duty, all respects
Due to a father's name—not Teraminta's ?
 Brutus. No, by the gods I swear, not Teraminta's !
No, Titus, by th' eternal fates that hang
I hope auspicious o'er the head of Rome,
I'll grapple with thee on this spot of earth
About this theme till one of us fall dead ;
I'll struggle with thee for this point of honour,
And tug with Teraminta for thy heart,
As I have done for Rome."

Doubtless plays of this kind exercised a bad influence on the mere acting of English plays, which is not yet dead. They seem to require mouthing, and the stage is a great supporter of tradition.* The passage just quoted, it is worth noticing, is in blank verse, and the question whether plays should be written in couplets or in blank verse was in Dryden's time much discussed. Dryden argued at great length in favor of rhyme, and wrote in rhyme ; then he abandoned it and denounced it ; then he tried it again : but the controversy on the matter I will not now review. The rhymed play is practically dead, but we must remember that we have in Milton's wonderful blank verse an argument in favor of that form of writing which Dryden's contemporaries did not have until 1667, and then there was every sort of prejudice at work to render them deaf to its harmonies. They did have, however, the beautiful blank verse of the older

---

* Davenant, who had seen "Hamlet" acted by men who had received Shakspere's instruction, gave hints to Betterton (1635–1710). Betterton was praised by both Pepys and Steele. That the heroic plays induced heroic acting we may learn from references in the *Spectator*, and from the delight with which Garrick was welcomed. See, for example, Cumberland's "Memoirs" (Amer. ed.), p. 47. Reference is made to his destruction of "the illusions of imposing declamation."

dramatists,* but their plays, it must be borne in mind, now
seemed most rude and obsolete.   Evelyn in his Diary,
Nov. 26, 1661, says : "I saw 'Hamlet, Prince of Denmark,'
played, but now the old plays began to disgust this refined age, since his Majesties being so long abroad."   In
Pepys we find frequent references to Shakspere.   "Macbeth " (Nov. 5, 1664) he thought "a pretty good play,"
and (Dec. 28, 1666) "a most excellent play for variety,"
and (Jan. 7, 1667) "a most excellent play in all respects,
but especially in divertissement, though it be a deep tragedy ; which is a strange perfection in a tragedy, it being
most proper here and suitable."   With "Hamlet " (Aug.
31, 1668) he was "mightily pleased."   "Midsummer-
Night's Dream " he thought (Sept. 25, 1662) the most insipid, ridiculous play "that ever he saw in his life."   "The
Merry Wives of Windsor " (Aug. 15, 1667) did not please
him "at all, no part of it."   "Othello " (Aug. 20, 1666) he
had "ever heretofore esteemed a mighty good play, but
having so lately read 'The Adventures of Five Houres,'
it seems a mean thing ;" and (Jan. 1, 1664) "saw the so
much cried-up play of 'Henry VIII. ;' which, though I
went with resolution to like it, is so simple a thing made
up of a great many patches, that, besides the shows and
processions in it, there is nothing in the play good or
well done."   Nov. 7, 1667, he saw the "Tempest," "an old
play of Shakspere's, . . . the most innocent play that ever I
saw ; and a curious piece of musique in an echo of half
sentences, the echo repeating the former half, while the
man goes on to the latter, which is mighty pretty.   The

---

* Blank verse had some adherents, however.   In Evelyn, Feb. 24, 1664,
" Dr. Fell, canon of Christ Church, preached before the king on 15 Romans,
2, a very formal discourse and in blank verse, according to his manner;
however, he is a good man."   Perhaps we have here the explanation of
Dr. Fell's mysterious unpopularity.

play has no great wit, but yet good above ordinary plays."

Certainly this is not the way in which Shakspere is regarded by people nowadays,* or at least these views are not openly defended, although the late German dramatist Benedix, imitating Rümelin, was even more severe in his denunciations. Yet Shakspere was frequently acted, and almost every one of the dramatists of this time found pleasure in writing his plays over for the new generation. Chapman, Beaumont and Fletcher, Webster, and others shared the same fate. Waller (1682) tried his hand at rewriting the fifth act of the "Maid's Tragedy." In the prologue he says :

> "Of all our elder plays
> This and Philaster have the loudest fame ;
> Great are their faults, and glorious is their flame.
> In both our English genius is expressed ;
> Lofty and bold, but negligently dressed.
> * * * *
> Our lines reformed, and not composed in haste,
> Polished like marble, would like marble last."

And in the epilogue he says :

> "Nor is't less strange, such mighty wits as those
> Should use a style in tragedy like prose.
> Well-sounding verse, where princes tread the stage,
> Should speak their virtue or describe their rage.
> By the loud trumpet, which our courage aids,
> We learn that sound as well as sense persuades.
> And verses are the potent charms we use,
> Heroic thoughts and virtue to infuse."

---

* We may add that it is not the way in which he is now acted. Pepys saw of Shakspere "Hamlet," "Othello," "Romeo and Juliet," "Tempest," "Taming of the Shrew," "Macbeth," "Merry Wives of Windsor,"."Twelfth Night," "Midsummer-Night's Dream," "Henry IV.," and "Henry VIII."—eleven in all. Of Beaumont and Fletcher, he saw twenty-four plays ; Shirley, nine ; Ben Jonson, five ; Ford, two ; and Massinger, two.

· Here is one of the king's speeches :

> " Courage our greatest failings does supply,
> And makes all good, or handsomely we die.
> Life is a thing of common use ; by heaven
> As well to insects as to monarchs given ;
> But for the crown, 'tis a more sacred thing ;
> I'll dying lose it, or I'll live a king.
> Come, Diphilus, we must together walk
> And of a matter of importance talk."

Compare this with Aspatia's speech in the original play. One of the maidens is working the story of " Theseus and Ariadne " in tapestry. She is dissatisfied with Ariadne's face :

> " Do it by me,
> Do it again by me, the lost Aspatia,
> And you shall find all true but the wild island.
> Suppose I stand upon the sea-beach now,
> Mine arms thus and my hair blown with the wind,
> Wild as that desert : and let all about me
> Be teachers of my story.   Do my face
> (If ever thou hadst feeling of a sorrow)
> Thus, thus, Antiphila ; strive to make me look
> Like sorrow's monument ; and the trees about me,
> Let them be dry and leafless ; let the rocks
> Groan with continual surges ; and behind me
> Make all a desolation." *

---

* I must apologize to Mr. Lowell for repeating here what he has said more forcibly in his article on Dryden.   He there quotes the passage given above to point the same moral, but there are no other lines in the play with half their beauty.   Even Theobald, the original hero of the "Dunciad," in the very middle of the last century, was struck by them. In his edition of Beaumont and Fletcher (1750), i. 32, note, he writes: "This is one of those Passages, where the Poets, rapt into a glorious enthusiasm, soar on the rapid wings of Fancy.   Enthusiasm," he adds, "I would call the very essence of Poetry."   Is it any wonder that Theobald was detested by his contemporaries ?

How does that passage compare with such a jingle as this?

> "Evadne's husband 'tis a fault
> To love, a blemish to my thought;
> Yet twisted with my life, and I,
> That cannot faultless live, will die!
> Oh! that some hungry beast would come
> And make himself Aspatia's tomb.
> If none accept me for a prey
> Death must be found some other way.
> In colder regions men compose
> Poison with art; but here it grows.
> Not long since, walking in the field,
> My nurse and I, we there beheld
> A goodly fruit which tempted me.
> I would have pluck'd; but trembling, she,
> Whoever eat those berries, cried,
> In less than half an hour dy'd.
> Some god direct me to that bough,
> On which these useful berries grow."

Shakspere was treated in the same way. Otway worked over "Romeo and Juliet" into a play of ancient Rome, which he called the "History and Fall of Caius Marius" (1680); but in justice to our ancestors, let it be said that both this play and Waller's revision were failures. The fact was, that the stage was dying; the only way in which the drama can exist is as a mirror of life. In the hands of the Elizabethan dramatists it did reflect the energy of an awakening nation. Marlowe and Shakspere saw about them great dreams of conquest, plans of discovery, joy in the new learning, the consciousness of religious freedom; and these things they reflected in their plays. The great poet is the man who sees the vast currents of thought which mark his time, without having his eyes blinded by the petty circumstances which dim our eyes to the higher vision. The critic, it may be said, is a sort of stammering guide who manages to get a glimpse of what the poet sees. Those writers who maintain that Bacon was Shakspere might as well affirm that Achilles was Homer.* They forget the very essential quality of a poet, which is to see the animating principles of things more clearly even than those who are taking an active part in them. That the possession of knowledge chills the ardor of the poet we see by comparing the second part of Goethe's "Faust," the great poem of this age, which is animated by a sort of scientific fervor, with the first part, which he wrote from his impressions as a poet.

When society becomes divided, when the social scheme grows confused, and religious freedom is turned into sectarianism, and patriotism into partisanship, the drama, which at its best reflects only a brightly glowing light, fades away. The absence of a single informing spirit is seen by the condition of tragedy in Dryden's time, and, for that matter, since. In the heroic plays which he wrote, an attempt was made to let the single passion of love suffice as an animating principle. In the "Indian Emperor" we have a mass of conflicting loves before us : Cortez falls in love with Montezuma's daughter ; Montezuma, with Almeria ; Almeria with Cortez, and this is a fair sample of the rest. In other plays he wrote in support of mere temporary interests : such was "Amboyna," 1673, a wretched piece of work, designed simply to inflame the English against the Dutch, with whom war had shortly before been declared. It represented some atrocities that had been committed fifty years before ; and yet even here the heroic sentiment prevailed, and the whole crime is ascribed to an unholy love. If the love of these characters is heroic, what can be said of their heroism ?

---

* If Bacon was Shakspere, who was Marlowe ?

Just as poor actors crack their voice in trying to make impressive what a really accomplished player would utter calmly, so did the writers of this time let their heroes break out in every form of extravagance. Some of these I have quoted in an earlier part of this book, and others may be added. Take this, for instance, from the "Conquest of Granada." Almanzor says :

> " Cut piecemeal in this cause,
>   From every wound I should new vigor take :
>   And every limb should new Almanzors make ;"

or this from Crown's " Juliana " (Crown, Mr. Lowell says, was once a student in Harvard College. He was a Nova Scotian by birth) :

> " Come, villains, level me right against the clouds,
>   And then give fire, discharge my flaming soul,
>   Against such saucy destinies as those
>   As dare thus basely of my life dispose ;
>   Then from the clouds rebounding I will fall,
>   And like a clap of thunder tear you all."

As Addison said in the *Spectator*, No. 40 : " As our heroes are generally lovers, their swelling and blustering upon the stage very much recommends them to the fair part of their audience. The ladies are wonderfully pleased to see a man insulting kings, or affronting the gods, in one scene, and throwing himself at the feet of his mistress in another."

These inventions were the work of what its owners called *wit*, and of their exclusive possession of that quality they spoke with the precise self-complacency which we show when we talk about the spirit of the nineteenth century ; and we may say, in general, that the disposition to dilate upon the admirable qualities of the present age is no more a healthy sign in the public at large than is boasting in private life, and, moreover, it is most common when second-rate work is performed. It is not when a soldier is charging the enemy that he brags about his bravery, and it is not when great work is doing in literature that writers take time to stop and call attention to their wit, as they did in Dryden's time, or to their general intelligence, as we do now.

It would be unfair to ascribe the tendency in current literature to deal with scarcely anything but love-stories to the heroic plays : other causes, which I need not enumerate, have contributed to this result ; but yet the exaggerated value given to the manifestation of passion which we find in the plays of that time doubtless intensified this natural tendency. In Dryden, Lee, and Otway—in their serious pieces, that is—we find, as I have said, that love is the only great animating principle. In the " Conquest of Granada," the " Indian Emperor," " Aureng-Zebe," " Venice Preserved," the " Orphan," " Tyrannic Love," we find more prominent than anything the impossible love-making. In the works of the greatest authors we find that life is regarded as a more serious and complex thing. Shakspere shows us other passions, ambition, jealousy, constancy, misanthropy, etc.; the dramatists who lived with him or followed him, like Chapman, even Beaumont and Fletcher, do not confine themselves to this one emotion ; and in Scott, what is poorest is the love-making of his tepid heroes and heroines. But in the last century we find some of the most important of the writers, such as Richardson—although, as we shall see, he in general expresses a very violent reaction from the artificial literature of this time—still celebrating the power of love, and the domestic tragedy carried down the same tradition, as in the " Stranger," for instance, and in the poorer work of later days.

However this may be, the love that was represented in

these heroic plays was a singular thing, as was not unnatural in view of its origin in the later tales of chivalry,
and its lack of harmony with the condition of society.
What this was may be seen in the comedies, which I shall
not treat at length.   At some other time it may be possible to point out the curious antithesis between comedy and
ideal poetry, and to show how the two have always appeared in sharp contrast at the times when literature has
flourished.   The magnificent farce of Aristophanes coincided in time with the glory of Æschylus and his successors; Molière, as Mr. Symonds says ("Renaissance in
Italy," v. 309), "portrayed men as they are before an
audience which welcomed Racine's pictures of men as the
age conceived they ought to be."   But in the drama of
the Restoration we see no such division of labor.   The
tragedy is, above all things, unreal, and the comedy takes
its revenge by exaggerating reality.   In contrast with the
metaphysical gallantry of the heroic plays, we have unparalleled grossness.   In neither branch do we see the
main object of the stage — "to show the very age and
body of the time, his form and pressure."   Artistically,
the wrong was equal on each side, but the distastefulness
of the comedy must be our excuse for passing it by.   An
excellent discussion of its main qualities is to be found in
Beljame's admirable book, "Le Public et les Hommes des
Lettres," Paris, 1881, to which I have frequently referred.

That the tragedians of the Restoration felt their incapacity for doing good work can hardly be affirmed.*
Nahum Tate, the same who wrote, with Dryden's aid, the
second part of "Absalom and Achitophel," rewrote "King

---

* Dryden, in the preface to "An Evening's Love," Scott's ed., vol. iii.,
p. 218, said: "I had thought . . . . to have shown . . . in what we may
justly claim precedence of Shakspere and Fletcher, namely, in heroic
plays."

Lear" as his contribution to the general polishing of Shakspere. The last act he wholly rewrote, and he gave the play
a happy ending. Lamb, in his "Essay on the Tragedies
of Shakespeare" (iii. 102): "Tate has put his hook in
the nostrils of this Leviathan, for Garrick and his followers, the show-men of the scene, to draw the mighty beast
about more easily. A happy ending!—as if the living
martyrdom that Lear had gone through,—the flaying of
his feelings alive,—did not make a fair dismissal from the
stage of life the only decorous thing for him. If he is to
live and be happy after, if he could sustain this world's
burden after, why all this pudder and preparation,—why
torment us with all this unnecessary sympathy? As if
the childish pleasure of getting his gilt robes and sceptre
again could tempt him to act over again his misused station!—as if at his years, and with his experience, anything was left but to die!"

In order that we may see the faults of our ancestors
in their proper light, I will quote a few lines from this
amended fifth act. Albany says:

> "To your majesty we do resign
> Your kingdom, save what part yourself conferred
> To us in marriage.
>   *Lear.*   Is't possible?
> Let the spheres stop their course, the sun make halt,
> The winds be hushed, the seas and fountains rest;
> All nature pause and listen to the change;"

and later, Lear says:

> "Cordelia then shall be a queen, mark that:
> Cordelia shall be a queen; winds, catch the sound,
> And bear it on your rosy wings to heaven.
> Cordelia is a queen."

And as for Lear's future, it is assured as follows; he says
to Gloster:

> " No, Gloster, . . .
> Thou, Kent and I, retired to some close cell
> Will gently pass our short reserves of time
> In calm reflection on our fortune's past,
> Cheer'd with relation of the prosperous reign
> Of this celestial pair; thus our remains
> Shall in an even course of thoughts be passed,
> Enjoy the present hour and fear the last."

And in the final speech of the play, as the green curtain
was rolling down, Edgar tells Cordelia that

> " Thy bright example shall convince the world
> (Whatever storms of fortune are decreed)
> That truth and virtue shall at last succeed."

These alterations of Shakspere would, perhaps, seem
more curious to us, if even we treated Shakspere as a man
who knew anything about the writing of plays. But the
text which he left is mauled and tossed about by different
actors, as if he were a sort of general theatrical provider,
from whom a bit here and there could be taken, as one
gets dresses or side-scenes from the people who let those
things. Colley Cibber's revision of " Richard III." still
holds the stage, with its

> " Off with his head ! so much for Buckingham !"

and,

> " Now, by St. Paul, the work goes bravely on ;"

and,

> " Richard's himself again."

And as for " Hamlet," who has ever seen Fortinbras come
in, bringing with him a flavor of practical life, as if a window were opened and fresh air were let into a sick-room ?

Dryden lent his hand to an alteration of the " Tempest,"
and his version of " Antony and Cleopatra," or " All for
Love," as he called it, is perhaps his best play. As singular
as any is the play, " The State of Innocence and Fall of

Man," a dramatization of Milton's "Paradise Lost." Certainly, to our ears, there is something unpardonable in the notion of clipping Milton's fine lines into the fashion of the couplet, as when Lucifer says :

> " Is this the seat our conqueror has given ?
> And this the climate we must change for heaven ?
> These regions and this realm my wars have got;
> This mournful empire is the loser's lot :
> In liquid burning, or on dry, to dwell,
> Is all the sad variety of hell."—I. 1.

Or when Lucifer (i., 1) says :

> " So, now we are ourselves again an host,
> Fit to tempt fate, once more, for what we lost;
> To o'erleap the ethereal fence, or if so high
> We cannot climb, to undermine his sky,
> And blow him up, who justly rules us now,
> Because more strong."

Or, act ii., scene 1, after an interlude, in which, according to the stage-directions, were expressed the sports of the devils : " as flights and dancing in grotesque figures ; and a song expressing the change of their condition; what they enjoyed before, and how they fell bravely in battle, having deserved victory by their valour, and what they would have done if they had conquered." We cannot help wishing that Dryden had composed this song. Then Adam, " as newly created, laid on a bed of moss and flowers by a rock," begins thus :

> " What am I ? or from whence ? For that I am
> I know, because I think." (*Cogito, ergo sum.*)

There is no need of going on with this. This cold-blooded way of looking at Dryden's poem reminds us of the way in which a great many foreign critics speak of Milton himself, and there would be nothing easier than to turn the " Paradise Lost " into abject ridicule. In spite of this curious compliment—for complimentary this treatment of the great epic was meant to be—Dryden had a great admiration for Milton; the cool admiration, I mean, which one has for a contemporary of whom one wholly disapproves. His inscription beneath the portrait of Milton, in Lord Somers's edition, proves this:

> " Three poets, in three distant ages born,
> Greece, Italy, and England did adorn:
> The first in loftiness of thought surpassed;
> The next in majesty; in both the last.
> The force of nature could no further go,
> To make the third, she joined the other two."

Sundry remarks of his in conversation are quoted, and here and there in his writings he expressed warm admiration for his greater contemporary. Yet his admiration was tempered by very evident contempt for Milton's inability or unwillingness to adapt himself to the time in which he lived. Still more important than Dryden's personal feeling is the knowledge of the opinion of Dryden's time, the general opinion of men of letters, concerning Milton. Every prejudice ran against him, as a Puritan and a defender of regicide, and it would, perhaps, not be an exaggeration to say that to those who were interested in literature his blank verse must have sounded very much as these lines may sound to all but the firmest adherents of Walt Whitman ("Leaves of Grass," p. 161, new edition):

" Here shall you trace in flowing operation,
In every state of practical busy movement, the rills of civilization:
Materials here under your eye shall change their shape as if by magic,
The cotton shall be picked almost in the very field;
Shall be dried, cleaned, ginn'd, baled, spun into thread and cloth before you;
You shall see hands at work at all the old processes and all the new ones;

You shall see the various grains and how flour is made and then bread
    baked by the bakers ;
You shall see the crude ores of California and Nevada passing on and
    on till they become bullion ;
You shall watch how the printer sets type, and learn what a composing-
    stick is," etc.

In a panegyric of Lee's, although one must remember
that much of the language of panegyrics was no more an
affidavit than are epitaphs, he says :

> " Milton did the wealthy mine disclose,
>   And rudely cast what you could well dispose :
>   He roughly drew, on an old-fashion'd ground,
>   A chaos ; for no perfect world was found,
>   Till through the heap your mighty genius shined :
>   He was the golden ore which you refined."

As a final extract from "The State of Innocence," I
shall quote part of Eve's soliloquy, after tasting the fatal
apple. You will notice the coquetry which Dryden has
introduced into the scene :

> " I love the wretch ; but stay, shall I afford
> Him part? already he's too much my lord.
> 'Tis in my power to be a sovereign now ;
> And, knowing more, to make his manhood bow.
> Empire is sweet ; but how if Heaven has spied ;
> If I should die, and He above provide
> Some other Eve, and place her in my stead?
> Shall she possess his love, when I am dead?
> No ; he shall eat, and die with me, or live :
> Our equal crimes shall equal fortune give."

Yet, naturally enough, the whole opera—for it corresponded
to that as much as to anything we know in the world of
art or literature—is not wholly made up of such scenes ;
still, these will show what things were possible in those
days, just as we may imagine some future student quoting
these lines to show the excesses of the present period :

> " Death !
> Plop.
> The barges down in the river flop:
> Flop, flop,
> Above, beneath,
> From the slimy branches the gray drips drop,
> As they scraggle black on the thin gray sky,
> Where the black cloud rack-hackles drizzle and fly
> To the oozy waters, that lounge and flop
> On the black scrag piles, where the loose cords plop,
> As the raw wind whines in the thin tree-top,
> Plop, flop." *

The poem ends thus :

> " Ugh, I knew !
> Ugh !
> So what do I care
> And my head is as empty as air—
> I can do,
> I can dare.
> Plop, plop,
> The barges flop
> Drip, drop.
> I can dare, I can dare !
> And let myself all run away with my head
> And stop.
> Drop
> Dead,
> Plop, flop,
> Plop."

---

* From " A Tragedy," by Theodore Marzials, in his " Gallery of Pigeons and Other Poems," p. 85. Mr. Stedman, in his " Victorian Poets," cites these lines to show the modernness of some later poets. He must have found it hard to stop quoting. Here is one passage, from a poem called " The Trout," p. 68, in which the bard out-Postlethwaites Postlethwaite:

> " All is a-gray, and the sky's in a glimmer,
> A glimmer as ever a sky should be;
> Silvery gray, with a silvery shimmer,

Yet to judge of any period by its faults alone would be like forming an opinion of a river by its low-water mark alone, and would, moreover, give us a very dark view of any age. We do not fix Homer's position by the catalogue of ships, or Shakspere's by his extravagant passages, and the age of Dryden deserves the same treatment. In general, the study of the pathology of literature is of use as showing vividly some of the tendencies that have prevailed at different times.

As examples of Dryden's finer style, I will quote these lines from "Aureng-Zebe" (act iv. sc. 1) :

> "When I consider life, 'tis all a cheat.
> Yet, fooled with hope, men favour the deceit,
> Trust on, and think to-morrow will repay.
> To-morrow's falser than the former day,
> Lies worse, and while it says, we shall be blest
> With some new joys, cuts off what we possesst.
> Strange cozenage! none would live past years again,
> Yet all hope pleasure in what yet remain,
> And from the dregs of life think to receive
> What the first, sprightly running could not give.
> I'm tir'd with waiting for this chemic gold,
> Which fools us young and beggars us when old." *

> Where shimmers the sun in the hazes a-shimmer,
> The shimmer of river, oh! river a-shimmer."

* Cf. "Macbeth" (act v. sc. 5):

> "To-morrow, and to-morrow, and to-morrow,
> Creeps in this petty pace from day to day,
> To the last syllable of recorded time;
> And all our yesterdays have lighted fools
> The way to dusty death. Out, out, brief candle!
> Life's but a walking shadow; a poor player
> That struts and frets his hour upon the stage,
> And then is heard no more: it is a tale
> Told by an idiot, full of sound and fury,
> Signifying nothing."

Or take this from the " Œdipus," written in conjunction with Lee, who wrote fine things amid his fustian :

> " Thou coward ! yet
> Art living ? canst not, wilt not find the road
> To the great palace of magnificent death,
> Though thousand ways lead to his thousand doors
> Which day and night are still unbarred for all."

This was written, you notice, in blank verse, and the fact that Dryden finally made up his mind in favor of blank verse, and wrote in that measure, turned the scale in favor of abandoning the couplets in tragedy. As Dryden said, in his prologue to " Aureng-Zebe " (1676) :

> " Not that it's worse than what before he writ,
> But he has how another taste of wit ;
> And to confess a truth (though out of time),
> Grows weary of his long-loved mistress, rhyme.
> Passion's too fierce to be in fetters bound,
> And nature flies him like enchanted ground.
> What verse can do he has performed in this,
> Which he presumes the most correct of his ;
> But spite of all his pride, a secret shame
> Invades his breast at Shakspere's sacred name :
> Awed, when he hears his god-like Romans rage,
> He, in a just despair, would quit the stage,
> And, to an age less polish'd, more unskill'd,
> Does, with disdain, the foremost honours yield."

He wearied of the couplet, and threw the weight of his authority on the other side. It was, after all, Dryden's critical writings that gave him a position as a representative writer. Lee surpassed him in certain kinds of tragedy; Etherege* in comedy; Otway, too, had a quality of direct pathos which Dryden never, or but very seldom, exhibited.

---

* See an interesting article on Etherege in the *Cornhill Magazine* for March, 1881.

The impression which Dryden left on the minds of his contemporaries, and the one which still survives, is this: that he was a man of great ability, and a wonderful craftsman. If he had been born in more poetical times he would have brought to the service of literature the same ability, and the sounder fervor of other men would have kept him from frittering away his power over such poor material as the heroic plays. We notice everywhere in his satirical and didactic poems his exceptional vigor. I have given some examples of this, and there are others:

> "Death in itself is nothing; but we fear
> To be we know not what, we know not where."

> "The secret pleasure of the generous act
> Is the great mind's great bribe."

> "Forgiveness to the injured does belong;
> But they ne'er pardon who have done the wrong."

Or such poetical touches as we find in the blank verse:

> "I feel death rising higher still and higher
> Within my bosom; every breath I fetch
> Shuts up my life within a shorter compass,
> And, like the vanishing sound of bells, grows less
> And less each pulse, till it be lost in air."

Antony, in "All for Love," says:

> "For I am now so sunk from what I was,
> Thou find'st me at my lowest water-mark.
> The rivers that ran in and raised my fortunes
> Are all dried up, or take another course:
> What I have left is from my native spring;
> I've a heart still that swells in scorn of Fate,
> And left me to my banks."

Here is one more picturesque passage:

> "You ne'er must hope again to see your princess,
> Except as prisoners view fair walks and streets,
> And careless passengers going by their grates."

Compare Dryden's best lines with some extracts from Lee's various plays.

From " Œdipus :"

> " May the sun never dawn,
> The silver moon be blotfed from her orb,
> And for an universal rout of nature
> Through all the inmost chambers of the sky
> May there not be one spark,
> But gods meet gods and jostle in the dark."

This is the sort of writing which has given Lee his reputation for writing fustian, but he could do better than this, and that he did so is undeniable, as these extracts will show.

From " Theodosius :"

> " *Leontini.* Thou art the only comfort of my age ;
> Like an old tree I stand among the storms,
> Thou art the only limb that I have left me ;
> My dear green branch, and how I prize thee, child,
> Heaven only knows !   Why dost thou kneel and weep ?"

> " *Varanes.*   Far be the noise
> Of kings and crowds from us, whose gentle souls
> Our kinder stars have steer'd another way.
> Free as the forest birds we'll pair together.
> *   *   *   *   *
> Together drink the crystal of the stream,
> Or taste the yellow fruit which autumn yields ;
> And when the golden evening calls us home,
> Wing to our downy nest, and sleep till morn."

> " *Theodosius.* Oh, were I proof against the darts of love,
> And cold to beauty as the marble lover
> That lies without a thought upon his tomb,
> Would not this glorious dawn of life run through me,
> And waken death itself ?"

> " *Varanes.* Though I have lived a Persian, I will fall
> As fair, as fearless, and as full resolved
> As any Greek or Roman of 'em all."

From " Cæsar Borgia :"

> " *Machiavelli.* The dead are only happy and the dying:
> The dead are still, and lasting slumbers hold 'em:
> He who is near his death, but turns about,
> Shuffles awhile to make his pillow easy,
> Then slips into his shroud and sleeps for ever."

And this,

> " *Machiavelli.* The occasion gives new life, fresh vigour to him ;
> E'en at the very verge of bottomless death,
> He stands and smiles as careless and undaunted .
> As wanton swimmers on a river's brink
> Laugh at the rapid stream."

From " The Rival Queens :"

> " *Alexander.* Oh, she is gone! the talking soul is mute !
> She's hushed, no voice or music now is heard !
> The power of beauty is more still than death ;
> The roses fade, and the melodious bird
> That waked their sweets has left them now for ever."

> " *Alexander.* How dead ! Hephæstion dead ! alas, the dear
> Unhappy youth !—But he sleeps happy,
> I must wake for ever :—This object, then,
> This face of fatal beauty,
> Will stretch my lids with vast, eternal tears."

From " Mithridates :"

> " Arm, arm, great Mithridates, the big war
> Comes with vast leaps, bounding o'er all the East,
> Which crouches to the torrent."

From " Sophonisba :"

> " Why do you stop ? Still as a statue low
> I stand, nor shall the wind presume to blow.
> Speak and it shall be night: not one shall dare
> To sigh, tho' on the rack he tortured were,
> Nor for his soul whisper a dying prayer."

These two extracts from " Mithridates " are also worthy of note :

> " *Masinissa.* Grant me, ye gods, before the hand of death
> Comes like eternal night with her dark wing

To bar the comfortable light for ever
From these my aged eyes; O, let me see
A grandchild of my prince's sacred blood,
To call him mine, to feel him in my arms,
To hear his innocent talk, and see him smile,
While I tell stories of his father's valour,
Which he in time must learn to imitate:
Grant me but this, you gods, and make an end,
Soon as you please, of this old happy man."

    " *Ziphanes.* Go then, thou setting star; take from these eyes
      *   *   *   *   *
    O take those languishing pale fires away,
    And leave me to the wide dark den of death."

It seems incredible that a man who wrote lines like these could compose such a passage as this:

" Wheels, stones, and all the subtlest pains of hell,
   With burning, reddest plagues about 'em dwell.
   About 'em! in 'em, through 'em, let 'em run,
   And flames with flames involved be swallowed down."

Yet, while we find occasional good lines in Dryden's plays, there is no one play, either tragedy or comedy, that deserves high praise. The most interesting part of them is the prologue, or the introductory essay, in which he used to discuss the best method of working, or some of the theories which were suggested by his critics or by himself.* I have given some examples, and it would be easy to find many more. We may leave this, however, and take into consideration some of the other sides of the drama. In the first place, all the tragedies were on the sufferings of kings; and, as Dryden said in his preface to the " Annus Mirabilis," in that poem was " incomparably the best subject I ever had, excepting only the Royal Family;" and

---

* He adopted the custom, doubtless, from the French tragedians, especially Corneille, who wrote a preface to each of his plays, explaining and defending his views. The dedications to the rich are the same in both, and for the same reason.

royal families were uniformly the subjects of these new plays. This was also the case in the French drama. Yet in the preface to his "Don Sanche" (1651) we find Corneille getting a glimpse of a truth which has since become a truism. He says: "Tragedy should excite both pity and fear. . . . Now since it is true that the latter feeling is only excited within us when we see our equals (*semblables*) suffering, when their misfortunes make us dread like sufferings for ourselves, is it not true that it might be more strongly excited by the sight of misfortunes befalling people in our own station of life, whom we resemble in every particular, than by those which drive from their thrones great monarchs, with whom we sympathize only so far as we are susceptible of the passions that cast them into this abyss, which cannot always be the case?" And elsewhere : "I venture to imagine that those who limited this sort of poem [the tragedy] to illustrious persons, did so only because they thought that the fortune of kings and princes was alone capable of such an action as the great master of the art prescribes. However, when he begins to discuss the qualities necessary for the hero of a tragedy, he does not touch upon his birth, and speaks simply of his life and character. He demands a hero who shall be neither vicious nor faultless ; he must be persecuted by some one with whom he is in close relations; he must be in danger of dying at the hand of some one whose duty it should be to save him — and I do not see why all this can happen only to one of royal birth, or that a lower station is exempt from these misfortunes." Voltaire, in his preface to the play, held up the cause of conservatism by saying that doubtless very sad misfortunes might befall simple citizens, " but they distress us much less than those which happen to monarchs, whose fate involves that of nations. A citizen may be assassinated as Pompey was, but the death of Pompey will always have a very different effect from that of a private citizen. If you treat the interests of a *bourgeois* in the style of Mithridates, you are guilty of impropriety ; and if you represent a terrible adventure befalling an ordinary man, in a familiar style, this diction, which suits the hero, ill-becomes the incidents."

The first writer of any prominence who chose any one for his subject outside of a royal family was Otway, whose "Orphan" (1680) and "Venice Preserved" (1682) long held the stage. The language of these plays is entirely different from that of Dryden's, and, as we shall see, is of itself worthy of attention ; but what I wish to mention, first of all, is the introduction of this new hero, and the abandonment of the king. This change was an indication of what was going to take place in the next century, and is but one of the instances which we shall find of the growth of democracy in literature. At this time, however, nothing of the sort was conjectured, and Otway, doubtless, wrote about private people from no desire to revolutionize letters. The poor man had but little chance to think of anything but the day before him, or, more probably, the night that was before him, and he manufactured gross comedies, and wrote two of the most memorable plays of the time.

These extracts may illustrate his manner. This is from "Venice Preserved :"

> "*Jaffier.* 'Tis now, I think, three years we've lived together.
>   *Belvidera.* And may no fatal minute ever part us,
> Till reverend grown, for age and love, we go
> Down to our graves, as our last bed, together;
> Then sleep in peace till an eternal morning.
>   *Jaffier.* When will that be ?
>   *Belvidera.*   I hope long ages hence,
>   *Jaffier.* Have I not hitherto (I beg thee tell me

Thy very fears) used thee with tender'st love?
Did e'er my soul rise up in wrath against thee?
Did I e'er frown when Belvidera smiled,
Or, by the least unfriendly word, betray
Abating passion?   Have I ever wronged thee?
 Belvidera.   No.
 Jaffier. Has my heart, or have my eyes e'er wandered
To any other woman?
 Belvidera.   Never, never—
I were the worst of false ones, should I accuse thee."

    *   *   *   *   *

Jaffier blesses her :

"Then hear me, bounteous Heaven;
Pour down your blessings on this beauteous head,
Where everlasting sweets are always springing,
With a continual, giving hand: let peace,
Honour, and safety always hover round her;
Feed her with plenty, let her eyes ne'er see
A sight of sorrow, nor her heart know mournings:
Crown all her days with joy, her nights with rest,
Harmless as her own thought; and prop her virtue
To bear the loss of one that too much loved,
And comfort her with patience in our parting.
 Belvidera. How, parting, parting?
 Jaffier.   Yes, forever parting;
I have sworn, Belvidera, by yon Heaven,
That best can tell how much I lose, to leave thee.
We part this hour forever.
 Belvidera.   Oh, call back
Your cruel blessing; stay with me and curse me!"

This from the " Orphan :"

" For all is hushed, as Nature were retired,
And the perpetual motion standing still:
So much she from her work appears to cease,
And every warring element's at peace,
All the wild herds are in their coverts couch'd;
The fishes to their banks or ooze repair'd,
And to the murmurs of the waters sleep;

The feeling air's at rest, and feels no noise,
Except of some soft breaths among the trees,
Rocking the harmless birds that rest upon them."

"Wished morning's come! and now upon the plains
And distant mountains where they feed the flocks,
The happy shepherds leave their homely huts,
And with their pipes proclaim the new-bórn day.
The lusty swain comes with his well-fill'd scrip
Of healthful viands, which, when hunger calls,
With much content and appetite he eats.
To follow in the fields his daily toil,
And dress the grateful glebe, that yields him fruits,
The beasts that under the warm hedges slept,
And weathered out the cold bleak night, are up,
And looking towards the neighb'ring pastures, raise
Their voice, and bid their fellow-brutes good-morning;
The cheerful birds, too, in the tops of trees
Assemble all in choirs and with their notes
Salute, and welcome up the rising sun."

Id., iv. 1.

For his heroics, *vide* "Orphan," iii. 1.

" *Castalio.* Who's there?
  Ernesto.   A friend.
  Castalio.   If thou art so, retire,
And leave this place, for I would be alone.
  Ernesto. Castalio! My lord, why in this posture,
Stretched on the ground? Your honest, true old servant,
Your poor Ernesto cannot see you thus;
Rise, I beseech you.
  Castalio.   If thou art Ernesto,
As by thy honesty, thou seem'st to be,
Once leave me to my folly.
  Ernesto.   I can't leave you,
And not the reason know of your disorders.
     ✿   *   *   *   *
  Castalio. Thou can'st not serve me.
  Ernesto.   Why?
  Castalio.   Because my thoughts
Are full of woman; thou, poor wretch, art past them.

Ernesto. I hate the sex.
   Castalio.   Then I'm thy friend, Ernesto.
I'd leave the world for him that hates a woman.
Woman, the fountain of all human frailty!
What mighty ills have not been done by woman?
Who was't betrayed the capitol? A woman.
Who lost Mark Antony the world? A woman.
Who was the cause of a long ten years' war,
And laid at last old Troy in ashes? Woman,
Destructive, damnable, deceitful woman!" etc.

Dr. Johnson said of one of his plays, the " Orphan,"
that it was " the work of a man not attentive to decency,
nor zealous for virtue ; but of one who conceived forcibly, and drew originally, by consulting nature in his own
breast."

This secret Otway had, and he shows a poetical quality,
too, in the " Poet's Complaint of his Muse," " part of which
I do not understand ; and in that which is less obscure I
find little to commend. . . . The numbers are harsh," as
Dr. Johnson said, but there is vigor in the following opening lines of the ode :

" To a high hill where never yet stood tree,
   Where only heath, coarse fern, and furzes grow,
     Where, nipped by piercing air,
   The flocks in tattered fleeces hardly graze,
     Led by uncouth thoughts and care,
   Which did too much his pensive mind amaze,
A wandering bard, whose Muse was crazy grown,
Cloyed with the nauseous follies of the buzzing town,
Came, look'd about him, sighed, and laid him down.
   'Twas far from any path, but where the earth
   Was bare and naked all as at her birth,
     When by the Word it first was made,
       Ere God had said :—
Let grass, and herbs, and every green thing grow
With fruitful herbs after their kinds, and it was so.

> The whistling winds blew fiercely round his head;
> Cold was his lodging, hard his bed;
> Aloft his eyes on the wide heavens he cast,
> Where, we are told, peace only is found at last;
> And as he did its hopeless distance see,
> Sighed deep and cried, 'How far is peace from me!'"

These lines will never be quoted for their harmony, but they are curious as a vivid description of scenery, at a time when scenery was as little studied as electricity. As a specimen of the way nature was frequently addressed, these lines may be noticed:

> "Weep then, once fruitful vales, and spring with yew!
> Ye thirsty barren mountains, weep with dew!
> *   *   *   *   *
> .Let mournful cypress, with each noxious weed,
> And baneful venoms, in their place succeed!
> Ye purling, querulous brooks, o'ercharged with grief,
> Haste swiftly to the sea for more relief," etc.

—John Pomfret, a pastoral, "Essay on the Death of Queen Mary," 1694.

This, I take it, is not an unfair example of the usual way of regarding nature at this time.* As Otway's poem goes on, it becomes very obscure, but the beginning at least is fine.

IV. To make a change from this subject to one akin to it, let us for a moment look at the songs of the drama of the Restoration. Here we come across a number of instances of the French influence. Yet it is worthy of notice that many of the songs in Dryden's plays are translations of French songs of the sixteenth century, the other models, the lyrics of the great English dramatists, being neglected. As an example of the change, we may com-

---

* For another example of the conventional treatment of nature, see Congreve's pastoral, "The Mourning Muse of Alexis," also on the death of Queen Mary; and Thackeray's amusing comments on it, in his "English Humourists."

pare the song which Rochester put into his version of Beaumont and Fletcher's "Valentinian," with the one in the original.   Here is Rochester's :

Nymph.

"Injurious charmer of my vanquished heart,
　　Canst thou feel love, and yet no pity know ?
Since of myself from thee I cannot part,
　　Invent some gentle way to let me go;
　　　For what with joy thou didst obtain,
　　　　And I with more did give,
　　　In time will make thee false and vain,
　　　　And me unfit to live."

Shepherd.

"Frail angel, that wouldst have a heart forlorn,
　　With vain pretence Falsehood therein might lie,
Seek not to cast wild shadows o'er your scorn,
　　You cannot sooner change than I can die;
　　　To tedious life I'll never fall,
　　　　Thrown from thy dear-lov'd breast;
　　　He merits not to live at all,
　　　　Who cares to live unblest."

Beaumont and Fletcher's song ran thus :

"Hear, ye ladies that despise,
　　What the mighty love has done;
Fear examples, and be wise:
　　Fair Calisto was a nun;
Leda, sailing on the stream
　　To deceive the hopes of man,
Love accounting but a dream,
　　Doated on a silver swan;
Danaë in a brazen tower,
Where no love was, loved a shower.

"Hear, ye ladies that are coy,
　　What the mighty love can do;
Fear the fierceness of the boy:
　　The chaste moon he makes to woo;
Vesta, kindling holy fires,
　　Circled round about with spies,

> Never dreaming loose desires,
>   Doting at the altar dies;
> Ilion, in a short hour, higher
>   He can build and once more fire."

You will notice the tone of gallantry in Rochester's, which is attractive enough, although it lacks the sort of musical dignity of the other. Indeed, as we all know, the cavaliers brought down the traditions of the early song-writers in a way that is sure to win admiration, but even the best of their work lacks the sort of classical finish which we find in the occasional lyrics of the drama-tists, such as, for instance, Peele's "His golden locks time hath to silver turned;" Green's "Ah, what is love? It is a pretty thing;" Dekker's "Art thou poor, yet hast thou golden slumbers;" Nash's "Spring, the sweet spring;" and his

> " Adieu; farewell earth's bliss,
>   This world uncertain is:
> Fond are life's lustful joys;
> Death proves them all but toys.
> None from his darts can fly:
> I am sick, I must die.
>   Lord have mercy on us!
>
> *   *   *   *   *
>
> " Beauty is but a flower,
>   Which wrinkles will devour:
> Brightness falls from the air;
> Queens have died young and fair;
> Dust hath closed Helen's eye;
> I am sick, I must die.
>   Lord have mercy on us!"

To say nothing of Shakspere's songs, Ben Jonson's, and the best of Beaumont and Fletcher's, as,

> " Roses, their sharp spines being gone,
>   Not royal in their smells alone,
>   But in their hue."

The earlier cavalier songs are good, such as those of Lovelace :

> " When love with unconfined wings;"

and the one "To Lucasta, on Going to the Wars :"

> " Tell me not, sweet, I am unkind ;"

or "To Althea from Prison ;" but in the play-writers we find a new quality, which would make it nearly impossible, for instance, to confound one of the songs of the later time with those that preceded them.

Take, for example, this one, by Congreve :

> " See, see, she wakes, Sabina wakes!
>   And now the sun begins to rise ;
> Less glorious is the morn that breaks
>   From his bright beams than her fair eyes.
>
> " With light united, day they give,
>   But different fates 'ere night fulfil;
> How many by his warmth will live !
>   How many will her coldness kill !

This one, by Etherege :

> " It is not, Celia, in your power
>   To say how long our love will last;
> It may be we, within this hour,
>   May lose those joys we now do taste:
> The blessed, who immortal be,
> From change of love are only free.
>
> " Then since we mortal lovers are,
>   Ask not how long our love will last;
> But, while it does, let us take care
>   Each minute be with pleasure past.
> Were it not madness to deny
> To live, because we're sure to die?
>
> " Fear not, though love and beauty fail,
>   My reason shall my heart direct:
> Your kindness now shall then prevail,
>   And passion turn into respect.

> Celia, at worst, you'll in the end
> But change a lover for a friend."

This, by Sedley :

> "Not, Celia, that I juster am
>   Or better than the rest;
> For I would change each hour, like them,
>   Were not my heart at rest.
>
> "But I am tied to very thee
>   By every thought I have:
> Thy face I only care to see,
>   Thy heart I only crave.
>
> "All that in woman is adored
>   In thy dear self I find—
> For the whole sex can but afford
>   The handsome and the kind.
>
> "Why, then, should I seek further store
>   And still make love anew?
> When change itself can give no more
>   'Tis easy to be true."

And this, by Rochester :

> "All my past life is mine no more,
>   The flying hours are gone;
> Like transitory dreams giv'n o'er
> Whose images are kept in store
>   By memory alone.
>
> "The time that is to come is not;
>   How, then, can it be mine?
> The present moment's all my lot,
> And that as fast as it is got,
>   Phillis, is only thine!
>
> "Then talk not of inconstancy,
>   False hearts, and broken vows;
> If I, by miracle can be
> This live-long minute true to thee,
>   'Tis all that Heaven allows."

We notice, in the first place, command of rhythms; take, for instance, this from one of Dryden's songs (from " King Arthur ") :

> " O Sight, the mother of desires,
>   What charming objects dost thou yield!
> 'Tis sweet when tedious night expires,
>   To see the rosy morning gild
> The mountain-tops and paint the fields.
> But when Clarinda comes in sight,
> She makes the summer's day more bright,
> And when she goes away, 'tis night;"

or this from " Cleomenes ; or, the Spartan Hero " (1692) :

> " No, no, poor suffering heart, no change endeavour;
>   Choose to sustain the smart, rather than have her;
> My ravish'd eyes behold such charms about her,
> I can die with her, but not live without her;
> One tender sigh of hers to see me languish,
> Will more than pay the price of my past anguish;
> Beware, O cruel fair, how you smile on me,
> 'Twas a kind look of yours that has undone me.

> " Love has in store for me one happy minute,
> And she will end my pain who did begin it;
> Then no day void of bliss, of pleasure, leaving,
> Ages shall slide away without perceiving:
> Cupid shall guard the door, the more to please us,
> And keep out time and death, when they would seize us;
> Time and death shall depart, and say, in flying,
> Love has found out a way to live by dying."

Charming as these verses of Dryden's are, they bear to our ears the marks of the decay of literature; and yet, while more vivid proofs might easily be found of the general inferiority, these lines of Mrs. Behn's on the death of Waller, which outdo the usual extravagance even of epitaphs, will show how well the age thought of itself :

"Long did the untun'd world in ignorance stray,
　Producing nothing that was great and gay,
　Till taught by thee the true poetic way;
　Rough were the tracks before, dull and obscure,
　Nor pleasure nor instruction could procure;
　Their thoughtless labours could no passion move,
　Sure, in that age, the poets knew not love.
　That charming god, like apparitions, then,
　Was only talked on and ne'er seen by men.
　Darkness was o'er the Muses' land display'd,
　And e'en the chosen tribe unguided strayed,
　Till by thee rescued from the Egyptian night,
　They now look up and view the god of light,
　That taught them how to love and how to write."

V. The extracts I have given will make it clear that the English stage was not in a healthy state at the end of the seventeenth century. I have passed over the most objectionable side on account of the impossibility of presenting it fairly. Mere denunciation of the faults of the English comedy of the Restoration would be idle, and since in the history of literature it was wholly sterile and left behind it no successor we may safely leave it untouched. The later development of the tragedies, as we have seen them in Lee and Otway, served as a model for succeeding playwrights in the next century; but the comedy forms a separate chapter, without a sequel, and what put an end to it, as much as anything, was a little volume of 288 pages, by the Rev. Jeremy Collier, entitled, " A Short View of the Immorality and Profaneness of the English Stage : Together with the Sense of Antiquity upon this Argument." This book appeared in 1698, running through three editions in the year of its publication.

The faults which it condemned at last brought their own punishment. When, twenty years before, Bunyan, in describing Vanity Fair, said, " at this Fair is at all times to be seen Jugglings, Cheats, Games, *Plays*, Fools, Apes, Knaves, and Rogues, and that of every kind," it was apparent that he expressed the opinion of the Puritans concerning the stage ; and for their opinion no one cared at all. No Puritan would have been listened to by the general public of those who professed an interest in letters. This denunciation of plays would have meant in those times political prejudice and religious bigotry. Collier, however, had this great advantage, that he was an ardent Tory, who was out of favor at court for his refusal to take the oath of allegiance to William after the Revolution of 1688, and had already been imprisoned in Newgate for his political writings. More than this, besides sturdily maintaining the rights of James II., he had given religious consolation to Sir John Friend and Sir William Parkyns when they were condemned to death for plotting against William ; and for giving these men absolution at the foot of the scaffold he had been blamed by the bishops, summoned before the court of the King's Bench, and for his contumacy in not recognizing the authority of this court he had been outlawed. This was the time he chose for stirring up another hornet's nest, by denouncing the most popular authors. He was, at any rate, sure not to be called a Puritan.

With regard to the immorality of the stage he had abundance of testimony, but he puts on the witness-stand only the works of Dryden, Wycherley, Congreve, D'Urfey, and Vanbrugh, and generally their latest writings, and from these examples proves his statements. He attacked their profanity with equal ardor and less judgment. For instance, in support of his charge that the writers, in their abuse of religion and Holy Scripture, "don't stop short of blasphemy," he says that "in the close of the play ['Mock Astrologer'] they make sport with Apparitions and

Fiends. One of the devils sneezes, upon this they give him the blessing of the occasion, and conclude *he has got cold by being too long out of the fire.*"

What Collier calls "the most extraordinary passage is this :

"'Carlos. *For your comfort, marriage, they say, is holy.*

"'Sancho. *Ay, and so is martyrdom, as they say, but both of them are good for just nothing but to make an end of a man's life.*'

"I shall make no reflections upon this. There needs no reading upon a monster. 'Tis shown enough by its own deformity."

Congreve, or, at least, one of his characters, spoke of Solomon as "wise by his judgment in astrology." "Thus," says Collier, "the wisest prince is dwindled into a gypsy !"

Sir Sampson Sampson is reminded of the strongest Samson of the name, "who pulled an old house over his head at last." "Here you have sacred history burlesqued, and Sampson once more brought into the house of Dagon to make sport for the Philistines !"

Every charge that he brings is supported by reference to all the plays of Greece and Rome, and while he shows blasphemy, as we have just seen, in English plays, it is part of his business to prove the absence of this in the plays of the ancients. But "there is one ill sentence in Sophocles. Philoctetes calls the gods κακοί, and libels their administration. This officer, we must understand, was left upon a solitary island, ill-used by his friends, and harassed with poverty and ulcers, for ten years together. These, under the ignorance of paganism, were trying circumstances, and take off somewhat of the malignity of the complaint."

He undertakes to prove that priests were ridiculed by the comic writers, and he even goes so far as to abuse Dryden because in "Cleomenes" one of the characters speaks disrespectfully of the Egyptian god Apis:

> "Accurs'd be thou, grass-eating, foddered god!
> Accurs'd thy temple! More accurs'd thy priests!"

He devotes thirteen pages to illustrating the manner in which English priests are turned to ridicule, and twenty-eight to show how priests were treated by Homer, Vergil, the Greek tragedians, Aristophanes, Plautus, Terence, Corneille, Molière (who "bring no priests of any kind upon the stage"), Racine, Shakspere, Ben Jonson, Beaumont and Fletcher; and then he goes on to prove, upon their accounts, "what right the clergy have to regard and fair usage." That they have received this elsewhere he makes clear by illustrations from the conduct of the Jews, the Egyptians, the Persian Magi, the Druids of Gaul, the priesthood of Rome, of France, of Hungary, Muscovy, Spain, Italy, etc.; and with every new point he lugs in the ancients and the rest of Europe.*

All of this seems sufficiently wide of the mark, and to tend simply to confuse what was very clear—namely, the corruption of the stage; yet, although Collier lacked all sympathy with artistic principles, and overshot his mark by putting all the blame for fashionable viciousness upon the stage, there are vigor, manliness, and intelligence in the book. To be sure, he blames Congreve for calling a coachman Jehu, and a parson Mr. Prig, and criticises

---

* The value of classical precedent at this time is most striking, though, perhaps, it is nowhere more vividly illustrated than here. With every new point the Greek and Roman writers are invoked to strengthen his arguments or to refute those of his enemies. No sooner have they passed off the stage in one paragraph than they are called back to dispose of something else. One is reminded of those clocks in which, every time the hour strikes, the apostles march out of one door, stalk across the stage, and then go in again.

Vanbrugh for neglecting the three unities ; but his general point is clear beneath even his accumulation of foreign testimony.

Naturally, the book excited great wrath. Almost all of those attacked directly, or by implication, made retort, but Congreve, who was distinctly a man of wit, showed none of it in his answer ; Vanbrugh did no better, and Collier, who certainly had the right on his side, had distinctly the best of the protracted arguments.* Dryden, almost if not quite alone, forbore to make reply, but in the preface to his "Fables" (1700) he said: "I shall say the less of Mr. Collier, because in many things he has taxed me justly ; and I have pleaded guilty to all thoughts and expressions of mine which can be truly argued of obscenity, profaneness, or immorality. If he be my enemy, let him triumph ; if he be my friend, as I have given him no per-

---

* John Dennis said : "Now there is no Nation in Europe, as has been observed above a thousand times, that is so generally addicted to the Spleen, as the English, and what is apparent to any observer, from the reigning distemper of the Clime, which is inseparable from the Spleen ; from that gloomy and sullen temper, which is generally spread through the nation, from that natural discontentedness which makes us so uneasie to one another, because we are so uneasie to ourselves : and lastly, from our jealousies and suspicions, which makes us so uneasie to ourselves and to one another, and have so often made us dangerous to the Government, and by consequence to ourselves. Now the English being more splenetick than other people, and consequently more thoughtful and more reflecting, and therefore more scrupulous in allowing their passions, and consequently things seldom hapning in life to move their passions so agreeably to their reasons, as to entertain and please them ; and there being no true and sincere pleasure unless these passions are thus moved, nor any happiness without pleasure, it follows, that the English to be happy, have more need than other people of something that will raise their passions in such a manner, as shall be agreeable to their reasons, that by consequence they have more need of the drama."—*Usefulness of the Stage* (1698), p. 12. These are not the words of a formidable antagonist.

sonal occasion to be otherwise, he will be glad of my repentance. . . . Yet it were not difficult to prove that in many places he has perverted my meaning by his glosses; and interpreted my words into blasphemy and bawdry of which they were not guilty; besides that he is too much given to horse-play in his raillery; and comes to battle like a dictator from the plough. I will not say 'The zeal of God's house has eaten him up;' but I am sure it has devoured some part of his good manners and civility." And he adds: "He has lost ground at the latter end of the day, by pursuing his point too far: . . . from immoral plays to no plays." *

---

* In 1719, a certain Bedford, chaplain to the Duke of Bedford, republished a book that first appeared in 1706, called "A Serious Remonstrance in behalf of the Christian religion against the horrid blasphemies and impieties which are still used in the English playhouse." Here is a sample of his arguments: "When God was pleased to vindicate His own honour, and show that he would not be thus affronted, by sending a most dreadful storm . . . yet, so great was the obstinacy of the stage under such signal judgments, that we are told the actors did in a few days after entertain again their audience with the ridiculous plays of the 'Tempest' and 'Macbeth,' and that at the mention of the chimneys being blown down the audience were pleased to clap at an unusual length . . . as if they would outbrave the judgment, throw Providence out of the chair, place the devil in his stead, and provoke God once more to plead his own cause by sending another calamity."

He accused playwriters of restoring Pagan worship by their reference to Cupid, Jupiter, Diana, etc., of encouraging witchcraft or magic; "for," he says, "by bewitching, magick, and enchanting, they only signify something which is most pleasant and desirable." He even detected blasphemy in Addison's "Cato," in lines like these:

> "This, this is life indeed! life worth preserving!
> Such life as Juba never felt till now!"

and

> "My joy! My best beloved! My only wish!"

Thirty years later, William Law, in his treatise, "On the Absolute Un-

That was scarcely an exaggeration of the result of the book. Societies for the encouragement of good morals took courage ; King William renewed the orders he had already given to prevent the licensing "any plays containing expressions contrary to religion and good manners ;" Queen Anne, at the beginning of her reign, helped the same cause. The erring comic writers purged their published works of some of their offensiveness ; and their later writings showed a new regard for decorum. Indeed, the popular feeling was so high that they had to shorten sail. The old Puritan spirit was revived, and the closing of the playhouses was urged in various quarters, which would have been but again to let one excess take the place of another. This bigotry would but have inspired another outbreak of indecency. Fortunately there were men living who were able to take sounder views, and to make a sort of compromise between the wits, as they called themselves, and the public. Sir Richard Blackmore, an absolutely uninspired poet, the Tupper of his age, had even preceded Collier in his attack on the corruption of the age, and had written voluminous epic poems for this excellent reason, "that the young gentlemen and ladies who are delighted with poetry might have a useful, at least a harmless, entertainment," such as they could not get from other poets ; but the remedy he prescribed no one could swallow—his books were practically unread. Addison was the man who reconciled literature and life. Let us see how he did this, and, first, how he was prepared for this arduous task.

---

lawfulness of the Stage," said that, in going to the theatre, "You are as certainly going to the devil's triumph as if you were going to those old sports where people committed murder and offered Christians to be devoured by wild beasts." And at the Shakspere Jubilee (1769), the heavy rains were attributed to the vengeance of heaven: *vide* Lecky, "England in the Eighteenth Century," i. 594, 595.

CHAPTER IV.

I. ADDISON was born in 1672 ; his father was a clergy-man, and, in 1683, Dean of Lichfield. At school he became intimate with Steele. The friendship then formed was of great service to English literature, by enlisting, as we shall see, in a common cause two able writers who supplemented each other admirably. Since then, however, their friendship has been a subject of dissension. This has happened because praise of one is supposed to imply blame of the other, and one who speaks approvingly of Steele's enthusiasm is imagined to be secretly condemning Addison's coolness.* Yet, since not all writers are admirable,

---

* Those who wish to settle the matter more fully will find a full discussion in Macaulay's essay on Addison, and John Forster's on Steele, in vol. ii. of his "Historical and Biographical Essays." Mr. Forster thought that Macaulay had set up Addison unduly, at Steele's expense, and he makes a warm defence of his favorite. With these two sources of information before him, the reader has a good chance of making up his mind fairly. Still, we should remember how hard it is fully to understand people as remote from us as, say, our next-door neighbors, and not be over-quick in deciding about people who lived nearly two hundred years ago. We always like to paint them in strong colors, to describe them with a single word. If, for instance, we read that so-and-so was avaricious, we picture him to ourselves sitting in a dark room, behind a barred door, counting his money-bags; whereas his avarice may have been a trait that showed itself only indirectly, by a certain hardness towards his friends. The surest way of ascertaining at a later day what a man was, is to find out the impression he made upon his friends, and double weight

let us be grateful for both. I do not know whether it was ever the fashion to make invidious comparisons between Beaumont and Fletcher, but if they escaped that fate they were rare exceptions. Goethe and Schiller, Wordsworth and Coleridge, whose names are commonly coupled, were not so fortunate.

In due time Addison became a student at Oxford, where Steele again met him. His first poetical essay was a short address to Dryden, for whom he composed the arguments prefixed to the several books of his translation of the "Æneid," and translated the greater part of the fourth "Georgic," which was published in the same volume with "An Account of the Greatest English Poets," and a translation from Ovid. The account of the poets, or, as he called it,

> " A short account of all the Muse-possesst,
> That down from Chaucer's days to Dryden's times,
> Have spent their noble rage in British rhymes,"

is a valueless production, from which I make a few extracts to show once more the manner of thought current at the time :

> " Chaucer first, a merry bard, arose,
> And many a story told in rhyme and prose ; ·
> But age has rusted what the poet writ,
> Worn out his language and obscured his wit ;
> In vain he jests in his unpolished strain,
> And tries to make his readers laugh in vain.

> " Old Spenser next, warm'd with poetic rage,
> In ancient tales amus'd a barbarous age ;

---

must be given to praise from his enemies. Applying this test, we find Addison a most lovable man. He was shy, and would never talk to more than one person at a time, but his conversation must have been delightful. For this we have the testimony of Pope and Swift, and many others. Steele said it was Terence and Catullus rolled into one, with something else that was neither of them, but Addison alone.

An age that, yet uncultivate and rude,
Where'er the poet's fancy led, pursued
Through pathless fields and unfrequented floods
To dens of dragons and enchanted woods.
But now the mystic tale that pleased of yore
Can charm an understanding age no more."

Shakspere is omitted ; the next poet is

" Great Cowley then (a mighty genius) wrote,
    *   *   *   *   *
He more had pleased us, had he pleased us less.
    *   *   *   *   *
Thy only fault is wit in its excess.
    *   *   *   *   *
Bless'd man ! who now shall be for ever known
In Sprat's successful labours and thy own."

Sprat, if we may interrupt Addison for a moment, not only edited Cowley and wrote his life ; he also imitated him. How he did this may be gathered from the following poem, which is avowedly in Cowley's manner, "On his Mistress Drown'd :"

" Sweet stream, that dost with equal pace
Both thyself fly, and thyself chase,
   Forbear awhile to flow,
   And listen to my woe.

" Then go, and tell the sea that all its brine
   Is fresh, compared to mine :
Inform it that the gentler dame,
Who was the life of all my flame,
   I' th' glory of her bud,
   Has passed the fatal flood.
Death by this stroke triumphs above
   The greatest power of love :
   Alas, alas, I must give o'er,
My sighs will let me say no more.
Go on, sweet stream, and henceforth rest
No more than does my troubled breast ;

And if my sad complaints have made thee stay,
These tears, these tears, shall mend thy way."*

From Sprat, Addison turned to Milton :

" Whate'er his pen describes, I more than see
Whilst every verse, arrayed in majesty,
Bold and sublime, my whole attention draws,
And seems above the critic's nicer laws."

Towards the end, he relapses into the customary civility
of the day, and praises " the courtly Waller," " harmonious bard," Roscommon, Denham, " artful Dryden," " harmonious Congreve," and " noble Montague." It would be
the height of unfairness to estimate Addison's critical
ability by this little poem ; it was but an exercise in expression wherein he echoed the language of the time. He
had not yet formed his own opinions.† While he was in

---

* Lee, in his " Sophonisba," has these lines :

" Near to some murmuring brook I'll lay me down,
Whose waters if they should too shallow flow
My tears shall swell them up till I will drown."

An early instance of these floods of tears is to be found in Montemayor's
" Diana Enamorada," 1542 ; Venice, 1568, p. 71 ; Engl. trans., by Bartholo-
mew Yong, London, 1598, p. 78: " What is it (thinke you) that makes the
greene grasse of this iland growe, and the waters (that encompasse it
roundabout) to encrease, but my ceaseless teares ?" The question is asked
by the deserted Belisa, who bemoans her faithless lover.

† It would be a great mistake to confound these verses, which are
scarcely more than an exercise in penmanship, with Addison's real work.
Yet it is a mistake that is constantly made with regard to writers, each
one of whom is apparently considered a complete unit from the time he
began to write until his death. In fact, however, the first compositions of
an author are generally valuable for showing what were the strongest
tastes of his parents and teachers. Thus, Dryden, who was one of the
clearest of writers, began with a copious accumulation of conceits ; Pope,
whose strength lay in wit and social satire, began with languid and artificial pastorals ; Wordsworth, with an echo of Goldsmith, conventional

process of forming them he was exposed to other influences ; and what some of these were we may gather from this title of a book published in 1687 : "Spenser Redivivus; containing the first book of the Faery Queen, His Essential Design preserv'd, but his Obsolete Language and Manner of Verse totally laid aside. Deliver'd in Heroick Numbers, by a Person of Quality." * At the same time flourished Thomas Rymer, whom Pope, according to Spence, called about the best critic we have ever had, and whom Macaulay calls the worst that ever lived. He wrote on Shakspere first, in "The Tragedies of the Last Age ; Considered and Examined by the Practice of the Ancients and the Common Sense of all Ages, 1678–92 ;" and secondly, in "A Short View of the Tragedy of the Last Age ; its Original Excellency and Corruption ; with some Reflections on Shakspear, and other Practitioners for the Stage, 1693." Judging things by the practice of the Ancients was, as we have seen, the fashion of that day. Addison, in his poem, says that henceforth the Simois and

> "rapid Xanthus' celebrated flood "

shall no

> "longer be the poet's highest themes,
> Though gods and heroes fought promiscuous in their streams ;"

but that, instead, they will sing of the battle of the Boyne. And the common-sense of all ages means generally the

---

heroics, and personification ; Victor Hugo, with praise of church and state. Every young man is brought up on the conservative teachings of his elders, and it is some time before he can overtake the best thought of his day, which is just in advance not only of beginners but of most teachers. The youth hears vaguely, if at all, of those who are introducing the novelties which are to be the commonplaces of the next generation ; he may sigh for them, but he hears them spoken of with dislike. Every father tries to turn the taste of his children to what he liked when young, and generally the revolt begins only when the young man has stepped out into the world.

* *Vide* Morley's "First Sketch of English Literature," p. 756.

prejudices of him who appeals to it. It certainly meant so in this case, for Rymer was most severe in what he said about Shakspere. It was "Othello" that he picked to pieces. "Why was not this called the tragedy of the handkerchief ? We have heard of Fortunatus, his purse, and of the invisible cloak long ago worn threadbare, and stowed up in the wardrobe of obsolete romances ; one might think that were a fitter place for this handkerchief than that it, at this time of day, be worn on the stage, to raise everywhere this clutter and turmoil." And, also, "the handkerchief is so remote a trifle, no booby on this side Mauritania could make any consequence from it." "There is nothing," he says, "in the noble Desdemona, that is not below any country kitchen-maid with us." ... "No woman bred out of a pig-sty could talk so meanly."

Her death, nevertheless, distresses him. "A noble Venetian lady is to be murdered by our poet, in sober sadness, purely for being a fool. No pagan poet but would have found some machine for her deliverance. Pegasus would have strained hard to have brought old Perseus on his back ; time enough to rescue this Andromeda from so foul a monster. Has our Christian poetry no generosity, no bowels? Ha, ha, Sir Launcelot ! Ha, Sir George ! Will no ghost leave the shades for us in extremity to save a distressed damsel?" And, finally, he says: "In the neighing of a horse, or in the growling of a mastiff, there is a meaning, there is as lively expression, and, may I say, more humanity, than many times in the tragical flights of Shakespeare." * With criticism of this sort for light reading,

---

* Some bold statements of Rymer's illustrative of the views then held concerning the province of tragedy are worth quoting : " We are to presume the greatest virtues where we find the highest rewards, and though it is not necessary that all heroes should be kings, yet, undoubtedly, all crowned heads, by poetical right, are heroes. This character is a flower,

there was evidently room for a man who should introduce some of the charm of civilization. Addison was busily fitting himself for the task. His acquaintance with Dryden brought him into contact with Congreve, who in his turn introduced him to Montague, then chancellor of the exchequer, and to Lord Somers, solicitor - general, who induced Addison to give up his plan of entering the church, and instead to prepare himself for political life. There is to be noticed a great change from the time when Dryden and his contemporaries were struggling for a living. Then writers could barely live by flattering the great; now the times had changed, and writers were sought by all of those in authority. The reason of this change is simple. Before the revolution of 1688, the king held his place by right of birth; his authority was not to be disputed. But with 1688, and the accession of William and Mary, the royal power depended on the will of the nation; parliamentary government established itself. The king selected for ministers men with influence; the ministers had to secure influence as best they might. Dryden's satirical poems had shown how great power a writer possessed, and with the development of the newspaper he

a prerogative, so certain, so indispensably annexed to the crown, as by no poet, or parliament of poets, ever to be invaded."

"If I mistake not, in poetry, no woman is to kill a man, except his quality gives her the advantage above him; nor is a servant to kill the master, nor a private man, much less a subject to kill a king, nor on the contrary. Poetical decency will not permit death to be dealt to each other, by persons whom the laws of duell allow not to enter the lists together." He made an exception, however, in favor of killing a pagan or a foreign prince.

Lord Shaftesbury, in his "Advice to an Author," 1710, speaks of the "Gothic Muse of Shakspeare, Fletcher, and Milton as lisping with stammering tongues, that nothing but the youth and rawness of the age could excuse."

became a more important person. Then, too, Montague, Earl of Halifax, who, with Prior, had written "The Country and the City Mouse," was a patron of letters. Somers had been prominent in encouraging the new edition of Milton; Dorset, too, the lord-chamberlain, had tried his hand at writing. Still, mere interest in literature would have done but little had not Dryden's "Absalom and Achitophel," and the controversies it aroused, shown how much power wit exercised. While Dorset and Montague were Whig patrons of letters, on the other side Harley and Bolingbroke encouraged writers to draw their morals in favor of Toryism. Thus, after the battle of Blenheim, 1704, Addison wrote his panegyric. You will remember that, in his lectures on the English Humorists, Thackeray mentions the angel's visit when Addison was asked to write about the victory: "Your wings seldom quiver at second - floor windows now." Marlborough, Addison said,

> "In peaceful thought the field of death surveyed,
> To fainting squadrons sent the timely aid,
> Inspired repulsed battalions to engage,
> And taught the doubtful battle when to rage.
> So when an angel by divine command,
> With rising tempests shakes a guilty land
> (Such as of late o'er pale Britannia passed),
> Calm and serene he drives the furious blast;
> And, pleased the Almighty's orders to perform,
> Rides in the whirlwind and directs the storm."

For this Addison was made commissioner of appeals, *vice* Mr. Locke; the next year Addison went to Hanover with Lord Halifax, and the year after was made under-secretary of state.

All these things came at a good time for Addison. No one ever grumbles at such luck, to be sure, but Addison, who in 1699 had been granted a pension of £300 in order that he might travel in preparation for diplomatic life, had lost it in 1702, when his friends went out of office. The battle of Blenheim, as we say, brought him into fame, however. It was John Philips who sounded the praises of Blenheim from the Tory side, or, as Dr. Johnson puts it, "with occult opposition to Addison."* Here is an example of his manner :

> "Now from each van
> The brazen instruments of death discharge
> Horrible flames, and turbid streaming clouds
> Of smoke sulphureous ; intermix'd with these
> Large globous irons fly, of dreadful hiss,
> Singeing the air, and from long distance bring
> Surprising slaughter . . . by sudden burst
> Disploding murderous bowels, fragments of steel,
> And stones and glass, and nitrous grain adust ;
> A thousand ways at once the shiver'd orbs
> Fly diverse, working torment and foul rout."

As a not unnatural consequence,

> "Unmanly dread invades
> The French astonied ; straight their useless arms
> They quit, and in ignoble flight confide,
> Unseemly yelling ; distant hills return
> The hideous noise."

It is not necessary to read more. You will notice that the lines are written in blank verse of the Miltonic pattern. And Philips, I may say by the way, was one of the first of the English poets to abandon the couplet and to take to the rival measure. In it he wrote the "Splendid Shilling," a burlesque, and a fifth Georgic, on "Cider," which

---

* Addison had tried his hand at the imitation of Milton, but without much success. *Vide* a piece out of Æn. iii. (Bohn's edition of Addison's Works, i. 38).

has been said to be a sound manual of instruction for the farmer. It may be doubted, however, whether the farmer would gather from these few lines that he was told to pick off superfluous fruit :

> " The wise
> Spare not the little offsprings if they grow
> Redundant, but the thronging clusters thin
> By kind avulsion, else the starveling brood,
> Void of sufficient sustenance, will yield
> A slender autumn, which the niggard soul
> Too late shall weep, and curse his thrifty hand,
> That would not timely ease the ponderous boughs."

The general reader will find his profit, too, in studying the poem :

> "Nor from the sable ground expect success,
> Nor from cretaceous, stubborn, and jejune ;
> The must of pallid hue declares the soil
> Devoid of spirit : wretched he that quaffs
> Such wheyish liquors ! oft with colic pangs,
> With pungent colic pangs, distrest he'll roar,
> And toss, and turn, and curse th' unwholesome draught." *

We shall see plenty of examples of this so-called Miltonic way of writing, as in Thomson's "Seasons," Cowper, Wordsworth, to name a few of the most prominent. Dr. Johnson bitterly opposed blank verse, and in his life of John Philips he said " he imitated Milton's numbers indeed, but imitates them very injudiciously. Deformity is easily copied ; and whatever there is in Milton which the reader wishes away, all that is obsolete, peculiar, or licentious is accumulated with great care by Philips. Milton's verse was harmonious, in proportion to the general state of our metre in Milton's age ; and if he had written after the improvements made by Dryden, it is reasonable to believe

---

* The poem was translated into Italian. This kind of writing was admired then, and previously, in Italy.

he would have admitted a more pleasing modulation of numbers into his work." This was the statement of a prejudiced man, but it is interesting to see what may be thought and stated with approbation in another time than our own.

At any rate, it will be clear that Addison did not have a serious rival in this miniature Milton. Philips, we are told, had admired Milton from his tender youth, but those who followed him doubtless belonged to the romantic half of mankind, who revolted from the reasonableness of those who clung to the heroic measure. Reasonableness had charms for Addison. In his preparations for diplomacy he made the usual tour of Europe, and, like many since his time, and a few before, he wrote a book about his travels. This volume has no great merit, although the descriptions are even now precise. As Doudan said, although Italy had not then been wholly cut up by the railroad, it seems as if not a nail had been driven in all Italy since Addison visited it. But a good many things have been driven into the heads of travellers since Addison went to Italy and compared the country, as he found it, with the descriptions he recalled from the Latin poets.

II. Nowadays the traveller who finds himself before St. Mark's in Venice dilates with various emotions. He has Ruskin's "Seven Lamps" and the "Stones of Venice" in his hand-bag, and the fact that he has learned to admire other things in architecture than the works of the ancients and the classical imitations of the Renaissance is another instance of the vicissitudes of taste. What was the rigorously enforced view of the times we are discussing, we may see, for instance, in Bishop Burnet's "Letters from Switzerland, Italy, and Some Parts of Germany, in the Years 1685 and 1686" (Rotterdam, 1687), p. 128. The worthy bishop says : "St. Mark's Church hath nothing to recommend it, but its great Antiquity, and the vast Riches of the Building, it is dark and low ; but the pavement is so rich a Mosaick, and the whole roof is also Mosaick, the outside and inside are of such excellent Marble, the Frontispiece is adorned with so many Pillars of Porphyry and Jasper, and above all with the four Horses of Corinthian Brass," etc.," that when all this is considered, one doth no where see so much cost brought together." "The Dome of Milan," he says, "hath nothing to commend it of Architecture, it being built in the rude Gothic manner " (p. 103).

Addison says of the beautiful cathedral at Sienna : "There is nothing in this City so extraordinary as the Cathedral, which a man may view with pleasure after he has seen St. Peter's, tho' 'tis quite of another make, and can only be looked upon as one of the Masterpieces of Gothic architecture. When a man sees the prodigious pains and expense that our forefathers have been at in these barbarous buildings, one cannot but fancy to himself what miracles of architecture they would have left us, had they only been instructed in the right way ; for when the devotion of those ages was much warmer than it is at present, and the riches of the people much more at the disposal of the priests, there was so much money consumed on these Gothic cathedrals, as would have finished a greater variety of noble buildings than have been raised either before or since that time." He then goes on to describe the very spouts, "loaden with ornaments ;" the windows, "formed like so many scenes of perspective, with a multitude of little pillars retiring one behind another ;" the great " columns " finely engraven with fruits and foliage "that run twisting about them from the very top to the bottom ;" the whole body of the church "chequered with different lays of white and black marble ;"

the pavement " curiously cut out in designs and Scripture-
stories and the Fruit cut with such a variety of figures
and over-run with so many little mazes and labyrinths of
Sculpture, that nothing in the world can make a prettier
show to those who prefer false beauties and affected ornaments to a noble and majestic simplicity."

Addison and Burnet did but express the average opinion
of their time* just as we all do when we praise what

---

* A century earlier these prejudices had not come into existence. Montaigne, in 1580, calls the cathedral at Florence "a magnificent structure,
one of the finest and most sumptuous churches in the world." See his
account in his "Journey into Italy," iv. 284 and 290. Of Sienna, he says,
"The cathedral church is very little inferior to that of Florence."

Lyly's "Euphues and his England," 1580, Arber's Reprint, p. 251:
"But first they came to Canterbury, an olde Citie—somewhat decayed, yet
beautiful to behold, most famous for a Catholic Church, the very Majestie
whereoff stroke them into a maze."

Coryat in his "Crudities" (edition 1611, p. 98) calls Milan cathedral an
"exceedingly glorious and beautiful church," and that at Amiens, "the
queene of al the churches in France and the fairest that ever I saw till
then" (Id. p. 12). Notice, too, his wild enthusiasm over the piazza and
church of St. Mark's (Id. pp. 171–216).

Evelyn, even as late as Oct. 25, 1644, says: "The Domo or Cathedral, both
without and within, is of large square stones of black and white marble
polished, of inexpressible beauty, as is the front adorned with sculptures
and rare statues. . . . The pulpit is beautified with marble figures, a piece
of exquisite work;" and the next May, "dined at Sienna where we could
not pass admiring the great church."

Of St. Mark's he said: "The Cathedral is also Gothic, yet for the pre-
ciousness of the materials," etc., "far exceeding any in Rome, St. Peter's
hardly excepted." "I much admired the splendid history of our Blessed
Saviour, composed all of mosaic. . . . The roof is of most excellent mosaic." "After all that is said, this church is in my opinion much too
dark and dismal and of heavy work." The prejudice against Gothic work
was not so bitter then as it became after the Restoration. Evelyn also
visited the cathedrals of Rouen and of Pisa. The latter, he says, is superb.
All the English cathedrals he admired warmly, Canterbury, Gloucester,

they condemned or overlooked. Every one held their view.* President de Brosses, in one of his letters from Venice, Aug. 26, 1739, says : "You know by reputation the palace of St. Mark's ; it is an ugly old fellow, if there ever was one, massive, sombre, and Gothic, in the most execrable taste. To be sure, the great inner courtyard has something magnificent in its construction. The doge lives in the palace, but he has the worst lodging of all the prisoners of state, for the ordinary prison, close by, is a thoroughly elegant and agreeable building. I do not care to linger there too long, however, and I make my way to the church of St. Mark's. You have imagined that this was an admirable place, but you are very much mistaken ; it is a sort of Greek church, low, impervious to light, in wretched taste both inside and out. It is surmounted by seven domes lined on the inside with mosaics on a gold ground, which make them look more like copper boilers than domes. . . . With the immense wealth spent there, it could not help being curious in spite of the diabolical workmen who have lent a hand to the work. From top to bottom, inside and out, the church is covered with pictures in mosaic on a gold ground. . . . With the exception of the colouring, which is tolerably well preserved by the nature of the material, there is nothing more pitiable than these mosaics ; fortunately the artisans took the wise precaution of writing above each piece what it was intended

---

etc. York cathedral he calls "a most entire and magnificent piece of Gothic architecture."

* Thus, in the *Spectator*, No. 415, Addison says : "Let any one reflect on the disposition of mind he finds in himself at his first entrance into the Pantheon at Rome, and how his imagination is filled with something great and amazing; and at the same time consider how little, in proportion, he is affected with the inside of a Gothic cathedral, though it be five times larger than the other; which can arise from nothing else but greatness of the manner in the one, and the meanness in the other."

to represent." The four horses above the entrance he calls the only thing about the building which is really worthy of admiration.

The baptistery at Florence is, he says, "a little less abominable than the cathedral of St. Mark's."[*] In 1753, Rousseau, in his letter on French Music, said that counter-fugues, double fugues, and other difficult fooleries that the ear cannot endure nor the reason justify, are evidently relics of barbarism and bad taste which survive, like the porticos of Gothic churches, to the disgrace of those who had the patience to construct them. Voltaire, too, "used Gothic architecture as the symbol for the supreme height of rudeness and barbarism."[†]

In another respect, Addison was a man of his time ; that is, in the way he regarded natural scenery. In one of his

---

[*] Smollett, in "Humphrey Clinker," p. 219 : "As for the minster [of York], I know not how to distinguish it, except by its great size and the height of its spire, from those other ancient churches in different parts of the kingdom, which used to be called monuments of Gothic architecture ; but it is now agreed that this style is Saracen rather than Gothic ; and I suppose it was first imported into England from Spain, great part of which was under the dominion of the Moors. Those British architects who adopted this style don't seem to have considered the propriety of their adoption." These buildings are suitable in hot countries on account of their coolness, but "nothing could be more preposterous than to imitate such a mode of architecture in a country like England. . . . The external appearance of an old cathedral cannot be but displeasing to the eye of every man who has any idea of propriety or proportion, even though he may be ignorant of architecture as a science : and the long slender spire puts one in mind of a criminal impaled, with a sharp stake running up through his shoulder. These towers, or steeples, were likewise borrowed from the Mahometans, who, having no bells, used such minarets for the purpose of calling the people to prayers. . . . There is nothing of this Arabic architecture in the assembly-room, which seems to me to have been built on a design of Palladio, and might be converted into an elegant place of worship."

[†] J. Morley's "Rousseau," i. 301.

letters, dated December, 1701, he wrote that he had reached Geneva after " a very troublesome journey over the Alps. My head is still giddy with mountains and precipices ; and you can't imagine how much I am pleased with the sight of a plain." This little phrase is a good illustration of the contempt for mountains, of the way they were re-garded as wild, barbaric, forgotten, useless excrescences.* This was not a temporary perversion of taste, however, like the detestation of Gothic architecture. The love of mountains is something really of modern, very modern, growth, the first traces of which we shall come across towards the middle of the last century. Before that time we find mountains spoken of in terms of the severest reprobation. Addison in his Italian travels writes from Thonon : " There are vistas in front of it [the town] of great length, that terminate upon the Lake. At one side of the walks you have a near prospect of the Alps, which are broken into so many steeps and precipices that they fill the mind with an agreeable kind of horror, and form one of the most ir-regular misshapen scenes in the world." As if, in a hap-pier world, the tops of mountains should be shaped like Corinthian columns ! Of Berne he says : " There is the noblest summer-prospect in the world from this walk ; for you have a full view of a huge range of mountains that lie in the country of the Grisons, and are covered with snow." This was about as warm an expression of admi-ration for mountain scenery as had been written up to that time. In the mediæval books of travel, in the ac-counts of the Crusades, we find nothing but horror ex-pressed of the Alps ; one German (1544) tells us at some length how his bones and his heart quivered as he stood at the top of the Gemmi.

---

* Howell, in a passage quoted below, calls mountains " excrescences of nature."

Evelyn is, perhaps, the single exception, and even he is not too remote from his times. He always mentions, though generally without adjectives, the different views of the Alps from various places ; but he found the journey over them very trying. After going over-night "through very steep, craggy, and dangerous passages to Vedra," . . . where "we had a very infamous, wretched lodging. The next morning we mounted again through strange, horrid, and fearfull craggs and tracts, abounding in pine-trees, and only inhabited by beares, wolves, and wild goates ; nor could we anywhere see above a pistol-shoote before us, the horizon being terminated with rocks and mountains, whose tops covered with snow seemed to touch the skies, and in many places pierced the clouds. . . . The narrow bridges in some places, made only by felling huge fir-trees and laying them athwarte from mountain to mountain over cataracts of stupendious depth, are very dangerous, . . . and in some places we passe between mountains that have been broken and fallen on one another, which is very terrible, and one had neede of a sure foote and steady head to climb some of these precipices, besides that they are harbours for beares and wolves, who have sometimes assaulted travellers. In these straights we frequently alighted, now freezing in the snow, and anon frying by the reverberation of the sun against the cliffs. . . . The next morning we returned our guide, and tooke fresh mules and another to conduct us to the Lake of Geneva, passing through as pleasant a country as that we had just travel'd was melancholy and troublesome." On the way to Martigny, they passed "between the horrid mountains on either hand." But later he says, "we sailed the whole length of the lake, about thirty miles, the countries bordering on it (Savoy and Berne) affording one of the most delightful prospects in the world—the Alps, covered with snow, though at a great distance yet showing their aspiring tops." And we find Evelyn continually speaking of beautiful views in England *—as, for one ex-

---

* But of the Riviera he said (p. 73): "All this coast (except a little at San Remo) is a high and steepe mountainous ground, consisting all of rock marble, without any grass, tree, or rivage, formidable to look on." Mountains, that is, he found intolerable.

Montaigne (iv. 263) had remarked of the country near Verona: "The road here [was] the roughest they had as yet traversed, and the scenery was wild and forbidding in the highest degree, both of which circumstances were owing to these same mountains."

So President de Brosses says of the Riviera (i. 47) that "there is always a precipice on one side, which seemed to my companions a very poor invention. There could be nothing more beautiful," he says, "than the appearance of all this shore. . . . There are nothing but well-built and populous towns and villages."

In one of Howell's letters (Nov. 6, 1621) to Sir J. H., from Lyons, he writes: "I am now got over the Alps and returned to France. I had crossed and clambered up the Pyraneans to Spain before; they are not so high and hideous as the Alps, but for our mountains in Wales, as Eppint and Penwinmaur, which are so much cried up among us, they are molehills in comparison of these: they are but pigmies compared to giants, but blisters compared to imposthumes, or pimples to warts. Besides, our mountains in Wales bear always something useful to man or beast—some grass, at least; but these huge, monstrous excrescences of nature bear nothing (most of them) but craggy stones: the tops of some of them are blanched over all the year long with snow, and those who drink the water have *goître*."

Compare letter cliv., in "Sir Charles Grandison," describing the passage of the Alps: At Pont Beauvoisin "we bid adieu to France, and found ourselves in Savoy, equally noted for its poverty and rocky mountains. Indeed, it was a total change of the scene. We had left behind us a blooming spring, which enlivened with its verdure the trees and hedges on the road we passed, and the meadows already smiled with flowers. . . . But when we entered Savoy, nature wore a very different face; and I must own that my spirits were great sufferers by the change. . . . The unseasonable coldness of the weather, and the sight of one of the worst countries under heaven. . . . At Lanebourg . . . every object which presents itself to view is excessively miserable."

ample, " what was most stupendious to me was the rock of
St. Vincent, a little distance from the town, the precipice
whereof is equal to anything of that nature I have seen
in the most confragose cataracts of the Alps, the river
gliding between them at an extraordinary depth. . . .
There is also on the side of this horrid Alp a very romantic* seat " (*horrid* = awful). I might quote many passages in which he speaks of beautiful views, but all that I
wish to point out here is the non-existence of the feeling
of admiration for mountain scenery. Nowadays, the fiercer
the mountains the warmer our raptures. As we go on, I
shall try to make clear the gradual change in men's feelings concerning this sort of natural beauty. We have
now ascertained what were the views that were current in
Addison's time and consequently authoritative over him.

III. Let us remember that what we understand as modern civilization was new then ; that all the thousand-and-
one particulars which make life comfortable were either
not known then, or were as new as the telephone is to us—
although we have this advantage, that we are accustomed
to inventions and that new wonders soon become commonplaces to us. Evelyn speaks of a nobleman's house
into which water was carried, as a princely mansion. The
streets were as dangerous as a drinking-saloon in a mining

Berkeley (Clarendon Press ed., iv. 68), speaking of crossing Mont Cenis
on New Year's Day, 1714, says that the rocks and crags, which were terrible then, "at the best are high, craggy, and steep enough to cause the
heart of the most valiant man to melt within him."

Winckelmann, however, admired them in 1755. See his "Life," by Carl
Justi, II. i. 7.

Compare with these Mr. Bryce's expressions about Ararat, with his quotation from Tournefort (a French botanist at the beginning of the eighteenth century) in his "Transcaucasia and Ararat" (pp. 231–233).

* This must be one of the first instances of the use of the word *romantic* (1654).

town on Saturday night. In 1679, Dryden was set upon and cudgelled by ruffians hired by Lord Rochester, because that nobleman quarrelled with the poet and his patron, Lord Mulgrave. In 1712, a band of young men calling themselves Mohocks committed various brutal assaults on unoffending people whom they met in the street, flattening their noses, gouging out their eyes, compelling them to dance until they dropped exhausted, rolling women in barrels, etc., beating the watch, etc. Horace Walpole, in 1752, wrote : "One is forced to travel even at noon as if one were going to battle." It was not till 1736 that London was lit ; before that time a lamp was put before every tenth house, from Michaelmas, Sept. 29, to Lady Day, March 25, and that only till midnight and on what were called dark nights, twenty days of every month, the rest being supposed to be lit by the moon. While crime was rampant, prisoners were put to death for trivial reasons, and those who were imprisoned were thereby sentenced to death by jail-fever. Women were publicly burned. Evelyn mentions somewhere in his Diary seeing a woman at the stake while he was on his way to look at some medals. Yet it would be impossible to draw a full picture of the social life of the time, although there is an abundance of material from which facts may be collected. When we come to the *Spectator* we shall see a number of social incidents mentioned and commented on.

What we notice is the newness at Addison's time of what we understand by modern life, and the enormous attraction of everything that stood for civilization and refinement. The age was in many ways gross, but it was working with all possible zeal for better things, and it sought aid from every direction. The people of that day had had enough of natural forces ; what they wanted was these natural forces tamed and softened, and they saw their ideal in the couplet, in Roman architecture, and in smooth landscapes. Hence we comprehend their abhorrence of the old dramatists of Gothic cathedrals, and it becomes clear to us how Addison could say that in viewing " huge heaps of mountains, high rocks and precipices, or a wide expanse of waters, we are not struck with the novelty or beauty of the sight, but with that rude kind of magnificence which appears in many of these stupendous works of nature" (*Spectator*, No. 412) ; and " we find the works of nature still more pleasing the more they resemble those of art. . . . Hence it is that we take delight in a prospect which is well laid out, and diversified with fields and meadows, woods and rivers ; in those accidental Landscapes of trees, clouds, and cities that are sometimes found in the veins of marble ; in the curious fretwork of rocks and grottos ; and, in a word, in anything that hath such a variety or regularity as may seem the effect of design, in what we call the works of chance " (No. 414).

Just as now we look to science as the future corrector of all evils, so they looked to literature ; and to expect of them that they should have looked with frank enthusiasm at lawless natural forces would be like asking men who have just been saved from shipwreck to sit on the rocks and admire the heavy surf.

IV. We have all this time been leaving Addison shivering at the foot of the Alps, which he detested ; yet these digressions may show that he was fitting himself to speak to the men of his time in an authoritative manner—not from so high a position that his words would be looked on as those of a man raised above all ordinary interests, but as those of one who had received the best training the time afforded. While Addison was getting his bookish training, Steele, his future coadjutor in the *Spectator*, was acquiring a practical knowledge of the world. He enlisted as a private in the Coldstream Guards, although, as he afterwards said, "when he mounted a war-horse, with a great sword in his hand, and planted himself behind King William III. against Louis XIV., he lost the succession to a very good estate in the county of Wexford, in Ireland, from the same humour which he has preserved ever since, of preferring the state of his mind to that of his fortune."

Lord Cutts, the colonel of the regiment, made Steele his secretary, and got him an appointment as ensign. Then Steele wrote his first book, "The Christian Hero;" as he said : "He first became an author when an ensign of the Guards, a way of life exposed to much irregularity ; and being thoroughly convinced of many things of which he often repented, and which he more often repeated, he writ, for his own private use, a little book, called 'The Christian Hero,' with a design principally to fix upon his own mind a strong impression of virtue and religion in opposition to a stronger propensity to unwarrantable pleasures ;" and, in short, he published it to have a stronger reason for conforming to his own best intentions. In this book he spoke of the heroism of the ancient world — for, as we saw in Collier's book, the ancients had to be appealed to in proof of everything—but the greatest praise he gave to the true Christian, whom he defined as "one who is always a benefactor with the mien of a receiver." The didactic flavor of the book he sought to relieve by a comedy, "The Funeral ; or, Grief à la Mode," in which he cleverly denounced affected mummeries of grief. He wrote other comedies, with a moral tone, in the new endeavor to let the theatre teach moral lessons ; in fact, Parson Adams said of Addison's "Cato" and Steele's "Conscious Lovers," that they were the only plays he ever heard of ; "and I must own," he says, "in the latter there are some things almost solemn enough for a sermon."

The great work of these two men, as well as the most lasting monument of their friendship, is the *Spectator.* The credit for the first thought of this belongs to Steele ; Addison had equipped himself for writing, but he needed some outside spur before revealing the stores of his intelligence and learning ; Steele had already written with this object in view, and he quickly seized the plan of publishing a brief daily paper.

The freedom of the press had been one of the most fortunate results of the revolution of 1688 ; at the end of the session of 1693, the Licensing Act expired, and was not renewed. Even before these formal measures had secured liberty, many new papers had been established, but these had led a precarious existence ; it was only when the censorship really disappeared that journalism fairly began ; the first fortnight after the final abolition of the censorship, May 3, 1695, saw the beginning, and a number quickly followed. These were wretched, meagre little things, appearing three times a week, printed sometimes on but one side of the leaf, and announcing the merest scraps of news. Soon came the *Flying Post,* with the news printed, and a blank space left for those who sent the paper to their friends in the country to add on it whatever they pleased ; and in 1702 the first daily paper appeared in London.

What these papers and their successors drove out was the pamphlet, written by Grub-street hacks. Politics had invaded the stage, where it appeared in the songs and the prologues and epilogues, but it was the anonymous and scurrilous pamphlets that had more especially busied themselves with this subject. Now, when discussion was free, and needed no longer to be carried on in the dark, journalism gradually attracted the ablest writers, and the days of the pamphlets were numbered. Journalism attained its power but slowly. The first man who thought of combining entertainment with information was one John Dunton,* who, March 17, 1690, began the publication of a penny paper, called first the *Athenian Gazette* and then the *Athenian Mercury*, or "A Scheme to answer a series of Questions Monthly, the Querist remaining concealed." The questions were such as might well have puzzled the Athenian Society : "Where was the soul of Lazarus for the four days he lay in the grave? Suppose Lazarus had an estate and bequeathed it to his Friends, whether ought he or his Legatees to enjoy it after he was raised from the dead?" "Where does extinguished fire go?" "Whether the torments of the damned are visible to the Saints? and *vice versa?*" "What became of the waters after the flood?" "Whether 'tis lawful for a man to beat his wife?"

Other questions were like these :

"Wherefore is it, that a piece of wood thrown from high to low into the water, together with a piece of lead, stone, or other hard and solid body of the same weight, both descending and falling at the same time on the water, and yet the lead, or a stone, will sink and the wood swim ?—*Ans.* The wood will not remain sunk in the water, but swim on the top thereof, because it is aerial, and the place of air is above the water ; the others will sink because they are terrestrial and aquatick ; but in the air the wood will descend as swift as either, because the air, as all other elements, except fire, do weigh in their natural place."

"Wherefore are we more timorous and fearful in the dark and in the night (especially if we are alone) than in the day-time, and in the light ? —*Ans.* Some do attribute this to the danger that may be apprehended by knocks and blows, when we cannot see from whence they come. [There

---

* In his "Life and Errors of John Dunton," i. 188, he tells us that he was walking in the street with a friend when the idea of this publication struck him. He at once exclaimed, "Well, sir, I have a thought I would not exchange for fifty guineas!"

7*

would seem to be more danger of these if we were not alone.] The true reason of this then is, that the great enemy of human kind, being the Prince and Lover of Darkness (as the Psalmist saith) walks in the darkness. [We have all felt sudden tremors in the dark] and the reason hereof may be that there is some evil spirit that we dread, without seeing of it."

" Why are the shadows of the sun more short at mid-day, than in the morning or at evening ?"

" Were all the creatures (as well as the serpent) vocal in Paradise as all the trees were in the Dodonian Wood ? Or was it the serpent only ? If the last, how came that to deserve the benefit of speech above the rest ? —*Ans.* The serpent only, which, in a few words, has but just outrivalled the mischief of such questions."

" Why should the serpent creep upon his belly, for his penalty ? Or did he walk upon his tail before ?"

" Whether is the more noble, man or woman ?"

Still, questions which we shall see later discussed in the *Spectator* are broached here, *e. g.* :

" Is it expedient that women should be learned ? — *Ans.* Knowledge puffeth up the mind ; therefore if women were learned, they would be prouder and more insupportable than before. Besides, a good opinion of themselves is inconsistent with the obedience they are designed for. Therefore God gave knowledge to Adam and not to Eve, who by the bare desire of knowledge destroyed all."

" Why are they not learned as men ; are they not capable to become such ? Why have they not solidity of judgment ?"

" Whether it is prudent to lodge in a room haunted by spirits ?—*Ans.* " A good man may, bad men should not tempt the Devil."

" Of what form was the serpent in Paradise, and whether such a sort of creature were not more likely to frighten than tempt Eve ? — *Ans.* To tempt a woman it is reasonable to conjecture that it had a man's face, for there are such snakes in Madagascar."

Dunton, and a few of his friends, forming the Athenian Society, as they called it, answered these and absurder questions with inexhaustible seriousness. It may be worth while to notice that one of this society was Samuel Wesley, Dunton's brother-in-law, and father of the founder of

Methodism. They were once badly deceived.* Thus, they were asked this question : "Since in your Advertisement you make it known that a Chyrurgeon is taken into your Society, I have thought fit to propound the following Question, withal assuring you that the matter of the Fact is true. A Sailor on board the Fleet, by an unlucky Accident broke his Leg, being in Drink, and refusing the assistance of the Surgeon of the Ship, called for a piece of new Tarpauling that lay on the Deck, which he rolled some turns round his Leg, tying up all close with a few Hoop-sticks, and was able immediately after to walk round the ship, never keeping his Bed one Day. I would know whether the Cure is to be attributed to the Emplastic Nature of the tarr'd and pitched Cloth bound on strait with the Hoop-sticks, &c., or rather whether it may not be solved according to the Cartesian Philosophy ?"

The concealed querist had the pleasure of receiving a serious though vague reply concerning fractures, tarred cloth, and Copernicus, from the club, who did not see that he spoke of a wooden leg.

Besides discharging this delicate duty, the paper—at first weekly, then twice a week—gave a list of books to be studied in such subjects as history, divinity, poetry, etc., English and foreign. This may seem to us its most important function: but the Marquis of Halifax used to read these questions and answers ; Sir William Temple used even to send questions ; and Dunton received poems from Tate and Defoe, and Swift sent his "Ode to the Athenian Society" to the society itself, with a request that they print it. His letter, which is published with the ode, will show how considerable was the reputation of this club.

---

* *Vide* Beljame, p. 272, who copies it from the original paper. Naturally, it was not reprinted in bound volumes.

Defoe was the most eminent of Dunton's* imitators, beginning the publication of his *Weekly Review of the Affairs of France: Purged from the Errors and Partiality of News-writers and Petty-Statesmen of all Sides.* This contained much serious political discussion in which Defoe did his best to make plain to his English readers the true condition of France, and at the end came a part of the paper called the *Mercure Scandale,* or later *Scandalous,* and then *Scandal, Club,* which contained answers to questions, the discussion of various social matters, attacks on drunkenness, swearing, duelling, etc.; the *Review* lived till May, 1713, but it is now known better as the model of the *Tatler* than for anything else.

You will notice the steps by which the periodical grew. Steele saw Defoe's success, and began the *Tatler;* this appeared at first three times a week, on post-days, as did the *Review.* But, while both journals supported the same side in politics, Steele made the political part subordinate to the social essays, while Defoe did the reverse. Steele, too, was at the time the director of the *London Gazette,* so that he had the first sight of political news. The political part faded away soon, after Addison had joined him— he began with No. 18—and the paper busied itself with

---

* Dunton visited this country in 1685-6, and thus described Cambridge in one of his letters: "This town is one of the neatest and best-compacted towns in the whole country. It has many stately structures and. well-contrived streets which for handsomeness and beauty outdoes Boston itself." At the college he "found eight or ten young fellows, sitting around, smoking tobacco, with the smoke of which the room was so full that you could hardly see, and the whole house smelt so strong of it, that when I was going upstairs, I said, this is certainly a tavern." The students, he adds, "could hardly speak a word of Latin, so that my comrade could not converse with them. They took us to the library, where there was nothing particular. We looked over it a little." This was the time he spoke of Bunyan. *Vide supra,* p. 35, note.

social matters. Steele saw, however, greater possibilities before himself and Addison, and so, Jan. 2, 1710–11, the *Tatler* was allowed to expire, and in the following March the first number of the *Spectator* appeared, simply as a literary journal, and every week-day, two important innovations.

It would be easy, but it would be unfair, to sneer at the *Tatler* and the *Spectator ;* it is true that some of the papers concern themselves with teaching rudimentary virtues, or the rudiments of the virtues, and that they are filled with praise of sentiments which we associate with copy-books. The essayist of the present time, as I think Mr. Leslie Stephen pointed out, has to leave the beaten track and show, for instance, how punctuality leads to the waste of time, how good-nature exposes a man to imposition, and to abuse by mischief-makers, etc., etc. Then they proved platitudes—platitudes meaning trite truths ; now we amuse ourselves by picking flaws in the demonstration.

In his "History of English Literature," Taine picks out some light, frivolous matter, and says that it is what English-speaking people call humor, leaving it to be understood that English-speaking people do not know what humor is—which is a hasty statement—and then he goes on to prove that Addison, beneath all his cultivation, is an Englishman, and has many sides which do not please the French. He has Protestant prejudices, he preaches, he treats his readers as if they were children, he refuses to discuss politics, etc., etc.; but these qualities combine to show how exactly fitted Addison was to fill the position he had chosen. Collier's remarks on the stage leave upon the reader an impression of an earnest but clumsy and angry theologian. It was in comparison with such men, and Collier was in many ways the best of the class, that Addison is to be judged. His

French contemporaries addressed a witty, polished public, capable of perceiving half-truths, sensitive to implication, full of literary tact and knowledge; Addison wrote for women who actually had nothing to read except the translation of long-winded romances, and for men who cared for nothing but open-air pleasures, or the plays of the time. How they were brought by ingenious variety and a due mixture of entertainment with instruction to become a reading public, we may learn from a few stray notices in contemporary publications. One man says that he used to collect his neighbors—"taking care not to alarm the country gentlemen by any premature mention of antiquities, he endeavored at first to allure them into the more flowery paths of literature. In 1709 a few of them were brought together every post-day in the coffee-house in the Abbey Yard; and after one of the party had read aloud the last published number of the *Tatler*, they proceeded to talk over the subject among themselves." And elsewhere, "the gentlemen met after church on Sunday to read the news of the week; the *Spectators* were read as regularly as the *Journal*." The "general reader" was now born, and was at once pampered. After Collier's harshness came gentle words like these: "I cannot be of the same opinion with my friends and fellow-labourers, the Reformers of Manners, in their severity towards plays; but must allow, that a good play, acted before a well-bred audience, must raise very proper incitements to good behaviour, and must be the most quick and most prevailing method of giving young people a turn of sense and good-breeding." Humor like this must have come as a revelation: Mr. Bickerstaff meets Ned Softly, who insists on reading to him a sonnet he had written upon a lady

"who showed me some verses of her own making, and is, perhaps, the best poet of her age:

"'To Mira, on Her Incomparable Poems.

I.

"'When dressed in laurel wreaths you shine,
And tune your soft melodious notes,
You seem a sister of the Nine
Or Phœbus' self in petticoats.

II.

"'I fancy when your song you sing,
(Your song you sing with so much art),
Your pen was plucked from Cupid's wing;
For, ah! it wounds me like his dart.'

"'Why,' says I, 'this is a little nosegay of conceits, a very lump of salt, every verse has something in it that piques; and then the *dart* in the last line is certainly as pretty a sting in the tail of an epigram, for so I think you critics call it, as ever entered into the thought of a poet.'— 'Dear Mr. Bickerstaff,' says he, shaking me by the hand, 'everybody knows you to be a judge of these things; and to tell you truly, I read over Roscommon's translation of Horace's "Art of Poetry" three several times before I sat down to write the sonnet which I have shown you. But you shall hear it again, and pray observe every line of it; for not one of them shall pass without your approbation :

"'When dressed in laurel wreaths you shine—'

'That is,' says he, 'when you have your garland on; when you are writing verses.' To which I replied, 'I know your meaning; a metaphor?'—'The same,' said he, and went on:

"'And tune your soft melodious notes—'

'Pray observe the gliding of that verse; there is scarce a consonant in it; I took care to make it run upon liquids. Give me your opinion of it.'—'Truly,' said I, 'I think it as good as the former.'—'I am very glad to hear you say so,' says he, 'but mind the next:

"'You seem a sister of the Nine—'

'That is,' says he, 'you seem a sister of the Muses; for if you look into ancient authors, you will find it was their opinion, that there were nine of them.'—'I remember it very well,' said I, 'but pray proceed.'

*　　　*　　　*　　　*　　　*　　　*

"'Pray observe the turn of words in these lines. I was a whole hour in adjusting of them, and have still a doubt upon me, whether in the second line it should be *your song you sing*, or, *you sing your song*. You shall hear them both :

> " ' I fancy when you sing your song,
>   (Your song you sing with so much art),'
or,
> " ' I fancy when your song you sing,
>   (You sing your song with so much art),' " etc.

Trifling of this sort must have been a delightful relief from the dull preaching of the other writers ; it was a new note to the people of those days, and while there have been plenty of writers who have. amassed statistics, and have spoken in praise of virtue and in denunciation of vice, those who may be called amusing are still few.   The *Tatler* began, doubtless, with no other plan in Steele's head than that of furnishing an entertaining paper; but when Addison joined him, as Steele said, " I fared like a distressed prince who calls in a powerful neighbour to his aid.   I was undone by my auxiliary ; when I had once called him in, I could not subsist without dependence on him."   Addison very early announced his plan in the *Spectator ;* in the tenth number, after having described in earlier papers the imaginary club to which the *Spectator* belonged, he says that his publisher has told him that three thousand are published every day, with probably twenty readers of each copy, so that he boasts of an audience of sixty thousand.   " Since I have raised to myself so great an audience, I shall spare no pains to make their instruction agreeable, and their diversion useful . . . to refresh their memories from day to day, till I have recovered them out of that desperate state of vice and folly into which the age is fallen. . . . It was said of Socrates,* that he brought

---

* A French translation of the *Spectator* (6 vols., Amsterdam, 1714-26), was entitled, *Le Spectateur, ou le Socrate moderne, où l'on voit un portrait naïf des mœurs de ce siècle.*

philosophy down from heaven, to inhabit among men; and
I shall be ambitious to have it said of me, that I have
brought philosophy out of closets and libraries, schools
and colleges, to dwell in clubs and assemblies, at tea-tables
and in coffee-houses. . . .

"Sir Francis Bacon once observes, that a well-written
book compared with its rivals and antagonists, is like
Moses' Serpent, that immediately swallowed up and devoured those of the Egyptians. I shall not be so vain as
to think that when the *Spectator* appears the other public
prints will vanish ; but shall leave it to my reader's consideration, whether, is it not much better to be let into the
knowledge of ones-self, than to hear what passes in Muscovy or Poland ; and to amuse ourselves with such writings as tend to the wearing out of ignorance, passion,
and prejudice, than such as naturally conduce to inflame
hatreds and make enmities irreconcilable ?"

The club which he described with such care in Nos. 1,
2, and 34 was doubtless intended for a sort of copy of the
Athenian Society. It survived in many of the imitations
of the *Spectator*, in the "Noctes Ambrosianæ," and in the
imaginary clubs of a number of magazines down to a very
recent date.

Addison had a great many arrows to his bow. At one
time he ridicules ladies' head-dresses : "There is not so
variable a thing in nature as a lady's head-dress. Within
my own memory I have known it rise and fall above thirty degrees. About ten years ago it shot up to a very great
height, insomuch that the female part of our species were
much taller than the men."

Similar social playfulness may be found in Nos. 101,
275, and 281. These papers certainly are not marked by
startling humor, though they have served as models for
countless imitators. However, Addison knew very well

what he was about, and never forgot that he was addressing a mixed audience, composed of people with very different tastes, and that to please this motley public he had
to intersperse the serious discussion of such matters as
the immortality of the soul, infidelity, Milton, with lighter
papers that should catch the attention of frivolous readers.
People who cared for nothing more serious than badinage
about the twirling of fans, or the ridiculous size of hoops,
or the placing of patches, had to be kept in good humor
with an abundance of such material in order to make the
Spectator a success. The light papers of this sort were
always in good taste according to the canons of that age,
and their number, though great, was not too large in view
of the follies they attacked.

There is one undeniable merit in the *Spectator*, and that
is the endless variety of the subjects treated. The essays
themselves will teach this better than the most copious
extracts.

V. The part that we should read last, and yet the one
that has had a very important influence on English literature, is the long discussion on Milton. We have already
noticed the indifference with which that great poet was
treated by his contemporaries and successors, and we have
seen evidence of the neglect with which most of the greatest English writers were treated in this modern dispensa-
tion. Yet already in the *Tatler* attention had been called
to Bacon, Spenser, Ben Jonson, Milton, and Shakspere, but
this was done by incidental references ; in the *Spectator*
Addison set seriously to work to put Milton in his proper
place. I say that we do not read these papers with delight, and, in proof of this assertion, I beg leave to quote
some of Addison's arguments in behalf of Milton's excellence. Take this, for instance : "The third qualification
of an epic poem is its greatness. The anger of Achilles

was of such consequence, that it embroiled the kings of Greece, destroyed the heroes of Troy, and engaged all the gods in factions. Æneas's settlement in Italy produced the Cæsars, and gave birth to the Roman Empire. Milton's subject was still greater than either of the former ; it does not determine the fate of single persons or nations, but of a whole species." That is to say, Aristotle says an epic poem must be this, that, and the other. Milton's poem is this, that, and the other ; *ergo*, it is an epic poem. In other words, he was using in his arguments the language of the schools.* Aristotle lay heavy over all the modern literature, and Horace's "Ars Poetica" was looked upon by every educated person as little else than an inspired work. All Europe lay in intellectual bondage, not to Greece so much as to the Latin Greece, which bore somewhat the same resemblance to the original that German-silver does to the nobler metal, whose name alone, without the brightness, the domestic imitation has taken.

Horace's dictum, "Ut pictura, poesis," was the first

---

* In his own day, and later, however, Addison seemed to be making concessions to the effeminacy of his age. Thus Dr. Johnson, in his " Life of Addison," says : " Had he presented ' Paradise Lost ' with all the pomp of system and severity of science, the criticism would perhaps have been admired, and the poem still have been neglected ; but by the blandishments of gentleness and facility he has made Milton an universal favorite with whom readers of every class think it necessary to be pleased."

Dr. Hurd (quoted in Knox's " Essays," No. 21) said : " For what concerns his criticism of Milton in particular, and as to his own proper observation, they are, for the most part, so general and indeterminate as to afford but little instruction to the reader, and are not infrequently altogether frivolous " ! Nowadays one would hardly call them frivolous.

Even towards the end of the last century, P. Stockdale said : " A sacrilegious contempt hath been expressed for that elegant critick's beautiful papers in the *Spectator*, on the ' Paradise Lost.' "—" Lectures on English Poets," i. 41 (1807, but written ten or twelve years earlier).

commandment ; the next, imitate nature ; the third and last, everything must announce and assist the cause of virtue : it was in compliance with this rule that King Lear climbed into his throne again ; that the "Maid's Tragedy" became a comedy ; that even now we see in old-fashioned plays a fortune and a bride awaiting the hero when, at about a quarter to eleven o'clock, all the actors form a semicircle on the stage and the green curtain shows signs of animation. Life, we all know, from reading moralists, is full of disappointment ; the youth starts out to set the world right and to earn wealth while he is young enough to enjoy it, but we are told that he finds his illusions destroyed on every side, that he loses his high ideals, and is content with comfortable compromise. We also instruct writers to paint life as they see it ; yet if one of them fails to make everything smooth at the end, and draws what we know to be the inevitable truth, we are disappointed, and we denounce the man who has learned his lesson as a foe to his kind. Possibly our grandchildren may find innocent amusement in discussing us.

At any rate, we do not make up our minds about the merit of a poem by the same processes as did those who read Addison's papers in the *Spectator ;* we do not keep one eye on the pseudo-Latin critics and one on the text to find warrant for our opinions ; yet, in writing as he did, Addison simply followed the legitimate methods of his time. By a singular turn of fate, while he seemed to be blocking the way by this old-fashioned lumber, he was really smoothing the path for us. We shall see in a moment how he did this. What prejudices Addison had to attack, besides those we have already seen, were such as we find in this passage from Dryden's dedication of his Juvenal and Persius (1692) : "As for Mr. Milton, whom we all admire with so much justice, his subject is not that of a heroic poem, properly so called : his design is the losing of our happiness ; his event is not prosperous, like that of all other epique works ; his heavenly machines are many, and his human persons are but two." That is the point ; I merely add this as a side-matter : "Neither will I justify Milton for his blank verse, though I may excuse him by the example of Hannibal Caro* and other Italians who have used it ; for, whatever causes he alleges for the abolishing of rhyme, . . . his own particular reason is plainly this, that rhyme was not his talent ; he had neither the ease of doing it nor the graces of it." Rapin, who held a position as a critic which no one of his successors has ever reached, said of Aristotle's laws : "There is no arriving at perfection but by these rules, and they certainly go astray that take a different course. . . . And if a poem made by the rules fails of success, the fault lies not in the art, but in the artist ; all who have writ of this art have followed no other idea but that of Aristotle ;" and of style : "What is good on this subject is all taken from Aristotle, who is the only source whence good sense is to be drawn, when one goes about to write." Addison, then, was compelled to prove that Milton was good by showing his conformity to Aristotelian rules, and this he did. .

We must remember that this superstitious respect for Aristotle is capable of very simple explanation. Our classical dictionaries tell us what that wonderful man accomplished, but fully to recount his influence would be almost to rewrite mediæval history. It filled not Europe alone. One writer says of him : "Translated in the fifth century of the Christian era into the Syriac language by the Nestorians who fled into Persia, and from Syriac

---

* Caro (1507–66) translated the "Æneid" into blank verse.

into Arabic four hundred years later, his writings furnished the Mohammedan conquerors of the East with a germ
of science, which, but for the effect of their religious and
political institutions, might have shot up into as tall a tree
as it did produce in the West; while his logical works, in
the Latin translation which Boethius, 'the last of the Romans,' bequeathed as a legacy to posterity, formed the
basis of that extraordinary phenomenon, the Philosophy
of the Schoolmen. An empire like this, extending over
nearly twenty centuries of time, sometimes more, sometimes less despotically, but always with great force, recognized in Bagdad and in Cordova, in Egypt and in
Britain, and leaving abundant traces of itself in the language and modes of thought of every European nation,
is assuredly without a parallel" (Blakesley, p. 1, quoted
in G. H. Lewes's "Biographical History of Philosophy,"
i. 245).

His position in Europe during the Middle Ages was
most firm. Marlowe's Dr. Faustus, at the opening of the
play of that name, bids himself "live and die in Aristotle's
works." "Aristotle's logic and physics, together with the
Ptolemaic system of astronomy, were then considered as
inseparable portions of the Christian creed" (Lewes, ii.
378). "In 1624 . . . the Parliament of Paris issued a decree banishing all who publicly maintained theses against
Aristotle; and in 1629, at the urgent remonstrance of the
Sorbonne, decreed that to contradict the principles of
Aristotle was to contradict the Church! There is an
anecdote recorded somewhere of a student, who, having
detected spots in the sun, communicated his discovery to
a worthy priest: 'My son,' replied the priest, 'I have read
Aristotle many times, and I assure you there is nothing of
the kind mentioned by him. Go rest in peace; and be
certain that the spots which you have seen are in your

eyes and not in the sun.'" He narrowly escaped being canonized for a saint. Bruno defied Aristotle, and said the earth revolved on its axis ; the Aristotelians affirmed that the earth did not move, and to confirm their views, after keeping Bruno six years in prison at Venice, they burned him in 1599.

The authority which Aristotle exercised in physics and logic ran over into literature, as we shall see more fully when we come to discuss Addison's " Cato ;" and possibly our grandfathers clung the more obstinately to his literary laws because they had been compelled to give ground elsewhere.* The necessity, then, under which Addison labored, of proving everything by Aristotle's rules has left those essays, after receiving the praise of several generations of men, to gather dust on forgotten shelves. They are like disused fords over a stream, which we look at from a car-window as we rattle over the new huge bridge. They have become curiosities.

As an example of this method, see the following extracts :

Spectator, No. 273 : " Having examined the Action of ' Paradise Lost,' let us in the next place consider the Actors. This is Aristotle's Method of considering, first the Fable, and secondly the Manners ; or, as we generally call them in English, the Fable and the Characters.

" Homer has excelled all the Heroic Poets that ever wrote, in the Multitude and Variety of his Characters.

* * * * * *

" Virgil falls infinitely short of Homer in the Characters of his Poem, both as to their Variety and Novelty. Æneas is, indeed, a perfect Character, but as for Achates, tho' he is stiled the Hero's Friend, he does nothing in the whole Poem which may deserve that title. Gyas, Mnesteus, Ser-

---

* Then, too, science is more pliant because it deals with facts and rests upon reason. Literature is slower to change, because it depends to a great extent on the emotions. Religion obviously moves the last of all. Our intellect may perceive the truth, but the emotions are the home of prejudice.

gestus, and Cloanthus, are all of them Men of the same Stamp and Character.

*   *   *   *   *   *

"If we look into the Characters of Milton, we shall find that he has introduced all the Variety his Fable was capable of receiving. The whole Species of Mankind was in two Persons at the Time to which the Subject of his Poem is confined. We have, however, four distinct Characters in these two Persons. We see Man and Woman in the highest Innocence and Perfection, and in the most abject State of Guilt and Infirmity. The two last Characters are, indeed, very common and obvious, but the two first are not only more magnificent, but more new than any Characters either in Virgil or Homer, or indeed in the whole Circle of Nature."

Even when Addison so far rises above the taste of his age as to praise the old ballads, he wears the fetters of conventional criticism :

Spectator, No. 70: "I know nothing which more shews the essential and inherent Perfection of Simplicity of Thought, above that which I call the Gothick Manner in Writing, than this, that the first pleases all kinds of Palates, and the latter only such as have formed to themselves a wrong artificial Taste upon little fanciful Authors and Writers of Epigram. Homer, Virgil, or Milton, so far as the Language of their poems is understood, will please a Reader of plain common Sense, who would neither relish nor comprehend an Epigram of Martial, or a Poem of Cowley: So, on the contrary, an ordinary Song or Ballad that is the Delight of the common People, cannot fail to please all such Readers as are not unqualified for the Entertainment by their Affectation or Ignorance; and the Reason is plain, because the same Paintings of Nature which recommend it to the most ordinary Reader, will appear Beautiful to the most refined.

"The old Song of ' Chevey Chase ' is the favorite Ballad of the common People of England; and Ben Johnson used to say he had rather have been the Author of it than of all his Works."

Then Addison quotes what Sir Philip Sidney said about it in his " Defence of Poesy," and goes on :

"The greatest Modern Criticks have laid it down as a Rule, that an Heroick Poem should be founded upon some important Precept of Morality, adapted to the Constitution of the Country in which the Poet writes. Homer and Virgil have formed their plans in this view."

*   *   *   *   *   *

" Earl Piercy's Lamentation over his Enemy is generous, beautiful, and passionate ; I must only caution the Reader not to let the Simplicity of the Stile, which one may well pardon in so old a Poet, prejudice him against the Greatness of the Thought.

> ' Then leaving Life, Earl Piercy took
>   The dead Man by the Hand,
> And said, Earl Douglas, for thy Life
>   Would I had lost my Land.
>
> ' O Christ ! my very heart doth bleed
>   With Sorrow for thy Sake ;
> For sure a more renownéd knight
>   Mischance did never take.'

That beautiful Line, *Taking the dead Man by the Hand,* will put the Reader in mind of Æneas's Behaviour towards Lausus, whom he himself had slain as he came to the Rescue of his aged Father."

Spectator, No. 74 : " If this Song had been written in the Gothic Manner, which is the Delight of all our little Wits, whether Writers or Readers, it would not have hit the taste of so many Ages, and have pleased the Readers of all Ranks and Conditions. I shall only beg Pardon for such a Profusion of Latin Quotations ; which I should not have made use of, but that I feared my own Judgment would have looked too singular on such a Subject, had not I supported it by the Practice and Authority of Virgil."

No. 85 : " I cannot for my Heart leave a Room, before I have thoroughly studied the Walls of it, and examined the several printed Papers which are usually pasted upon them. The last Piece that I met with upon this Occasion gave me a most exquisite Pleasure. My Reader will think I am not serious, when I acquaint him that the Piece I am going to speak of was the old Ballad of the *Two Children in the Wood,* which is one of the darling Songs of the common People, and has been the Delight of most Englishmen in some Part of their Age.

" This Song is a plain simple Copy of Nature, destitute of the Helps and Ornaments of Art. The Tale of it is a pretty Tragical Story, and pleases for no other Reason but because it is a Copy of Nature. There is even a despicable Simplicity in the Verse ; and yet because the Sentiments appear genuine and unaffected, they are able to move the Mind of the most polite Reader with Inward Meltings of Humanity and Compassion. The Incidents grow out of the Subject, and are such as are the most proper to excite Pity ; for which Reason the whole Narration has something in it very

moving, notwithstanding the Author of it (whoever he was) has deliver'd
it in such an abject Phrase and Poorness of Expression, that the quoting
any part of it would look like a Design of turning it into Ridicule. But
though the Language is mean, the Thoughts, (as I have before said,) from
one end to the other are natural, and therefore cannot fail to please those
who are not Judges of Language, or those who, notwithstanding they are
Judges of Language, have a true and unprejudiced Taste of Nature. The
Condition, Speech, and Behaviour of the dying Parents, with the Age, Innocence, and Distress of the Children, are set forth in such tender Circumstances, that it is impossible for a Reader of common Humanity not to be
affected with them. As for the Circumstance of the Robin-red-breast, it
is indeed a little poetical Ornament; and to show the Genius of the Author amidst all his Simplicity, it is just the same kind of Fiction which
one of the Greatest of the Latin Poets has made use of upon a parallel
Occasion; I mean that Passage in Horace, where he describes himself
when he was a Child, fallen asleep in a desart Wood, and covered with
Leaves by the Turtles that took pity on him." *

---

* To judge what was thought of this appeal in behalf of simplicity, one
may read what was said by Dr. Johnson, in his "Life of Addison:" "He
descended now and then to lower disquisitions; and by a serious display
of the beauties of 'Chevy Chase' exposed himself . . . to the contempt
of Dennis, who, considering the fundamental position of his criticism, that
'Chevy Chase' pleases, and ought to please, because it is natural, observes
'that there is a way of deviating from nature by bombast and tumour,
which soars above nature and enlarges images beyond their real bulk; by
affectation which forsakes nature in quest of something unsuitable; and
by imbecility, which degrades nature by faintness and diminution, by ob-
scuring its appearances and weakening its effects.' In 'Chevy Chase'
there is not much of either bombast or affectation; but there is chill and
lifeless imbecility. The story cannot possibly be told in a way that shall
make less impression on the mind."

Godwin, in his "Enquirer" (1797), p. 353, showed that even he could
be conservative on occasion; he speaks of Addison's "far-famed and ridiculous commentary upon the ballad of 'Chevy Chase.'"

This was not the only time that he frowned on the new literature (p.
326): "If we compare the style of Milton to that of later writers, and particularly to that of our own days, undoubtedly nothing but a very corrupt
taste can commend it."

Again, p. 339: "The age of Charles II. is regarded by modern critics with

The papers about Milton were naturally much admired at the time ; they came out on Saturdays, and so furnished Sunday reading of an agreeable kind. In Germany, however, their influence was greater than at home. Up to this time German literature was something unknown ; yet, in its own way, Germany was going through the motions of having a literature with the same conscientiousness that our fellow - countrymen showed when every man who wrote was an American Pope, or an American Byron, or what not. Gottsched, a great man in the last century (1700–66), has been much laughed at in this. He was a critic who, in his day, did good service to letters, but who is principally known to us now for having been a steadfast supporter of French influence in Germany, and as an opponent of Bodmer (1698–1783), of Zürich, who was the head of what was called the Swiss school. For many years the literary warfare between these two men raged furiously, until finally real literature appeared, when their discussions faded into obscurity. Yet they were by no means fruitless. The two schools agreed that poetry consisted in imitating nature, but the Leipsic school said that the way to do this was by following the dictates of reason, and they hence praised the French : the Swiss, on the other hand, affirmed that the reason had nothing to do with it ; that the poet must possess a creative power,

---

neglect and scorn ; though perhaps no age, except that of George III., was ever so auspicious to the improvement of English prose ; [so far he commands assent] as none certainly has been adorned with higher flights of poetry."

After all, the literary conservatism of such men as Voltaire and Godwin admits of simple explanation. Reason, which made them intolerant of the errors of mankind, and inclined them to become political reformers, also made them intolerant of the misty, emotional side of the new Romanticism. They demanded, above everything, clearness.

which they called *Phantasie,* or the imagination ; that what was wonderful was not only a means, but also the end and object of poetry ; and they praised Milton and the Greeks, recommending that they be studied. Both parties agreed that poetry must be useful, instructive, didactic. The Swiss urged the study of the poets they praised ; Gottsched recommended the imitation of those he admired. The quarrel then went on, Gottsched decrying Milton, and Bodmer, who translated these essays in the *Spectator,* praising him. In time Gottsched was driven from the field, and, although Bodmer was not a man who was able to lead, he at least deserves credit for pointing out the path which Germany was to follow. Gottsched's plan was to let France be for Germany what Greece was for Rome, and he worked eagerly in support of this notion ; but he succumbed, not before Bodmer, but before the current of the time. Bodmer's notion was that the imagination should be the slave of utility, and that the way of accomplishing this was by the fable ; this is bringing up at the starting-point with a vengeance.*

But outside of all this there lay on Gottsched's side, as was to be expected, contempt for Homer in comparison with Vergil, and exaggerated praise of Horace, Boileau, the French tragedians, and French literature. Bodmer,

---

* The deliberate way in which fables were reached is expounded by Goethe. *Ut pictura, poesis,* was affirmed, and the poet began with comparisons and descriptions. But the imitation of nature demands choice, and so he chose what was most striking ; this was what was most new, and finally what was wonderful. It was necessary that his work should have some improving influence on mankind, and, as there was nothing more wonderful than talking beasts, fables were selected as a favorite method of conveying instruction ; they combined nature, wonder, and utility. This all sounds, however, a good deal like an excuse for the fable, which was sufficiently attractive from its unfailing moral. *Vide* Goethe, "Dichtung und Wahrheit," i. 6.

and his ally Breitinger, on the other hand, were never tired of praising Homer, Ariosto, Tasso, Milton, and Saspar, as they called Shakspere. This was the side that triumphed, and when finally Germany began to count in literature it was under the inspiration of England rather than of France that her authors began to write ; the main importance of Lessing, who derived much from England, as a critic was that he hopelessly expelled the imitation of classic French writers from Germany. Towards the end of the last century Germany repaid its debt with accumulated interest, by carrying out the theories of the best English writers, by seeing and preaching the superiority of those who did not follow French models and by joining with them in the study of the long-neglected past. Later we shall come to see the influence which Bürger and Goethe, etc., had on Scott and Coleridge. Then we shall perceive more clearly that, when Addison was proving how good the " Paradise Lost " was, with an air as if he were dancing the minuet, he was really aiding the work of the writers who, a century later, were abolishing all the traces of the school to which Addison belonged when he wrote formally. The discord between Gottsched and Bodmer seems, in some respects, like a tempest in a teapot ; but it was really the foreboding of a great revolution. Bodmer tried to compress the whole inspiration of " Paradise Lost " within the six lines of a fable and its twenty lines of moral, but, naturally enough, he failed in this attempt to bottle the ocean.

So long as we bear in mind that these crude discussions were the beginning of a momentous reform in literature, they acquire an importance which otherwise we should be only too ready to deny them. They were not a mere interchange of prejudices, they were the first dim gropings after better things. We must remember that scarcely

anything is ludicrous in itself except any person's belief
that in him alone does wisdom reside. What was most
strongly impressed upon these German writers, as, indeed,
upon Addison himself, was the great need of rudimentary
education, and the desirability of finding rules which
might be of universal application ; and since they made
these out of the remarks of critics,rather than out of the
study of original writers, they very soon fell into confusion. At all times, indeed, the didactic critic is in danger
of being left behind by the intellectual movements of his
time. The critics stand up for precedent, and creative
writers try to improve on precedent. This, however,
leads us far away from Addison and his solemn remarks
on Milton.

We have seen how, when he was most formal, and was
defining the epic by the rules of Aristotle, he was unconsciously paving the way for another method of thinking
and writing. In those papers about Sir Roger de Coverley he was, to a considerable extent, laying the foundations
of the English novel. At that time fiction was in an un-
promising condition. In No. 37 of the *Spectator* we find
a list of books which a lady had collected, and it is interesting to make use of this glimpse which Addison gives
us of the life of the time. Of novels, we find here " Cas-
sandra," " Cleopatra," " Astræa," " The Grand Cyrus,"
"Pembroke's Arcadia," a volume mysteriously referred
to as " a book of novels," " Clelia," Mrs. Manley's " The
New Atalantis," a book which no lady would have in
her library now, and Steele's " Christian Hero "— for
the most part, books which no one would read now except from a sense of duty. At this time, Richardson
(1689–1761) was still in a printing-office, Fielding (1707–
54) a child, and Smollett (1721–71) not yet born. In
other words, what we know as the English novel did

not exist. It would be too much to say that Addison founded it by his little sketches in the *Spectator*. To give him all the credit for it would be unfair. Other causes contributed, which I shall speak of in a moment, but Addison helped it in two ways: first, by drawing those many little scenes of real life which keep the *Spectator* ever fresh before us; and, secondly, by aiding the general uplifting of the *bourgeoisie* into prominence. As we have seen, it was imagined that nothing but kings and very high nobles were deserving of a writer's attention, in the time of the tales of chivalry and the heroic drama. When the comic writers began to write about citizens, it was with the object of holding them up to the scorn of the nobility. The women were represented as vicious, and the men as ridiculous. They were looked upon as fair game for the wits. As in time the political power of the citizens made itself felt, they began to be esteemed fit subjects for fiction. So long as the only persons who are prominent are lords, dukes, and earls, they will be the only persons who are reflected in what we may call recognized literature. We must remember that underneath the stratum of literature with which we are supposed to be familiar as a part of our education, there are the chap-books, the ballads, the stories which in their time have delighted the populace, and which were only frowned upon by those eminent persons who deigned to give them any attention. These writings show the directions of popular taste—not, I trust, its amount.

When Addison drew such scenes as Sir Roger at the theatre—

Spectator, No. 335: "We convoy'd him in safety to the Play-house, where, after having marched up the Entry in good order, the Captain and I went in with him, and seated him betwixt us in the Pit. As soon as the House was full, and the Candles lighted, my old Friend stood up and looked about him with that Pleasure, which a Mind seasoned with Humanity naturally feels in itself, at the Sight of a Multitude of People who seem pleased with one another, and partake of the same common Entertainment. I could not but fancy to myself, as the old Man stood up in the Middle of the Pit, that he made a very proper Center to a Tragick Audience. Upon the entring of Pyrrhus, the Knight told me, that he did not believe the King of France himself had a better Strut. I was indeed very attentive to my old Friend's Remarks, because I looked upon them as a Piece of natural Criticism, and was well pleased to hear him at the Conclusion of almost every Scene, telling me that he could not imagine how the Play would end. The while he appeared much concerned for Andromache; and a little while after as much for Hermione; and was extremely puzzled to think what would become of Pyrrhus.

"When Sir Roger saw Andromache's obstinate Refusal to her Lover's Importunities, he whisper'd me in the Ear, that he was sure she would never have him; to which he added, with a more than ordinary Vehemence, You can't imagine, Sir, what 'tis to have to do with a Widow. Upon Pyrrhus his threatning afterwards to leave her, the Knight shook his Head, and muttered to himself, Ay, do if you can. This Part dwelt so much upon my Friend's Imagination, that at the close of the Third Act, as I was thinking of something else, he whispered in my Ear, These Widows, Sir, are the most perverse Creatures in the World. But pray, says he, you that are a Critick, is this Play according to your Dramatick Rules, as you call them? Should your People in Tragedy always talk to be understood? Why, there is not a single Sentence in this Play that I do not know the Meaning of.

"The Fourth Act very luckily begun before I had time to give the old Gentleman an Answer: Well, says the Knight, sitting down with great Satisfaction, I suppose we are now to see Hector's Ghost. He then renewed his Attention, and, from time to time, fell a praising the Widow. He made, indeed, a little Mistake as to one of her Pages, whom at his first entering, he took for Astyanax; but he quickly set himself right in that Particular, though, at the same time, he owned he should have been very glad to have seen the little Boy, who, says he, must needs be a very fine Child by the Account that is given of him. Upon Hermione's going off with a Menace to Pyrrhus, the Audience gave a loud Clap; to which Sir Roger added, On my Word, a notable young Baggage!

"As there was a very remarkable Silence and Stillness in the Audience during the whole Action, it was natural for them to take the Opportunity of these Intervals between the Acts, to Express their Opinion of the Players, and of their respective Parts. Sir Roger hearing a Cluster of them praise Orestes, struck in with them, and told them, that he thought his Friend Pylades was a very sensible Man; as they were afterwards applauding Pyrrhus, Sir Roger put in a second time; And let me tell you, says he, though he speaks but little, I like the old Fellow in Whiskers, as well as any of them. Captain Sentry seeing two or three Waggs who sat near us, lean with an attentive Ear towards Sir Roger, and fearing lest they should Smoke the Knight, pluck'd him by the Elbow, and whisper'd something in his Ear, that lasted till the Opening of the Fifth Act. The Knight was wonderfully attentive to the Account which Orestes gave of Pyrrhus his Death, and at the Conclusion of it, told me it was such a bloody Piece of Work, that he was glad it was not done upon the Stage. Seeing afterwards Orestes in his raving Fit, he grew more than ordinary serious, and took occasion to moralize (in his way) upon an Evil Conscience, adding, that Orestes, in his Madness, looked as if he saw something."

—When, I say, he drew such scenes as this, he was unconsciously setting a model for future novelists. I do not mean that he deliberately chose one of a dozen different ways of describing the scene, and that later writers, seeing his success, determined to write in the same way; but, rather, that he wrote in the manner that was natural to him, and that this was the English way when unaffected by the deliberate copying of other people. So far as it is safe or possible to distinguish the distinctive characteristics of the different countries of Europe, one of the main qualities of English literature is this semi - humorous observation — we find it in Chaucer, Shakspere, Addison, Fielding, Thackeray, Dickens, Scott, Sterne, Jane Austen, and in the first novel of the " Franklin Square Library " on which our hand happens to fall. We are so accustomed to it, that we do not fairly notice it until we have been occupying ourselves with something else, just as we do not observe the freshness of the open air until we come out into it from a close room. We are struck by it, as we are struck by a certain logical coherence and sense of form in the French ; by the poetical flavor of the imaginative writings of the Germans, and by the tremendous passion which the Russian writers are bringing into literature. These are faint and crude generalizations, to be sure, like our notions of a German with a round face, blue eyes, and light hair; or a sallow Frenchman; or a red-cheeked Englishman—but we are surprised, and justly surprised, when we make a mistake in a foreigner's nationality. When we come to speak of Defoe we shall make further investigations into the paternity of the English novel; here we must confine ourselves to the discussion of Addison's contribution to this wonderful result, which we have before us in the *Spectator*. And this includes, besides the practical work we see in the sketches of Sir Roger de Coverley and his friends, the attention he has given to the life he saw about him. One of the most important things, indeed, for a writer to do is to speak of what he knows, and he is pretty sure to know best what he has himself seen. Addison aided this movement in every way in his power. He wrote about life as he saw it, and his *Spectator* is a classic work. He succeeded, too, without very definitely knowing what he was doing. He was not trying to be a realist; he aimed at improving the minds and tastes of his contemporaries, and to get a hearing he made himself simple; he showed them what they were, how they acted in society, what their foibles were, and put his little word of advice in here and there, where its influence would be felt before the reader knew that he was swallowing moral medicine.

That the influence of the *Spectator* was great we learn from a number of contemporary sources. Tickell said of it (preface to his edition of Addison): "The world became insensibly reconciled to wisdom and goodness, when they saw them recommended by him with at least as much spirit and elegance, as they had been ridiculed for half a century." Sir Richard Blackmore said: "It was with great Pleasure and Satisfaction that Men, who wished well to their Country and Religion, saw the People delighted with Papers which lately came abroad as daily Entertainments; in which rich Genius and polite Talents were employ'd in their proper Province, that is, to recommend Virtue and regular Life, and discourage and discountenance the Follies, Faults, and Vices of the Age; . . . Nor was it without good Effect, for the People in some measure recover'd their true Relish, and discern'd the Benefit and moral Advantages as well as the Beauties of these daily Pieces, and began to have profane and immodest Writings in Contempt."*

Dr. Thomas Rundle said of Addison: "To him we owe that swearing is unfashionable, and that a regard to religion is become a part of good-breeding. . . . He had an art to make people hate their follies, without hating themselves for having them; and he showed gentlemen the way of becoming virtuous with a good grace." This was the credit which belongs to the moral reforms of the *Spectator;* as some one has said, it brought the laughers on the side of virtue, and it did more, in that it taught wise moderation. It checked licentiousness and it withheld bigotry, the two opposing forces. It civilized England more, perhaps, than any one book.

As to that form of success which interests publishers first of all, we know that this was very satisfactory. At the beginning, 3000 copies were published; this number rapidly grew to 20,000, and sometimes to 30,000—equal, doubtless, to 200,000 now—and the bound volumes, in octavo, at two guineas, and then a pocket-edition, were sold in enormous quantities. Each edition consisted of 10,000

---

* "Essays," ii. 268 (ed. 1717).

copies, and more than 9000 copies of the first four volumes had been sold before the *Spectator* ceased to appear. It was sold at one penny until August, 1712, when a tax was imposed on papers, and its price was doubled. Its fame spread to the Continent; in France, Marivaux wrote French *Spectators* (1722); in Germany, there were a number of imitations; * Italy, too, followed in the same path.† All of these were inspired, in the first place, by

---

* The first to appear in German was the *Discurse der Maler* (Zürich, 1721). This was written by a society of which Bodmer and Breitinger were at the head (*vide* Biedermann, " Geschichte des XVIII᷉ᵉⁿ Jahrhunderts," II. i. 429). He says that Gervinus mentions two earlier ones, the *Vernünftler* (1713) and the *Lustige Fama* (1718), but that he has not been able to find anything about them. *Der Patriot* (Hamburg, 1724) speedily followed, and Gottsched's *Vernünftige Tadlerinnen* (Leipsic, 1725).

The history of these publications in Germany closely resembles that of the English originals and imitations. Five thousand copies of the *Patriot* were sold, besides bound volumes. There were three editions of Gottsched's periodical. The subjects treated and the ends desired were very much the same. There was the same zeal, for, according to Biedermann, there were 182 publications started before 1760. In literary merit no comparison can be made.

Even in Russia the influence of the *Spectator* was felt. "Again, the first satirical review to appear in Russia, which she [Catherine II.] secretly patronized, followed in the footsteps of Addison's *Spectator* " (*Academy*, March 25, 1882, p. 210, in a translation of a letter to *Le Livre*, making mention of Veselowski's book on the influence of Western civilization on Russian literature).

Alexander Romald, " Tableau de la Littérature Russe " (St. Petersburg, 1872), p. 67, mentions " une foule de publications périodiques qui parurent de 1769 à 1774. . . . Le meilleur de tous était le *Peintre*, dans lequel des articles de critique et de polémique alternaient avec d'autres ayant un fond plus sérieux."

And *vide* Courrière, "Histoire de la Littérature Contemporaine en Russie " (Paris, 1875), p. 37.

† Gozzi's *Osservatore* (1761–62).

the translations of the *Spectator* itself into those different tongues. Indeed, nothing like its popularity had been known before in English literature, and the only thing which can be compared with it is the wonderful success of the "Waverley Novels." What it did in England in establishing a form of literature which is barely extinct yet, we shall soon see. Dec. 6, 1712, it ceased to appear, although it was resumed June 18, 1714, appearing thrice a week till Dec. 20 of the same year, when it finally closed. It was speedily followed by the *Guardian*, which appeared, in fact, before the eighth volume of the *Spectator*, under the direction of Steele, who determined "to have nothing to manage with any person or party ;" but Steele was a philosopher by fits and starts, and political feeling ran so high that he soon gave up that paper and took up the *Englishman*, in which his fervor had full swing in attacking Swift's *Examiner*. The first volume of the *Guardian* contains many good essays by Berkeley, Pope, and Tickell, and the second many by Addison.

In England, the number of successors of the *Spectator* was very great, although now the very names of most are forgotten. The *Censor*, the *Hermit*, the *Surprize*, the *Silent Monitor*, the *Inquisitor*, the *Pilgrim*, the *Restorer*, the *Instructor*, the *Grumbler*, the *Freethinker*, the *Anti-theatre*, the *Weaver*, etc. Even the names of those for which Addison and Steele wrote are known only to scholars, and very properly, for these are but the fringes of scholarship ; the main thing is to understand what the Essay was, and what part it has played in English literature. Therefore we shall not take up the essays at any length until we come to Dr. Johnson's *Rambler;* that does stand out above the general crowd. And since numbers are sometimes of use in conveying information, I will add that between 1709 and 1809 there were two hundred and fourteen pub-

lications of the sort we have been discussing ; one hundred
and six between the *Tatler* and the *Rambler*, forty-one
years ; and between the *Rambler* and 1809 just the same
number ; in the fifty-nine years since then they have ceased.

Yet the fame and the influence of the *Spectator* survive.
These light papers, which Addison wrote with doubtless
but little understanding of their value, now belong to the
English classics, while what he regarded as his most important contribution to literature, his " Cato," lives only
in a few quotations, and is mentioned now principally as
one of the few specimens in English literature of a play
written according to the rules. To be sure, these rules
had but little direct influence on English literature, but
no one can understand the character of the drama of that
nation without knowing what it was *not*, and in what
ways it differed from that of other countries.

CHAPTER V.

WE know that it was flung in the face of the English dramatists that they did not regard the *rules*, which for three hundred years were spoken of in Europe with as much reverence as the Ten Commandments, and were obeyed with incomparably more zeal. It may be worth while, then, to take "Cato" for our excuse, and under the shield of his good name to examine these rules, and see what it was that moulded the drama of parts of continental Europe from the revival of letters down to a time within the memory of men still living. To do this it is not necessary to go into the history of the miracle-plays and mysteries which abounded in the Middle Ages, under slightly varying forms, in Italy, France, Spain, England, and Germany ; we may turn at once to the early attempts to revive the drama at the time of the Renaissance, for all testimony seems to show that the drama revived as a wholly independent thing amid the general resuscitation of literary interests. Indeed, the fact that then plays were first written more with a desire to have a full showing in the various departments of intellectual work than from an intense feeling seeking dramatic expression—just as some people buy the books which they think they ought to care for, and not the books they want — this fact, I say, poisoned the stream at its fountain-head.

I quote from Mr. Symonds's "Renaissance in Italy"

some interesting and acute remarks on the conditions necessary for the full and natural development of the drama. He says : "Three conditions, enjoyed by Greece and England, but denied to Italy, seem necessary for the poetry of a nation to reach this final stage of artistic development. The first is a free and sympathetic public, not made up of courtiers and scholars, but of men of all classes—a public representative of the whole nation, with whom the playwright shall feel himself in close *rapport*. The second is a centre of social life—an Athens, Paris, or London—where the heart of the nation beats and where its brain is ever active. The third is the perturbation of the race in some great effort, like the Persian war, or the struggle of the Reformation, which unites the people in a common consciousness of heroism. Taken in combination, these three conditions explain the appearance of a drama fitted to express the very life and soul of a puissant nation, with the temper of the times impressed upon it, but with a truth and breadth that renders it the heritage of every race and age. A national drama is the image created for itself in art by a people which has arrived at knowledge of its power, at the enjoyment of its faculties, after a period of successful action. Concentrated in a capital, gifted with a common instrument of self-expression, it projects itself in tragedies and comedies that bear the name of individual poets, but are, in reality, the spirit of the race made vocal." *

But the Italians saw great tragedies in antiquity, and so sat down to compose great tragedies for modern times. Let us not laugh at them ; we see the same error about us, unless, indeed, we happen to be committing it ourselves. When we hear or say that the "Nibelungen Lied"

---

* "Renaissance in Italy," v. 112. See also his "Greek Poets" (Amer. ed.), ii. 1 et seq.

or the "Chanson de Roland" is quite as fine as the "Iliad" and the "Odyssey," we are making our bow to antiquity, and attempting to show that we are as good as the Greeks, and that our early writers are as good as theirs. We are using old-fashioned standards of measurement—or at least misusing them.

The first regular Italian tragedy was Trissino's "Sofonisba," which was finished in 1515, and six times printed before its first performance in 1562.* Trissino was an eager advocate of the improvement of Italian literature, but he saw only one way of accomplishing his object—*i. e.*, by copying the ancients. He wrote an epic poem, "Italia Liberata," in blank verse, in which he turned his back on the method adopted by Ariosto and subsequently followed by Tasso, and tried his best to imitate Homer. This was a complete failure ; but his "Sofonisba," although it really had no success on the stage, did have an influence on dramatic literature. It is to be noticed that it was printed six times before it was acted : this statement suffices to show the difference between a real drama and a literary drama, just as now a certain number of English poets write plays in book-form and fancy they are improving the English stage, forgetting that fitness for representation is the only true test of a play, as readableness is of a novel. Certainly, if the English drama is to be revived, this will be done by plays on the boards, not by books on the shelves.

In his "Sofonisba," Trissino † followed very closely

---

* So Mr. Symonds. Elsewhere it is stated that it was performed in 1515, but not repeated until 1562. It has been acted in Italy within a few years.

† Trissino was not alone ; Rucellai wrote his "Rosmunda" in generous rivalry. Symonds ("Renaissance in Italy," v. 236) says : "These two dearest friends, when they were together in a room, would jump upon a bench and declaim pieces of their tragedies, calling upon the audience to decide

what we took to be the practice of the ancients. I have already spoken of the enormous influence of Aristotle; it was now about to appear in a new quarter. Trissino wrote an "Ars Poetica," made up out of Aristotle and Horace, and applied these rules with the utmost rigor in this play. The rules, or the three unities, as they were afterwards called, were the unity of action—which different writers took to mean a number of different things, as we shall presently see — unity of time, which demanded that the action should take place within twenty-four hours; and unity of place, which was taken to mean that the scene should not be transferred beyond the palace, temple, or dwelling where the action was supposed to occur.* The only one of these rules which commanded universal assent was the unity of time, for the unity of place was interpreted in various ways, sometimes being taken as forbidding change of scene within the limits of an act. All of these rules were followed in their literal sense by Trissino in his "Sofonisba," and they were introduced into France by Mairet, who wrote a "Sophonisba," which was produced at Rouen in 1629. Before this the French plays had coquetted with the unities, and many of them were closely modelled on those of Seneca; but the "Sophonisba," coming with all the authority of Italy behind it, firmly established the rules on the French stage. All

---

between them on the merits of their plays." The "Rosmunda" was acted at about the same time with the "Sofonisba." It is not now easy to detect which was the better. The "Rosmunda" is unmistakably a dull play. The author, lest his characters should break some rule by action, keeps them apart, declaiming to echo-like confidants.

Speron Sperone, Giraldi, Dolce, while they studied Greek originals, all agreed that Seneca had much improved on the Greek methods. Their plays contained no tragic solemnity, no lyric beauty—nothing but mangled plots and cold declamation.

* *Vide* Simpson's "Dramatic Unities," p. 8.

the great French tragedies, down to Victor Hugo's "Cromwell" and "Hernani," were written in obedience to them.
Even Voltaire was one of their warmest defenders.

The history of the growth and decay of the unities is
full of interest, as illustrative of the general course of
pseudo-classicism in literature. Their value was one of
the most important of the tenets of this school, and it was,
in France at least, one of the longest-lived. As was just
stated, they were not absolutely novel in France ; when
they were firmly planted there, the ground had been already prepared for their reception. Mellin de St. Gelais
had translated Trissino's "Sofonisba," with the dialogue
in prose and the chorus alone in verse, and this rendering
had been acted before Henry II., at Blois, in 1559. There
had been, too, other versions of this play.* Moreover, the
dramatists of the Pleiad, *cir.* 1550, in their transcripts of
ancient tragedies, had observed the unities, more, doubtless, from imitation than from deliberate effort. There
were other dramatists whose influence lay in the opposite direction ; the most important of whom was Hardy
(1560–1631), who wrote six or eight hundred plays—for
authorities differ. Fontenelle says that this statement
will cease to surprise any one who reads them. Hardy
nobly disregarded the unities in many of his dramas, in
this following the Spanish rather than the classic or the
Italian stage. For, as Lope de Vega said, before he
wrote he locked up with six keys the "Ars Poetica," and
turned Terence and Plautus out of his study.† The medi-

---

* *Vide* Ebert, "Entwickelungsgeschichte der franz. Tragödie," p. 138.

†   "Y quando he de escribir una Comedia,
        Encierro los preceptos con seis llaves ;
        Saco a Terencio y Plauto de mi estudio,
        Para que no me den voces, que suele
        Dar gridos la verdad en libros mudos."
        —*Arte de Hacer Comedias.* Obras sueltas iv. 406.

ocrity of Hardy threw the victory into the hands of his antagonists, who could bring antiquity and all the authority of Italy against his lax principles and crude workmanship. Catherine de Médicis, it must be remembered, opened the court to the more refined influences of Italy, and dramatic companies from that country gave performances in France between 1570 and 1577.

There were many indications of the impending rule of the unities. Mairet, before he wrote his "Sophonisba," in the preface to his "Silvanire" (1625), urged their adoption because, he said, they would enable the spectator to see the action of the play as if it really were going on before him, and hence would be spared the trouble of trying to make out how the actor, speaking at Rome in the last scene of the first act, should be in Athens at the beginning of the next act.[*] Segrais says it was Chapelain who made the change by recommending it to Mairet;[†] and doubtless the authority of Chapelain, who was a minister, and of high repute as a man of taste, weighed for something, but it was far from being all. In politics he, with all of his generation who had received the new learning, was busy in extirpating the remains of feudalism, the memories of chivalry, the vestiges of the Middle Ages, and the romantic drama stood for all these things with them, and they sturdily maintained what they took to be the modern side. Discipline, which, as Fournier says ("Littérature Indépendante," p. 22), is the character-

---

[*] *Vide* Bizos, "Étude sur Mairet," p. 125.

[†] "Ce fut Monsieur Chapelain qui fut cause que l'on commença à observer la règle des 24 heures dans les Pièces de Théâtre (et parce qu'il faloit premièrement le faire agréer aux Comédiens, qui imposoient la loi aux Auteurs); Il [doubtless, Chapelain] communiqua la chose à M. Mairet, qui fit la Sophonisbe, qui est la première Pièce où cette règle est observée."—*Anec.* i. 161.

istic quality of the seventeenth century in France, conquered here as everywhere. No one man made the change : it was a widespread movement, although it might have been seriously modified, if not thwarted, had Hardy been a man of real genius.

As we shall see, Corneille could not withstand the general sentiment of his contemporaries, though in his heart he yearned for the freer treatment and more copious material of the Spanish stage. The critics for once got matters into their own hands, and they clipped the wings of poetry. Trissino, Malherbe, and Voltaire were all rather critics than poets.*

In order to know what the unities were, let us see what Aristotle said on the subject, and how his words were interpreted by different writers.

Aristotle, in his "Poeticon," said : "Tragedy is the imitation of a grave and complete action possessing magnitude ; (clothed) in pleasing language, independently of the (pleasurable) ideas (suggested) in its other parts ; set forth by means of persons acting, and not by means of narration ; and through pity and fear effecting the purification of those passions. . . . The most important, however, of these (requisites) is the setting together of the incidents " (vi.).

"It will then be granted that tragedy is the imitation of a perfect and complete action, possessing magnitude ; for there may be a whole which has no magnitude. But a whole is that which has a beginning, a middle, and an end. The beginning is that which, of necessity, follows nothing else, but after which something is bound to be, or to be produced. The end, on the contrary, is that which naturally comes after something else, either necessarily or

---

* See Prölss, "Geschichte des neueren Dramas," ii. 1, 45 ; and Ebert, *passim.*

for the most part, but after which there is nothing else. The middle, however, is that both before and after which there is something else. It is necessary, then, that well-combined fables should neither begin whence, nor end when, chance may dictate, but should be composed according to the above-mentioned forms " (vii.).

"It is fit, then, that—just as in other imitative arts the imitation is the imitation of one single thing—the story, also, since it is the imitation of an action, should be that of one whole and complete action ; and that the parts of the transactions should be so combined that, any of them being transposed or taken away, the whole would become different and disturbed."

The first question one asks after reading this, even in English, is, what does it mean ? And there has been no lack of answers. Corneille said : "I maintain that the unity of action consists, in comedy, in the unity of the intrigue, or of the obstacles offered to the designs of the principal personages ; in tragedy, in the unity of peril, whether it be that the hero sinks under it or extricates himself from it. I do not, of course, maintain that it is not allowable to admit several perils in the one, and several intrigues or obstacles in the other, provided that, in freeing himself from the one, the personage falls of necessity into the others " ("Troisième Discours").

Voltaire ("Remarques sur le Troisième Discours") : "We think that Corneille here understands by unity of action and of intrigue a principal action, to which the various interests and the private intrigues are subordinate, forming a whole composed of several parts, all tending to the same object."

La Harpe says : "Aristotle desires, and all the legislators on the subject have followed him in this, that a character be the same at the end as at the beginning."

Lessing, more clearly ("Hamburg. Dramaturgie," 38) : "There is nothing that Aristotle has more strongly recommended to the poet than the proper composition of his story. . . . He defines the story as the imitation of an action, and the action is, in his opinion, the connection of the incidents. The action is the whole, the incidents are the component parts of the whole ; and as the excellence of any complete whole depends upon the excellence of its several parts and their combination, so also is a tragic action more or less perfect in proportion as the incidents—each for itself and all conjointly—are in harmony with the purposes of the tragedy." It is clear that there is no great divergence of opinion about this rule : the playwright is directed to observe coherence in his story, to make it of one piece, so to speak, and this no one doubts ; and although La Harpe's rule is scarcely to be found in Aristotle, it is so undeniable that it goes into circulation without question.

The unanimity with which this rule was obeyed inspired full belief in the second rule, that of unity of time, which was taken to mean that the whole action must be supposed to take place within twenty-four hours. This inconvenient rule depended on these remarks of Aristotle: "Moreover, [the epos differs from the tragedy], as regards length ; for the latter attempts, as far as possible, to restrict itself to a single revolution of the sun, or to exceed it but little, whereas the epos is indefinite as regards time, and in this respect differs from tragedy " (v.).

No sooner had the unities become the law in France than Corneille began to chafe under them. In 1636 ("Troisième Discours ") he wrote : " For my part, I find that there are subjects so hard to confine within the limits of so short a time, that not only would I allow them the full twenty-four hours, but I would even take advantage of the liberty

accorded by the philosopher to exceed them in some measure, and would without hesitation go as far as thirty
hours." Voltaire, in commenting on this, says : "The
unity of time is founded not only on the laws of Aristotle, but on those of nature. It would, in fact, be extremely proper that the action should not extend beyond the
time required for representation. . . . It is clear, however, that this merit may be sacrificed to a much greater
one — that, namely, of interesting the audience. If you
can cause more tears to flow by extending your action
twenty-four hours, take a day and a night, but do not go
beyond that. If you did, the illusion would be too much
impaired."

The attempt of Corneille to secure thirty hours failed,
however, and the dramatists bound themselves up by the
rigid rule of twenty-four hours. Into what trouble their
pedantry brought them we may see by examining a single instance, Corneille's "Cid." The writer said : "The
unities must be preserved, there can be no doubt about
that, but we must have thirty hours." Let us see what
in this case thirty hours brought forth. The heroine's
father gives the hero's father a box on the ear. He
is consequently challenged to a duel by the hero, and
killed. The heroine, although she still loves him, demands
his life in satisfaction from the king, who orders him to
join the campaign against the Moors. From this he returns victorious, having performed many valiant deeds,
and having made two of their kings prisoners. The im-
placable heroine still demands his life, whereupon he is
commanded to meet another lover in single combat, the
condition being that she shall marry the survivor. He
is naturally successful in this ; he disarms his rival, spares
his life, and the heroine at last agrees to forgive him.
Corneille saw that the incidents were rather crowded,

and that the "Cid" well deserved two or three days of rest after his campaign before being called upon to fight another duel. "But there," he says, "you see the inconvenience of the rule." As the Academy said in passing judgment on the play : "The poet, in trying to observe the rules of art, has chosen rather to sin against those of nature." After that reproof Corneille followed the rules more closely, and throughout the French classic drama we find an impossible and inartistic huddling of incidents under the compulsion of this *obiter dictum* of Aristotle's. It would have been natural, one might think, to examine the Greek plays and see how they dealt with the problem, and whether they were ever allowed greater license. But against this we may put the comparative ignorance of Greek even in such a man as Voltaire ; and, secondly, the superstitious adoration of Aristotle, which was so great that, if any violations of his rules had been pointed out, the answer would doubtless have been made that those who broke his rules were bad Greeks.*

Yet when Lessing began his attack on the rules, about one hundred years ago, he did what should have been done long before: he went back to the Greek plays. And what do we find in them ? Take the "Agamemnon," for instance ; in that play, as Schlegel put it, "we have the whole interval between the destruction of Troy and the hero's arrival at Mycenæ. In the 'Trachinia' of Sophocles the voyage from Thessaly to Eubœa is made three times. In the 'Suppliants' of Euripides, during one choral ode an army is supposed to march from Athens to Thebes to fight a battle, and the general returns victorious." The appeal to the Greek dramatists was consequently misleading.

---

* As indeed happened in France; *vide* Ogier, "Ancien Théâtre Français," vol. viii.

Even more marked transgressions may be found. In the "Alcestis," that heroine and Hercules descend to the lower regions, and, although that journey is said to be easy and short, they returned thence, which is proverbially difficult.

Lessing said of the dramatists who obeyed the unities: "It is true that these writers pride themselves on the most scrupulous regularity; but they are also the ones who either put so wide a construction on their rules that it is scarcely worth while to call them rules at all, or they observe them in so awkward and constrained a way, that one is more shocked to see them observed than if they were not observed at all." He takes Voltaire's "Merope" to pieces, and asks: "Of what use is it to the poet that the incidents of each act, supposing them really to happen, should not occupy more time than the performance of the act really demands; and that this time, together with that allowed for the pauses, should not even extend to a full revolution of the sun? Is that a reason for supposing that he has observed the unity of time? He has obeyed the words of the rule, but not the spirit; for what he puts into one day might possibly be performed in that time, but no sensible man would do it in that time. Physical unity of time is not enough, moral unity must be there too; for if this is violated every one will notice it; whereas the other may be destroyed without general notice."

To us, whose minds are made up, these remarks, which coincide with our way of thinking, seem not only convincing, but also sufficiently obvious; yet, as I have said, for three hundred years they were not spoken in France, and, as we have seen, every means was taken to urge the opposite views by precept and example.

Having seen the fervor with which these opinions were upheld, we shall not be surprised to learn that in the "Poeticon" of Aristotle there was no mention of the third rule, the unity of place.* The invention of this must be put down to the account of the French critics, on which side of the account the reader must decide for himself. Corneille groaned beneath this rule, and urged that the whole

---

* No one will for a moment imagine that the trifling fact that Aristotle never said anything that has come down to us that can be perverted into support of the unity of place made that law any the less binding. D'Aubignac, in his "Pratique du Théâtre" (1669), said: "Les ignorants et les personnes de faible esprit, s'imaginent que l'unité de lieu répugne à la beauté des comédies. . . . Aristote, dans ce qui nous reste de sa Poétique, n'en a rien dit, et j'estime qu'il la négligée, à cause que cette règle était trop connue de son temps."

On the unity of time, he wrote in favor of limiting the action to twelve hours: "La raison en est certaine et fondée sur la nature du poème dramatique, car ce poème, comme nous avons dit plusieurs fois, n'est pas dans les récits, mais dans les actions humaines, dont il doit paraître une image sensible. Or, nous ne voyons point que régulièrement les hommes agissent avant le jour, ni qu'ils portent leurs occupations au-delà; d'où vient, que, dans tous les états, il y a des magistrats établis pour réprimer ceux qui vaguent la nuit, naturellement destinée au repos."

Riccoboni, in explaining the horrors and bloodshed of the Shaksperian plays, says ("Historical and Critical Account of Theatres in Europe," English transl., p. 171): "The principal character of the English is that they are apt to be plunged in contemplation [they "are gentle, humane, extremely polite, but generally pensive to excess"], as I said before. It is owing to this their pensive Mood that the Sciences of the most sublime Nature are by the Writers of that Nation handled with much Penetration, and that Arts are carried to that Pitch of Perfection which they are now arrived at; because their native Melancholy supplies them with that Patience and Exactness which other Countries have not. . . . To pursue my reasoning; I believe that were there to be Exhibited on their Stage Tragedies of a more refined Taste, that is, stripped of those Horrors that sully the stage with Blood, the audience would perhaps fall asleep. The Experience which their earliest Dramatic Writers had of this Truth, led them to establish this Species of Tragedy, to raise them out of their contemplative Moods, by such bold Strokes as might awaken them."

of a play should be represented within the limits of one town. "Of course," he says, "I should not wish the stage to represent a whole town; that would be somewhat too vast, but merely two or three particular places enclosed within its walls." Voltaire held a similar view. He says:

"We have before said that the imperfect construction of our theatres—handed down from the days of our barbarism to the present time—has made the rule of unity of place almost impossible. The conspirators cannot conspire against Cæsar in his own cabinet; people do not talk about their most secret interests in a public place; the same scene cannot represent at once the front of a palace and that of a temple. The stage ought to be so arranged as to bring before the eye all the particular places where the scene is laid, without injury to the unity of place. Here a part of a temple; there the vestibule of a palace; a public square; streets in the background—in short, everything necessary for presenting to the eye all that the ear ought to hear. The unity of place is the whole view which the eye can embrace without difficulty."

But this is a clumsy contrivance. Even this accumulation of architectural monuments, like those on the cover of the atlases, representing civilization, can be of but little service, and we need not wonder that in his "Brutus" Voltaire was forced to resort to the transparent device of having two of the characters "*supposed* to have quitted the audience-chamber and to be in another apartment in Brutus's house." In his "Semiramis," the tomb of Ninus is brought into the drawing-room! However, it is idle work killing the dead. The unities have gone to the curiosity chamber, along with the Ptolemaic system of astronomy and the notion that all languages are derived from the Hebrew. The theory had its strong side, however, although in Italy it helped to produce nothing of

importance. In France it inspired a love for smoothness of
form and neatness of execution. It is, of course, impossible
to imagine what would have been the course of literature
in France if it had not prevailed there, because it did prevail there from seeming abundantly good to those who
were in power.* Remember that it stood for light and
truth in contrast with what seemed to the men of that day
the detestable barbarism of the Middle Ages, and that the
task of that time, as of all times, was to attain higher civilization. Their sole beacon was the light from antiquity, the rays of which were supposed to be concentrated
in Aristotle, and they obeyed him as earnestly as possible. Their yearnings for greater freedom they probably
repressed as proofs of an unregenerate nature, and if we
find their classic plays dull, it is easy to see what they
thought of ours. Here is Voltaire describing an English
play—and bear in mind that Voltaire was not only one of
the ablest men of his time, but of any time, and that, although he was not averse to misrepresentation when
there was anything to be got by it, he was intellectually
honest. He says ("Introduction to Semiramis," Œuvres,
v. 194): "I am very far from justifying the tragedy in
everything: it is a rude and barbarous piece. . . . The
hero goes mad in the second act, and his mistress in the
third. The prince slays the father of his mistress, pre-

---

* La Motte and Fontenelle, among others, however, agreed in detesting
the unities, long monologues, confidants, and the use of rhyme in plays,
and were consequently cordially hated by their contemporaries, notably by
the critics.

Fontenelle defended the moderns; we too shall become ancients, he
says, "on nous admirera avec excès dans les siècles à venir."—"Dieu sait
avec quel mépris on traitera en comparison de nous les beaux-esprits de
ce temps-là, qui pourront bien être des Américains."—Sainte-Beuve, "Causeries du Lundi," iii., 332.

tending to kill a rat, and the heroine throws herself into the river. They dig her grave on the stage; the grave-diggers jest in a way worthy of them, with skulls in their hands; the hero answers their odious grossness by extravagances no less disgusting. Meanwhile, one of the characters conquers Poland. The hero, his father, and mother drink together on the stage; they sing at table, they wrangle, they fight, they kill; one might suppose such a work to be the fruit of the imagination of a drunken savage. But in the midst of all these rude irregularities, which to this day make the English theatre so absurd and so barbarous, there are to be found in 'Hamlet,' by a yet greater incongruity, sublime strokes worthy of the loftiest geniuses. It seems as if nature had taken a delight in collecting within the brain of Shakspere all that we can imagine of what is greatest and most powerful, with all that rudeness without wit can contain of what is lowest and most detestable."

One is tempted here to go on to a comparison between English and French tragedy; but this would take us wholly away from our path. It concerns us now to consider simply the fate of these laws. In France, they survived the general wreck of the Revolution; Sundays were banished, and the week brought into the decimal system; * religion was abolished; kings and aristocrats were murdered—but, as Brandes pointed out, "While in all external matters France is inclined to change, and in following this inclination knows no limits or moderation, it is yet in all literary matters exceedingly conservative, recognizing authority, maintaining an academy, and observing moderation. The French had overthrown their

---

* It will be remembered that this demolition of the Sabbath is sometimes brought up in all seriousness as an argument against substituting the metre and the gramme for the yardstick and ounce.

government, hanged or banished the odious aristocrats, established a republic, carried on war with Europe, done away with Christianity, decreed the worship of a Supreme Being, deposed and set up a dozen rulers, before it occurred to any one to declare war against the Alexandrine verse, before any one ventured to question the authority of Corneille or Boileau, or to feel any doubt that the observance of the three unities was absolutely essential to the preservation of good taste. Voltaire, who had but little respect for anything in the heaven above or in the earth beneath, yet respected the Alexandrine. He turned tradition topsy-turvy ; made his tragedies attacks upon the powers they had hitherto supported, namely, the right of kings and of the church ; from many of them he excluded love, which previously had formed the main interest in real tragedy ; he tried to follow in Shakspere's footsteps : but he did not venture to shorten his line by a single foot, to make the least alteration in the conventional method of rhyming, or to make the action last more than twenty-four hours, or to lay it in two different places in one play. He did not hesitate to wrench the sceptre from the hand of kings, or to tear the mask from the face of priests, but he respected the traditional dagger in Melpomene's hand and the traditional mask before her face."

Voltaire, it must be remembered, had a very sincere detestation of wilfulness and obscurity, and great love of neat workmanship and literary polish. In good part through his authority, the unities survived in France until Victor Hugo began to write plays.* The preface to " Cromwell "

---

* It must not be forgotten how often the rules were questioned, and with ever-growing force, by successive dramatists in the last century. It was probably Voltaire's influence that maintained them so long, for there were many able men, less authoritative than he, however, who were attacking them by precept and example. The full history of the pro-

(1827) was a violent attack upon them, but it was over his
"Hernani" that the fight was really fought and the victory won. Of course there had been men who objected
to the rigid rules, such as La Motte (1672–1731), but his
objections were without influence ; it was Victor Hugo
who fairly broke these chains. Feb. 25, 1830, this play
was first acted, amid wild confusion. Théophile Gautier,
in his "Histoire du Romantisme," says :

　　"How can any one imagine that this line,

　　　　　　　"Est-il minuit ?—Minuit bientôt,"

should have called forth a tempest, and that the fight
lasted three days ? The phrase seemed trivial, familiar,
indecorous : a king asks what's o'clock, like a private citizen, and they tell him, as if he were a ploughboy, *midnight*."

The rules fell with a crash into unrecognizable ruin.
In Italy, a play of Manzoni's, "Il Conte di Carmagnola"
(1820), was the first to break the charmed regulations, but
Victor Hugo destroyed the citadel after the outposts had

---

tracted discussion concerning them belongs rather to the study of French
than of English literature. (*Vide* Charles Formentin's "Essai sur les
Origines du Drame Moderne en France." Paris, 1879.) The most important of these writers were Diderot, Beaumarchais, Mercier, Sedaine, etc.
It yet remains true that, while these men skirmished bravely, Victor Hugo
routed the enemy and won the victory.

In his "Bijoux Indiscrets," chap. xxxviii., Diderot said, speaking of the
classic stage: "En admirez-vous la conduite ? Elle est ordinairement si
compliquée que ce serait un miracle qu'il se fût passé tant de choses en si
peu de temps. La ruine ou la conservation d'un empire, le mariage d'une
princesse, la perte d'un prince, tout cela s'exécute d'un tour de main.
S'agit-il d'une conspiration, on l'ébauche au premier acte, elle est liée,
affermie au second ; toutes les mesures sont prises, les obstacles levés, les
conspirateurs disposés au troisième ; il y aura incessamment une revolte, un
combat, peut-être une bataille rangée, et vous appelez cela : conduite, intérêt, chaleur, vraisemblance."

'surrendered. The length of the struggle between reason and reasonableness shows how hard it is to expel bigotry, pedantry, obstinacy, and all the respectable vices.

To return to Addison's " Cato," which was published in 1713: its only interest is, so to speak, an archæological one, as an example of a rare phenomenon, and as a proof of the spread of waves of thought. We see that it took about two hundred years for the form devised by Trissino to reach London, it having reached Paris in one hundred and twenty years; and the wave that overwhelmed France made but a slight ·disturbance in England,* for, at the most, less than a dozen plays can be counted among those written after this model, and Otway's " Venice Preserved " and Congreve's " Mourning Bride " may well be counted out. The only other at all well known, excepting Lillo's " Fatal Curiosity," is Johnson's " Irene " (1749), and if Johnson's fame depended on that play his name would have been lost long since.†

---

* *Vide* " Lectures on Poetry," delivered 1711, at Oxford, by Dr. Trapp, of whom Dr. Young wrote, " Satire I., Works," iii. 106 :

> " If at his title Trapp had dropp'd his quill
> Trapp might have passed for a great genius still.
> But Trapp, alas ! (excuse him if you can)
> Is now a scribbler, who was once a man."

This, however, probably refers to his political pamphlets. He warmly defended the unities.

† Yet it is curious to observe that two thirds of Browning's plays observe the unity of time — viz., " Pippa Passes," " The Return of the Druses," " A Blot on the Scutcheon," " Colombe's Birthday," " Luria," and " In a Balcony." The " Blot on the Scutcheon " was written in five days, as was also " The Return of the Druses " (*vide Academy*, Dec. 24, 1881). It would be hard to say that Browning deliberately sought this unity. It doubtless came from what we may call the instantaneousness of his intellectual processes. He almost always chooses for his subject a single mood or passion.

What you will have noticed here, as I trust elsewhere, is the close connection between the literary tenets of the time and the general condition of thought. To be sure, these do not always precisely coincide. We find the regular drama existing throughout the French Revolution, only giving way later before the attacks of the Romanticists, yet, in general, the widespread views of a period affect immediately the literary methods; in this case, too, the first leisure was devoted to making the drama over again. The task of our ancestors was establishing civilization and driving out barbarism, and what seemed to them one of their first duties was expelling barbarism from literature. What they thought barbarous, the Gothic architecture, mountains, and certain forms of poetry, we have learned to enjoy. If we bear these things in mind, and watch the growth of modern feelings during the last century, we shall get to understand the present better. There is, too, an advantage in studying a period of unbrilliant performance, that it gives an opportunity to see how opinions grow.

As to the play itself, and the excitement it produced, it was enormously admired. The political condition only added to the excitement; party feeling ran high, and, as Macaulay said, it was hoped that " the public would discover some analogy between the followers of Cæsar and the Tories, between Sempronius and the apostate Whigs, and between Cato, struggling to the last for the liberties of Rome, and the band of patriots who still stood firm round Halifax and Wharton." The Tories, however, were not to be outdone ; each side determined to find nothing but compliments for itself in the political setting. Pope wrote that the applause " of the Whig party, on the one side, was echoed back by the Tories on the other, and after all the applauses of the opposite faction, Lord Boling-

broke sent for Booth, who played *Cato,* into his box, and
presented him with fifty guineas in acknowledgment (as
he expressed it) for defending the cause of liberty so well
against a perpetual dictator."ᣟ

Bishop Berkeley was at the performance with Addison,
"and two or three more friends in a side-box, where we
had a table and two or three flasks of Burgundy and
champagne, with which the author (who is a very sober
man) thought it necessary to support his spirits. . . . Some
parts of the prologue, written by Mr. Pope, a Tory, and
even a Papist, were hissed, being thought to savour of
Whigism, but the clap got much the better of the hiss "
(*Academy,* Sept. 6, 1879).

Even in Dr. Johnson's time, the "Cato" had come to
be regarded as "rather a poem in dialogue than a drama,
rather a succession of just sentiments in elegant language
than a representation of natural affections, or of any probable or possible in human life." And Dr. Johnson said :
"About things on which the public thinks long, it commonly attains to think right ;" and now, having thought
longer, the public has attained to think that it will not
read "Cato," and I need dwell on it no longer.

Its effect was to lend the authority of Addison's name
to this formal way of writing plays. In Germany, Gottsched * wrote " Der Sterbende Cato " (written 1731, pub-

---

* Gottsched was by no means satisfied with Addison's work ; *vide* Riccoboni, "Account of Theatres " (Engl. transl.), 226 et seq.: "I was at first
advised literally to translate Addison's 'Cato,' but as I was resolved to
stick to the rules of the drama, I found he fell far short in regularity to
the French tragedy. The English are indeed great masters both of thought
and expression ; they know wonderfully well how to sustain a character,
and enter surprisingly into the heart of man ; but as to the conduct of the
Fable they are very careless, as appears from all their dramatic compositions," etc. ; and "the scenes are very ill-connected together; the actors
go and come without any apparent reason ; sometimes the stage, is quite

lished 1732), in imitation of this and a French play by
Deschamps (1715), and in England the tradition of the
Elizabethan drama was rendered fainter than ever. If we
are inclined to condemn Addison, we must remember that
what he was really endeavoring to supersede was the
exaggerations of Dryden, Lee, and their contemporaries
of the post-Restoration stage. In the place of rant he put
a sort of decorous eloquence. The play reads not so much
like the work of a poet as like that of an intelligent and
able man, who has deliberately made up his mind to write
a tragedy, and who has put a number of dignified thoughts
into the most elegant language he could find. Addison's
intelligence was sufficient to save him from gross faults,
but not enough to inspire him to write a real tragedy.

---

empty," etc.   Hence he combined the English and the French models, and
wrote his own " Cato."

Gottsched's play went through ten editions by 1757 (Koberstein, v. 286,
note 10). Freiherr von Bielefeld said: "Es sei eine Tragödie, die in allen
Sprachen der Welt schön sein würde" (Koberstein, *loc. cit.*).

CHAPTER VI.

I. THE never-ending question suggests itself here, What is real poetry? We cannot help wondering how it is that such frigid propriety as fills the " Cato " should have given full satisfaction to our grandfathers and grandmothers. And while we may be willing to acknowledge that the " Cato " was admired quite as much because Addison wrote it as for anything else, this does not explain its long success. The question, too, comes up again with regard to Pope, who was the head of the poetical school of his time. Nowadays the reading world may be said to be divided into classes, one of which avers that Pope was a great poet, while the other wonders how it is possible to call him a poet at all. It may well be that these contending foes will very nearly agree concerning what they find in Pope ; what divides them is the proper definition of poetry. It would be a difficult matter to furnish this. Various attempts have been made to do it, but I know none that satisfies every one, and there would seem to be this objection to all definitions : that they must be made by judging past methods of writing poetry, and next year there may be found a new way which will not accord with the rule. Moreover, they will be made to suit but a single period. In fact, however, this discussion would not only take us into a very confused region, but it would be wanton straying from the work we have now before us, which is looking at what was liked in the last century, and trying to find its relation to what went before and what has followed it.*

In general, we are inclined to make such a definition of poetry as shall include the work of the poets we like and exclude most of the rest. Those who demand that poetry shall be compact of imagination, that it shall arouse or charm the emotions, rather than give a cooler intellectual delight, may give Pope all the credit his admirers claim for his intelligence—to state it broadly—without consenting to place him among the singers who delight us in a very different way. As contrasted with these singers, as we may call them, among whom any one may place his favorite—say Keats, Byron, Shelley, Tennyson, Browning, or Mrs. Browning—Pope may be called a talker, or rather a converser. He is the best of conversers, and there is a great deal implied in that title : wit, tact, knowledge of men and the world, wisdom, a clever tongue—and all of these things Pope had. In short, he is the flower of the period which we are studying ; not necessarily the greatest man, for Dryden leaves upon the reader an impression of magnitude, of being greater than what he accomplished, which we do not feel about Pope, who was perfectly successful in putting what was best of himself into literature, and into classical literature. The aim of the period in which he lived was to let reasonableness, common-sense, have full sway, and nowhere did it find fuller expression in English literature than in Pope.

The period was an interesting one in respect to the man of letters, whose position, however, was not secure, although the *Spectator* had created a large reading public. It may

* In the *Contemporary Review* for December, 1881, and January, 1882, are two interesting articles by Mr. Alfred Austin, discussing Mr. Matthew Arnold's definition of poetry as a criticism of life.

·be worth while to see how it was that writers gradually acquired independence. We have seen how in the reign of Queen Anne, the Augustan age of English literature, as it is called, authors were rewarded ; but, while it is probably true that this was in some measure due to the fact that their patrons had a disinterested love of litera-· ture, it must not be forgotten that the higher rewards were given for value received. Addison's various appointments were in return for work accomplished with the pen, and the politics of the writers of this time had much to do with their success. Dryden's satires had shown (as I have said) how great was the power of an able pen, and those who were in authority sought to get these valuable allies on their side. Thus Locke, who had been suspected of connection with Shaftesbury's treason, had left England to avoid trouble in 1683, and had returned after the arrival of William of Orange in 1689, was within a week offered an ambassadorship, which he declined, and was soon made commissioner of appeals. What literature could have done for him, we may perceive from the fact that he sold the copyright of his famous "Essay" for £30. This place was of the nature of a sinecure, and the pay, £1000 a year. Locke, who had shown great interest in the practical matters of politics, worked hard at the duties of the position when these were enlarged, but resigned it when he felt unable to give them full attention. He was succeeded by Prior, the poet. Prior, the story runs, was the son of a joiner, who, when his father died, fell under the charge of his uncle, who intended to let his education end with studying under the famous Dr. Busby, at Westminster school ; but the Earl of Dorset happened to see him reading Horace, which so gratified him that he sent him to Cambridge. In 1691, when twenty-five years old, he was sent as secretary to the embassy to the congress at the Hague, and again, in 1697, to another embassy to negotiate the treaty of Ryswick; the next year he was given the same office at the court of France. Before succeeding Locke he was under-secretary of state for a short time. Sir Isaac Newton was, in 1695, by the influence of his friend Charles Montague, earl of Halifax, made warden of the mint, with a salary of £600; and in 1699 he succeeded to the mastership, with a salary of from £1200 to £1500, and this position he held until his death in 1727. This position was given to him not merely in admiration of his mathematical labors, but partly in return for his defence of the authorities of the University of Cambridge before the high-commission court, where they were summoned to answer for their refusal to admit Father Francis Master of Arts on the king's (James II.) mandamus, without his taking the oaths. He was twice elected to Parliament. Steele, as we have seen, held various positions under government. From 1694 to 1699 Defoe was employed as accountant to the commissioners of the glass-duty for his aid to the government, and Defoe wrote a countless number of political writings. Indeed, we are only too ready to overlook most of the political work which literary men did in those days. Prior not only wrote a number of odes (one of them, 1706, in Spenser's stanza, and avowedly in imitation of his style), epistles, prologues, etc., full of political references; he also contributed to the *Examiner*, a Tory journal. Congreve sang victories, mourned the death of Queen Mary, and was made a commissioner for licensing hackney-coaches. Vanbrugh went to France as a sort of spy, and was locked up in the Bastile for nearly two years. Indeed, it would be hard to find one of the writers of this time who did not devote his pen to the service of one of the political parties, and sometimes of both: Ambrose Philips, Rowe, Gay, Stepney, Eusden, Hughes,

Garth, Arbuthnot, Blackmore, Tickell, Shadwell—the list could be made very long—were all of them rewarded in one way or another : the instances I have given will show what I mean by this.

That the writers were necessary to the politicians is clear from the rewards they received, and is explained by a brief examination. The debates in Parliament, it will be remembered, could not at that time be reported. Even in 1745, they were printed in the *Gentleman's Magazine* as the " Discussions in the Senate of Lilliput." The Lords were called *Hurgoes ;* Lord Hardwicke, Hurgo Hickrad ; the archbishop of Oxford, the Archbishop of Oxdorf. In the Clinabs (Commons), Wyndham was Yamdahm ; Fox, Feaucs, etc. Degulia stood for Europe, Mildendo for London, Blefuscu for France, the Jacomites for the Jacobites. In the *Scots' Magazine,* Sir Robert Walpole was Marcus Tullius Cicero ; Pulteney, Cato, etc. Consequently, the only way in which the public could be kept in close relations with Parliament—and in the last resort the support of the public was necessary—was by means of the newspapers, pamphlets, political poems, etc. Ministers themselves wrote for the papers, and they were compelled to secure some authors as their allies, as well as to keep others in their pay to prevent their going over to the opposite camp. Nowhere do we find the whole current of intrigue between politicians and authors more clearly related than in Swift's " Journal," or more distinctly illustrated than by his career. He was Vicar of Laracor, in Ireland, when he wrote his first political tract, the " Dissensions in Athens and Rome " (1701), in which the politicians of his time were disguised under ancient names, with application to the existing state of affairs. In this paper he urged a just balance of power at home as necessary for preserving the freedom of the state. This was in 1701, when Swift was thirty-four years old. Halifax and Somers, when they had ascertained who wrote it, received him with great warmth and many promises of support—indeed, proposed him for a bishopric. But they could not keep their promises, which filled Swift with bitter disappointment ; so that, when the Whigs went out and the Tories came in, he hastened from the obscurity of Ireland to London in order to see for himself how matters stood. Naturally his appearance on the scene was of great service to him. The absent are always wrong, the French say, and the absent are pretty sure not to be in the way of picking up promotion which is eagerly contended for by many applicants. The Whigs were profuse with apologies and new promises, and the Tories, eager for such an ally, tempted Swift in every way in their power. He had, meanwhile, given further proof of his ability, though scarcely of respect for the conventional side of ecclesiasticism, by writing his "Tale of a Tub" (taking the hint, doubtless, from a writing of Fontenelle's, "History of Mero and Enegu"— Rome and Geneva). Harley's flatteries gave Swift great satisfaction. He says : "He has desired to dine with me. . . . I mean he has desired me to dine with him on Tuesday, and, after four hours' being with him, set me down at St. James's coffee-house in a hackney-coach. All this is odd and comical, if you consider him and me. He knew my Christian name very well ;" and Oct. 14, 1710 (three days later) : "I stand with the new people ten times better than ever I did with the old, and forty times more caressed." Consequently Swift went over to the "new people," and he was of infinite service to them. Of his ability it is hard to speak too highly, and his change of party by no means implies moral worthlessness. Such a change nowadays is commonly understood. Mr. Gladstone, for instance, is by no means a type of the im-

moral renegade, yet his position at present is in direct opposition to that which he took on entering public life, yet
we can see and respect the steps by which he changed his
views. We can also see and watch Swift's, in his statement : "They call me nothing but Jonathan ; and I said
I believed they would leave me Jonathan as they found
me, and that I never knew a ministry do anything for
those whom they make companions of their pleasures :
and I believe you will find it so ; but I cannot." What
he wanted is definitely stated, and his life was embittered
by his failure, although his friends did their best for him,
but in vain. I do not care to sit in judgment on Swift's
political changes. I wish merely to show the relations between writers and politicians at this time. Each side, in
making a bargain, naturally tried to make the best bargain
it could. There is, of course, no reason why a man of letters should be averse to putting his pen to political writing—and in many ways at this time it was of service by
securing free discussion—but on literature the effect was
not so unmistakably beneficial. Authors had to be obsequious to the political leaders, and they were continually
bringing themselves into notice by dedicating their works
to those in authority.* Halifax, Bolingbroke, Godolphin,
the Duke of Ormond, when in power, received dedica-

---

* Cf. Schiller's dedication of " Dom Karlos ;" *vide* " Thalia," vol. i. (1787):

" DURCHLAUCHTIGSTER HERZOG :

" Gnädigster Herr,—Unvergesslich bleibt mir der Abend wo Eure Her-
zogliche Durchlaucht Sich gnädigst herabliessen, dem unvollkommenen
Versuch meiner dramatischen Muse, diesem ersten Akt Dom Karlos, einige
unschätzbare Augenblicke zu schenken, Theilnehmer der Gefühle zu
werden, in die ich mich wagte, Richter eines Gemähldes zu sein das ich
von IHRES GLEICHEN zu unterwerfen mir erlaubte," etc.

Corneille dedicated his " Cinna " to a M. de Montauron for one thousand
pistoles (Guizot, " Corneille," p. 181).

tions as one nowadays receives Christmas cards. The first
volume of the *Spectator* was dedicated to Somers ; the
second, to Halifax ; the third, to Henry Boyle ; the fourth,
to Marlborough ; the fifth, to Earl Wharton ; the sixth,
to the Earl of Sunderland ; the seventh, to Mr. Methuen,
English ambassador at the court of Savoy. These dedications are not so cringing as some in the previous century, but they are very fulsome. Young, in his maturer
years, excised from the later reprints of his poems the
dedications he had written when he began his literary career. Pope, too, who denounced the habit warmly in his
" Epistle to Dr. Arbuthnot," wrote in these terms about
Halifax :

> " Proud as Apollo on his forked hill,
>   Sat full-blown Bufo, puffed by every quill ;
>   Fed with soft dedication all day long,
>   Horace and he went hand in hand in song."

Thus, in a " Letter from Italy," Addison spoke to him of
" lines like Virgil's or like yours." And Congreve wrote:

> " O had your Genius been to Leisure born,
>   And not more bound to aid us than adorn !
>   Albion in verse with ancient Greece had vied,
>   And gained alone a fame, which, then, seven States divide."

Pope himself said of him, in his preface to the translation
of Homer, " of whom it is hard to say whether the advancement of the polite arts is more owing to his generosity or his example." Pope goes on :

> " His library (where busts of poets dead
>   And a true Pindar stood without a head)
>   Received of wits an undistinguished race,
>   Who first his judgment asked, and then a place :
>   Much they extolled his pictures, much his seat,
>   And flattered every day, and some days eat :
>   Till grown more frugal in his riper days,
>   He paid some bards with port and some with praise."

Yet, while Pope* did rap what was a great fault, we must not take these dedications too literally ; we should set down part of their language to mere formality, like that which is used in the ending of a letter, where one man calls himself the obedient servant of, it may be, his deadliest enemy.

Another misfortune of this dependence of the writers on the government was this, that much of their time was taken up in work that could have been as well performed by some one else equally well. Possibly, however, this was better than starving to death, which, as we shall soon see, was the ever-ready alternative. Then, too, ministries went out and new parties went in, so that, although dancing attendance on ministers kept Swift from literature for fourteen years, the interval between the "Tale of a Tub" and "Gulliver," the enforced leisure which Addison enjoyed gave him an opportunity to write the *Spectator.* A more serious matter was the way in which even a man like Swift could be forced to bend his neck to the yoke to taste the sweets of flattery and power, and then be dismissed to live and die in Ireland, "like a poisoned rat in a hole," as he said.

With the advent of the ministry of Sir Robert Walpole, in 1721, the Augustan age of literature ceased, and those who wrote for a living dropped from the company of courtiers to the gutter, one may say almost without exaggeration. George the Second, like the rest of the Hanoverian kings, cared nothing for literature, and his minister was very indifferent to it, and when he came into power he had already condemned literary men as practical politicians, very much as they have been condemned in this country in more recent times. Whatever writing he wanted done was intrusted to low scribblers, and that

---

* And cf. Pope again in the *Guardian*, No. 4.

was not a great deal. With his accession to power, government patronage ceased. It was not that one side went in when the other went out: they were all outs. The literature of the last century is full of references to the direful effects this change had on the fortunes of authors. Swift ("To Mr. Gay," 1731) calls him "Bob, the poet's foe." But, in general, the old arts of fascinating the great were tried on him, though without success. Savage, whose life was full of misery, after squandering whatever money he was able to get, published a panegyric on Sir Robert Walpole, for which he received the sum of twenty guineas; but that was a singular exception, moderate as the gift was. His friends, too, solicited Walpole for the promise of the next place, not exceeding £200 a year, that should become vacant. The promise was made, with the statement that "it was not the promise of a minister to a petitioner, but of a friend to his friend." Yet the promise, whatever it might be called, was never kept. Savage tried writing a poem in honor of the Prince, but nothing came of it. The Queen, however, gave him a pension of £50 a year, which ceased at her death. These few lines from Dr. Johnson's life of him, which may well be read for the light it throws on the condition of literary men at that time, show to what stress writers were sometimes driven, though this abject penury was in great measure Savage's own fault: "He lodged as much by accident as he dined, and passed the night sometimes in mean houses which are set open at night to any casual wanderers, sometimes in cellars, among the riot and filth of the meanest and most profligate of the rabble, and sometimes, when he had not money to support even the expenses of these receptacles, walked about the streets till he was weary, and lay down in the summer upon the bulk, or in the winter, with his associates in poverty, among the ashes of a glass-house." During a considerable part of the time in which he was writing "Sir Thomas Overbury," " he was without lodging and often without meat ; nor had he any other conveniences for study than the fields or the streets allowed him ; there he used to walk and form his speeches, and afterwards walk into a shop, beg for a few moments the use of the pen and ink, and write down what he had composed upon paper which he had picked up by accident." To be sure, Savage's habits were such as at any period of the world's history would have brought him to such straits, but his was not an exceptional fate. Steele, who, to be sure, was never a model of economy, died in want and obscurity in 1729. Savage, Steele, and Ambrose Philips were walking together one evening, when they were met by a man who told them there were some suspicious-looking fellows in waiting at the end of the street, probably bailiffs, and urged any one who might have business with them to go home by some other way. They all turned and ran.

Or take Thomson's life as that of a man who found patrons. He came to London, but his pocket was at once picked and his letters of introduction stolen. The blame for that, however, cannot be justly put on Sir Robert Walpole. He sold the manuscript of his "Winter" to buy a pair of shoes. It was dedicated to Sir Spencer Compton, whom he afterwards visited by request. He writes of this visit : "He received me in what they commonly call a civil manner ; asked me some commonplace questions ; and made me a present of twenty guineas."

"Spring" was dedicated to the Countess of Hertford, " whose practice it was to invite every summer some poet into the country, to hear her verses and assist her studies. This honor was one summer conferred on Thomson, who took more delight in carousing with Lord Hertford and his friends than assisting her ladyship's poetical operations, and therefore never received another summons." He afterwards travelled on the Continent with a pupil ; on his return, he was given the place of secretary of the briefs, and composed an unreadable poem on "Liberty ;" but his patron soon died. However, he was given a small pension, £100, and managed to be put into another office.*

Less successful was Johnson's friend, Mr. Boyse, who lay in bed because his clothes were in pawn.† Johnson collected enough, by separate sixpences, to get them out, and in two days they were back. Once he was nearly starving, and "some money was produced to purchase him a dinner, he got a bit of roast beef, but could not eat it without catchup, and laid out the last half-guinea he possessed in truffles and mushrooms, eating them in bed, too, for want of clothes, or even a shirt to sit up in."

The refining influence of letters may be gathered from this anecdote : "Another man . . . made as wild use of his friend's beneficence, . . . spending in punch the solitary guinea which had been brought him one morning ; when resolving to add another claimant to a share of the bowl, besides a woman who always lived with him, and a footman who used to carry out petitions for charity, he borrowed a chairman's watch, and pawning it for half-a-crown, paid a clergyman to marry him to a fellow-lodger in the wretched house they all inhabited, and got so drunk over the guinea bowl of punch the evening of his wedding-day, that having many years lost the use of one leg, he now contrived to fall from the top of the stairs to the

---

* This was when the Prince of Wales was in the opposition, and with a small purse made an attempt to collect adherents among literary men. Mallet also got a pension.

† *Vide* Life in Anderson's " Poets," x. 329.

bottom, and break his arm." In this condition Johnson brought him relief.

Johnson, too, had himself known what were the difficulties in the way of the young author, for he and Savage were sometimes so poor that they could not pay for a lodging, and had wandered together whole nights in the streets. One night in particular, he and Savage strolled about inveighing against the minister, and resolved they would stand by their country.

As these are well-attested historical facts, we can understand the allusions in the novelists to the wretchedness of authors.

In "Humphrey Clinker," Smollett gives an account of a collection of authors, who met on Sunday, the only day they were safe from arrest, at the house of one S., who welcomed them to his table. They were men who had translated, collated, and compiled for more reputable authors, and had now set up for themselves. The most learned had been expelled the university for atheism, had prepared an orthodox confutation of Lord Bolingbroke, but had been meanwhile presented to the grand jury as a public nuisance for blaspheming in an alehouse on the Lord's day. A Scotchman was there who gave lectures on the pronunciation of the English language. There was a Piedmontese who wrote a humorous satire on the "Balance of the English Poets." A sage who labored under the ἀγροφοβία had written on agriculture, though he did not know hominy from rice.* Another Cockney, who had never left London, was engaged in writing his travels through Europe and a part of Asia, etc., etc. Fielding, in his "Joseph Andrews" (lib. iii. chap. iii.), gives an account of the miseries of a poor author: "Many a morning have I waited in the cold parlours of men of

---

* *Vide* "Notes and Queries," July 6, 1861, p. 7.

quality ; when after seeing the lowest rascals in lace and embroidery . . . admitted, I have been sometimes told, on sending in my name, that my lord could not possibly see me this morning. . . . The profits which booksellers allowed authors for the best work was so very small, that certain men of birth and fortune some years ago, who were the patrons of wit and learning, thought fit to encourage them further by entering into voluntary subscriptions for their encouragement. Thus Prior, Rowe, Pope, and some other men of genius received large sums for their labours from the public. This seemed so easy a method of getting money, that many of the lowest scribblers of the times ventured to publish their works in the same way ; and many had the assurance to take in subscriptions for what was not writ and never intended." Mallet (whose name was changed by himself from Malloch) for a long time assumed to be writing a life of the Duke of Marlborough ; as a reward, the Duchess left him £1000, and he also had for the same reason a pension from the family, but he had not written a line. The papers had before this been intrusted to Steele, who had pawned them. Boswell quotes Dr. Johnson's mention of a man named Cooke,* who translated Hesiod, and lived twenty years on a translation of Plautus, for which he was always taking subscriptions.

Fielding's Wilson took to translating, but " contracted a distemper by my sedentary life, in which no part of my body was exercised but my right arm, which rendered me incapable of writing for a long time." Smollett mentions an author who, on the pretext of meaning to make a short journey, borrowed a horse, which he at once sold,

---

* It was this Cooke who introduced Foote to a club in these words : " This is the nephew of the gentleman who was lately hung in chains for murdering his brother."

and, in addition, stole his publisher's boots. As for Savage, it is told of Lord Tyrconnel, when Savage was living with him, that, "having given him a collection of valuable books, stamped with his own arms, he had the mortification to see them in a short time exposed to sale upon the stalls, it being usual with Mr. Savage, when he wanted a small sum, to take his books to the pawnbroker." He was continually getting subscribers for new editions of his writings, which were never printed. The translators were the lowest of all, as Fielding implies. One, who undertook a translation of Lucretius, wrote out a new version of the first page, and then copied all the rest from a published work.

How different all this crapulous misery is from the condition of things in the beginning of the century is very clear. Then a writer held a high social position, and afterwards he sank low, until, in the course of time, he managed to get into relations directly with the public. We shall see later how this happened.

That literature should have been looked upon as a disgraceful profession is not, under the circumstances, surprising. Even in the older times, Congreve had affected to despise his literary success. Voltaire, who was anxious to see everything and every one, made him a visit, and spoke about the Englishman's plays, but Congreve treated them as trifles, and asked his visitor not to speak of them. "Sir," said Voltaire, " if you had the misfortune of being nothing but a gentleman, I should never have come to see you." But now literature was despised for very different and more respectable reasons. Society could hardly be expected to smile on Savage, for instance, who, " if he was entertained by a family, nothing was any longer to be regarded there but amusement and jollity." " He was an incommodious inmate; for, being accustomed to an irregular life, he could not confine himself to any stated hours, or pay any regard to the rules of a family, but could prolong his conversation till midnight, without considering that business might require his friend's application in the morning ; and when he had persuaded himself to retire to bed, was not, without equal difficulty, called up to dinner : it was therefore impossible to pay him any distinction without the entire subversion of all economy, a kind of establishment which, wherever he went, he always appeared ambitious to overthrow." This is, of course, an exceptional case, such as might happen nowadays, and does happen every night of the week. Horace Walpole was very unwilling to be looked on as a man of letters. As Macaulay said, " he did not like to have anything in common with the wretches who lodged in the little courts behind St. Martin's Church, and stole out on Sunday to dine with their bookseller." When Mann congratulated him on the learning shown in his " Catalogue of Royal and Noble Authors," Walpole wrote : "I know nothing. How should I ? I who have always lived in the big busy world ; who lie abed all the morning, calling it morning as long as you please ; who sup in company ; who have played at faro half my life, and now at loo till two or three in the morning ; who have always loved pleasure ; haunted auctions. . . . How I have laughed when some of the magazines have called me the learned gentleman. Pray don't be like the magazines." But Horace Walpole was a very genteel person, who did not represent the whole view of society. His letters are full of contemptuous references to most of the writers of his time, viz.: "I had rather have written the most absurd lines in Lee, than ' Leonidas ' or the ' Seasons.' " " The third and fourth volumes of ' Tristram Shandy ' are the dregs of nonsense, and have universally met the contempt they deserve." In short, he was an industrious dilettante who should be living now in the present age of æstheticism.

The relations of Pope to the public need to be studied carefully, for while, when he began to write, government encouragement of literature was at its height, he outlived that, and saw most of the contemporaries of his later years in the misery I have described. The fact that he belonged to the Church of Rome stood in the way of his holding a position under government. The laws against Papists were very severe at that time. Thus ("Lecky," i. 298, etc.) : "An act was passed in 1699, by which any Catholic priest convicted of celebrating mass, or discharging any sacerdotal function (except in the house of an ambassador), was made liable to perpetual imprisonment,"* and a reward of £1000 was offered for conviction. The same punishment was to be inflicted on any Papist who kept school or undertook the education of the young. No parent could send a child abroad to be educated in the Catholic faith, under a penalty of £100, which went to the informer. "All persons who did not, within six months of attaining the age of eighteen, take the Oath, not only of Allegiance, but also of Supremacy, and subscribe the declaration against transubstantiation, became incapable of either inheriting or purchasing land, and the property they would otherwise have inherited passed to the next Protestant heir." All persons in any civil or military office, all members of colleges, teachers, preachers, lawyers of every grade, were compelled to take the Oath of Supremacy, which was distinctly anti-Catholic, as well as the Oath of Allegiance and the declaration against the Stuarts. At any time the oath could be required of any Catholic who was suspected of disaffection. Whoever refused was debarred from appearing at court, or

---

* Lecky's "History of the Eighteenth Century," i. 298 et seq.

even coming within ten miles of London, from holding any office or employment, from keeping arms in his house, from travelling more than five miles from home without special license, and from bringing any action at law or suit in equity, under pain of forfeiting all his goods.

In the English provinces, Virginia proscribed Puritans and Catholics ; Massachusetts proscribed and persecuted Episcopalians and Quakers ; but the Quaker provinces and Rhode Island established complete religious freedom, and in 1632 Maryland, founded by the Catholic Lord Baltimore, established this precedent of toleration, limited, however, to believers in the Trinity. The Protestants, however, got the upper hand, and in 1704 "enslaved" the Catholics.

While the laws in England were thus rigorous, they were seldom put into effect ; the Catholics in fact enjoyed toleration, and possibly, as Lecky suggests, the fact that a Roman Catholic was at the head of English literature may have tended towards encouraging milder views. Yet there was the danger that the laws might be turned against Pope at any moment.

As he said ("Imitation of Horace," lib. ii. ep. ii.) :

> "Bred up at home, full early I begun
> To read in Greek the wrath of Peleus' son.
> Besides, my father taught me, from a lad,
> The better art to know the good from bad :
> (And little sure imported * to remove,
> To hunt for truth in Maudlin's learned grove.)
> But knottier points, we knew not half so well,
> Deprived us soon of our paternal cell ;
> And certain laws, by sufferers thought unjust,
> Denied all posts of profit or of trust :
> Hopes after hopes of pious Papists failed

---

* *Peu importait*, cf. Dryden ("Marriage à la Mode," iii. 1): "It imports me to practise what I shall say to my servant when I meet him."

> While mighty William's thundering arm prevailed.
> For right hereditary taxed and fined,
> He stuck to poverty with peace of mind;
> And me the Muses helped to undergo it;
> Convict a papist he, and I a poet." *

Yet Pope was essentially a man of letters and not a politician. Harley, in 1714, offered him a place under government if he would consent to change his religion; yet, although he was by no means a fervent Catholic, he declined this proposal, one reason being that he was unwilling to pain his parents. Halifax, possibly with a view to being sung by Pope, proposed a pension, but this was declined, as was a similar offer from Craggs of one of £300 a year out of the secret funds.

Certainly these things should be remembered to Pope's credit, especially at the present time, when, besides being out of favor as a poet, his moral character has been riddled by the discoveries of those who have made a searching examination of his life, writings, and papers. He has been found guilty of the most complicated lying that can be imagined, and he stands in contrast not with living men—many of whom are not wholly free from this vice, which is encouraged by the fact that it makes no difference how often a man is discovered in falsehood, he is eagerly believed the next time he perjures himself— but with the faultless beings whom we find in biographies.

As soon as Pope began to write he got into communication with Tonson, the publisher of Dryden's "Virgil," and it was in a volume of Tonson's miscellanies that Pope's pastorals appeared in 1709. There was this advantage for Pope, that Tonson no longer enjoyed a monopoly; he had a formidable rival in Lintot. These two men

---

* As if these were equal faults in the eyes of the government.

pushed each other hard. Tonson published Shakspere's plays, Lintot brought out his poems. Lintot announced Pope's translation of the "Iliad," Tonson offered the "First Book," translated by Tickell. They both wrote to Young to secure his work, and in answering their letters he misdirected them, so that the one to Tonson fell into Lintot's hands, and *vice versa*. The matter was complicated by the fact that the one sent to Lintot, but written for Tonson, began : "That Bernard Lintot is so great a scoundrel, that," etc.

Pope's "Pastorals"* have scarcely sufficient literary

---

* Pope was recommended to write the fourth pastoral by William Walsh, a famous critic of the time (1663–1708). He it was who urged Pope to try to be a *correct* poet. He had been recommended to the public by Dryden, who said he was the best critic in the nation ; and Pope wrote of him :

> "To him the wit of Greece and Rome was known,
> And every author's merit but his own ;
> Such late was Walsh—the Muses' judge and friend,
> Who justly knew to blame or to commend ;
> To failings mild, but zealous to desert,
> The clearest head and the sincerest heart."

Walsh is one of the few men who wrote sonnets in English between Milton and the Wartons (about 1750):

> "What has this bugbear Death that's worth our care ?
> After a life of pain and sorrow past,
> After deluding hopes and dire despair,
> Death only gives us quiet at the last ;
> How strangely are our love and hate misplaced !
> Freedom we seek and yet from freedom flee,
> Courting those tyrant sins that chain us fast ;
> And shunning death that only sets us free.
> 'Tis not a foolish fear of future pains,—
> Why should they fear who keep their souls from stains ?
> That makes me dread thy terrors, Death, to see ;
> 'Tis not the loss of riches or of fame,

merit to detain us long.   Lines like these cannot move us now :

> " Hear how the birds, on every blooming spray,
>   With joyous music wake the dawning day !
>   Why sit we mute, when early linnets sing,
>   When warbling Philomel salutes the spring?
>   Why sit we sad when Phosphor shines so clear,
>   And lavish nature paints the purple year ?"

Or these :

> " All nature mourns, the skies relent in showers,
>   Hush'd are the birds, and closed the drooping flowers ;
>   If Delia smile, the flowers begin to spring,
>   The skies to brighten, and the birds to sing."

It is sufficiently clear that these lines—and they are fairly representative of the whole—are but a faded transcript of some old pattern.   They show the smooth copying of some other original rather than genuine love of the country or real passion :

> " For her the flocks refuse their verdant food,
>   The thirsty heifers shun the gliding flood,
>   The silver swans her hapless fate bemoan
>   In notes more sad than when they sing their own ;
>   In hollow caves sweet echo silent lies
>   Silent, or only to her name replies."

All this is as truly sham sentiment as it is faulty natural history.   It is part of the pastoral poetry of which mention was made above.   It had its origin in the reaction of modern life against the Middle Ages, in the negation of chivalry, mysticism, and asceticism which distinguished the Renaissance,* and the struggle of the

---

> Or the vain toys the vulgar pleasures name,
>   'Tis nothing, Celia, but the losing thee !"

It is the last line, with its smirk and bow to Celia, that betrays the date of composition.

* *Vide* Symond's " Renaissance in Italy," v. 245.

southern races, with their love of clearness, against the murky emotions of northern Europe. In Italy, as we have seen, the movement, after bearing fruit in a number of poems in Latin and Italian, and flowering in the pastoral dramas of " Aminta " and the " Pastor Fido," faded away into the Arcadias of the last century, and the Italian opera. From Italy, as we saw, they passed through the rest of Europe ; even Cervantes wrote a pastoral novel, the " Galathea," and the pastoral existed for a long time as the legitimate expression, artificial as it seems to us, of the love of nature. Real nature they could not endure, this artificial copying of it was looked upon as an admirable form of literature. In English literature, we find the earliest traces of it in Sidney and Spenser. Spenser's " Shepherd's Calendar " (1579) (the name was applied commonly to a sort of almanac, with recipes and astrological notes suited to rustics) consists of twelve eclogues.* " Æglogai, as it were αἰγῶν or αἰγονόμων λόγοι, that is 'Goatherd's Tales,' " is Edward Kirke's explanation of their name. Spenser really said something in this way ; he pretended to be a shepherd, calling himself Colin Clout ;† Hobbinoll being Gabriel Harvey ; Cuddie, possibly Edward Kirke. These were real names ; Hobbinoll, for instance, in a note, is called " common and usuall." The poems, one for each month, beginning with January, are on different subjects. Some are simply love-poems ; three or four others are translations from Marot or imitations of Theocritus, Bion, or Vergil. Two contain well-told fables—the " Oak and the Briar," and that of the " Fox and the Kid," which expresses the dissatisfaction of the populace with the clergy,

---

* "This being, who seeth not the grossness of such as by colour of learning would make us believe, that they are more rightly tearmed Eclogai, as they would say, extraordinarie discourses of unnecessary matter."

† From Skelton and Clément Marot.

and the suspicions felt concerning Romish intrigues ; and then there is, of course, a poem in honor of the fair Eliza. Two " are burlesque imitations of rustic dialect and banter." *   One is a funeral tribute to a great lady ; another is a complaint of the way in which poets were neglected by the great.   Three of them abuse the misconduct of the clergy and denounce Rome.   This brief description will suffice to show that Spenser's treatment of the pastoral had at least this advantage, that it was used to convey something to the reader besides ingenious rhapsodies. After his time, we see it as a conventional form used by many poets, as in Milton's "Lycidas," Congreve's poem on the death of Queen Mary, and even Shelley's "Adonais," and Mr. Arnold's "Thyrsis."   As Dr. Johnson said ("Life of Ambrose Philips "), " there had never, from the time of Spenser, wanted writers to talk occasionally of Arcadia and Strephon."   Yet this is not a precise statement.   Later writers used some of the pastoral machinery, to be sure, and Arcadia became as truly part of the classical territory as the region of that name was part of classical geography, and Strephon and Doris were its inhabitants ; but the pastoral, as sung by alleged shepherds, did not exist without interruption, and it was ridiculed by certain poets.   Marlowe wrote " The Shepherd to his Love," " Come Live with Me and Be my Love," † in answer to which Raleigh (?) wrote (" The Milk-maid's Mother's Answer ") the " Nymph's Reply:"

> " If that the world and love were young,
>   And truth in every shepherd's tongue,
>   These pretty pleasures might me move
>   To live with thee and be thy love."

---

* Church's "Spenser," English Men of Letters Series.
† Reprinted in the "Compleat Angler," 1653, and so made popular.

Each stanza of the answer ridiculed the corresponding one of the original. Marlowe's poem was printed in the "Passionate Pilgrim" (1549)—*i. e.*, stanzas 1, 2, 3, and 5. This bore only Shakspere's name on it at first, but, in 1600, Marlowe's. It was very popular, and was imitated by Donne ("The Bait"), and by Herrick ("To Phillis: to Love and Live with Him ").*

Among the miscellaneous poems of the dramatist Robert Greene (1550–92) we find a burlesque, called "Doron's Eclogue, joined with Carmela's."

"*Doron.*   Sit down, Carmela; here are cobs for kings,
            Sloes black as jet or like my Christmas shoes,
            Sweet cider, which my leathern bottle brings;
            Sit down, Carmela, let me kiss thy toes.

"*Carmela.* Ah Doron! ah my heart! thou art as white
            As is my mother's calf or brinded cow;
            Thine eyes are like the glow-worm in the night;
            Thine hairs resemble thickest of the snow.

            "The lines within thy face are deep and clear
            Like to the furrows of my father's wain," etc.

Yet this, to our ears, is scarcely more absurd than Pope's

---

* Donne's ran thus:

    "Come live with me and be my love,
    And we will some new pleasures prove
    Of golden sands and crystal brooks,
    With silken lines and silver hooks.

    "There will the river whispering run
    Warm'd by thine eyes more than the sun;
    And there the enamoured fish will stay
    Begging themselves they may betray," etc.

Herrick's thus:

    "Live, live with me and thou shalt see
    The pleasures I'll prepare for thee;
    What sweets the country can afford
    Shall bless thy bed, and bless thy board."

rehandling of the pastoral. By a singular coincidence, Ambrose Philips also composed pastorals ; he it was who became immortalized in the words *namby-pamby*, for such lines as this:

> " Dimply damsel, sweetly smiling." *

---

* " To Miss Margaret Pulteney, Daughter of Charles Pulteney, esq. April 27, 1727 :

> " Dimply damsel, sweetly smiling,
> All caressing, none beguiling,
> Bud of beauty, fairly blowing," etc.

In the *Golden Treasury*, No. cxii. p. 111, is his poem " To Charlotte Pulteney," May 1, 1724 :

> " Timely blossom, infant fair,
> Fondling of a happy pair,
> Every morn and every night
> Their solicitous delight," etc.

It is rather pretty.

Compare Ambrose Philips's poems to the Pulteney children with Marot's " Pour la Petite Princesse de Navarre, à Mme. Marguerite:"

> " Voyant que la Royne, ma mère,
> Trouve à present, la ryme amère,
> Ma dame, m'est prins fantasie
> De vous monstrer qu'en poësie
> Sa fille suis. Arrière prose,
> Puis que renier maintenant j'ose.

> " Pour commencer donc à renier :
> Vous pouvez, ma dame, estimer
> Quel joye à la fille advenoit,
> Sachant que la mère venoit," etc.
>
> D'Héricault's ed., p. 85.

And with Ronsard, " Gayeté," No. vii. (ed. Blanchemain, vi. 396) :

> " Enfant de quatre ans, combien
> Ta politesse a de bien !
> Combien en a ton enfance
> Si elle avoit cognoissance
> De l'heur que je dois avoir
> Et qu'elle a sans le scavoir," etc.

Lamb says (" Works," iii. 178): " To the measure in which these lines

It was applied to him by Henry Carey * (author of "Sally in Our Alley," and "Chrononhotonthologos"). That two men should at the same time try their hand at this species

---

are written the wits of Queen Anne's days contemptuously gave the name of Namby Pamby, in ridicule of Ambrose Philips, who has used it in some instances, as in the lines on Cuzzoni, to my feeling at least, very deliciously; but Wither, whose darling measure it seems to have been, may show that in skilful hands it is capable of expressing the subtilest movements of passion. So true it is, which Drayton seems to have felt, that it is the poet who modifies the metre, not the metre the poet." These are the lines " To Signora Cuzzoni " to which Lamb refers :

> " Little syren of the stage,
> Charmer of an idle age;
> Empty warbler, breathing lyre,
> Wanton gale of fond desire,
> Bane of every manly art,
> Sweet enfeebler of the heart!
> O, too pleasing in thy strain,
> Hence to southern climes again;
> Tuneful mischief, vocal spell,
> To this island bid farewell;
> Leave us as we ought to be,
> Leave the Britons rough and free."

* Henry Carey: " He led a life free from reproach, and hanged himself Oct. 4, 1743." In his poems (3d ed., 1729, p. 55) we find " Namby-Pamby; or a Panegyric of the New Versification :"

> " All ye poets of the age!
> All ye witlings of the stage,
> Learn your jingles to reform,
> Crop your numbers and conform :
> Let your little verses flow
> Gently, sweetly, row by row.
> Let the verse the subject fit,
> Little subject, little wit,
> Namby-Pamby is your guide
> Albion's joy, Hibernia's pride.
> *   *   *   *
> Now the venal poet sings

of composition is, perhaps, a little strange, unless we remember that it was, so to speak, awaiting the writers of the day. It gave pleasure, however, to readers; for the Arcadia it described was, after all, a relief from the intellectual and didactic region towards which poetry was moving. As Steele said in the *Guardian*, No. 22: "It transports us into a kind of fairy - land, where our ears are soothed with the melody of birds, bleating flocks, and purling streams; our eyes enchanted with flowery meadows and springing greens; we are laid under cool shades, and entertained with all the sweets and freshness of nature. . . . The first reason is, because all men like ease. . . . A second reason is our secret approbation of innocence and simplicity. . . . This is the reason why we are so much pleased with the prattle of children. . . . A

> Baby clouts and baby things,
> Baby dolls and baby houses,
> Little misses, little spouses,
> Little playthings, little toys,
> Little girls, and little boys.
>   * * * *
> Now methinks I hear him say
> Boys and girls come out to play," etc.

As to "Sally in Our Alley," Carey, in the 3d edition of his poems, p. 127, prefaces the poem with the remark that he meant "to set forth the beauty of a chaste and disinterested passion even in the lowest class of humanity." He noticed a young shoemaker's prentice making holiday with his sweetheart, showing her Bedlam, puppet-shows, and flying-chairs, and all the elegance of Moorfields. He gave her a collation of buns, cheese-cakes, gammon of bacon, stuffed beef, and bottled ale. The author followed them through the crowd, and afterwards wrote his poem, but "being young and obscure, was very much ridiculed by some of his acquaintance for this performance; which nevertheless made its way into the polite world and amply recompensed him by the applause of the divine Addison who was pleased more than once to mention it with approbation." This is but one of many incidental proofs of Addison's sound taste and kindheartedness.

third reason is our love of the country." These remarks surprise us; Pope's and Philips's pastorals seem to us more artificial than a brick house ; yet, for three hundred years poems as vague as these gave our ancestors the feeling of being out-doors. To our thinking, they are as much like nature as the smoke of pastilles is like fresh air.

Philips's pastorals were praised by Addison in the *Spectator* (No. 523) : "He has given a new life and a more natural beauty to this way of writing by substituting in the place of these Antiquated Fables, the superstitious Mythology which prevails among the Shepherds of our own Country." This praise galled Pope. Among other things he had given his doll-like shepherds classical names, pluming himself on his resemblance to Vergil, while Philips imitated Spenser, so far as preserving such names as Hobbinoll, Colinet, etc., may imply imitation. Pope's method of redeeming himself was characteristically ingenious. He sent, anonymously, to Steele a paper for the *Guardian* (No. 40), in which he gave ironical praise to Philips for all that was poorest in his pastorals, and found pretended fault with himself, and did all this so slyly that it was only after it was printed that his real design became evident. Steele, before printing, showed the paper to Pope, who assented to its publication. Addison is reported to have been annoyed by this incident, and it does not seem surprising. He had praised Philips's " Distressed Mother," the play which so moved Sir Roger, and he had always spoken well of Philips's work ; possibly, too, the fact that this writer did try to preserve a faint ray of what is called local color may have attracted him.* However this may be, further com-

---

* Pope is also suspected, though on no good evidence, of having instigated Gay to write his mock pastorals, " The Shepherd's Week," in parody of Philips. It seems quite as likely that Gay wrote this for his own

plications arose between him and Pope. Dennis, it will be remembered, had made an onslaught on Addison's "Cato." Pope took upon himself the task of crushing

---

amusement, for he was by no means a solemn person. Swift, who cared but little for conventional poetry, once said to him that a Newgate pastoral—*i. e.*, something in the form of a pastoral with the grim truth of life as shown by criminals—would be an amusing thing, and Gay wrote the "Beggar's Opera." The "Shepherd's Week," although meant for a caricature, was taken to be a serious picture from real life. So, too, the *Guardian*, No. 40, which was written by Pope, was for a long time supposed not to be ironical. Hannah More (*vide* Elwyn's "Pope," i. 254) detected the imposition, but she said almost every one else differed from her. Of course, those directly concerned had seen through Pope's device long before, but they were not anxious to spread the fact abroad. Philips himself hung up a stick at Buttons's to whip his brother-Arcadian with, as he said, in case they should ever meet there.

It is curious to notice that the Italian pastoral poets were turned to ridicule in the same way by the writers of burlesque, Berni, Folengo, and Romolo Bertini.

To return to Gay's pastorals, Gay said of them : " Thou wilt not find my shepherdesses idly piping upon oaten reeds, but milking the kine, tying up the sheaves, or, if the hogs are astray, driving them to their styes. My shepherd gathereth none other nosegays but what are the growth of our own fields ; he sleepeth not under myrtle shades, but under a hedge ; nor doth he vigilantly defend his flocks from wolves, because there are none."

Here is an example of his burlesque :

> " If by the dairy's hatch I chance to hie,
> I shall her goodly countenance espy,
> For there her goodly countenance I've seen,
> Set off with kerchief starched and pinners clean.
> Sometimes, like wax, she rolls the butter round,
> Or with the wooden lily prints the pound.
>
> * * * * *
>
> But now, alas ! these ears shall hear no more
> The whining swine surround the dairy door ;
> No more her can shall fill the hollow tray
> To fat the guzzling hogs with floods of whey.
> Lament, ye swine ! in grunting spend your grief,
> For you, like me, have lost your sole relief.
>
> * * * * *

Dennis, and wrote a foul-mouthed pamphlet of personal abuse of the poor old critic, whom he represented as raving in a garret over the failure of his attack on the "Cato." The criticisms themselves were not answered at all. Addison got Steele to write a note to Lintot disavowing all connection with this, and saying that, if he took notice of Mr. Dennis's criticisms, it should be in such a way as to give Mr. Dennis no cause of complaint. He added that he had refused to look at the pamphlet when it was offered to him, and that he had expressed his disapproval of this mode of attack. It is not made clear that he knew that Pope had written the attack, but Pope took umbrage at the implied reproof, and thus was laid the foundation of a famous literary quarrel.*

II. Although Addison agreed with posterity in being indifferent to Pope's pastorals, and differed from it in praising Philips's, he warmly commended Pope's "Essay on Criticism" in the *Spectator* (No. 253, Dec. 20, 1711). Praise from Addison was something to be grateful for. He stood at the head of English men of letters at this time, and his position and his age—he was fifty years old, while Pope was twenty-four — authorized him to warn Pope against denunciations of his fellow-writers. To be sure, those whom Pope had attacked were men whom the world has agreed to forget or to remember with contempt, such as Dennis, Sir Richard Blackmore, and Luke Milbourne, but it would have been better for Pope's name if he had shown some of Addison's forbearance. After this slight reproof, Addison had nothing but commendation.

> After the good man warned us from his text,
> That none could tell whose turn it would be next,
> He said that heaven would take her soul, no doubt,
> And spoke the hour-glass in her praise—quite out."

* *Vide* Mr. Leslie Stephen's " Pope," English Men of Letters Series, p. 53.

He said, after speaking of the friendships between literary men in ancient times : " In our own country a man seldom sets up for a poet, without attacking the reputation of all his brothers in the art. The ignorance of the moderns, the Scribblers of the age, the decay of poetry, are the topics of detraction with which he makes his entrance into the world. . . . I am sorry to find that an author, who is very justly esteemed among the best judges, has admitted some strokes of this nature into a very fine poem : I mean ' The Art of Criticism,' which was published some months since, and is a masterpiece in its kind."

Pope wrote a letter thanking Addison for his kind notice, saying : " Though it be the highest satisfaction to find myself commended by a writer whom all the world commends, yet I am not more obliged to you for that than for your candour and frankness in acquainting me with the error I have been guilty of in speaking too freely of my brother moderns."

Addison says : " The observations follow one another like those in Horace's ' Art of Poetry.' . . . They are some of them uncommon, but such as the reader must assent to, when he sees them explained with that elegance and perspicuity in which they are delivered. As for those which are the most known, and the most received, they are placed in so beautiful a light and illustrated with such apt allusions, that they have in them all the graces of novelty, and make the reader, who was before acquainted with them, still more convinced of their truth and solidity." He gives, too, many examples of Pope's excellence, ending with these words : " I cannot conclude this paper without taking notice that we have three poems in our tongue, which are of the same nature, and each of them a masterpiece in its kind ; the ' Essay on Translated Verse,' the

'Essay on the Art of Poetry,' and the 'Essay on Criticism.'" The comparison with those two other books is likely to be less understood as a compliment at present than it was at the time when it was written. The "Essay on Criticism" is still a classic, while the others are seldom read. The "Essay on Translated Verse" was written by Lord Roscommon (1633–84), and published the year of his death. It is best known to posterity by two lines, for which Pope gets all the credit; just as in our times all the good jokes, old and new, are ascribed to Lamb and Sidney Smith. The lines are these :

> " Immodest words admit of no defence ;
> For want of decency is want of sense."

Other familiar lines of his are :

> " And choose an author as you would choose a friend."

> " The multitude is always in the wrong."

The final couplet, too, of this passage is sometimes quoted:

> " But who did ever in French authors see
> The comprehensive English energy?
> The weighty bullion of one Sterling line,
> Drawn to French wire, would through whole pages shine."

This was one of the hand-books of the literary movement of the time succeeding the Restoration, and it is interesting to examine the faults he condemns, such as these:

> " Absurd expressions, crude, abortive thoughts,
> All the lewd legion of exploded faults."

Yet Roscommon ventured to denounce the couplet, for he said :

> " Of many faults, rhyme is perhaps the cause;
> Too strict to rhyme, we slight more useful laws,
> For that in Greece or Rome was never known,
> Till by barbarian deluges o'erflown ;" etc.

* * * * *

" But now that Phœbus and the Sacred Nine,
With all their beams on our bless'd Island shine,
Why should not we their ancient rites restore,
And be what Rome or Athens were before ?"

And here he inserts twenty-seven lines of his own, written in the Miltonic manner,* and ends with the wish :

" O may I live to hail the glorious day,
And sing loud pæans through the crowded way,
When in triumphant state the British Muse,
True to herself, shall barbarous aid refuse,
And in the Roman majesty appear,
Which none know better, and none come so near."

Roscommon also translated Horace's " Ars Poetica " into blank verse.

The other piece which Addison mentions was by John Sheffield, Duke of Buckinghamshire (1649–1721), who, when he was Earl of Mulgrave, wrote the " Essay on Satire," a part of which Rochester suspected to have been written by Dryden, and accordingly had him beaten by hired ruffians. Sheffield also made over Shakspere's " Julius Cæsar " according to the unities. His " Essay on Poetry," 1682, begins thus :

---

* " Have we forgot how Raphael's numerous prose
Led our exalted souls through heavenly camps,
And marked the ground where proud apostate thrones
Defied Jehovah ! Here, 'twixt host and host,
(A narrow but a dreadful interval)
Portentous Sight ! before the cloudy van
Satan with vast and haughty strides advanced,
Came towering armed in adamant and gold." Etc.

This is probably the first imitation of Milton extant. Roscommon died in 1684, in which year this essay was published. His own blank verse in the translation of the " Ars Poetica " is most crabbed.

Samuel Say (" Poems," London, 1745) has an imitation of Milton dated 1698.

"Of all those arts in which the wise excel,
Nature's chief masterpiece is writing well:"

and he proceeds to give the rules for writing well.

"Here I shall all the various sorts of verse,
And the whole art of poetry rehearse;
But who that task would after Horace do?
The best of masters, and examples, too!
Echoes at best, all we can say is vain,"

he adds, with truth. He goes on to mention, "first, then,
of songs;" "next, Elegy, of sweet, but solemn voice;" "a
happier flight, and of a happier force, are Odes, the Muses'
most unruly horse;" "satire;" "the Stage." Of this last
he says:

"The unities of action, time, and place,
Which, if observed, give plays so great a grace,
Are, though but little practised, too well known
To be taught here, where we pretend alone
From nicer faults to purge the present age,
Less obvious errors of the English stage."

This is a bad beginning, but what he has to say about
the writing of plays is well worth a moment's attention,
as when he says:

"Who can choose but pity
A dying hero, miserably witty?
But, oh! the dialogues, where jest and mock
Is held up like a rest at shuttlecock;
Or else like bells, eternally they chime,
They sigh in simile and die in rhyme."

He says:

"Shakspere and Fletcher are the wonders now:
*   *   *   *   *   *
Their beauties imitate but not their faults,
First, on a plot employ thy careful thoughts."

He warns against perfect characters:

"There's no such thing in nature, and you'll draw
A faultless monster which the world ne'er saw."

And finally, in speaking of the epic, he says :

> "Read Homer once, and you can read no more ;
> For all books else appear so mean, so poor,
> Verse will seem prose ; but still persist to read,
> And Homer will be all the books you need."

This brief recapitulation will make clearer the relation of Pope's poem, the "Essay on Criticism," to contemporary literature. It is sufficiently remarkable as the work of a young man of but twenty-two, but the merit lies in the execution, not, as we might think without examination, in the conception. What lay nearest at hand was Boileau's poem, "L'Art Poétique" (1674), which was translated as early as 1680, and published in 1683, with revisions by Dryden, with whose works it is commonly printed.* Naturally, at the time of the Renaissance, one of the most important questions had been how men should write, and, as we have seen, since it seemed as if the ancients had alone known the answer, the moderns had gone back to those who had spoken with the most authority. We have seen the enormous influence of Aristotle ; Horace, too, was scarcely less respected. His "Ars Poetica" held the position in regard to literature that Euclid has held in astronomy. It was in 1567 that Thomas Drant made the first English translation of that poem. About 1603, Ben Jonson made another translation † in exceedingly

---

* With English names, put in as illustrations, in place of the French ones employed by Boileau.

Cf. Oldham's Horace, "His Art of Poetry," imitated in English (1684), " putting Horace into a more modern dress, than hitherto he has appeared in—that is, by making him speak as if he were living now. I therefore resolved to alter the scene from Rome to London, and make use of English names of men, places, and customs, when the parallel would decently permit."

† *Vide* "To the Readers of Sejanus," p. 137, where he says he shall speak of ancient drama "in my observations upon Horace, his Art of

rugged verse. The first of the moderns to write a code
of laws for literature was Trissino,* the same man whose
"Sofonisba" lent such additional gloom to European tragedy. In France, there were many who taught the same
lesson. Yet, it is to be noticed, the greatest writers of
Italy and of England came before these new teachers
of the way to write. Petrarch, Boccaccio, Ariosto, like
Chaucer, Spenser, and the great Elizabethan dramatists,
owed nothing to the rigid rules which men like Trissino, Boileau, and Pope were to preach as a new gospel.
Even in France, the first fruits of the Renaissance were,
although of moderate literary value, of the same kind.
Du Bellay, Belleau, and Ronsard were first deposed by
Malherbe, and then thrown into the shade by the great
French classic writers, and were neglected until about
a century ago, when the chains were broken ; and since
then these older writers have received the praise which
is their due. The reason of this change becomes plain
on consideration. The first effect of the revival of letters was purely stimulating ; and in the place of the
meagre traditional lore, the scraps of antiquity which
formed the whole supply of the Dark Ages, there were
given them the magnificent literatures of the ancient
world, and they turned with fervor to their writing. In
their enthusiasm, they did not break loose from the Mid-

Poetry, which, with the text, I intend shortly to publish." These observations are lost. In his "Timber, or Discoveries Made upon Men and Matters," he speaks of Aristotle as a great critic, and of the need of the unity
of action in the drama, but says nothing of the other rules. They were
unknown in England at this time. They first came into England through
Dryden's praise of Bossu and Rapin.

Webbe, Puttenham, etc., make no mention of these rules, and they were
continually groping for statements of this kind.

Sidney, to be sure, had commended them in his "Defence of Poesy,"
but without effect.

dle Ages. They took the material that lay ready to the hand. In Italy, Ariosto, for instance, did not scorn the romances of chivalry. Shakspere wrote about Hamlet or Macbeth as freely as about Julius Cæsar ; it was only later that Otway found it necessary to alter the mediæval "Romeo and Juliet" into a play of ancient Rome. The early pedantic attempts to translate Greek originals, such as the Italian version of the "Œdipus,"* Dolce's "Jocasta," Gascoigne's rendering of this same "Jocasta," and Jodelle's "Cleopatre" and "Didon," clearly implied breaking allegiance to the native traditions, although there was no avowed hostility between the classic leaven and the abundant native material, such as arose later. When this first fervor died out, and people turned to books for directions about writing rather than for a sympathetic glow, the rules were deemed of the utmost importance; pedants got into power, and pseudo-classicism held full sway over the literature and taste of modern Europe. This deliberate wooden imitation of classical models was then, so to speak, the sober second-thought of the Renaissance : the first was one of delight, and it inspired great works in Italy and England ; the other followed, correcting, pruning, revising, mistaking pallid faultlessness for perfection, but yet teaching correctness and precision. All of this was, it must be remembered, for the Italians the resumption of an interrupted growth, a restoration of shattered continuity ; but elsewhere it was a foreign importation. In France, various circumstances, especially the Hundred Years' War, broke the connection between the Middle Ages and modern times, and the greater literature of that country belongs to the classical period and its legitimate successors. In England and in Spain, this movement was less marked than in

---

* By Giovanni Andrea dell' Anguillara.

. Italy, just as the earthquake that destroyed Lisbon was marked only by an unusually high tide on the English coast. We thus see more clearly the coherence of the literature of different countries the more closely we examine that of any one. They were, and are, all fellow-workers in the great task of clearing away the Middle Ages, a process not yet completed, for no new system has yet been announced which we are to obey. This has advanced by three steps, the Renaissance, the Reformation, and Revolution.* The age of Pope was in literature a time of Reformation. We need not fear to think that we are living in one of Revolution, of which the outbreak of Romanticism was but a preliminary riot. Certainly the time is ripe for it ; the present unceasing imitation of everything that has found success before shows, by its being an artistic process, that the old methods are dead, and writers cannot forever go on pretending that they are somebody else. Let us not be alarmed ; we need only to take courage from observing the groundlessness of the fears that agitated our ancestors when the school of Pope was overthrown. It seemed to them as if the world were relapsing into savagery, especially when it no longer was possible to bind up all truth in a book. There is a constant yearning of the human race to take a printed volume as the sole receptacle of truth about literature and art, and a constant discovery that this wish is unattainable. Yet here, as everywhere, other people's experience is worthless.

As to Pope's version of the poetic art, it survives as the last and best of the many manuals, as Boileau's does in France. I have mentioned Pope's predecessors. Boileau had many more.† His own "Art Poétique" is now a most

---

* Symonds, "Renaissance in Italy," v. 530.

† Eustace Deschamps (1338–1415), the "Jardin de Plaisance et les Fleurs de Rhétorique" (1547), Pierre Fabri, Th. Sébilet (1548), Jacques

readable poem in the original. Although Boileau, when charged with writing merely an imitation of Horace, replied that this was scarcely a fair statement, inasmuch as but fifty or sixty lines out of eleven thousand could be called imitations, he was inexact, because the whole poem was really founded on Horace. It was an adaptation of the Roman poet's "Ars Poetica." Pope's "Essay on Criticism," as I have said, was of the same literary family. It has been very highly praised, and it has been attacked with equal ardor. Dr. Johnson called it one of Pope's greatest works ; Warton said it was a masterpiece ; De Quincey found fault with it ; Hazlitt said it was a double-refined essence of wit and sense ; and Elwyn, his latest editor, attacks it most indiscreetly, putting

---

Pelletier (1555), Vauquelin de la Fresnaie (*cir.* 1576, published 1605), Pierre de Laudrun d'Aigalliers, Ronsard, Mlle. de Gournay, etc.; *vide* Goujet, "Bibliothèque Française," iii. 459. Vauquelin de la Fresnaie (the first French satirist) wrote in his "Art Poétique " (Œuvres, i. 90):

> "Tu peux encore faire une sorte d'ouvrage,
> Qu'on peut nommer forest ou naturel bocage :
> Qu'on fait sur le cham, en plaisir, en fureur,
> Un vers qui de la Muse est un Avancoureur
> Et que pour un sujet ou court par la carriere,
> Sans bride gallopant sur la mesme matiere,
> Poussé de la chaleur, qu'on suit à l'abandon,
> D'une grand' violence et d'un aspre randon.
>
> Stace fut le premier en la langue Romaine,
> Qui courut librement par cette large plaine.
> Comme dans les forests les arbres soustenus
> Sur les pieds naturel, sans art ainsi venus.
> Leur perruque jamais n'ayant esté coupee,
> Sont quelquefois plus beau qu'une taille serpee.
> Aussi cette façon en beauté passera
> Souvent un autre vers qui plus limé sera."

This quotation, however, does Vauquelin no justice ; he was not often so wide of the mark. See his "Idillies," liv. ii. 9, 12, and 24.

on Pope all the blame which belongs to the age in which
he lived.　It is hard not to admire the poem as a work of
art, however much we may differ in our views of the rules
he inculcates.　In execution, compare it with these lines
from the translation of Boileau :

> "Whate'er you write of pleasant or sublime,
> Always let sense accompany your rhyme :
> Falsely they seem each other to oppose ;
> Rhyme must be made with reason's laws to close :
> And when to conquer her you bend your force,
> The mind will triumph in the noble course,
> To reason's yoke she quickly will incline,
> Which, far from hurting, renders her divine :
> But if neglected will as easily stray,
> And master reason which she should obey.
> Love reason, then ; and let whate'er you write
> Borrow from her its beauty, force, and light," etc.

This is clumsy work by the side of the facile grace of
the lines with which Pope's " Essay on Criticism " * opens :

> " 'Tis hard to say if greater want of skill
> Appear in writing or in judging ill ;

---

* Of course the commentators have been over this poem ; they have
proved that where Pope wrote

> " When first young Maro in his boundless mind
> A work t'outlast immortal Rome designed,"

" the word *outlast* is improper ; for Virgil, like a true Roman, never dreamt
of the mortality of the city " (Wakefield).

More amusing is this comment :

> " Some on the leaves of ancient authors prey,
> Nor time, nor moths, e'er spoiled as much as they."

" This is a quibble.　Time and moths spoil books by destroying them.
The commentators only spoiled them by explaining them badly.　The edi-
tors were so far from spoiling books in the same sense as time, that by
multiplying copies they assisted to preserve them " (Elwyn).　With more
justice they point out obscure and prosaic lines.

But of the two less dangerous is th' offence
To tire our patience than mislead our sense.
Some few in that, but numbers err in this,
Ten censure wrong for one who writes amiss;
A fool might once alone himself expose,
Now one in verse makes many more in prose.
　'Tis with our judgments, as our watches, none
Go just alike, yet each believes his own;
In poets as true genius is but rare,
True taste as seldom is the critic's share," etc.

The "Windsor Forest" (published in 1715) need not occupy our attention. Yet Wordsworth, in one of his prefaces, reprinted in the second volume of his prose works, where he assaulted the literature of the time we are now considering, said that, "excepting the 'Nocturnal Reverie'* of Lady Winchelsea, and a passage or two

---

* For Lady Winchelsea, *vide* Ward's "English Poets," iiL 27:

"In such a night, when every louder wind
Is to its distant cavern safe confined,
And only gentle Zephyr fans his wings,
And lonely Philomel, still waking, sings,
Or from some tree, framed for the owl's delight,
She hollowing clear, directs the wanderer right,—
In such a night, when passing clouds give place,
Or thinly veil the heaven's mysterious face,
When in some river, overhung with green,
The waving moon and trembling leaves are seen,
When freshened grass now bears itself upright,
And makes cool banks to pleasing rest invite,
Whence spring the woodbine and the bramble-rose,
And where the sleepy cowslip sheltered grows,
Whilst now a paler hue the foxglove takes,
Yet chequers still with red the dusky brakes,
Where scattered glow-worms,—but in twilight fine,—
Shew trivial beauties, watch their hour to shine,
While Salisbury stands the test of every light,
In perfect charms and perfect beauty bright;

in the 'Windsor Forest' of Pope, the poetry of the period intervening between the publication of the 'Paradise Lost' and the 'Seasons' does not contain a single new image of external nature, and scarcely presents a familiar one from which it can be inferred that the eye of the poet has been steadily fixed upon his object, much less that his feelings had urged him to work upon it in the spirit of genuine imagination." It is not easy to decide what are the

> When odours, which declined repelling day,
> Through temperate air uninterrupted stray;
> When darkened groves their softest shadows wear,
> And falling waters we distinctly hear;
> When through the gloom more venerable shows
> Some ancient fabric awful in repose;
> While sunburned hills their swarthy looks conceal,
> And swelling haycocks thicken up the vale;
> When the loosed horse now, as his pasture leads,
> Comes slowly grazing through the adjoining meads,
> Whose stealing pace and lengthened shade we fear,
> Till torn-up forage in his teeth we hear;
> When nibbling sheep at large pursue their food,
> And unmolested kine rechew the cud;
> When curlews cry beneath the village walls,
> And to her straggling brood the partridge calls;
> Their short-lived jubilee the creatures keep,
> Which but endures, whilst tyrant man doth sleep;
> When a sedate content the spirit feels,
> And no fierce light disturbs, whilst it reveals;
> But silent musings urge the mind to seek
> Something too high for syllables to speak;
> Till the free soul to a composedness charmed,
> Finding the elements of rage disarmed,
> O'er all below a solemn quiet grown,
> Joys in the inferior world, and thinks it like her own;
> In such a night let me abroad remain,
> Till morning breaks and all's confused again;
> Our cares, our toils, our clamours are renewed,
> Our pleasures, seldom reached, again pursued."

passages in the " Windsor Forest " that he meant. Gray, one might say, should be excluded from this condemnation. Parnell,* too, was, in his way, a new voice.

---

* Parnell is the first of the school of Young and Blair; *vide* his " Night-Piece on Death."

Goldsmith, in his "Life of Parnell," *cir.* 1763, says: "It is indeed amazing, after what has been done by Dryden, Addison, and Pope, to improve and harmonize our native tongue, that their successors should have taken pains to involve it into pristine barbarity. These misguided innovators have not been content with restoring antiquated words and phrases, but have indulged themselves in the most licentious transpositions, and the harshest constructions, vainly imagining, that the more their writings are unlike prose, the more they resemble poetry. They have adopted a language of their own, and call upon mankind for admiration. All those who do not understand them are silent, and those who make out their meaning are willing to praise, to show they understand. From these . . . affectations the poems of Parnell are entirely free." The " Night-Piece," he says, " deserves every praise; and I should suppose, with very little amendment, might be made to surpass all those night-pieces and church-yard scenes that have since appeared."

Yet, in the Elizabethan period, which, as a friend of mine suggests, held the various characteristic traits of later times in solution, we find examples of this quality, as in Fletcher's

> " Hence, all you vain delights,
>   As short as are the nights
>   Wherein you spend your folly!
> There's nought in this life sweet,
> If man were wise to see 't,
>   But only melancholy,
>   Oh, sweetest melancholy!
> Welcome, folded arms, and fixed eyes,
> A sight that piercing mortifies!
> A look that's fastened to the ground,
> A tongue chain'd up without a sound!
> Fountain heads, and pathless groves,
> Places which pale passion loves!
> Moonlight walks, when all the fowls
> Are warmly housed, save bats and owls!

The "Rape of the Lock" (1712, and enlarged, 1714) has been praised very highly, and is generally much admired. De Quincey calls it "the most exquisite monument of playful fancy that universal literature offers." Hazlitt: it "is the most exquisite filigree work ever invented. . . . It is the perfection of the mock heroic;" and many echoing forms of this commendation may be accumulated by the curious. Yet, it would seem as if it was only when the heroic is admired that the mock-heroic can be fully appreciated, and if one goes the other must go with it. However this may be, I may as well own frankly that I am unable to admire the poem. It is, of course, clever, but I fail to get such delight from its lines as has rewarded the eminent men who have written about it. It is impossible to avoid the thought that patriotism is in part the cause of this admiration. Warton says ("Elwyn," ii. 116) : "If some of the most candid among the French critics begin to acknowledge that they have produced nothing in point of sublimity and majesty equal to the 'Paradise Lost,' we may also venture to affirm that in point of delicacy, elegance, and fine-turned raillery, on which they have so much valued themselves, they have produced nothing equal to the 'Rape of the Lock.'" The French speak with equal enthusiasm of Boileau's "Le Lutrin" (1674), and every new Italian editor of Tassoni's "La Secchia Rapita" (1624) proceeds at once to demolishing Boileau's pretensions.* The Italian poem is long,

---

A midnight bell, a parting groan !
These are the sounds we feed upon ;
 Then stretch your bones in a still gloomy valley,
 Nothing's so dainty sweet as lovely melancholy."

* La Harpe, in reviewing a French translation of Pope's works, says : "'Le Lutrin' est un chef d'œuvre poétique, une de ces creations du grand talent, dans laquelle il a su faire beaucoup dè rien." On the other hand,

consisting of twelve cantos of about sixty stanzas each, and narrates imaginary wars, with an abundance of denunciations of the author's enemies; Boileau's mock-heroic, in describing the controversy over the proper place for a reading-desk, blames several common ecclesiastical faults, and Pope's is too well known to need describing. If the French have never written anything superior in delicacy and fine-turned raillery to this poem, then their literature has not done them justice.

This passage is pleasing enough, where Ariel, the chief of the sylphs, says:

> " Our humbler province is to tend the fair,
>
> *   *   *   *   *
>
> To save the powder from too rude a gale,
> Nor let th' imprisoned essences exhale;
> To draw fresh colours from the vernal flowers;
> To steal from rainbows ere they drop in showers
> The brightest wash; to curl their waving hairs,
> Assist their blushes, and inspire their airs;
> Nay oft, in dreams, invention we bestow,
> To change a flounce or add a furbelow."

But whatever levity there may be here, it disappears, and the smile that accompanies it gives way to an unpleasant leer, when we come to such heavy-handed social satire as this:

> " Whether the nymph shall break Diana's law,
> Or some frail china-jar receive a flaw;
> Or stain her honour, or her new brocade;
> Forget her prayers, or miss a masquerade."

Yet, barring these faults, it is certainly an agreeable squib. It was first written without any mention of the sylphs; these were an afterthought. Some critics find a

---

one may examine the " Rape of the Lock," " et l'on verra cinq chants absolument dénuées d'action, de caractères, de mouvement, d'intérêt, d'idées, et de variété."

close connection between them and the fairies in the
"Tempest ;" they say that it is a very appropriate continuation of Shakspere's fairy-land, which may mean that
the description of them in this poem is something like
what Shakspere would have written had he lived in the
more prosaic age. This is, of course, a question which
no one can answer with certainty, but there is room for
modest doubt. Fairies do not follow the fashions ; when
hoops and patches come in, wings do not necessarily go
out, and I find it hard to trace any family connection between

> " Come unto these yellow sands,
>   And then take hands :
>   Courtesied when you have and kissed
>   The wild waves whist
>   Foot it featly here and there," etc.,

and

> " Know then unnumbered spirits round thee ply,
>   The light militia of the lower sky :
>   These, the unseen, are ever on the wing,
>   Hang o'er the box, and hover round the ring," etc.

And this is not merely saying, what needs not to be
said, that Pope is not Shakspere; there is an absolute lack
of resemblance between the imagination of the one and
the artificial invention of the other. Pope's sylphs lend
the charm of cleverness to his verse, and any further claim
in their behalf seems to me monstrous. Still, a poem may
be less good than Shakspere's best passages, and yet have
merit ; and, if we do not try to rate the " Rape of the
Lock " too high, it will be possible to enjoy it. We
should laugh at a Frenchman who maintained that Boileau's mock-heroic was to be compared with Shakspere's
poetical songs. No one could entertain the notion for a
moment, yet there is no wide difference between Boileau
and Pope here ; each is able, in his own way, and as con-

temporaries — for contemporaneousness does not always follow the dates of the almanac any more than isothermal lines do parallels of latitude—they were inspired by the same subjects. This, too, is to be borne in mind with regard to alleged imitations of one poet by another. Because one nation does at some time what another did a few years earlier, it by no means follows that it is inspired by imitation, any more than does the fact that I, who put on my thick coat day before yesterday, had any desire, conscious or unconscious, of imitating my fellow-countryman in Chicago who put his on two days earlier. He was the first to be exposed to the northwest blast, that is all. Of course, one nation may impose its authority on another by virtue of its success ; thus, the brilliant civilization of Italy made its literary tenets only the more authoritative, but the movement spread, too, as the natural effort to find something to take the place of the enthusiasm of the Renaissance. They tried to arrange their knowledge, and they made it an idol to which almost everything was sacrificed. It seems not to be worth while, then, to trace the lineage of the mock-heroic poems. They were as natural as shadows. Given the heroic, and the mock-heroic follows; the parody following the original as night follows day.

This work brought Pope a great deal of fame, although it added but little to his wealth. He had also published his translation of the first book of Statius, some versions of Chaucer in imitation of Dryden, his " Eloisa to Abelard," " Sappho to Phaon," etc., but he was far from rich. His father had a fortune of about £10,000, and when he died, in 1717, he left his son an income of three or four hundred pounds ; but Catholics paid double taxes, and probably there was a good deal of fanatic zeal in the way these taxes were assessed and collected. We have seen that Pope had nothing to do with government aid to authors. Most writers of the time published their books by subscription,* with flattering dedications. Pope now cast about for some way of securing independence by his literary labors. He determined to make a translation of the "Iliad." The booksellers made generous offers, and Pope accepted that of Lintot,† who proposed that the book be sold by subscription, he himself undertaking to supply each subscriber with his copies, to bring the work out in six volumes quarto, and to pay to Pope all the product of the subscription and, besides, £200 for each volume. He, of course, reserved for himself the profits of the succeeding editions, and on these he grew rich and was able to leave a valuable property for his heirs. There were five hundred and seventy-five subscribers, who took six hundred and fifty-four copies, so that Pope received £5320 4s. The success of this venture emboldened him to undertake the translation of the "Odyssey," which he accomplished with the aid of two young assistants, Browne and Fenton. For the two poems he received £9000—over £3500 for the "Odyssey," after paying Browne £500 for doing eight books and notes, though he declared, in a note, that he had done but three; to Fenton £200. He did four, but confessed to only two. This is the first instance of a large sum being paid to an author for his work, and it may be compared with the £1200 or £1300 paid Dryden for his "Virgil."

This success made Pope's position secure. The ten years' work made him a rich man, entirely independent of the government and of patrons. As we have seen, in the

---

* The 1688 edition of Milton was one of the first books published in this way. Dryden's "Virgil" and the volumes of the *Tatler* were also published by subscription.

† For Tonson, he undertook an annotated edition of Shakspere, also published by subscription.

condition of things at that time, this was most fortunate. For an additional proof listen to these lines of Swift's, from his "Libel on the Rev. Dr. Delany and Lord Carteret" (1729), ii. 89 :

> " Deluded mortals ! whom the great
> Choose for companions *tête-à-tête ;*
> Who, at their dinners, *en famille,*
> Get leave to sit whenc'er you will,
> Then boasting tell us where you dined,
> And how his Lordship was so kind ;
> How many pleasant things he spoke,
> And how you laughed at every joke ;
> Swear he's a most facetious man,
> That you and he are cup and can ;
> You travel with a heavy load,
> And quite mistake preferment's road.
> Suppose my Lord and you alone,
> Hint the least interest of your own ;
> His visage drops, he knits his brow,
> He cannot talk of business now :
> Or mention but a vacant post,
> He'll turn it off with, ' Name your toast :'
> Nor could the nicest artist paint
> A countenance with more constraint.
>
>   *   *   *   *
>
> When wearied with intrigue of state
> They find an idle hour to prate,
> Then should you dare to ask a place,
> You forfeit all your patron's grace,
> And disappoint the sole design
> For which he summoned you to dine.
> Thus Congreve spent in writing plays,
> And one poor office * half his days ;
> While Montague, who claimed the station
> To be Mæcenas of the nation,
> For poets open table kept,
> But ne'er considered where they slept :

---

* Commissioner for licensing coaches.

Himself as rich as fifty Jews
Was easy though they wanted shoes.

    *   *   *   *

Thus Steele, who own'd what others writ,
And flourish'd by imputed wit,
From perils of a hundred jails,
Withdrew to starve and die in Wales.
Thus Gay, the Hare with many friends,
Twice seven long years the Court attends;
Who under Tales conveying truth,
To virtue form'd a princely youth : *
Who paid his courtship with the crowd
As far as modest pride allowed;
Rejects a servile usher's † place,
And leaves St. James's in disgrace.
Thus Addison, by lords caressed,
Was left in foreign lands distressed;
Forgot at home, became for hire
A travelling tutor to a squire;
But wisely left the Muses' hill,
To business shaped the poet's quill;
Let all his barren laurels fade :
Took up himself the courtier's trade,
And, grown a minister of state,
Saw poets at his levee wait.
Hail, happy Pope! whose generous mind
Detesting all the statesmen kind,
Contemning courts, at courts unseen,
Refus'd the visits of a queen.
A soul with every virtue fraught,
By sages, priests, or poets taught;
Whose filial piety excels
Whatever Grecian story tells ;
A genius for all stations fit,
Whose meanest talent is his wit;
His heart too great, though fortune little,
To lick a rascal statesman's spittle;

---

* The young Duke of Cumberland (1726).
† Gentleman usher to the Princess Louisa.

Appealing to the nation's taste,
Above the reach of want is placed;
By Homer dead was taught to thrive,
Which Homer never could alive;
And sits aloft on Pindus' head,
Despising slaves that cringe for bread."

The rest of the poem is worth reading, for what it shows us of Swift's experience with courts.* Swift had been of

---

* " True politicians only pay
For solid work, but not for play;
Nor ever choose to work with tools
Forged up in colleges and schools:
Consider how much more is due
To all their journeymen than you.
At table you can Horace quote,
They at a pinch can bribe a vote:
You show your skill in Grecian story,
But they can manage Whig and Tory:
You as a critic are so curious
To find a line in Virgil spurious;
But they can smoke the deep designs,
When Bolingbroke with Pulteney dines.
Besides, your patron may upbraid ye,
That you have got a place already;
An office for your talents fit,
To flatter, carve and show your wit,
To snuff the lights, and stir the fire,
And get a dinner for your hire.
What claim have you to place or pension?
He overpays in condescension."

Then, after some bitter words on Walpole, he goes on:

" But I, . . .
Can lend you an allusion fitter:
*   *   *   *
' Go to affect a monarch's ends.
From hell a viceroy-devil ascends,—
His budget with corruptions crammed,
The contributions of the damned,

great service to Pope at the beginning of his translation in the way of getting him subscribers, for he was at that time of great influence. "He instructed a young nobleman that the best poet in England was Mr. Pope, a Papist, who had begun a Homer into English verse, for which, he must have them all subscribe, 'for,' says he, 'the author shall not 'begin to print, till I have a thousand guineas for him.'" You will notice that, at the beginning of the collection of subscribers, Oxford and Bolingbroke were in power, and Swift was their strongest ally in the press. When the first volume appeared, 1715, Bolingbroke was in exile, Oxford under impeachment, Swift in angry retirement at his deanery. Yet Pope managed to keep out of political storms. He was careful in this part of his life not to ally himself with one party, and he kept himself free from compromising dedications, from principle and doubtless from policy. In No. 4 of the *Guardian*, as I have said, he denounced the servility which many literary men showed in the letters of dedication, saying : "This prostitution of praise is not only a deceit upon the gross of mankind, who take their notion of characters from the learned, but also the better sort must by this means lose some part at least of that desire of fame which is the incentive to generous actions. . . . Even truth itself in a dedication is like

---

Which, with unsparing hand, he strows
Through courts and senates as he goes,
And then at Beelzebub's black hall
Complains his budget was too small.'
Your simile may better shine
In verse, but there is truth in mine;
For no imaginable things
Can differ more than gods and kings,
And statesmen by ten thousand odds
Are angels just as kings are gods."

an honest man in a disguise or vizor-mask, and will appear a cheat by being dressed so like one. Though the merit of the person is beyond dispute, I see no reason that because one man is eminent, therefore another has a right to be impertinent, and throw praises in his face," etc., etc.

When the "Iliad" was finished, with the sixth volume in 1720, Pope dedicated it to neither Whigs nor Tories, who had been equally civil to him, but to Congreve, thus exhibiting an honorable neutrality. Before this time, to be sure, Steele had dedicated "The Tender Husband" to Addison, 1705, and Gay, 1713, his "Rural Sports" to Pope, but these were less important. The "Iliad" was, one may almost say, a publication of importance to the whole nation. In his preface, too, which appeared in the first volume in 1715, he paid compliments not only to men of various sorts, but also of different parties. "Mr. Addison was the first whose advice determined me to undertake this task; who was pleased to write to me on that occasion in such terms as I cannot repeat without vanity. I was obliged to Sir Richard Steele for a very early recommendation of my work to the public. Dr. Swift promoted my interest with that warmth with which he always serves a friend. The humanity and frankness of Sir Samuel Garth are what I never knew wanting on any occasion. I must acknowledge, with infinite pleasure, the many friendly offices, as well as sincere criticisms of Mr. Congreve." "I must add the names of Mr. Rowe, and Dr. Parnell." "But what can I say of the honor so many of the great have done me." "His grace the Duke of Buckingham." "The Earl of Halifax was one of the first to favor me; of whom it is hard to say whether the advancement of the polite arts is more owing to his generosity or his example." "Such a genius as my Lord Bolingbroke, not more distinguished in the great scenes of business, than in all the useful and entertaining parts of learning, has not refused to be the critic of these sheets and the patron of their writer; and that the noble author of the tragedy of 'Heroic Love,' George Granville, Lord Lansdowne, has continued his partiality to me, from my writing pastorals to my attempting the Iliad." And the list might be made longer.

Of the translation itself I shall not speak at any length. We have already taken into consideration the style of this period, contrasting it with that which it succeeded. There we saw how every period demands its own translation of the great masterpieces of antiquity and other nations; and we compared Pope's work with Chapman's, and that of the many of the present time. I may add here, that the number of the competitors for our favor is another proof of the unsettled condition of literature. We are all trying over the old methods in the lack of any great present inspiration which shall sweep everything before it. Since we see nothing in the present, our attention naturally reverts to the past, and we try to be as simple as the ballad-writers, or like Chaucer, or Milton, or to rival Pope —*quot homines tot sententiæ.* Moreover, the tendency towards prose translations is in obedience to the dictates of precise scholarship, and the general despair of ever finding a satisfactory poetical form. In Pope's time, there was no doubt about the poetical form to be adopted, and Chapman had his choice of all the metres.

III. When the translation was finished Pope found himself a rich man. He bought, in 1719, his famous place at Twickenham, which, as Walpole said, he " twisted and twirled and rhymed and harmonized," " till it appeared two or three sweet little lawns, opening and opening beyond one another, and the whole surrounded with impenetrable woods." His life here is to be found described

in Mr. Leslie Stephen's volume in the "English Men of
Letter Series." I will only say here that he lived in comfort, or, as he put it,

"... thanks to Homer since I live and thrive,
　Indebted to no Prince or Peer alive."

Yet he saw princes and peers in abundance. Indeed,
he is said to have fallen asleep at his own table when the
Prince of Wales was talking to him, and many of the
most eminent men of England were numbered among his
guests. Such were Swift, Gay, Atterbury, Arbuthnot;
politicians like Bolingbroke, Murray, Lyttelton, Wyndham,
Lord Oxford, Lord Peterborough, etc. Later we shall
find Pope's exultation over the joys of life as he tasted
them at his villa. Yet he was not happy, and the cause
of his unhappiness was his detestation of the poor writers
of his time. This detestation he put into verse, and the
"Dunciad" has secured the unhoped-for immortality of
numerous petty writers of the first half of the last century.
Whether they were worth the pains that were taken to
demolish them, is an open question. The poem is one of
the English classics, and has been highly praised by numerous critics, yet the impression that it leaves on the
reader is not a pleasant one. Pope would have resented
the notion that he was not a civilized writer, yet here we
find him indulging in abuse of all sorts of persons, most
of them to the last degree insignificant, and those who
were of importance were unjustly attacked. Yet, good or
bad, even granting that they were all bad, Pope's temper
in this poem is exactly that of the furious pamphleteers
whom he wished to depose, of the hack-writers whom he
never looked upon as fellow-beings. It has been remarked
by the wise that the foolish are not yet extinct—still the
world has found a *modus vivendi* with these people, and
has learned at any rate to observe them without excessive

loss of temper.　They are now as vexatious, annoying, and pretentious as they were in Pope's time, yet what should we think of a man who devoted the best years of his life to abusing them?　Disproportionate anger is as unfortunate as disproportionate enthusiasm, and Pope's fury against incompetence and foolishness is very far from the temper with which a man of the world, a truly civilized person, regards these inevitable qualities.　If he had been galled by seeing folly rewarded, incapacity triumphant, there might have been some excuse, but even then anger would not be becoming; as it was, however, he, the leading literary man of England, one might say of Europe, went out of his way to attack a number of wretched, scribbling starvelings, to ridicule some whose only fault was inability to do anything, and to denounce others whom he should have had the intelligence to rate higher.　Pope had done much to raise the tone of litera-ture; he had taught authors how they might break with servility and rise to independence, and then at last he made use of the position he had acquired with much honor to throw discredit on letters, not so much by exposing petty men as by degrading himself to something near their level.　This, of course, does not apply to the execu-tion of his work, but to the rude, brutal spirit that ani-mated it.　Thus in the second book, when, a monarch of Dulness having been chosen, games are instituted in his honor—for, like everything else, the humor is heroic and pseudo-classical.　Some of the games are simply disgust-ing, but one of the least objectionable is thus described: Dulness with her court descends

> " To where Fleet Ditch with disemboguing streams
> Rolls the large tribute of dead dogs to Thames,
> The king of dykes than whom no sluice of mud
> With deeper sable blots the silver flood.

' Here strip, my children ! here at once leap in,
Here prove who best can dash thro' thick and thin,
And who the most in love of dirt excel,
Or dark dexterity of groping well,' " etc.

Here is the description of some who sought the prize,
"a pig of lead to him who dives the best :"

"Next plunged a feeble, but a desp'rate pack,
With each a sickly brother at his back :
Sons of a day ! just buoyant on the flood,
Then numbered with the puppies in the mud.
Ask ye their names ?   I could as soon disclose
The names of these blind puppies as of those."

Literature is scarcely honored by such support as this.

Pope always maintained that the provocation came
from his enemies, and certainly they had adopted enraging
measures.   They said of him, " he is one whom God and
nature have marked for want of common honesty ;" "great
fools will be christened by the names of great poets, and
Pope will be called Homer ;" "a little abject thing," and
this gem : " Let us take the initial letter of his Christian
name, and the initial and final letters of his surname, viz.,
A, P, E, and they give you the same idea of an Ape as
his face." "A squab short gentleman—a little creature
that, like the frog in the fable, swells and is angry that it
is not allowed to be as big as an ox." Yet this was but a
part of the regular language of the critics of the day, and
called for no especial answer, certainly no answer in kind.
Dryden had been called an ape, an ass, a frog, a coward, a
knave, a fool and a thing in very much such language as
that used about Pope.   Thus, "Poet squab endured with
Poet Maro's spirit ! an ugly croaking kind of vermin
which would swell to the bulk of an ox." These were the
words of Luke Milbourne, a persistent foe of Dryden, but
how did Dryden answer him ?   In the preface to his

"Fables " (" Versions of Chaucer, Boccaccio, and Ovid "),
we find this passage :

"As a corollary to this preface, in which I have done
justice to others, I owe somewhat to myself : not that I
think it worth my time to enter the lists with one Milbourn and one Blackmore, but barely to take notice that
such men there are who have written scurrilously against
me, without any provocation. Milbourn, who is in orders,
pretends amongst the rest this quarrel to me, that I have
fallen foul on priesthood : if I have, I am only to ask pardon of good priests, and am afraid his part of the repara-
tion will come to little. Let him be satisfied that he shall
not be able to force himself upon me for an adversary. I
contemn him too much to enter into competition with him.
His own translations of Virgil have answered his criticisms
on mine. If (as they say, he has declared in print) he prefers the version of Ogilby to mine, the world has made
him the same compliment ; for it is agreed on all hands,
that he writes even below Ogilby : that, you will say, is
not easily to be done ; but what cannot Milbourn bring
about ? I am satisfied, however, that while he and I live
together, I shall not be thought the worst poet of the age.
It looks as if I had desired him underhand to write so ill
against me ; but upon my honest word I have not bribed
him to do me this service, and am wholly guiltless of his
pamphlet. 'Tis true, I should be glad, if I could persuade
him to continue his good offices, and write such another
critique on anything of mine : for I find by experience he
has a great stroke with the reader, when he condemns any
of my poems, to make the world have a better opinion of
them. He has taken some pains with my poetry ; but nobody will be persuaded to take the same with his. If I
had taken to the church (as he affirms, but which was
never in my thoughts) I should have had more sense, if

not more grace, than to have turned myself out of my benefice by writing libels on my parishioners.—But his account of my manners and my principles are of a piece with his cavils and his poetry : and so I have done with him for ever."

Certainly this disposes of Milbourne more completely than does Pope's resuscitation of him, and his new vengeance in the "Dunciad," when he adorns Smedley, the successful diver, with cassock, surcingle, and vest :

> " ' Receive,' he said, ' these robes which once were mine,
> Dulness is sacred in a sound divine.' " *

Yet Dryden had shown his power of using verse as a means of attack, and notably in the three lines of brief description of his publisher, Tonson, which he wrote when that gentleman had refused him an advance of money :

> " With leering looks, bull-faced, and freckled fair,
> With two left legs, and Judas-coloured † hair,
> And frowsy pores, that taint the ambient air."

"Tell the dog," Dryden said to the messenger, "that he who wrote these can write more." But these were sufficient. In his "Mac Flecknoe," Dryden set the example of the satirical poem which Pope afterwards followed, and in the second part of the "Absalom and Achitophel" he resumed the attack on Shadwell ; but Dryden, in all his attacks, preserved his self-possession, his superiority to his subject,

---

* *Vide* Renan: "Il y a chez lui (Lammenais) trop de colère et pas assez de dédain. Les conséquences littéraires de ce défaut sont fort graves. La colère amène la déclamation, et le mauvais gout ; le dédain, au contraire, produit presque toujours un style délicat. La colère a besoin d'être partagée ; elle est indiscrète, car elle veut se communiquer. Le dédain est une fine et délicieuse volupté qu'on savoure à soi seul ; il est discret, car il se suffit " (" Essais de Morale et de Critique," p. 188).

† "Amboyna," act i. sc. i., Beaumont says : "I do not like his oath, there's treachery in that Judas-colour'd Beard."

while Pope lost his. For Dryden's coarseness in some parts of his denunciation of his foes there is more excuse than for Pope's, which is less robust, and less to be pardoned by consideration of the usual language of the time. Dryden retained his superiority to his victims, Pope lowered himself to ribaldry. Dryden, as I said, maintained his self-possession, and any loss of self-possession is fatal, or at least injurious, to artistic performance. We do not want the actor,* by excess of emotion, to become speechless when he should be speaking, or the lyric poet to burst into prose, or the painter to be blinded by tears so that he cannot distinguish his colors; and especially are we repelled when a great man gives way in public to undue wrath. There is nothing dignified in anger, there is dignity in self-control; and the reader of the "Dunciad" is sure to be struck by the curious exhibition it offers us of Pope's state of mind concerning paltry writers, who only needed to be neglected to perish.

All the satirical writers of France and England write with a certain violence, as if they composed their verses to the inspiration of the beating of a bass-drum; but here we have the additional fire of wrath with unworthy objects. It will be fairer, however, to judge of this from the study of the evidence. We shall then find, as in nearly all that Pope wrote, abundant example of his wit and ingenuity. Dryden, it will be remembered, celebrates the appointment of Elkanah Shadwell as Flecknoe's successor on the throne of the kingdom of Dulness, and he describes the ceremonies at his coronation. Pope chose for his successor Theobald, the first writer on Shakspere who took the pains of studying the contemporary literature. Pope

---

* *Vide* Diderot, "Paradoxe," viii. 384, and Lessing, "Hamburger Dramaturgie" (3tes Stück). Mrs. Kemble has also some interesting remarks on the subject in her "Records of a Girlhood," p. 246.

had himself prepared an edition of Shakspere ; it appeared in six large quarto volumes, for which Pope received £217 12s. The work was sold at first for a guinea a volume, but out of the seven hundred and fifty copies printed one hundred and forty remained unsold, and were disposed of at 16s. apiece. Pope's work as an editor was valueless. He, to be sure, said some good things in his preface,* where he gave evidence of very sincere and warm admiration for Shakspere. His plays, compared with those of modern times, are, he says, like an "ancient, majestic piece of Gothick architecture, compared with a neat modern building : the latter is more elegant and glaring, but the former is more strong and more solemn." His emendations are worthless. Thus he is amazed by Shakspere's frequent use of the double comparative, as "more better," which Theobald showed was not a misreading ; and the best proof of Theobald's accuracy, though he did not go far, is this, that Warburton, Pope's editor and admirer, accepted many of his suggestions in the revision of Pope's edition. Pope, too, marked with quotation-marks all the lines that seemed to him particularly fine. Theobald naturally incurred Pope's particular hostility by criticising his Shakspere, and was first chosen for the favorite of Dulness ; but afterwards, in a later edition (1743), he was deposed and Colley Cibber was put in his place. Cibber was a writer of light and somewhat amusing plays, and of an 'Apology' for his own life, which is still entertaining. As Mr. Leslie Stephen states it : "Pope owed him a grudge. Cibber, in playing the 'Rehearsal,' had introduced some ridicule of the unlucky 'Three Hours after Marriage.' Pope, he says, came behind the scenes foaming and choking with fury, and forbidding Cibber ever to repeat

---

* "To judge, therefore, of Shakespeare by Aristotle's rules is like trying a man by the laws of one country who acted under those of another."

the insult. Cibber laughed at him, said that he would repeat it as long as the 'Rehearsal' was played, and kept
his word. Pope took his revenge by many incidental hits
at Cibber, and Cibber made a good-humoured reference to
this abuse in the 'Apology.' Thereupon Pope, in the new
'Dunciad,' described him as laughing on the lap of the
goddess, and added various personalities in the notes.
Cibber straightway published a letter to Pope, the more
cutting because still in perfect good-humour, and told the
story about the original quarrel. He added an irritating
anecdote in order to provoke the poet still further. . . .
The two Richardsons once found Pope reading one of
Cibber's pamphlets. He said, ' These things are my diversion ;' but they saw his features writhing with anguish,
and young Richardson, as they went home, observed to
his father that he hoped to be preserved from such diver-
sions as Pope had enjoyed." The change showed more
bad temper than judgment. Theobald, although chosen
for an unworthy motive, was undeniably dull, but Cibber,
who was selected for the same reason, was certainly not
dull. If he had been, he would have been overlooked. To
us of a later generation, there is not only a feeling of disappointment in seeing this man of genius killing flies with
fury, there is also a wearisome monotony about the flies
he has killed, as we see them pinned to the pages of the
"Dunciad." Shoals of notes are necessary to explain who
Smedley is, who Concanen, who Osborne, who Arnall, and
when we have learned who they all are we cannot care for
the uninteresting collection. Doubtless the buzz of this
one, or the persistent return of the other to the galled
spot, was enraging, but there is little profit for us in hearing how this one infuriated Pope, or what a torment the
other was. Two lines are devoted to one man, named
Ralph—

> " Silence, ye wolves, while Ralph to Cynthia howls,
> And makes night hideous ; answer him, ye owls,"—

whose early attempts at writing poetry are mentioned in
Franklin's too brief autobiography. Bentley, who was a
great scholar — indeed, one of the last of great English
scholars—is attacked as if he were wretchedly incompe-
tent, and put in the same line with the other men who
were really worthless. I have spoken of the first two
books ; in the third is a description of the impending rule
of dulness over the world, and especially over Great Britain (ii. 178). The fourth book was added under Warburton's influence. It turned to ridicule pedants and people
interested in collecting memorials of the past, a pursuit
that was then looked upon as proof of a morbid taste ; but
it is confused, and, to our thinking, it shares the fault it
denounces by being dull. The book and the poem ends
with the famous apostrophe, which Pope could not repeat
without emotion, and which has been warmly admired by
Dr. Johnson and Thackeray. Thackeray, indeed, went so
far as to say " no poet's verse ever mounted higher than
that wonderful flight with which the 'Dunciad' concludes :"

> " She comes, she comes ! the sable throne behold
> Of night primeval and of chaos old," etc. (ii. 199).

Certainly such praise seems strange. I will not go into
any description of the torrent of abuse which this poem,
not unnaturally, brought down on Pope's head. Many of
the people whom he attacked retorted in kind, and literature was still further defiled by a multitude of squibs in
denunciation of this abusive poet. As we have seen, the
poem occupied him more or less for nearly the last twenty
years of his life, and Pope was continually adding new
names and new notes to this Rogues' Gallery, proving that
the other boy began the quarrel, and urging that other

poets of acknowledged fame had also risen in their might against their persecutors, but none of them had so far shared the errors he condemned as Pope did. Boileau had spoken with severity, and Régnier with frankness, but neither with the cold grossness which mars the "Dunciad," which, in spite of its occasional clever lines, is a blot on the literature of the time—a proof of the thinness of the polish on which they prided themselves. There breathes through the poem not merely Swift's coarseness, but the brutal spirit which darkens the middle of the last century —the same thing which stained the comedy of the Restoration, faded away under Addison's influence, and appeared again here, and in some of the novels of the period that was then opening. The whole movement in England towards this pseudo-classicism did not properly agree with the conditions of the native English spirit. We have seen how in Addison it was an artificial rule imposing on a man of the best natural taste, and in Pope's "Dunciad" it showed most lamentably its incapacity to purge the Englishman of his innate tendencies. The proper home—by adoption, to be sure—of the whole change was France. It was an exotic in England.

IV. Yet what England failed to attain in literary polish—and Pope cannot be said to be wanting in this—it made up in the acquisition of certain things which were of more importance in the development of civilization. The freedom which England won by the Revolution of 1688 made it the home of philosophical thought. France and England were at that time the leading intellectual centres of Europe, and so of the world. Italy was sunk in sloth and intellectual torpor. Between 1450 and 1525 it had discovered the glories of Greek art and literature, and had communicated its knowledge to Europe. What the Renaissance in Italy did was to re-establish the dignity, the importance of human nature, and to break with the absolutism of the Middle Ages. Before its splendor ceased, it, as we saw, fell to worshipping Latin models, and it taught this less important lesson to neighboring countries. Then, as an Italian writer, Algarotti, said of his nation, "the one who had got up early before the others, and drudged a good deal, might rest somewhat in the daytime." But the artistic enjoyment of life that fascinated Italy was followed by a strong reaction in favor of authority, and this was most strongly expressed by Spain, where the literary rules which arose in Italy took the least hold on the writers. Spain, by means of the Jesuitism which was the Catholic counter-wave to the Reformation, asserted the divine right of monarchy, and freedom was crushed out of the greater part of Europe. As Hillebrand * says, "Think of the difference between the mediæval conception of sovereignty and the one which was the soul of Louis XIV., nay, even of the Protestant James I. of England, and down to the smallest German and Italian princelings of that time ; between the vanity of the feudal royalty of the Middle Ages, with its almost independent vassals, and the uniformity of the modern monarchy with its passive obedience and its *l'État c'est moi.*" The failure of the Spanish Armada in 1588 preserved the freedom of England from the direct yoke of Spain, and although its literary influence, as we have seen it in Euphuism, and in the long romances, was considerable—and, for that matter, we shall soon see it again when we come to study the origin of the English novel—in England the absolutism of monarchs was completely overthrown by the revolution of 1688. England remained free to scientific workmen, and freedom is the very breath of

---

* *Vide* his invaluable "History of German Thought" (Amer. ed.), p. 10 et seq.

scientific work. The English philosophy, from Bacon to
Newton and Locke, was what inspired the French literature of the last century. In England itself it had less
influence on the literature. Various causes combined to
bring about this result. For one thing, all the most famous French writers of the last century were interested
in philosophy, and they carried out the English notions
with a relentless logic that soon transported them into a
sort of pure ether out of a world which has no such easy
solution for its problems as logic, while in England the
test of suitability of the philosophy to practical affairs
was continually applied. Another interesting contribution to literature from England was the appearance, early
in the last century, of the love of nature which we shall
soon begin to trace, and the assertion of the people, as
distinguished from a literary circle, in literature. The
pseudo-classicism which we have been studying did not
recognize anything but a cultivated class. Literature was
a freemasonry of which the founders were Horace and an
imaginary Aristotle. The populace was merely a dim
background against which were to be seen kings and
lords, who were studied by men of letters. Even now the
literary class is derided by men of action, as a collection
of useless idlers, and the feeling was much more natural
one hundred and fifty years ago. But in England and
Spain the influence of the Roman classicism was weaker
than elsewhere. In Spain, the people were kept in subjec-
tion by the reactionary rule of a priesthood which stamped
out all the Spanish love of adventure and conquest together with literature and the arts, just as Puritanism in
England threw back the fine arts and endangered the free
growth of literature for a long time, but the natural yearning of the populace for literary expression was not wholly
lost. There was bigotry, and there was enthusiasm, too,

which conquered classicism, and English literature rose in power from the French rules that for some time seemed to the careless observer to be triumphant.

The empirical philosophy inspired a sort of free thought, as was inevitable. Europe, in breaking with the Middle Ages, gave a violent wrench to the continuity of the Church of Róme. While every century brings forth some new peril to an historic Church, it brings, too, the added weight of greater antiquity ; the Church can point back to a greater past ; it accumulates dignity. Even heretics cannot look with indifference on the long history of Catholicism. Its age alone inspires reverence. Suddenly, however, a remoter past was discovered with qualities in which Christianity had no share, and old beliefs were quickly shattered, or at least shaken. We nowadays have learned to respect history, but in Pope's time history meant a record of degradation ; the Middle Ages were a black chasm between two periods of light—its learning was but the mumbling of ignorance, its religion, superstition. The populace, we must understand, was unconscious of these discoveries, but the cultivated felt them most keenly. It is no wonder that the Jesuits regarded the new learning with abhorrence ; in their eyes it was full of mischief to all that they held dear. In Italy, the Church had been carried away by the sweetness of the new pleasure-loving creed, but it was soon called to a sense of its responsibilities. In France and Germany, religious wars raged for a long time. In England, when the Reformation was complete, religion found itself confronted by the new spirit which questioned, by the new doubts of men who could find no authority in the past. They had to draw their reasons from recent discoveries ; the old, uninquiring faith was gone, they were forming a new creed : "Philosophy, hitherto in alliance with Christianity, began to show indications of a possible divorce. Though philosophers might use the old language, it became daily more difficult to identify the God of philosophy with the God of Christianity. How could the tutelary deity of a petty tribe be the God who ruled over all things and all men? How could even the God of the mediæval imagination, the God worshipped by Christians when Christendom was regarded as approximately identical with the universe, be still the ruler of the whole earth, in which Christians formed but a small minority, and of the universe, in which the earth was but as a grain of sand on the seashore? Or how, again, could the personal Deity, whose attributes and history were known by tradition, be the God whose existence was inferred by philosophers from the general order of the universe; or regarded as a necessary postulate for the discovery of all truth? If there was no absolute logical conflict between the two views, the two modes of conceiving the universe refused to coalesce in the imagination."* Moreover, as Mr. Stephen goes on to show, "the great astronomical and geographical discoveries enlarged men's conceptions of the Infinite." The world became acquainted with the fact that there were three hundred million Chinese who, it was tauntingly asserted, would be damned because " they knew nothing of an event which, so far as they were concerned, might as well have happened on the moon." The vast majesty of the universe was unfolded to men who, as Mr. Stephen says, had hitherto been able to " think of their little planet as itself the universe, consisting of a little plain, a few miles in breadth, and roofed by the solid vault carrying our convenient lighting apparatus. . . . Through

---

* *Vide* L. Stephen's " History of English Thought in the Eighteenth Century," i. 81, etc.

the roof of the little theatre on which the drama of man's history had been enacted, men began to see the eternal stars shining in silent contempt upon their petty imaginings." The question was how to combine nature, as it was so rapidly unfolded, with the old creed. The whole controversy cannot be described here—perhaps the best account of it is to be found in the book from which I have been quoting, Leslie Stephen's " History of English Thought in the Eighteenth Century." We have to do with but a small part of it—namely, that part which inspired Pope's " Essay on Man."

The Deists in England who led the attack on orthodoxy were a despised set. Newton, after his astronomical discoveries, and his assertion, since confirmed by the spectroscope, that probably all the celestial bodies were composed of substances like those known in the earth, devoted himself to the interpretation of the prophecies. All the great men,* with scarcely an exception, devoted themselves to upholding the orthodox belief, to reconciling it with the new discoveries, and they were attacked only by obscure writers, whose morals and manners condemned their arguments, who were detested for their vulgarity. Even Addison forgot some of his urbanity in speaking of them (*Spectator*, No. 186). Swift mentioned them with contempt ; and in the " Dunciad " Pope hurled scorn at them, but in time he came under the influence of Lord Bolingbroke, and was fascinated by that nobleman's philosophy. Bolingbroke wrote down his views on religious matters when the religious controversy was over, and his position saved him from contempt, but his immunity was especially due to the fact that the question had ceased to be a burning one. Pope was a free-thinker, although he de-

---

* Locke, Bishop Butler, Berkeley, Bentley, Waterland, and Warburton.

12*

tested the avowed free-thinkers. There is no inexplicable inconsistency in this : of course, not all of the English members of Parliament who vote against the admission of Mr. Bradlaugh would consent to be burned at the stake in defence of the Church of England. Pope's Catholicism sat lightly on him, and he was familiar with the intellectual movement of his time, which had been caught in snatches by the earlier deists and put to such ignoble use as the ridicule or demolition of stray texts. Bolingbroke's inspiration in the " Essay on Man " is well known, and some commentators have gone to work to show how great is Pope's indebtedness to his friend, even in the very matter of language, for half lines are often found in the poem which were taken from Bolingbroke's prose. He borrowed thoughts and phrases, too, from Shaftesbury. One example out of many is to be found in Leslie Stephen's "Pope" (p. 167), and more examples are given in Elwyn's notes. These need not occupy us. The poem is chiefly interesting as a readable statement of the form which infidelity took in the minds of some English thinkers of the last century. It is an exceedingly inconsistent statement, because what Bolingbroke had gathered rather at random was further confused by Pope's disinclination to thorough systemization, and by his aversion to open infidelity, which in England especially has always implied contempt for the social system. That Pope was greatly agitated by the accusations of infidelity that were brought against the poem is well known. He did not publish it under his name at first, but waited to observe the effect it might have on the public. Yet it is not surprising that the general public failed to detect the deism of the " Essay," because not only are there inconsistencies in the poem, but there are many passages of such brilliant and eloquent appeal in behalf of virtue that they might well disarm criticism. It was far from being a religious poem, like the "Paradise Lost." It was an attempt, as Pope said, "to vindicate the ways of God to man."* We can see by the "Essay on Man" how the horizon had been widened by the many discoveries, and the consequent discussions. Whatever may have been the condition of Bolingbroke's mind, Pope's was in a state of flux concerning the subjects he treated in this poem. As Mr. Stephen says, "Pope felt and thought by shocks and electric flashes." Hence he accumulated a number of heterogeneous thoughts, from which no coherent system can be formed. After all, it makes little difference what a poet writing on such a subject believes; what makes a poem is the clearness and fervor with which he expresses what he has to say, whether his message be one of hope or of hate, of belief or doubt, of optimism or pessimism. Pope lacked any animating belief ; he was impressed by a number of theories that were in the air and that he had come across in his reading, and he had a wonderful gift of expression. Consequently we find some of the commonplaces of his day admirably stated.

Every reader has noticed the extreme cleverness with which Pope puts many of the disconnected thoughts of the "Essay," and this success has kept it alive to the present day. In its time it was accused of unorthodoxy and of incoherency, but the energy of the best passages has always found admirers. They are still part of the classics of the language.

Pope's literary workmanship was always good, but the taste of the present time requires cooler praise to be given to the total performance. Where he is first is in his epis-

---

* Milton, "Paradise Lost," i. 26, had said, "Justify the ways of God to man."

tles and satires, although at times even here, as in the "Dunciad," he is open to the charge of finding fault with poverty rather than with more serious crimes, and of condemning opposing politicians with more malice than wisdom. Still, our withers are unwrung, and we may get an excellent notion of the heat of political feeling at the time of Walpole's administration, and of the social gossip at that time, from these pages, which supplement the memoirs of Pope's contemporaries.

We notice that these satires are very unlike the rugged Juvenalian satires of the earlier English poets. The model which had the most influence on Pope was the work of Boileau, whose collected works were put into English in 1708. Boileau adopted the Horatian form, and his satires and epistles are full of translations from Horace, with application to contemporary persons and matters. Pope's predecessors — Hall, Donne, and Oldham — were inspired by a sort of assumed indignation against crimes which they exaggerated with theatrical fury. Pope was inspired by genuine feeling, even though we may perceive that his anger was, as Mr. Mark Pattison says, perverse and one-sided. He always had a concrete object for his wrath ; he did not build up men of straw to knock down with fine-sounding lines. Yet, to quote again from Mr. Pattison, "That poetry which is to be permanent must deal with permanent themes. Satirical is not more than any other poetry absolved from this obligation. Satire, even when individual, must never lose sight of just and noble ends. Of all petty things nothing is so petty as a petty quarrel. Pope too often allows the personal grudge to be seen through the service of public police which he puts on his work. He tries to make us think he is descending from a superior sphere to lash scribblers, who had not only sinned against taste by their foolish verses, but had out-

raged his moral sense by the scandalousness of their lives.
. . . The thin disguise of offended virtue is too often a
cloak for revenge. His most pungent verses can always
be referred back to some personal cause of affront—a line
in *The Bee*,* or a copy of verses upon him which was
handed about in manuscript. He knowingly threw away
fame to indulge his piques."

It was in this part of Pope's work that the French influence is most clearly visible. The tendency to modernize
the classic poets had already appeared. Oldham's versions
of Juvenal and Horace with contemporary references, and
Dryden's version of Boileau's "L'Art Poétique," were examples of this tendency to apply foreign poems to domestic circumstances. Rochester's "Allusion to the Tenth
Satire of the Fifth Book of Horace" was the first regular
example in English of what Pope afterwards brought to
perfection. In France, satire had found a home where it
flourished even more than in England. The first to introduce there this method of writing was Vauquelin de la
Fresnaie (published 1612), who declared : "Donc il ne
faut douter que la Satyre ne soit une espece de poësie, qui
sera merveilleusement plaisante et profitable en nostre
François, pouveu qu'on s'abstienne de diffamer personne
en particulier, et qu'on ne se licentie par vengeance on
autrement à faire des vers pleins de medisance, d'iniure,
et de menterie, tels que sont les Cocqs-à-l'Asne" (i. 130).
Yet Vauquelin's numerous satires have more historical
than poetical value; they lack the vigor of those of
D'Aubigné's, and the animation of Régnier's. We notice
in France the swiftness with which that country became
civilized after the long wars of the sixteenth century.
We find Corneille and Racine almost treading on the heels

* A weekly pamphlet for which Budgell (*inter alios*) wrote.

of Hardy, just as in England we see the *Spectator* and Pope's neat verse following a rugged past. This will show us how eager was the yearning, of cultivated men at least, for civilization. Boileau wás a most useful ally in clearing away the encumbrances of the past, and his satirical poems still remain as models of neat and dexterous verse. The best qualities of Pope—condensation and intellectual clearness—we find in Boileau, who lacks Pope's occasional roughness of temper and personal bias. How good Pope was at his best we may see in the "Epistle to Dr. Arbuthnot," which is really Pope's masterpiece.

Since Boileau's and Pope's satirical writings, in spite of great changes in the popular taste, still hold their place as classics, we may form a more complete notion of their success in their own day, when these two writers said in the best form what their contemporaries were most anxious to hear. Boileau's message on literary matters was almost omnipotent in France, and through France almost everywhere in Europe, until a comparatively recent time ; and though in his own country, since the outbreak of romanticism, his reputation has suffered, his great literary skill is still admired. Of course it is not merely his word that controlled the taste of this great people—he was but the best mouthpiece of the prevailing sentiments ; but his wit and skill lent additional force to what he had to say. In very much the same way Pope's name is given to the whole of the English literary movement of the last century, though with great inaccuracy, as I shall presently try to show. Since both these writers especially distinguished themselves in satirical poetry, one cannot help wondering what it was in the conditions of their times that made satire so powerful a weapon. A satirist nowadays—one who should write in verse, at least—would be laughed at for his pains. This form of writing was subsequently tried, to be sure, by Gifford in his "Baviad" and his "Mæviad," by Byron in his "English Bards and Scotch Reviewers," to mention the most prominent examples, but these writers only galvanized what was a dead form. An attack on the satire had been already made by Bowles in his edition of Pope (1797), when he asked whether the attitude of the satirist is one which any individual can assume towards his fellow-men. This attitude of condemnation of our fellow-men is taken by every person living, at home and abroad, in private talk, in letters, and in public writing, but its mode of expressing itself is changed. Mr. Pattison says that just as the prophet comes forward to rebuke sin, so does the satirist deliver the judgment of society on social conduct, literary taste, and such matters as the law does not attempt to cover. That is true, but the prophet and the satirist would now both be laughed at. Society has taken the control of the matters that formerly interested satirists into its own hands. It has become a democracy where every man is invited to contribute what he knows, and no one is permitted to rise and speak, as if from an upper-story window, to the populace below. And that, I take it, was what the satirist did. It was all very well when education was confined to comparatively few, and the general bent was towards rudeness, but nowadays no such self-exaltation could be endured. Satire has become the possession of the populace ; it does not belong to a privileged class. We should be as impatient of a professional satirist as we are of any one who undertakes to give instruction in etiquette ; and yet the present day is not wholly indifferent to matters of deportment, as any one may see by reading the novels of the last century.

As we noticed a few moments ago, the whole poetical movement of the eighteenth century is generally said to have been made under Pope's influence. But the exact truth of this statement may well be doubted. For one thing, we find frequent proof of what Mr. Symonds states ("Renaissance in Italy," v. 2) : " It seems to be a law of intellectual development that the highest works of art can only be achieved when the forces which produced them are already doomed, and in the act of disappearance." Only in this way, perhaps, can the artist get the perspective without losing the original inspiration; but, whatever the reason, we see this law confirmed by all our observation. Dante expressed all the majesty of the Middle Ages just as they were about to disappear forever. Even in Shakspere's lifetime, the Elizabethan drama, in the hands of his contemporaries, was beginning to decline, and, at the very moment when Pope had routed his adversaries, had proved and illustrated the neatness of his chosen form and the power of his cool common-sense in the discussion of many baffling questions, the rule of his formal verse began to be doubted, and new voices were heard discussing strange problems.* Cowper, to be sure, said that Pope

"made poetry a mere mechanic art,
And every warbler had his tune by heart,"

but this statement shows the exaggeration of first attempts at organized revolt, and fails to do sufficient justice to some of the contemporary resistance to his influence. Swift, for instance, represented a very differ-

---

* Allan Ramsay, the painter, and son of the poet, April 29, 1778 (*vide* Boswell's " Johnson "), said: " I am old enough to have been a contemporary of Pope. His poetry was highly admired in his lifetime, more, a great deal, than after his death." Johnson: "Sir, it has not been less admired since his death; no authors ever had so much faith in their own lifetime as Voltaire and Pope; and Pope's poetry has been as much admired since his death as during his life: it has only not been as much talked of; but that is owing to its now being more distant, and people having other writings to talk of."

ent form of art. Gay's view of life was very unlike that
of Pope, and Prior, whom we have already caught trying
to imitate Spenser, wrote little poems for which he was
much more indebted to French poetry than to English.
A fuller study of the growth of other forms, even in
Pope's time, we must delay until we turn to the study
of the poetical outbreak towards the end of the century,
when we shall have occasion to notice various indications
that many writers were seeking greater freedom than reason and formality could give them. Now, laying aside the
poetry for a while, let us observe what was done in prose
at this time.

CHAPTER VII.

THE most striking and important appearance in the English literature of this period is that of the novel. Let us see how this came into existence and how it flourished. To do this it will not be necessary to refer to the stories of the later Greek writers, to discuss Apuleius's "Golden Ass," or Lucian's novelettes, still less to make extracts from the recently discovered Egyptian novels, or to begin an argument as to whether the books of Job and Ruth are or are not ancient Hebrew novels—all of these questions have their value, but they need not trouble us now. We may take it for granted that the telling of stories is one of the fundamental attributes of the human race. In the Middle Ages, our ancestors had a number of stories, chiefly in poetical form, for their delectation. Such were, first, those treating religious subjects, as versions of the Old and New Testaments, lives of saints and martyrs, and the accounts of pious men and women — *e. g.,* "The Journey of St. Brandanus to the Earthly Paradise" (*cir.* 1121), the "Life of the Blessed Virgin," the "Life of Thomas à Becket" (by Garnier, *cir.* 1182), the "Story of the Seven Sleepers," the "Life of St. Elizabeth," etc. Secondly, Norman and Breton mythical and historical tales, such as "Le Roman du Rou," "Robert le Diable," "Richart sans Paour," of Norman origin ; of Breton origin, the stories about Brutus, the Trojan, the Knights of the Holy Grail — about Merlin, Lancelot, Perceval, etc. Thirdly, the Frankish romances,

about Charles the Great, " Le Roman d'Alexandre" (*cir.*
1150), a paraphrase of Curtius, with flattering references
to Louis VII. and Philip Augustus; the "Roman de Troie,"
"Le Livre du Preux et Vaillant Jason," the "Contes" and
"Fabliaux," short stories, the prose *conte* being distinguished from the rhymed *fabliau* by its greater length.
Their subjects were countless and varied, and are especially
to be noticed for this—that while the romances were in a
great measure, though not exclusively, the possession of
the higher classes, the *fabliaux* were the exclusive property of the populace. No precise description can be given
that shall apply to all. It is well to notice that they referred to the incidents of every-day life, which were narrated in a comic way. In them we find the originals of
some of Chaucer's least poetical tales, and of some of the
stories that are still handed down from one age to another by word of mouth ;* they turned to ridicule all pre-

---

* The wanderings of stories form an interesting part of literary history.
The fact is, that there is nothing rarer than originality, and a good novel
in one language is sure to be translated into every other. A curious instance of the wide use of a single plot may be seen in the travels of the
story of the "Widow of Ephesus." It gets its name from the narrative as
it appears in Petronius; but it is also a Chinese tale, as well as Persian
and Arabian and Turkish. Its earliest appearance in India was in the
Pantchatantra, and it probably was carried to neighboring countries by
the Buddhists. It entered Europe in the collection, the "Seven Sages,"
and speedily found its way into many *fabliaux.* The old story was told by
Eustace Deschamps (in the fourteenth century), Brantôme (1527–1614),
dramatized by Pierre Brinon (1614), and was told over again half a century later by La Fontaine, in one of his *contes.* St. Evremond (1678) has a
translation of the same story in Petronius; in 1682 it was again dramatized;
1702, by La Motte; 1714, a comic opera; Voltaire, in "Zadig" (1747);
Rétif de la Bretonne (1734–1806), in one of his "Contemporaines;"
Alfred de Musset, in "La Coupe et les Lèvres" (1832).

It appeared in Italy and Spain with the "Seven Sages." It early made
its appearance in England and Scotland in metrical romances of the thir-

tensions to greatness and excessive uprightness; they were the streak of realism that always exists in the human race, and most strongly when contrasted with artificial pomp. Many of the stories thus told probably described actual incidents, or some that, perhaps, had been handed down by tradition from very remote times; others may be traced to the "Gesta Romanorum" and other collections of stories made up from the Greeks and from Eastern nations: the Crusades helped to introduce these. "Reynard the Fox" is very possibly a combination into a coherent whole of a number of stories, the origin of which is like that of "Bre'r Fox" and "Bre'r Rabbit" in the Southern States, and like the many similar stories told in various remote and separate regions. Later in the Middle Ages, we come across the allegorical stories, of which the "Roman de la Rose" is the best known.* Of course this

---

teenth, fourteenth, and fifteenth centuries; in a separate volume in 1665; in Jeremy Taylor's "Holy Dying" (1651); Chapman dramatized it in his comedy, "The Widow's Tears," early in the seventeenth century; J. Ogilby (died 1676) wrote a poem narrating the story; Charles Johnson, a farce (1730); Goldsmith, in his "Citizen of the World" (published in 1762).

In Germany, we find it *inter alios* in Gellert, Wieland, Musäus, and Chamisso; Lessing began a play with this plot (*vide* Grisebach, "Die treulose Wittwe," Stuttgart, 1877).

Voltaire knew that the Chinese were familiar with this story; *vide* his "Sottisier" (Paris, 1881), p. 22. A French translation of the Chinese version had been published by a Jesuit priest in 1736.

* An interesting chapter of literary history would be a full discussion of allegories in literature during and since the Middle Ages. In the "Roman de la Rose" allegorical personages abound, drawn as crudely as the figures in ancient illustrations who are labelled on the placard issuing from their mouths. In the mysteries, too, we come across them. This proved to be a long-lived literary form. In the heroic romances of Mlle. de Scudéry, for instance, we find instances of its survival, as in the "Carte du Tendre," which was once famous for its ingenious representation of

is a very crude and incomplete description of mediæval literature. I can show now merely the abundance of material, the general lines in which it ran, in the course of the fifteenth century, when prose began to be written more freely. In this new guise the old romances had even greater popularity. These versions appeared in Germany, England, and France, and the latest of the tales of chivalry was the "Amadis de Gaule," of which I have already spoken. This book, which may be read in Southey's modern English version, differs from the others in that it and its many successors continued popular even when chivalry had already faded away. They are not so much inspired by knighthood after the manner of the people's *poetry* (*Volkspoesie*) ; they describe it with artistic enthusiasm. These novels were admired in Germany, France, and Spain until "Don Quixote" (1605–15) gave them their death-blow. Thus we read in Burton's "Anatomy of Melancholy" (1621) : "If they read a booke at any time, 'tis an English chronicle, 'Sir Huon of Bordeaux,' or 'Amadis de Gaule,' a playe - booke, or some pamplett of newes ;" and elsewhere he speaks of "such inamoratos as read nothing but play-books, idle poems, jests, 'Amadis de

---

the tender passion. This notion was not original with her. Livet, in his "Précieux et Précieuses," p. 173, says that Charles Sorel, author of "Francion," in another book had described something of the kind, as had another writer. All this belongs rather to French literature, but it has a meaning for us when we recall the corresponding treatment of his story by Bunyan, in his "Pilgrim's Progress." What the French writers had done profanely, he did in behalf of religion, so that this wonderful book is one of the last expressions of mediævalism in English literature. In art there correspond with it the quaint decorations of cathedrals, and some of the old illustrations of MSS.—*e. g.*, P. Lacroix, "Vie Réligieuse et Militaire au Moyen Âge," etc., p. 448, the reproduction of an old picture in a missal of the "Fortress of Faith," besieged by heretics and the impious, and defended by the Pope, etc.

Gaul,' the 'Knight of the Sun,' the 'Seven Champions,' 'Palmerin de Oliva,' 'Huon of Bourdeaux,' etc. Such many times prove in the end as mad as 'Don Quixote.'" "Don Quixote" had been put into English by Thomas Shelton (1612–20). The original Amadis was a genuine expression of chivalry just as it was about to disappear, and it was really of enormous influence on later literature. It not only inspired numerous successors, it affected the style of historians, just as Sir Walter Scott's novels altered the whole method of historical writing, made bulky volumes fascinating, and history picturesque. In Italy, however, these tales of chivalry lost their hold on the people. Dante, Petrarch, Boccaccio, and Ariosto all show intimacy with them, but the literary tendency ran in the direction of the brief, concise tale, in a few words, of some adventure. For one thing, the classics expelled these impossible romances, and the inclination of the Italians towards the peaceful arts and commerce made them intolerant of the vast impossibilities which seemed entrancing to less polished nations. Even Ariosto and Pulci, when they chose the romances for their subject, wrote about them in a mocking spirit ; and Boiardo civilized them, so to speak, when he wrote his "Orlando." But they disappeared from literature before the *novella*, the most characteristic form of Italian literature. It was built up on the French *fabliaux*, and on the short stories that reached Europe from the East, in the "Hitopadeṣa." This work, Dunlop states (*vide* his "History of Fiction," i. 382), was preserved by an Indian king as one of his greatest treasures. In time a Persian king (at the end of the sixth century) sent a learned physician into India to get a copy of this famous book. This physician accomplished his object by inducing an alleged sage to steal the book, the bribe he employed being "a promise of intoxication." The physician translated the book into Persian, thence into Syriac and Arabic; about 1100 it was translated from Arabic into Greek, in the thirteenth century from Greek into Latin, thence into German, Spanish, and Italian, and from Italian into English in 1570. This, we must understand, is merely one of the streams that supplied the abundant material of the Italian novelists. Curiously enough, the *novella* never developed into the modern novel — that production seems to belong only to nations which have had a drama: it is the modern version of the play. Yet these short stories of the Italian novelists supplied the English dramatists with abundant subjects.* Shakspere's "Twelfth Night," "Romeo and Juliet," "Othello," "Measure for Measure," "Merchant of Venice," "Much Ado about Nothing," "Cymbeline," are to a greater or less extent derived from Italian stories, and what is true of Shakspere is true of many of his contemporaries and successors. On the modern novel these short stories had but little influence.

The tales of chivalry, especially those about Amadis and his successors, had a long popularity, and they, as I have said, were only finally crushed by "Don Quixote," in which we find that the parody keeps close to the text of the "Amadis." Yet Cervantes did not begin this attack on the crumbling tales of chivalry. The *picaresque* novels, as they are called, had already made their appearance, and these it may be well to describe at some length,

---

* Boccaccio was translated in full in 1620, but many of his stories— Bandello's and Cinthio's — had been translated in William Paynter's "Palace of Pleasure" (1566). The first volume contains sixty novels, and the second thirty-four. The stories, however, came through the French, being taken from Belleforest's French version, as T. North's "Plutarch" was taken from Amyot's translation.

because they undoubtedly had vast influence on the English novel; and they acquired this, it is well to notice, by not being simply destructive, but by being constructive, by bringing forward new ideals and new subjects. No one of the picaresque novels approaches the greatness of "Don Quixote," which is really inimitable, and is now read for itself without care for what it says about chivalry. It was what was latent in the early novels that has been developed by subsequent writers. No complicated form of literature steps forth at once in a condition of completeness; the drama makes its way to excellence only by successive changes, and the novel advances only gradually. Of course this is the only way in which works of art attain excellence; and in the picaresque stories we catch the modern novel, so to speak, in the bud, and we shall be able to trace its modifications down to the most recent times.

That the tales of chivalry were fascinating, that they encouraged the imitation of some of the deeds and many of the emotions that inspired chivalry, is not only in itself probable, but it is confirmed by outside evidence. The novel and society, for that matter, play, as it were, into each other's hands. The novel pictures society, and society sees itself mirrored in the novel, and takes its image for a model or a warning. Hence the power of a novel as a moral teacher. Indeed, literature is a phonographic sheet on which are expressed the thoughts and emotions of all ages, and in the novel we catch society as it really was and is, rather than as it was when it was especially endeavoring to be magniloquent. Nowadays we continually find in the newspapers that two boys, aged eleven and thirteen, were found in the train going to New York, each armed with a shot-gun and a bowie-knife, and provided with his father's pocket-book, their intention being to shoot buffaloes and fight Indians, and that they were inspired thereto by reading dime-novels. In the same way, Cortez and Pizarro,* when they came to America, not only felt the genuine greed of conquerors, but compared them-

---

* Prescott, "Conquest of Peru" (ed. 1868), i. 190, and "Conquest of Mexico" (Phila. 1874), i. 47.

In 1543, Charles the Fifth prohibited the introduction of books of chivalry into the American colonies, and forbade their being printed or even read there. In 1555, the Cortes presented to the king a petition (that required only the royal signature to become law), urging the destruction of these romances. Thus (Prescott, "Biographical and Critical Essays," pp. 143 and 634): "Moreover, we say that it is very notorious what mischief has been done to young men and maidens, and other persons, by the perusal of books full of lies and vanities, like Amadis and works of that description, since young people especially, from their natural idleness, resort to this kind of reading, and becoming enamoured of passages of love or arms, or other nonsense which they find set forth therein, when situations at all analogous offer, are led to act much more extravagantly than they would otherwise have done. And many times the daughter, when her mother has locked her up safely at home, amuses herself with reading these books, which do her more hurt than she would have received from going abroad. All which redounds not only to the dishonour of individuals, but to the great detriment of conscience, by diverting the affections from holy, true and Christian doctrine, to those wicked vanities with which the wits, as we have intimated, are completely bewildered. To remedy this, we entreat your Majesty that no book treating of such matters be henceforth permitted to be read, that those now printed be collected, and burned, and that none be published hereafter without special license; by which measures your Majesty will render great service to God as well as to your kingdoms," etc.

Cf. "Eastward Ho" (by Chapman, B. Jonson, and Marston), iii. 2 (1605), "I tell thee, gold is more plentiful there than copper is with us." ... "Why, men, all their dripping-pans ... are pure gold; and all the chains with which they chain up their streets are massy gold; all the prisoners they take are fettered in gold; and for rubies and diamonds, they go forth on holidays and gather them by the sea-shore, to hang on their children's coats and stick in their caps, as commonly as our children wear saffron-gilt brooches and groats with hoals in them."

And Sidney, "Defense of Poesy:" "Truly I have known men, that even

selves with the dragon-slayers whose deeds had fired their
imagination from boyhood.　We know, for instance, that
the Mississippi was discovered by De Soto when he was
searching for the fountain of youth—the Eldorado, as it
was called, seemed to fulfil every promise ; and we may be
sure that the conquest of Mexico or Peru would not have
formed the romantic story that it did if its conquerors had
not been fed on romance.　We denounce them for their
cruelty to their enemies, but the tales they' had read were
full of the slaughter of heretics.　They, like the rest of
the world, breathed the air of their time.　Or, if we desire further proof, it may be found without difficulty.　In
one of the early novels, in the picaresque style, published
in France (" Histoire Comique de Francion," ed. Delahays,
1858, p. 128) : " It became my pastime to read nothing
but books of chivalry, and I must tell you that this occu-
pation sharpened my courage and gave me unparalleled
desires to seek adventures in the wide world.　For it
seemed to me that it would be as easy with one blow to
cut a man in two, as it would be to cut an apple.　I was
full of sovereign content when I saw a horrible massacre
of giants cut into mincemeat.　The blood which flowed
from their wounds formed a stream of rose-water in which
I bathed most deliciously ; and sometimes I imagined that
I was the youth who kissed the maiden with green eyes
like a falcon.　I use the language of those true chronicles.
In a word, my mind was full of nothing but castles, or-
chards, combats, enchantments, delights, and love-making,
and when I remembered that this was all nothing but fiction, I said that it was wrong to blame reading of this

---

with reading Amadis de Gaul, which God knoweth, wanteth much of a
perfect Poesy, have found their hearts moved to the exercise of courtesy,
liberality and especially courage."

kind, and that henceforth it was but to lead the sort of life most akin to that described in these books; thereupon I began to blame the vile conditions of the men of this century, whom I have to-day in great honor." Then he describes at great length his reaction from the restraints of the bourgeois society which was beginning to acquire power.

Let us now see what the picaresque * novel was, and perhaps we shall be able to make out how it came into existence. The first one, the "Lazarillo de Tormes," was written by Mendoza, in his twenty-first year, when he was a student at the University of Salamanca, but first published only in 1553 (being delayed possibly from fear of the Inquisition). Mendoza, who was born early in the sixteenth century (1503–75), was one of the distinguished men of his time, as a diplomatist and a historian. With those sides of his character, however, we have nothing to do. We shall examine only his work as a novelist. The hero, who tells the story in the first person, and whose name is that of the book, is the son of a miller who lived on the banks of the Tormes. His father dies early, and the boy, when eight years old, makes his first start in life. "About this time, a blind man came to lodge at the house, and thinking that I should do very well to lead him about, asked my mother to part with me for that purpose. My mother recommended me strongly, stating that I was the son of an excellent man who died in battle against the enemies of our faith." (He had been found guilty of stealing grain from his customers; he had "joined an armament then preparing

---

* *Picaro* is a rogue. The word is well defined in an interesting article in the *Cornhill* for June, 1875, p. 671 : "The picaro is not necessarily a thief, or a cheat, or an impostor, but one who has no scruple about lying, cheating, or stealing, under the slightest possible circumstances." The distinction is most subtle.

against the Moors, in the quality of mule-driver to a gentleman ; and in that expedition, like a loyal servant, he,
along with his master, finished his life and services together." His father, " being convicted of bleeding his customers' sacks, suffered with such exemplary patience the
reward appointed by the law in cases of that nature, that
his friends have ground to hope he is among the number
of the saints " [cd. 19, 1777] : the reward consisted in his
" being whipt through the whole town, and the city arms
imprinted on his shoulders.") " She confided me to his care
as an orphan boy, and entreated him to use me with kindness.   The old man promised to receive me, not as a servant, but as a son; and thus I commenced service with my
new though blind and aged master." The way in which the
blind man fulfilled his promise was as follows : " We left
Salamanca, and having arrived at the bridge, my master
directed my attention to an animal carved in stone in the
form of a bull, and desired me to take him near it. When
I had placed him close to it, he said, ' Lazaro, if you put
your ear close to this bull, you will hear an extraordinary
noise within.'   In the simplicity of my heart, believing it
to be as he said, I put my ear to the stone, when the old
man gave my head such a violent thump against it, that I
was almost bereft of sense, and for three days after I did
not lose the pain I suffered from the blow." This experience opened his eyes to the ways of the world he was
entering.   Moreover, his blind master nearly starved him.
He used to carry his food in a linen knapsack, and give
the boy a few scraps, and then close the bag ; the boy
made a small rip in the seam of the bag and would take
out choice pieces of meat, bacon, and sausage, and then
close the seam. Moreover, " all that I could collect, either
by fraud or otherwise, I carried about me in half-farthings ; so that when the old man was sent for to pray,

and they gave him farthings (all of which passed through my hands, he being blind), I contrived to slip them into my mouth, by which process so quick an alteration was effected, that when they reached his hands they were invariably reduced to half their original value. The cunning old fellow, however, suspected me, for he used to say, ' How the deuce is this ? ever since you have been with me they give me nothing but half-farthings ; whereas before, it was not an unusual thing to be paid with halfpence, but never less than farthings. I must be sharp with you, I find.'" The old man was unusually careful of his jar of wine, and the boy was forever trying to outwit him, and get a chance to drink of it. Soon he was detected and the old man used to fasten it to himself by a string attached to the handle. Consequently, the young rogue got a large straw and drew the wine through it. After that, the blind man kept it between his knees, and held his hand over the mouth. The boy consequently bored a little hole into the bottom, which he closed very delicately with wax. "At dinner time, when the poor old man sat over the fire, with the jar between his knees, the heat, slight as it was, melted the little piece of wax, and I, feigning to be cold, drew close to the fire, and placed my mouth under the little fountain in such a manner that the whole contents of the jar became my share. When the old man had finished his meal, and thought to regale himself with his draught of wine, the deuce a drop did he find, which so enraged and surprised him, that he thought the devil himself had been at work ; nor could he conceive how it could be. ' Now, uncle,' said I, ' don't say that I drank your wine, seeing that you have had your hand on it the whole time.'" But the old man felt all over the jar, and found out the trick that had been played on him, but said nothing. The next time the boy was stealing the wine, the blind man raised the jar and broke it over the boy's face, bruising him severely, and afterwards the old man was perpetually maltreating the boy. When bystanders would remonstrate, he would narrate the boy's rogueries so that those who listened would say, "Thrash him well, good man; thrash him well; he deserves it richly!" The boy's revenge consisted in leading the blind man over the worst roads, over the sharpest stones, and through the deepest mud. "It is true that my head and shoulders were subjected in consequence to the angry visitations of his staff; and though I continually assured him that his uneasy travelling was not the result of my ill-will, but for the want of better roads, yet the old traitor had too much cunning to believe a word I said." Among his other tricks, when his master was once cooking a sausage, this boy stole the sausage and substituted a turnip, for which he was again beaten. The next day was wet, and as he led the blind man on his round of begging, the boy devised this ingenious plan, which he thus narrates: "On our return we had to pass a small stream of water, which with the day's rain had grown quite large. I therefore said, 'Uncle, the brook is very much swollen; but I see a place a little higher, where by jumping a little we may pass almost dry-shod.' 'Thou art a good lad,' said the old man; 'I like you for your carefulness. Take me to the narrowest part, for at this time of year, it would be dangerous to get our feet wet.' Delighted that my plot seemed to succeed so well, I led him from beneath the arcades, and led him to directly opposite to a pillar, or, rather, to a large stone post, which I observed in the square. 'Now, uncle,' said I, 'this is the place where the brook is narrowest.' The rain was pouring down, and the man was getting very wet; and whether it was by his haste to avoid it, or, as is more probable,

Providence at that moment deprived him of his usual cunning, that he might fall into my snare, and give me my revenge, he believed me and said, 'Now place me opposite the spot, and do you jump yourself.' I placed him directly opposite the pillar so that he could not miss it, and leaping over myself, I placed myself just behind the post, whence I shouted, 'Now, master, jump as hard as you can, and you will clear the water.' The words were hardly out of my mouth when the poor old rogue started up as nimbly as a goat, took a step or two backwards to get an impetus, which lent his leap such force, that instead of alighting on soft ground, as he supposed he should do, he gave his poor bald pate such a smash against the pillar that he fell to the ground without sense or motion. 'Take that, you unhappy old thief,' said I, 'and remember the sausage;' then leaving him to the care of the people who began to gather, I took to my heels as swiftly as possible through the town gates, and before night reached Torrejos. What became of the old man afterwards I don't know, and neither did I ever give myself any pains to find out."

After thus getting rid of one master, the boy ran until he got to a place called Maqueda, where he fell in with a priest, into whose service he entered. But " the old blind man, selfish as he was, seemed an Alexander the Great, in point of munificence, in comparison with this priest, who was, without exception, the most niggardly of all miserable devils I have ever met with. It seemed as if the meanness of the whole world were gathered together in his wretched person. It would be hard to say whether he inherited this disposition, or whether he had adopted it with his cassock and gown." (This last sentence was stricken out by the Inquisition.) Here the boy went through another course of starvation, smelling the string of onions in the garret and sucking the dry bones on which the priest had meagrely dined. At mass, the priest watched every coin that fell into the plate. The bread and wine left from the church he would lock up in a chest, saying, "'You see, my boy, that priests ought to be very abstemious in their food. For my part, I do think it a great scandal to indulge in food and wine as many do.' But the curmudgeon lied most grossly, for at convents and funerals, when we went to pray, he would eat like a wolf, and drink like a mountebank ; and now I speak of funerals—God forgive me, I was never an enemy to the human race but at that unhappy period of my life, and the reason was solely, that on these occasions I obtained a meal of victuals. Every day I did hope and pray that God would be pleased to take his own. Whenever we were sent for to administer to the sick, the priest would of course desire all present to join in prayer. You may be certain I was not the last in these devout exercises, and I prayed with all my heart that the Lord would take pity on the afflicted, not by restoring him to the vanities of life, but by relieving him from the sins of this world ; and when any of these unfortunates recovered—the Lord forgive me—in the anguish of my heart I wished him a thousand times in perdition ; but if he died no one was more sincere in his blessings than myself. During all the time that I was in this service, which was nearly six months, only twenty persons paid the debt of nature, and these I verily believe that I killed, or, rather, that they died of the incessant importunity of my prayers."

Once, however, when the priest was away, a tinker, or, as he thought, an angel in the guise of a tinker, came along, whom the young rogue told that he had lost the key of the chest, and the man fitted one for him, so that he had access to the loaves. But, of course, he had to

help himself only sparingly after his first hungry thefts
were discovered. Then he stole some more, and made
holes in the chest as if rats had been at it. When those
holes were stuffed up he made new ones. His master was
amazed. " What can it mean?" he asked ; "as long as I
have been here, there have never been rats before." And
he might say so with truth ; if ever a house in the kingdom deserved to be free from rats it was his, as they are
seldom known to appear when there is nothing to eat.
Then the priest set a trap, but the boy stole the cheese
and ate it with more of the bread. Then some one suggested that the food was stolen by a snake, and the priest
was forever jumping up to find the snake. Meanwhile
the boy slept with the key in his mouth for the sake of
safety ; but one night his breath made it whistle, and the
priest, feeling sure that now he had caught the snake by
its hissing, came with a club, and meaning to kill it, but
he hit the boy on the head, bruising him severely, and
finding the key. As soon as the boy had recovered he
was discharged by his master, who said, " No one will ever
doubt that you have served a blind man ; but as for me,
I do not require so diligent or so clever a servant." Then
he betakes himself to Toledo, and enters the service of a
new master, a grandee of great splendor, who is also inclined to practise starvation. " He had an air of ease and
consequence" which persuaded the boy to think that this
was just the situation he desired. But this esquire, though
he made to the world a great show of elegance, was really
without a penny. The boy then was thrown on his wits,
and had to beg his food from door to door. The supply
he gathered in this way he shared with his master, for
whom he feels very genuine sympathy. Soon, however,
a law was passed against vagrancy, and they both began
to suffer ; but the master managed to get a little money,

which they spent in food, but the landlord came for his rent and the esquire disappeared, leaving the boy to shift for himself. With his fourth master, a friar, he stayed but a little while ; and then he entered the service of a dealer in Papal indulgences, the description of whose performances gave the writer an opportunity to make some remarks which did not please the Inquisition. This new master he detected in his impositions, so that he left him in disgust. Then he entered the service of a chaplain, and made a little sum of money by selling water, after which he became the servant of an alguazil, and married an ignoble woman. Here the novel was left in an unfinished state, although its publication was soon followed by that of a continuation by another hand, with more adventures; one of which was that the hero was saved from shipwreck and dressed so as to represent a merman, and was so exhibited in many towns of Spain. He finally escaped, and after some adventures reached a hermitage. The original hermit died soon after, and this hero assumed his dress and lived on the contributions of the charitable people of the neighborhood—an incident which is also to be found in "Gil Blas," in the history of Don Raphael (v. i.).

I describe this story at some length, because it is the earliest of the picaresque novels, and is remarkable in many ways. Not only is the whole tone diametrically opposite to that of the tales of chivalry, but the book is worthy of attention for the way in which it breaks a wholly new path for literature. In itself it is curious, and as the leader of one of the great movements in modern writing it is deserving of great respect. It had no predecessor, but the author managed to see and to put down some of the characteristics of the life about him. The Spanish peasant had acquired importance in the wars that had devastated that country in the protracted struggle against the Moors, and the numberless proverbs in "Don Quixote" show how his character had been formed, how he had learned wisdom in the only way in which wisdom can be learned, through experience ; and they prove how unlike his practical good-sense was to the fantastic notions of the Spanish knights, who were still under the delusion of the splendor of chivalry. In the reign of Ferdinand and Isabella, several knights went into foreign parts, " in order to try the fortune of arms with any cavalier that might be pleased to venture with them, and so gain honor for themselves, and the fame of valiant and bold knights for the gentlemen of Castile." And Ticknor says : " Castillo, another chronicler, tells us gravely, in 1587, that Philip II., when he married Mary of England, only forty years earlier, promised that if King Arthur should return to claim the throne he would peaceably yield to that prince all his rights ; thus implying, at least in Castillo himself, and probably in many of his readers, a full faith in the stories of Arthur and his Round Table." Yet alongside of these fantastic people was the populace, made up of shrewd men living by their wits, compressing their wisdom into proverbs, which you will notice are always abundant in a subjected race or class. Prosperous people never make proverbs; they have leisure, or, at least, freedom for discussion ; but among the oppressed they are current as convenient, easily remembered condensations of the lessons of life. They pass from mouth to mouth as safe expressions, when long denunciations or asseverations would be full of danger. This quality, perhaps, combines with their brevity and picturesqueness in making proverbs popular among the uneducated. Notice their abundance in the East, in Spain, and Russia, and among the former slaves in the South. The nature of the people struck Mendoza, aristocrat though he was, and this was strange enough when we consider how rare it is for a writer to see through the mists of the literary atmosphere of his times. Yet when a man has this power, when living in an artificial time—and it is the inevitable tendency of all literary movements to become artificial, to substitute mechanism for originality—the reaction is a great one, and in the most unreal times we find an undercurrent which only assumes importance in the works of men of ability, reacting violently against the accepted forms. When Pope writes pastorals, and poetry becomes didactic, Swift paints the gross side of reality ; when chivalry fires the brains of half the world, the other half is telling ribald anecdotes or beginning to draw pictures of actual life. To be amazed at the contrast is like being amazed at the existence of comedy alongside of tragedy, or that shadows are black when the sun is shining bright. It is only in a fog that there are no contrasts of light and shade.

Another important trait of these novels is the fact that their writers went back to the people for their subject; and even now we daily speak of the people as if they were a race, valuable, to be sure, to the curious student of natural history, but in other respects remote from ourselves. Without referring to the political bearings of this misunderstanding, I will merely say that literature, which is not a thing apart from human interests, follows the same path with political changes, and that the whole course of literature at the present time is in the direction of democracy. Certainly the novel has shown the way, and the most important original literary form of modern times has owed the greater part of its strength to the fact that it has studied humanity, and where it has, in the natural course of events, grown artificial, it has found new strength by returning to the study of real life. We shall have further instances of this as we go on with our investigation of literature.

That the "Lazarillo" was popular cannot be doubted. It ran through Spain like wildfire ; it was translated into French, English, and German. The first English translation appeared in 1586—thirty-three years after the first publication—and was followed by many more. The nineteenth appeared in 1777 (the twentieth in 1789), which is about ten editions a century, or one every ten years. Naturally enough, the success of this novel inspired other writers to the imitation of this form of writing. One of the finest was Matthew Aleman's "Life of Guzman de Alfarache" (1599), of which twenty-five Spanish editions soon appeared, as well as two French translations, one by Le Sage ; a German translation in 1615 ; and English translations in 1623, 1630, 1634, and 1656, under the name of "The Rogue, or the Life of Guzman de Alfarache."* The hero is the son of a Genoese merchant, who had settled in Spain. After his death, the young fellow runs away from home and begins his adventures. On reaching Madrid, he starts in life as a beggar, and comments on the motley crowd that passes him as he stations himself at the street-corner. Soon he sets up as a sharper, and is forced to betake himself to Toledo, where he plays the part of a man of fashion until all his money is lost or spent, when he goes to Barcelona, and thence, *via* Genoa, to Rome, the paradise of beggars. One of the most amusing of the incidents is his ingenuity in painting his leg in such a way that it deceived a cardinal, who imagined him very ill, and had him taken to his own house to be cared for by physicians. One of them Guzman overhears declaring the ailment is a fraud—he

---

* Fielding says "The Spanish Rogue" was Jonathan Wild's favorite book (" Jonathan Wild," chap. iii.).

had once already been flogged when detected in this deception by neglecting to whiten his ruddy cheeks—and
Guzman runs in, acknowledges his sins, but shows the
doctors that it will be much more lucrative for them to
pretend to carry him through a long illness. To this
they consent, and he gradually becomes a miraculous
cure. He remains here long as a page, playing various
tricks, then he makes his way through Italy back to
Spain, where he marries. This marriage proves unfortunate, and after his wife's death Guzman enters the university of Alcala, in order to obtain a benefice. He
marries again ; a worthless wife she proves to be, but
no worse than her husband, who finally, when he and
his wife are banished from Madrid, becomes the cham-
berlain of an old lady, but manages her affairs so ill
that he is arrested and sent to the galleys. His fellow-
slaves try to engage him to enter a plot to deliver the
vessels to the corsairs ; he betrays the plot, receives his
freedom for a reward, and employs his time in writing
his life. This story, too, like "Gil Blas" and "Don
Quixote," contains many episodes. The fashion of episodes was long lived. We find them in Fielding and
Smollett, in Goethe's "Wilhelm Meister," and in "Sandford and Merton."

Then comes the "Life of Paul the Sharper," by Que-
vedo (1580–1645), one of the most distinguished men of
his day. He was a profound scholar, and an eminent
writer on moral and political philosophy, as well as a
famous poet, who, at the age of twenty-three, was honored
by the praise of Lipsius and all his learned contemporaries.
He is of interest, too, as the first man who is mentioned in
history as having gone to live in a hotel in order to be
freed from domestic cares. He must have known other
counter-sorrows, if the account of the inns of the time con-

tained in most of the picaresque novels are to be believed, and the accuracy of their writers may be attested by all who have travelled in Spain. This novel is perhaps the wittiest of all.* It begins thus : " I was born at Segovia; my father's name was Clement Paul, a native of the same town ; I hope his soul is in heaven. I need not speak of his virtues, for these are unknown, but by trade he was a barber, though so high - minded that he took it for an affront to be called by any name but that of a tonsor of beards, or the gentleman's hair-dresser. They say he came of a good stock,—and it must have been a vine-stock,—as all his actions showed a remarkable affection for the refined blood of that glorious genealogical tree." But I shall quote no more. I have not forgotten that we are studying English, not Spanish, literature. There were, besides, " La Picara Justina " (1605) ; and the " History of the Life of the Esquire Marcos de Obregon " (1618), which was of great service in the construction of " Gil Blas."

That the picaresque novels owed much, especially the earliest of them, to the Italian stories, we may readily believe. But they differ from the originals, if originals they were, by the fact that they compose a long and coherent novel, the different chapters of which remind us of some of the separate Italian tales. In justice to the Spaniards, we must remember the greatness of the step they made in making whole novels, and in tracing the gradual modifications of character which are required in stories of this sort. Those I have mentioned, however, were not all. Cervantes wrote some short stories: his " Exemplary Novels " abound in the humor of the picaresque school, and, as I have said, the " Don Quixote " contains much that is inspired by them,

---

* This " Paul the Sharper " was translated in 1657.

especially the whole of Sancho Panza's relation to the Don. His cowardice, shiftiness, and comic treatment of everything are part of the same thing. There is, of course, this great difference, that "Don Quixote" is one of the great books of the world, while the others are but clever tales.

The picaresque novels, as I have said, spread over Europe, and inspired countless imitations. Even in Germany the inspiration was felt. Grimmelshausen (1625–76) wrote his "Simplicissimus" (1668), the hero of which, in one of the continuations, retires to a desert island, where he lives for some time. We shall have occasion to refer to this incident when we speak of "Robinson Crusoe." This novel inspired many others of a similar kind. In France, too, the picaresque novels had great influence. The best of the French imitations was Sorel's "Histoire Comique de Francion" (1622 and 1633), a book now nearly forgotten, but in its time enormously admired.* Sorel wrote another volume, "Le Berger Extravagant," ridiculing the pastoral stories. In the "Francion" we have the life of a rogue told with great fidelity, and the story is especially valuable for the light it throws on the life of the time. All the complicated society of France, early in the seventeenth century, is mirrored here; whole classes of people pass before us in review, a chapter, for instance, being devoted to a delineation of the literary men of that day.† Then came

---

* In English, by several hands, 1703.

† Sorel, in "L'Ordre et l'Examen des Livres Attribués à l'Auteur de la Bibliothèque Française" (quoted in Demogeot, "Litt. française au XVII⁰ Siècle," p. 327, note): "Nos romans comiques sont chacun autant d'originaux qui nous représentent les caractères les plus supportables et les plus divertissants de la vie humaine, et qui n'ont point leur sujet des gueux, des voleurs, et des faquins, comme Gusman, Lazarille, et Buscon; mais des hommes de bonne condition, subtils, généreux, et agréables . . . et, de ce côté, nous n'avons rien à envier aux étrangers."

Scarron's "Roman Comique" (1651), which tells of the
adventures of a company of strolling players. They had
just left one town because their doorkeeper had murdered
an officer, and they reach another, and agree to act that
night in the tennis-court. Since, however, the full company was not expected until the next day, they are in
some distress about the smallness of their number—two
men and one woman. One of the men, however, says that
he once performed a play alone, acting as king, queen, and
ambassador in a single scene. Their clothes, too, are another source of trouble, for the key of the wardrobe is in
the hands of one of the other party. An official, however,
solves the matter by giving the actress a robe of his wife's,
and the coats of two young men who are playing tennis.
So the play begins, and goes on with some interruptions,
the young men, who have finished their match, rushing on
the stage to reclaim their clothes. This matter excites a
tumult, in which the audience takes part. The story runs
on, the company is invited out to supper, the actress is
abducted, and the pursuit of her is what takes up most of
the rest of the book. There is love-making, too, and a
comical description of the absurdities of the incongruous
characters, and much space is devoted to exaggerated
accounts of their misfortunes. The book contains many
episodes in the shape of love-stories, the scenes of which
are laid in Spain. The story, it will be seen, is distinctly
comic, and the manners of provincials, always despised by
Parisians, are turned to ridicule.* Another book of the
same class is Furetière's "Roman Bourgeois," which describes the ridiculous courtship by a counsellor of the

---

* Boileau did not like Scarron's travesties, but he had a good word for
the "Roman Comique," as well as for "Gil Blas," though he despised the
"Diable Boiteux."—Sainte-Beuve, "Causeries du Lundi," ii. 357.

daughter of a rascally attorney. It is more or less a caricature. The greatest of the French stories, and one of the greatest of novels, was Le Sage's "Gil Blas" (1715-35), the scene of which is laid in Spain, and the characters are Spanish, though the book itself is, in all essentials, French. Its dependence on the Spanish novels, even to borrowing some of the incidents, has been often noticed.

Now, at last, we come to the English novel, and this long digression will not have been without service if it shows, by analogy, how certain it is that the Spanish novels must have had some influence on English literature. Lyly's "Euphues" had died of its own elegance, and its few successors, notably Greene's "Dorastus and Fawnia," had left no permanent mark. The English novel in no way rose from that artificial soil. We have seen that the "Lazarillo" was translated into English in 1586, and with that book "the Spanish rogue" acquired the right of citizenship in English letters. Those books had, however, formidable rivals in the translations of the Italian novelists, where so many of the dramatists found their plots, and novel-writing was less common when the stage was crowded with plays, just as now, when novels swarm everywhere, plays are rare. Yet there were some imitations of the Spanish stories. Thomas Nash (1558-1600) wrote a novel of a somewhat similar kind — to judge from the few pages given in an appendix to one of the volumes of Dr. Nott's edition of Surrey's poems — called "Jack Wilton."* Another, and possibly a more important imitation, was "The English Rogue" (part 1 by Richard Head [died 1678], 2, 3, and 4 by Francis Kirkman, two minor dramatists), which was possibly a reaction against some now forgotten "Amadis" novels, diluted

---

* See also *Observer*, No. xxxix.

fragments of chivalry, such as " The Famous, Delectable, and Pleasant Hystorie of the Renowned Parismus, Prince of Bohemia," by Emanuel Ford, London, 1598, which soon ran through thirteen editions, one as late as 1732 ; also his " Ornatus and Artesia," and Henry Roberts's " Pheander, or the Maiden Knight" (1595) * (not in Allibone ; *vide* Wolff, " Gesch. des Romans," p. 221-22, and Dunlop, ii. 384).

"The English Rogue" appeared in 1665, 1668, and 1671 (two parts). The whole title is " The English Rogue Described, in the Life of Meriton Latroon, a Witty Extrava-

---

* There had been, too, a great many short popular stories, called novels, sometimes merely jest-books (Mark Lemon's, in Golden Treasury Series, is the latest of these publications). Such were "Tarleton's Jests" (1611); "Merrie Conceited Jests of George Peele" (1627). Thomas Deloney's "Pleasant History of John Winchcomb in his younger yeeres called Jack of Newberrie, the famous and worthie clothier of England : declaring his life and love, together with his charitable deeds and great hospitality : and how he set continually five hundred poore people at worke, to the great benefit of the Common-wealth : worthy to be read and regarded," licensed 1596, and soon printed, is a curious mixture of novel and jest-book. With but a feeble plot, it is scarcely more than a collection of incoherent stories. Thomas Deloney was a great ballad-maker, and, Warton says, one of the original actors of Shakspere's plays. In the preface of the "Tinker of Turvey," five or six short stories of faithless wives, the writer says a good wife may find it as well worth reading as " Robin Hood," " Clim a the Clough," " Tom Thumb," " Fryer and the Boy," and " Sir Irenbras." Now, such of these as are known are the reading of infants. " Jack the Giant-killer" is from "Sir Geoffrey of Monmouth." " Valentine and Orson " was once a popular story. See, too, Goethe's " Aus Meinem Leben " (30 vol. ed., Stuttgart, 1858), p. 30, where he speaks of the romances he read when young. May not Scott's novels be gradually sinking in this way to younger readers? The change is not in romance alone; A. De Morgan (*Notes and Queries*, July 17, 1858) says that boys of eighteen now read Newton's " Principia," which not a dozen men in Europe could read at its first appearance.

gant. Being a Compleat History of the Most Eminent
Cheats of both Sexes." Motto,

> " Read, but don't Practice: for the Author findes,
>   They which live Honest have most quiet mindes."

The mere title shows that this book is an imitation of the
picaresque stories ; and, if doubt were possible, it would
be removed by one of the commendatory poems, by one
N. D., who says :

> " Guzman, Lazaro, Buscon,* and Francion,
>   Till thou appeard'st did shine as at high Noon.
>   Thy Book's now extant; those that judge of Wit,
>   Say, They and Rablais too fall short of it.
>   How could't be otherwise, since 'twas thy fate,
>   To practise what they did but imitate," etc.

The hero recounts his tricks at considerable length, and
without a trace of the humor of his Spanish predecessors.
He was a bad boy at home and at school, and of course
he ran away, soon joining a band of gypsies, whose cant
language he describes at some length. He leaves them
and becomes a professional beggar, until "a tradesman
of no mean quality, passing by, took a strong fancy to
me," and carried him home to take him into his service.
Here he plunges into various excesses, which form an
incoherent combination of villanies. He leaves England
and travels in Ireland. Then, "having now gotten a
round sum of money by me, I borrowed wherever I
could, so crossing St. George's Channel and landed at
Chester, I took up my quarters at a very graceful inn, and
gave out immediately that I had an hundred head of Cattel coming. The Master of the house, taking notice of
my extraordinary Garb, and believing the report which I
had caus'd to be spread abroad, lodg'd me with much re-

---

* Buscon is another name for Paul the Sharper.

spect in one of the best Chambers of his house. The wind favoured my design as much as I could desire, for it blew East North East, by which no Shipping could come out of Ireland. One day I came to my landlord, and telling him that by reason of the non-arrival of my Cattel, I was disappointed of Moneys, and therefore I desired him to lend me ten pounds, and he should satisfie himself in the first choice of the best of my beasts when they came, and swore to him I would perform my promise to him upon the word of a Gentleman. So that without any scruple he lent me the money. Being Market-Day I bought an excellent gelding with Furniture thereunto belonging, with Sword and Pistols, and in this Equipage mounted I took my leave of my credulous Landlord, without speaking a word to him," etc. We notice the total lack of vivacity in this narration, and its enormous inferiority to the Spanish stories. The poor author beats his brain to find incidents, but his dreary pen leaves them all heavy. The hero served a notable revengeful trick on the turnkey of Ludgate, he played a freak upon a jeweller, he put a notable cheat upon a gentleman, he cheated a scrivener, he was revenged on a broker, he cozened a rich usurer, etc. Suddenly he is in Newgate, and (1650) condemned to be transported to Virginia ; he is wrecked on the coast of Spain, and then starts anew, this time of his own will, for the East Indies, but the ship is captured by Turkish pirates, and he is sold in the market-place ; he regains his liberty, however, and pushes on to the East Indies, where he marries a native woman. Here the part written by Head comes to an end. Kirkman's continuation begins with another man's memories of his life and its misdeeds. The book is prolonged with the full confessions of a number of evil-doers of both séxes. A certain amount of information may be got of the life of the time ; but, though the book is of infinitely less literary merit than the French and Spanish stories, the vulgar tale shows the effect that the picaresque novels had.

While "The English Rogue" belongs to a low depart-ment of literature, what strikes any one who reads it is its resemblance to Defoe's secondary novels, as Lamb called them. It is true that these stories are floated by the "Rob-inson Crusoe;" if that novel had never been written, we should know but little of "Colonel Jack," "Roxana," and "Captain Singleton." Fortunately, however, they survive, and we can trace the foundations of the English novel in them as in "The English Rogue," although these founda-tions were laid in miry places. Defoe had from nature what he calls his "natural infirmity of homely, plain writ-ing," but he did not invent—although he often gets the credit for it—the art of writing about the lives of vicious people. In his volume on Defoe, in the "English Men of Letters Series," for instance, Mr. Minto says : "Defoe is spoken of as the inventor of the realistic novel ; realistic biography would, perhaps, be a more strictly accurate de-scription." In fact, Defoe invented neither; he found the realistic biographical novel already made, and he adapted the form to his own ends. He did this with great skill, for while he was not a great artist, he was a wonderful craftsman. That is to say, he studies his fellow-creatures from the point of view of their relations to society ; he writes as a reformer with a direct practical end, with the end that was foremost in the minds of his generation, that of promoting civilization. Take his "Robinson Crusoe," for example ; full as it is of fine things, as when Robinson sees with terror the print of a human foot upon the sand, it is singularly devoid of any expression of the feeling of vast loneliness that would weigh down on the spirit of any such hero in a novel of the present day. The prob-

lem that lay before him, and which he accomplished, was
how to make himself over from a worthless person into a
peaceable, God-fearing citizen. The shadow of the municipal law and of the English Sunday seems to lie over
the lonely island. The moral of the book, in short, is this :
If a man in solitude, with a few scraps from a wreck and
an occasional savage, dog, and cat to help him, can lead so
civilized a life, what may we not expect of good people in
England with abundance about them ? This moral is what
now makes the value of the book as a means of education
for boys, that they may see, as Rousseau put it, that the
stock of an ironmonger is better than that of a jeweller,
and glass better than diamonds.* Indeed, the whole book
appeals to a boy's imagination by its continual reference
to practical difficulties and by the absence of a larger
imagination. Of the influence of this book it is hardly
necessary to speak, for its position as a classic for boys is
still firm. It appeared in 1719, and was soon followed
by many English imitations, one of which was the " Life
and Adventures of Peter Wilkins " (1750), by Robert
Paltock, but it had a much larger following abroad. A
French translation appeared in 1720–21; in 1720 it was put
into German and soon into Italian. Everywhere the book
was much admired, but nowhere so much as in Germany.
By 1760 forty "Robinsonaden," as they were called, were
published, including a German (1722), an Italian (1722),
a "Schlesischer Robinson," and one of almost every country; the clerical "Robinson" (1723); a medical, a Jew-
ish, a moral, a learned, a poetic "Robinson ;" the "Girl
Robinson ;" "Robinson, the Bookseller ;" an "Invisible
Robinson," etc. Twenty-one more, indeed, appeared after 1760, exclusive of those written solely for children, the

---

* "Émile," liv. iii.

best known of which is Campe's "Swiss Family Robinson," who, it will be remembered, land in wash-tubs nailed together between planks—a device which throws considerable light on a German's notion of the ocean in a storm.

It is Defoe's other novels that had more influence on English literature, or at least inclined more towards the direction which English literature was to follow. In his "Colonel Jack" (1722), for instance, we are once more in the line between the picaresque novel and the English novel made up of the study of character and the combination of incident. The hero tells in autobiographical form the story of his life, and it is impossible to pass by his chronicle without quoting a few lines to show of how good material the book is made. The hero, who has gentle blood in his veins, is brought up amid thieves and pickpockets, whose arts he has soon learned to practise. The moral agnosticism of the poor fellow, who was brought up to believe the picking of pockets a legitimate business, like anything else, is well given ; he has no struggle with his conscience, he simply does as he is bid, although when older he regrets that his victims suffer the agony of losing large sums. At one time he returns a stolen pocket-book for the sake of the reward. The gentleman becomes interested in him, and talks with him thus :

" ' What is your name ?' says he—' But hold, I forgot,' said he; ' I promised I would not ask your name, so you need not tell me.'

" ' My name is Jack,' said I.

" ' Why, have you no surname ?' said he.

" ' What is that ?' said I.

" ' You have some other name besides Jack,' says he, ' han't you ?'

" ' Yes,' says I ; ' they call me Colonel Jack.'

" ' But have you no other name ?'

" ' No,' said I.

" ' How come you to be called Colonel Jack, pray ?'

" ' They say,' said I, ' that my father's name was Colonel.' ·

"'Is your father or mother alive?' said he.

"'No,' said I, 'my father is dead.'

"'Where is your mother, then?' said he.

"'I never had e'er a mother,' said I.

"This made him laugh. 'What,' said he, 'had you never a mother; what then?'

"'I had a nurse,' said I, 'but she was not my mother.'

"'Well,' says he to the gentleman, 'I dare say this boy was not the thief that stole your bills.'

"'Indeed, sir, I did not steal them,' said I, and cried again.

"'No, no, child,' said he, 'we don't believe you did. This is a clever boy,' says he to the other gentleman, 'and yet very ignorant and honest; 'tis pity some care should not be taken of him, and something done for him; let us talk a little more with him.' So they sat down and drank wine, and gave me some, and then the first gentleman talked to me again.

"'Well,' said he, 'what wilt thou do with this money now thou hast it?'

"'I don't know,' said I.

"'Where will you put it?' said he.

"'In my pocket,' said I.

"'In your pocket,' said he; 'is your pocket whole? sha'n't you lose it?'

"'Yes,' said I, 'my pocket is whole.'

"'And where will you put it when you come home?'

"'I have no home,' said I, and cried again.

"'Poor child!' said he; 'then what dost thou do for thy living?'

"'I go of errands,' said I, 'for the folks in Rosemary-lane.'

"'And what dost thou do for a lodging at night?'

"'I lie at the glass-house,' said I, 'at night.'

"'How, lie at the glass-house! have they any beds there?' said he.

"'I never lay in a bed in my life,' said I, 'as I remember.'

"'Why,' says he, 'what do you lie on at the glass-house?'

"'The ground,' says I, 'and sometimes a little straw, or upon the warm ashes,'" etc.

Here Defoe describes one of the performances of a young rascal:

"How he did to whip away such a bag of money from any man that was awake and in his senses, I cannot tell; but there was a great deal in it, and among it a paper full by itself. When the paper dropt out of the bag, 'Hold,' says he, 'that is gold!' and began to crow and hollow like a mad boy. But there he was baulked, for it was a paper of old thirteenpence halfpenny pieces, half and quarter pieces, with ninepences, and fourpence halfpennies—all old crooked money—Scotch and Irish coin; so he was disappointed in that: but as it was, there was about £17 or £18 in the bag, as I understood by him; for I could not tell money, not I."

These inadequate quotations must suffice to show the similarity in the subjects between the Spanish picaresque stories and Defoe's novels; they bear, too, a striking resemblance to some of the scenes in Grimmelshausen's "Simplicissimus."* And "Colonel Jack" is not the only

---

* For example, Erstes Buch, Capitel 8:

" *Einsiedel.* Wie heissestu?

" *Simplicius.* Ich heisse Bub.

" *Eins.* Ich sihe wohl, dass du kein Mägdlein bist; wie hat dich aber dein Vater und Mutter gerufen?

" *Simp.* Ich habe keinen Vater oder Mutter gehabt.

" *Eins.* Wer hat dir dann das Hemd geben?

" *Simp.* Ei, mein Meuder.

" *Eins.* Wie heisset dich dann dein Meuder?

" *Simp.* Sie hat mich Bub geheissen, auch Schelm, ungeschickter Tölpel und Galgenvogel.

" *Eins.* Wer ist dann deiner Mutter Mann gewest?

" *Simp.* Niemand.

" *Eins.* Bei wem hat dann dein Meuder des Nachts geschlafen?

" *Simp.* Bei meinem Knan.

" *Eins.* Wie hat dich dann dein Knan geheissen?

" *Simp.* Er hat mich auch Bub genennet.

" *Eins.* Wie hiesse aber dein Knan?

" *Simp.* Er heisst Knan.

" *Eins.* Wie hat ihn aber dein Meuder gerufen?

" *Simp.* Knan und auch Meister.

" *Eins.* Hat sie ihn niemals anders genennet?

" *Simp.* Ja, sie hat.

" *Eins.* Wie dann?

" *Simp.* Rülp, grober Bengel, volle Sau und noch wol anders, wann sie haderte.

" *Eins.* Du bist wol ein unwissender Tropf, dass du weder deiner Eltern noch deinen eignen Namen nicht weist!

example ; the "Memoirs of a Cavalier," which Dr. Johnson thought genuine, the "Captain Singleton," and I may
even include the "History of the Plague," which has to
be shown up every few years for an imaginary account,
and the "Moll Flanders" and "Roxana"—all the genuine
novels of this list describe vicious characters and adventurous careers.   As in the Spanish novels, the most striking thing is the picturesque setting ; the novels, indeed,
are like some of the modern French pictures—the French
novels are mainly satirical, and Defoe's contain practical
morality. He always teaches a lesson. We have seen
how he did this even in his "Robinson Crusoe." One of
the few exceptions is when, after the Spanish ship was
wrecked with all on board, Robinson says : "Such were
these earnest wishings, 'That but one man had been
saved !   O that it had been but one !'   I believe I repeated the words, 'O that it had been but one !' a thousand
times ; and my desires were so moved by it that when I
spoke the words, my hands would clinch together, and my
fingers press the palms of my hands, that if I had had any
soft thing in my hand, it would have crushed it involuntarily ; and my teeth in my head would strike together,
and set against one another so strong, that for some time
I could not part them again."   And, chap. viii. : "Before,
as I walked about, either on my hunting, or for viewing
the country, the anguish of my soul at my condition would
break out upon me on a sudden, and my very heart would
die within me to think of the woods, the mountains, the
deserts I was in ; and how I was a prisoner, locked up
with the eternal bars and bolts of the ocean, in an unin-

"*Simp.* Eia, weist dus doch auch nicht.

"*Eins.* Kanstu auch beten ?

"*Simp.* Nain, unser Ann, und mein Meuder haben als das Bett gemacht."

habited wilderness without redemption. In the midst of
the greatest composures of my mind, this would break out
upon me like a storm, and made me wring my hands, and
weep like a child. Sometimes it would take me in the
middle of my work, and I would immediately sit down
and sigh, and look upon the ground for an hour or two
together, and this was still worse to me; for if I could
burst out into tears, or vent myself by words, it would
go off; and the grief, having exhausted itself, would
abate."

These passages show that Defoe was by no means insensible to the romantic interest of the situation he described with such great skill, but in general he confined
himself, as we all know, to the description of facts. His
homely narratives—that is, all his stories except "Robinson Crusoe"—have always belonged to the lower stratum
of literature, but the spirit that inspired them has never
become wholly extinct. He, to be sure, limited himself to a sordid method, to the dexterous adaptation, as
Mr. Minto says, of means to ends; but his unwearying
realism is still one of the main forces in the English
novel.

While it is only the "Robinson Crusoe" that floats
Defoe's other novels, this stands outside of the regular
progress of the fiction of England, which soon grew famous in the hands of Richardson. We all know how this
peaceful printer, at the age of fifty-one, suddenly burst
into authorship, and became one of the most famous
writers of his time. His own account of this step is well
worth consideration, especially because at first sight it
seems to show that his treatment of the novel was
wholly fortuitous, and in no way dependent upon what
his predecessors had accomplished. In a letter to Aaron
Hill, he said that the foundation of the story of "Pa-

mela," * in which the heroine withstands the solicita-
tions of her master, and finally induces him to marry
her, was an anecdote which he had heard some twenty-
five years earlier. The way in which he happened to
write it was this : " Mr. Rivington and Mr. Osborne,
whose names are on the title-page, had long been urging
me to give them a little book (which, they said, they
were often asked after) of familiar letters on the useful concerns in common life ; and, at last, I yielded to
their importunity, and began to recollect such subjects
as I thought would be useful in such a design, and formed
several letters accordingly. And, among the rest, I thought
of giving one or two as cautions to young folks circum-
stanced as Pamela was. Little did I think, at first, of
making one, much less two volumes of it. But, when I
began to recollect what had, so many years before, been
told me by my friend, I thought the story, if written in an
easy and natural manner, suitable to the simplicity of it,

---

* Pamĕla, it is often pronounced now, although Richardson doubtless
said Pamĕla. Thus in an introductory poem we find, "Sweet Pamela, for
ever blooming maid." And in the verses the heroine writes to her fellow-
servants :

> "My fellow-servants dear, attend
> To these few lines which I have penned ;
> I'm sure they are from your honest friend
> And wisher-well, poor Pamela."

Pope, however, "To Miss Blount, with works of Voiture," has

> "The gods to curse Pamela with her prayers."

Fielding says ("Joseph Andrews," bk. iv. chap. xii.): "They had a
daughter of a very strange name, Pamĕla or Pamĕla ; some pronounced it
one way, and some the other."
In "A Remedy for Love," Sidney has

> "Philoclea and Pamela sweet,
> By chance in one great house did meet."

might possibly introduce a new species of writing, that might possibly turn young people into a course of reading different from the pomp and parade of romance-writing, and dismissing the improbable and marvellous, with which novels generally abound, might tend to promote the cause of religion and virtue. I therefore gave way to enlargement ; and so Pamela became as you see her. But so little did I hope for the approbation of judges, that I had not the courage to send the two volumes to your ladies, until I found the books well received by the public.

"While I was writing the two volumes, my worthy-hearted wife, and the young lady who is with us, when I had read them some part of the story, which I had begun without their knowing it, used to come into my little closet every night, with—'Have you any more of Pamela, Mr. Richardson ?' 'We are come to hear a little more of Pamela,' etc. This encouraged me to prosecute it, which I did so diligently, through all my other business, that, by a memorandum on my copy, I began it Nov. 10, 1739, and finished it Jan. 10, 1739–40."

If any book seems to have been written independently it was this. Yet it is important to notice that, by his own confession, he was desirous of writing something "that might possibly turn young people into a course of reading different from the pomp and parade of romance - writing, and dismissing the improbable and marvellous, with which novels generally abound, might tend to promote the cause of religion and virtue." We find him, then, obeying the spirit of his time by reacting against the decaying romantic novels, the heroic romances which were in the lady's library mentioned by the *Spectator*, and following the bent of part of his contemporaries by teaching the importance of virtue. To Richardson the heroic romances seemed absurd and exaggerated. He was tired of the lovesick emperors of imaginary countries and the fantastic princesses, and determined to show what were the dangers really surrounding human beings ; and he took the only means in his power of doing this. He described life as he knew it. Defoe, there can be no doubt, struck a lower class of readers, and indeed, even now, when, naturally enough, there is a strong tendency to admire any work in the past that seems animated by the modern spirit, his novels are simply the reading of the curious. If further proof is needed of Richardson's dependence on laws stronger than any man's whim, it may be found in the fact that there were, as Erich Schmidt says, Richardsonians before Richardson. The most celebrated of those was Marivaux (1688-1763), who published a French *Spectator* in 1722, and in 1731 published his novel "Marianne," which he left unfinished—the completion being added by Mme. Riccoboni, a few years later.*

This story is very much like those of Richardson. The heroine loses her parents at an early age, and is taken care of by the curé of the village near by until her sixteenth year, when his sister is called to Paris to attend a relative at the point of death. She takes Marianne with her— who recounts her own adventures—to find her some employment. But the curé's sister is taken ill and dies ; the curé himself falls into a state of imbecility and has spent all his money, so that Marianne could not think of returning to him. She turns for succor to a monk to whom her friend had recommended her on her death-bed. She is intrusted to a man with a fine reputation for benevo-

---

* There is no ground for affirming that Richardson had read it. Fielding had, however. In "Joseph Andrews" (1742), bk. iii. chap. i., he says: "The same mistakes may be found in Scarron, the 'Arabian Nights,' the 'History of Marianne,' and 'Le Paisan Parvenu.'" Of the "Paysan Parvenu" a translation appeared in 1735.

lence, who is, however, a monster of hypocrisy. After
some harrowing scenes with this infamous persecutor, one
day, on her way home from mass, she sprains her ankle,
and is carried to the house of a M. Valville, who, it is unnecessary to add after saying that the heroine had sprained
her ankle, falls at once madly in love with her. This
young gentleman is the nephew of the unvenerable villain
who assumes to be her protector, and there is much misunderstanding between the two gentlemen concerning
each other's intentions. Marianne finds refuge in a convent, where a benevolent lady, who overhears her story,
establishes her. This benevolent lady soon confides to
Marianne that she is in much distress because her son has
just refused an advantageous marriage on account of his
attachment for a young girl who had been carried into
her house after a slight accident. Marianne confesses that
she is the person, but, while she declares that she returns
his affection, she promises to do all in her power to deter
him from such an unequal alliance. Valville, however,
does not agree to this, and his mother consents to the marriage. All seems happily concluded, when Marianne is
reduced to despair by learning that Valville has fallen
madly in love with another woman, and Marivaux's part
of the story concludes with a nun's recital of her own woes,
with the purpose of distracting Marianne from the contemplation of her own sufferings. The continuation puts
an end to the long episode about the nun, and narrates
how the woman with whom Valville is in love is an unworthy intriguer. He means to elope with her to England, but is prevented and put in the Bastile. An officer
falls in love with Marianne, but she, at any rate, is constant and refuses him. Valville is taken sick, and Marianne hastens to the Bastile to nurse him. He repents
his errors and renews his attachment; it is discovered

that she belongs to a very noble family, and they at last marry happily.

The main idea of this novel is the same as that of Richardson's "Pamela," that virtue and honesty triumph over all persecutions; but in Marivaux's novel the uprightness is of a higher kind than Pamela's rigid, calculating, bargaining virtue. Marianne is a loving person who is willing to sacrifice herself and never see her lover if she stands in the way of his prosperity; Pamela is simply looking out for her own advantage. In spite of this difference between the two books, they are sufficiently alike in intention and in choice of subject. They show how similar causes produce similar results. Yet this novel had no imitators in France, where a few years later Richardson was hailed with warmth as the founder of a new school.

In France, too, I may say here, there had been an earlier reaction against the heroic novel, in Mme. de La Fayette's story, "La Princesse de Clèves," a calm narrative of social complication, as different as possible from the heroic novels, with their pompous, inflated love-making. Yet the most complete modification appeared in England; the "Princesse de Clèves" belonged to a more refined society than that of England, and Lee's play of that name (1681) was a base travesty of a beautiful novel. The reaction that appeared in England was characteristic of that country because made up of the elements that existed there. As I have said, the middle class was more important because more powerful there than anywhere, and as it grew into prominence it became impatient of the aristocratic literature which was fashionable, and the new novel became a study of the middle classes. Its moral turn was that which was popular with these people. It recalls that of the *Spectator*, just as the incidents are like the brief sketches which Addison and Steele were fond of writing. The picaresque novels, it need scarcely be said, had no influence on Richardson, though we shall soon see them again inspiring other writers. He was simply giving human interest to fiction which for a long time had been occupied with the intrigues of aristocrats. Marivaux's novel was almost an accidental occurrence, though the result of similar causes, while Richardson founded a school. Princes and princesses had to give way to human beings, when royal authority could be made by act of parliament, and naturally curiosity was diverted to those who had the power which was expressed by the parliament. In England, too, the great change from feudalism to the modern industrial society was completed, and naturally the novel which pictured this society was written there.

CHAPTER VIII.

I. The stage, too, had taken notice of the change. We have seen how artificial was Addison's "Cato," yet it set a literary fashion. If even Addison, whose taste was so much above that of his contemporaries, could write that cold tragedy, need we wonder that Thomson, who drew inspirations for his poems from Milton and Spenser, should have written a severely classical tragedy? One line of it ran, "Oh! Sophonisba; Sophonisba, oh!" which some one in the pit turned to ridicule by shouting out, "Oh! Jemmy Thomson, Jemmy Thomson, oh!" and which Fielding again laughed at in his "Tragedy of Tragedies; or, the Life and Death of Tom Thumb the Great" (1730–31), in the line, "Oh! Huncamunca, Huncamunca, oh!" This burlesque of Fielding's is not unamusing. It is prefaced with a long essay, with mock references to Aristotle and Horace, and there are notes containing extracts from the tragedians who are most frequently parodied, and caricatures of the pompous critics. Thus, "Act i. sc. i., the Palace; *Doodle, Noodle:*

> "*Doodle.* Sure such a day as this was never seen!
> The sun himself, on this auspicious day,
> Shines like a beau in a new birthday suit:
> This down the seams embroidered, that the beams,
> All nature wears one universal grin.

"Note.—Corneille recommends some very remarkable day wherein to fix the action of a tragedy. This the best of our tragical writers have understood to mean a day remarkable for the serenity of the sky, or what we generally call a fine summer's day: so that, according to this exposition, the same months are proper for tragedy which are proper for pastoral. Most of our celebrated English tragedies, as *Cato, Mariamne, Tamerlane,* etc., begin with these observations on the morning. Lee seems to have come the nearest to this beautiful description of our author's."

And then he quotes from Lee's tragedies some of his passages of this sort:

> " The sun, too, seems
> As conscious of my joy, with broader eye
> To look abroad the world, and all things smile
> Like Sophonisba."

Noodle replies:

> " This day, O Mr. Doodle, is a day,
> Indeed!—A day we never saw before,
> The mighty Thomas Thumb victorious comes;

" Note.—Dr. B—y reads, The mighty Tall-mast Thumb. Mr. D—s, The mighty Thumbing Thumb. Mr. T—d reads, Thundering. I think Thomas more agreeable to the great simplicity so apparent in our author."

Scene II.

> " *King.* Let nothing but a face of joy appear;
> The man who frowns this day shall lose his head,
> That he may have no face to frown withal.
> Smile Dollallolla—Ha! what wrinkled sorrow
> Hangs, sits, lies, frowns upon thy knitted brow?"

And in a note on this last line we find:

> " Repentance *frowns* on thy contracted brow."—Soph.
> " *Hung* on his clouded brow, I mark'd despair."—Ibid.
> " A sullen gloom
> *Scowls* on his brow."—Busiris.

Here again is a parody of a sufficiently common fault of the tragedians. The ghost of Tom Thumb's father appears to King Arthur, and says:

> " Oh! then prepare to hear—what but to hear
> Is full enough to send thy spirit hence.

Thy subjects up in arms, by Grizzle led,
Will, ere the rosy-fingered morn shall ope
The shutters of the sky, before the gate
Of this thy royal palace, swarming spread.
So have I seen the bees in clusters swarm,
So have I seen the stars in frosty nights,
So have I seen the sand in windy days,
So have I seen the ghosts on Pluto's shore,
So have I seen the flowers in spring arise,
So have I seen the leaves in autumn fall,
So have I seen the fruits in summer smile,
So have I seen the snow in winter frown.

" *King.* Damn all thou hast seen! Dost thou beneath the shape
Of Gaffer Thumb, come hither to abuse me
With similes, to keep me on the rack?
Hence—or by all the torments of thy hell,
I'll run thee through the body, though thou'st none.

" *Ghost.* Arthur, beware! I must this moment hence,
Not frighted by your voice, but by the cock's!
Arthur, beware! beware! beware! beware!
Strive to avert thy yet impending fate;
For if thou'rt killed to-day,
To-morrow all thy care will come too late."

And when Noodle comes to announce that Tom Thumb
has been swallowed by "a cow, of larger than the usual
size," he enters the scene with these words :

" Oh! monstrous, dreadful, terrible, oh! oh!
Deaf be my ears, forever blind my eyes!
Dumb be my tongue! feet lame! all senses lost!
Howl, wolves; grunt, bears; hiss, snakes; shriek all ye ghosts!

" NOTE.—These beautiful phrases are all to be found in one single
speech of *King Arthur, or the British Worthy.*

" Chrononhotonthologos," produced in 1734, is another
mock tragedy, by Henry Carey, author of " Sally in Our
Alley." This " most Tragical Tragedy that ever was
Tragedized by any Company of Tragedians " begins in
an antechamber of the palace, where Rigdum Funidos

learns that the King is asleep. The King, on awakening, threatens to banish Somnus from his dominions. There is to be eternal pantomime to keep mankind from sleep. In the midst of the pantomime a guard cries :

> " To arms! to arms! great Chrononhotonthologos!
> Th' antipodean powers from realms below
> Have burst the solid entrails of the earth ;
> Gushing such cataracts of forces forth
> The world is too incopious to contain 'em."

Chrononhotonthologos takes the King of the Antipodes, who walks with his head where his feet should be. The King is invited to take some wine in the tent of his general, Bombardinion ; he assents, and expresses a desire for something to eat. Bombardinion to the cook :

> " See that the table constantly be spread
> With all that Art and Nature can produce.
> Traverse from pole to pole ; sail round the globe ;
> Bring every eatable that can be eat :
> The king shall eat tho' all mankind be starved."

A quarrel arises. The King kills the cook and strikes his general :

> " *Bombardinion.* A blow! Shall Bombardinion take a blow ?
> Blush, blush, thou sun! Start back then rapid ocean !
> Hill, vales, seas, mountains! All commixing crumble,
> And into Chaos pulverize the world ;
> For Bombardinion has received a blow,
> And Chrononhotonthologos shall die."

And he kills him. A physician is brought, who says :

> " My lord, he's far beyond the power of physic ;
> His soul has left his body and this world.
> " *Bombardinion.* Then go to 'tother world and fetch it back.
> And if I find thou triflest with me there,   [*Kills him.*
> I'll chase thy shade thro' myriads of orbs,
> And drive thee far beyond the verge of nature.

Ha! call'st thou, Chrononhotonthologos?
I come! your faithful Bombardinion comes!
He comes in worlds unknown to make new wars,
And gain thee empires num'rous as the stars."   [*Kills himself.*

These two pieces were the destructive part of the new feeling, and this found further expression in George Lillo's (1693–1739) tragedy, "The London Merchant, or the History of George Barnwell," which was brought out in 1731, ten years before Richardson's "Pamela" was published. It marks in the history of the stage the same change which Richardson introduced into the novel. Yet the comparison must not be carried too far; they agree in the most devoted respect for morality, but in art poor Lillo is the merest bungler, and by the side of Richardson he makes but a poor show.

The play itself was what the Germans call epoch-making; first, because it was written in prose, and secondly, because of the plot, which was taken from an old ballad,* that "of 'George Barnwell,' an apprentice of London, who thrice robbed his master, and murdered his uncle in Ludlow," thus bringing a citizen on the stage as hero. The plot is, briefly, the story of the young apprentice, who gets into bad company, and to stealing money, and murder, so that the last scene is the place of execution, "The gallows and ladders at the further end of the stage." To us this seems a sufficiently common plot, yet, at the time it

---

* "A Yorkshire Tragedy" (1608) is sometimes mentioned as an early play with the modern spirit, but it must be remembered that it was written long before the heroic drama existed. Not even in France were there rules at that time. It was a dramatization of a story told in a ballad.

John Home's "Douglas" (1756) was founded on the ballad of "Gil Morrice." The play keeps close to the unities. Of Lillo's other plays, "Fatal Curiosity" (1737) observes the unities; "Arden of Feversham" does not.

was produced, the fact that the play had nothing to do with kings and heroes was enough to make it the object of very genuine curiosity. "The witlings," we are told, called it "a Newgate Tragedy," and even proposed to receive it with scorn, but they were overcome by its pathos and disarmed of their ill-will. The prologue, by Mr. Cibber, Jun., was an ingenious petition for a kind hearing :

> "The Tragic Muse, sublime, delights to show
> Princes distrust, and scenes of royal woe;
> In awful pomp, majestic, to relate
> The fall of nations, or some hero's fate.
>   *　　*　　*　　*　　*
> Upon our stage indeed, with wish'd success,
> You've sometimes seen her in a humbler dress;
> Great only in distress. When she complains
> In Southern's, Rowe's, or Otway's moving strains,
> The brilliant drops that fall from each bright eye,
> The absent pomp, with brighter gems, supply.
> Forgive us then, if we attempt to show,
> In artless strains, a tale of private woe.
> A London 'Prentice ruined is our theme,
> Drawn from the fam'd old song that bears his name.
> We hope your taste is not so high to scorn
> A moral tale, esteem'd e'er you were born.
>   *　　*　　*　　*　　*
> Though art be wanting, and our numbers fail,
> Indulge the attempt in justice to the tale."

Fully to understand the importance of this play in the history of literature, we must recall the extremely artificial nature of the heroic drama, with its unities, and the necessity that was imposed on it of concerning itself only with princes and heroes.* We have seen how the

---

* As Kuno Fischer has well condensed it, the stage had modelled itself on society with its rigid distinctions of rank. Princes and heroes belonged to tragedy; the middle class to comedy, peasants to the pastorals. See his "Lessing als Reformator der deutschen Sprache" (Stuttgart: Cotta, p. 73).

dramatists groaned under their self-imposed chains, how Corneille entreated in vain for thirty hours, and suggested that it was possible to take an interest in the fate of common people. What Corneille had said in 1651 Lillo repeats in the prefatory letter to this play : " If Princes, &c., were alone liable to misfortunes, arising from vice, or weakness in themselves, or others, there would be good reason for confining the characters in tragedy to those of superior rank ; but, since the contrary is evident, nothing can be more reasonable than to proportion the remedy to the disease. I am far from denying that tragedies, founded on any instructive and extraordinary events in History, or well-invented Fable, when the persons introduced are of the highest rank, are without their use, even to the bulk of their audience. . . . I have attempted, indeed, to enlarge the province of the graver kind of poetry, and should be glad to see it carried on by some abler hand."

Still, the success of the play settled the question whether or not the novelty was justifiable, although it, of course, did not put an end to all cavilling. One of the comments upon it, in the old edition, is ascribed to a " Living Authoress," who says, with a certain scorn, " Mr. Lillo being a tradesman, was perhaps thereby influenced to describe scenes in humble life ; beyond which his knowledge could only exist in theory"—although it would be fair to ask how much the ordinary writers of tragedies knew of Eastern emperors, and whether the heroic plays were bits of heroic autobiography. " . . . Though not founded on the distresses of the great, yet Colly Cibber eagerly received this Pathetic Drama, which was soon patronized by the Mercantile Interest, and after its first run of twenty successive nights in the summer, was also frequently represented to crowded houses during the following winter.

" Mr. Pope allowed that the Fable was well conducted ; the Language. natural, and if sometimes elevated above the simplicity of the characters, yet it never was mean, nor deviated from propriety of. style calculated to affect the heart."

Yet it is a most wretched play ; to the last degree stilted, with a sort of melodramatic *tremolo* running through it.* For instance, take the speech of Mr. Thorowgood, in answer to the good Mr. Trueman, who has remarked that, according to his observation,

" those countries, where trade is promoted and encouraged, do not make discoveries to destroy, but to improve mankind, by love and friendship ; to tame the fierce and polish the most savage," etc.

"*Thorowgood.* 'Tis justly observed : the populous east, luxuriant, abounds with glittering gems, bright pearls, aromatick spices, and health-restoring drugs : The late-found western world glows with unnumbered veins of gold and silver ore. On every climate and on every country, heaven has bestowed some good peculiar to itself. It is the industrious merchant's business to collect the various blessings of each soil and climate, to enrich his native country.—Well ! I have examined your accounts : they are not only just, as I have always found them, but regularly kept, and fairly entered. I commend your diligence. Method in business is the surest guide. He who neglects it, frequently stumbles, and always wanders perplexed, uncertain, and in danger. Are Barnwell's accounts ready for my inspection ; he does not use to be the last on these occasions."

Or this, when Barnwell is about to murder his uncle :

" Murder my uncle ! Yonder limpid stream, whose hoary fall has made a

---

* His prose, which is, rather, a tremulous blank verse, resembles some that we find in Dryden's plays, and, indeed, held its ground down to an undetermined period in this century. Dryden, for instance, has (" Amboyna," iii. 1): " Dead with grief ; with these two hands I scratch'd him out a grave ; on which I placed a cross, and every day wept o'er the ground where all my Joys lay bury'd. The manner of my Life who can express ! The Fountain Water was my only Drink, the crabbed Juice and Rind of half-ripe Lemmons my only Food, except some Roots ; my House the widow'd Cave of some wild Beast," etc.

natural cascade, as I pass'd by, in doleful accents seem'd to murmur, murder. The earth, the air, and water, seem'd concerned; but that's not strange," etc.

Then the uncle appears, his imagination "fill'd with ghastly forms of dreary graves, and bodies changed by death," etc.

"[*Enter* GEORGE BARNWELL *at a distance.*]

"O death, thou strange mysterious power, seen every day, yet never understood, but by the uncommunicative dead, what art thou?" etc.

When he gets to the end of his sentence, Barnwell rushes forward and stabs him; he falls wishing blessings on

"My dearest nephew; forgive my murderer, and take my fleeting soul to endless mercy." *

"*Barnwell.* Expiring saint! O murder'd, martyr'd uncle!" etc.

The heroic language survived in the following passages, and doubtless helped to redeem the play in the eyes of its critics:

"*Maria.* Why are your streaming eyes still fixed below, as though thou'dst give the greedy earth thy sorrows, and rob me of my due? Were happiness within your power, you should bestow it where you pleased; but in your misery I must and will partake.

"*Barnwell.* Oh! say not so, but fly, abhor, and leave me to my fate. Consider what you are: how vast your fortune, and how bright your fame: have pity on your youth, your beauty, and unequalled virtue, for which so many noble peers have sighed in vain. Bless with your charms some honourable lord. Adorn with your beauty, and by your example improve, the English court, that justly claims your merit; and so shall I quickly be to you as though I had never been.

* * * * * * * *

"*Barnwell.* Ere I knew guilt or shame, when fortune smiled, and when

---

* In the ballad, this incident is more curtly narrated:

"Sudden within a wood,
   He struck his uncle down,
And beat his brains out of his head;
   So sore he crackt his crown."—Percy's "Reliques."

my youthful hopes were at the highest; if then to have raised my thoughts to you, had been presumption in me never to have been pardoned, think how much beneath yourself you condescend to regard me now.

"*Maria.* Let her blush who, professing love, invades the freedom of your sex's choice, and meanly sues in hopes of a return. Your inevitable fate hath rendered hope impossible as vain. Then why should I fear to avow a passion so just and so disinterested?

* * * * * * * *

"*Barnwell.* So the aromatic spices of the East, which all the living covet and esteem, are with unavailing kindness wasted on the dead."

It will be seen that a thrifty tradesman was lost in George Barnwell. The earnest moral aim of the play fell in with the popular spirit, but its main importance was that it introduced a hero from private life.* Otway, to be sure, had done this, for no man is ever the first to do anything, but Lillo went lower, and selected an apprentice of London, who is a much less romantic person than a Venetian conspirator. The moral tendency had been shown by Southern, Rowe, and Addison—the same moral tendency that inspired the *Spectator;* Lillo not only enforced that, but he opened the stage to contemporary interests. Lillo continued in the same path which he had had the good fortune to open; he wrote his "Fatal Curiosity," which Fielding brought out in 1736, writing a prologue for it which contained these lines:

"No fustian hero rages here to-night;
No armies fall to fix a tyrant's right:

---

* In his "Réflexions Historiques et Littéraires sur les Différents Théâtres de l'Europe" (Amsterdam, 1740), p. 132, Riccoboni mourns the defection of the English from what he calls the reform of the stage which Addison's "Cato" had so well begun: "On s'était imaginé que cette tragédie en avait donné la loi au Théâtre Anglois, mais les tragédies nouvelles, que l'on a données depuis dans leur ancien goût, et particulièrement une des dernières qui a pour titre 'Georges Barnevelt,' et que a eu un si grand succès ne nous font pas présumer qu'ils puissent jamais changer."

From lower life we draw our scene's distress,
Let not your equals move your pity less."

Edward Moore, in 1753, brought out the "Gamester;" and Cumberland wrote a number of plays continuing the reaction against the French dramatic rules. The influence of Lillo's reform was felt in England less than in France and Germany, because in England, as we have seen, the French rules were less revered than on the continent. We have seen how little the unities were regarded by the English writers, and teaching morality by the plays certainly does not improve the stage. The novel absorbed more general interest, and the theatre languished.

In France, this new step found many admirers and imitators, the most important of whom was Diderot, who (vii. 95) compared the scene between Maria and Barnwell in prison with the "Philoctetes" of Sophocles, as the hero is heard shrieking, and also translated Moore's "Gamester." Diderot's own plays were written in direct opposition to the classical views of his time, but they were not successful. "The Natural Son," taken, without acknowledgment, from Goldoni's "A True Friend," is certainly as vapid a play as ever was written, and was a complete failure on the stage (written 1757, brought out 1771). "The Father of the Family" (written 1758, acted 1761) is better, and was, at least in Germany and Italy, popular. But, as Mme. de Staël said, "Diderot, in his plays, put the affectation of nature in the place of the affectation of convention." It was not so much Diderot's own plays as what he wrote about acting that aided the revolution in taste which, in his way, Lillo had begun. To be sure, Diderot very strongly urged that plays should directly inculcate morality, forgetting, as Mr. Morley says ("Diderot," 215), that "exhortation in set speeches always has been, and always will be, the feeblest bulwark against

the boiling floods of passion that helpless virtue ever invented, and it matters not at all whether the hortatory
speeches are placed on the lips of Mr. Talkative, the son
of Saywell, or of some tearful dummy labelled the Father
of the Family." In other respects he was wiser ; his rule
was, " Watch nature, follow her simple and spontaneous
guiding," and he enforced this in many ways, in condemning the French classic drama. " The dialogue," he
said, " is all emphasis, wit, and glitter ; all a thousand
leagues away from nature. Instead of artificially giving
to their characters *esprit* at every point, poets ought to
place them in such situations as will give it to them.
Where in the world did men and women ever speak as
we declaim? Why should princes and kings walk differ-
ently from any man who walks well? Did they then
gesticulate like raving madmen? Do princesses when
they speak utter sharp hissings?" (" Bijoux Indiscrets,"
ch. xxxviii.) It was in the criticism of details that he was
wisest and that his influence was most widely felt.* One
reason was that the great romantic revival was to draw
its life from the Dark Ages, which Diderot † hated, as did

---

* He said (Morley's " Diderot," p. 226) that, first, a domestic or bourgeois
tragedy must be created ; secondly, the conditions of men, their callings
and situations, the types of classes, in short, must be substituted for mere
individual characters ; thirdly, a real tragedy must be introduced upon the
lyric theatre ; and that, finally, the dance must be brought within the forms
of a true poem.

Diderot wrote plays that brought into literature the sufferings of the
middle classes, as they then began to be put upon canvas by Greuze.
This connection between painting and literature may be often seen. The
Dutch painters were much admired, for instance, in England and Spain.
Louis XIV. could not tolerate them. A full exposition of the analogy be-
tween the two arts would take up too much space.

† It would not be exact to say that all the influence which moved Diderot
in this direction came from Lillo alone. Destouches (1680–1754) in his

all the Encyclopædists. He, however, broke open the road which literature was about to follow.

Diderot's influence on Lessing was very great, and this showed itself not only in the German's onslaught on the so-called tragedy, which is a model of literary criticism, but also in his creative work, where he closely copied the English models, and with more ability than was shown by Diderot, who was a critic above all things. We left the German stage, when we last spoke of it, in the care of Gottsched, who had brought out his play, " Der sterbende Cato " (1732), modelling himself on Addison's play, doubtless with special delight that he could appeal to Addison's example ; for, as we saw, his opponents, Bodmer especially, made great use of Addison's defence of Milton in their attack on the French school. If the literature of this period was everywhere artificial, an invention of the cultivated classes, nowhere was this more the case than in Germany. There the divorce between the aristocracy

---

" Glorieux," and La Chaussée (1692–1754), preceded him in this movement. Riccoboni wrote of the latter : " La Chaussée a inventé un nouveau genre de comédie ; elle avait toujours représenté les incidents domestiques des bourgeois, des gens aisés et quelquefois même des artisans. Il y a cependant dans la société une espèce de personnages qui sont exclus d'une action comique ; on croit les gentilshommes et les grands seigneurs d'une haute naissance, trop élevés pour entrer dans les situations domestiques qui ont toujours été le partage de la comédie ; ils ne peuvent pas non plus agir dans le tragique, parce qu'ils ne sont pas assez grands pour chausser le cothurne, que n'appartient qu'à des princes et à des actions héroïques. Ce sont ces mêmes personnes, qui occupent, si l'on peut se servir de ce terme, une espèce de niche isolée et un certain milieu entre le rang élevé de la tragédie et le populaire de la comédie, que M. de la Chaussée a imaginé de faire entrer dans une action, qui puisse avoir tantôt l'intéressant de la tragédie et tantôt les situations de la vie civile entre des gens de condition, et qui conserve aussi le caractère de la comédie " (Lettre à Muratori).

But it is to be noticed that La Chaussée kept to the unities !

and the people was complete; the language even was
neglected, and French became the common medium of
communication, with which all the writers were familiar
and many used exclusively. But the seed which Bodmer
sowed bore good fruit, and the nation turned gradually
away from France and learned to read and study English
writers. This tendency prevailed throughout the last
century. We see it referred to in Goethe's autobiography, and in old libraries we find a number of German
reprints of English books, such as Goldsmith and Ossian,
and countless translations of popular writers. We find
mention, too, of occasional translations of single plays of
Shakspere. "Julius Cæsar" was put into German in 1741,
but into Alexandrines, however. Lessing, who was born
in 1729, welcomed the new movement, and wrote his "Miss
Sara Sampson" (1755), the very name of which indicates
its pedigree. This play belongs to the same school with
"George Barnwell" and the "Gamester;" it is what the
Germans call a "bürgerliches Trauerspiel." One of his
friends, Ramler, wrote to Gleim, "The audience sat for
four hours like statues, and dissolved in tears."[*]

Here the tearfulness of the last century may be said to
begin. Indeed, these plays were called *la comédie larmo-
yante* as well as *bourgeoise*, and the sentimentality which
appeared in them and novels was one of the early reac-
tions against the omnipotence of reason.[†] Judging from

---

[*] Schröder, later known as the actor of Shakspere, and who held in
Germany much the same place as Garrick in England, was then but ten
years old, and played the little girl, Arabella.

[†] Compare the French enthusiasm over Rousseau. Thus, Taine, "L'Ancien
Régime," p. 210: "On bâtit dans son parc un petit temple à l'Amitié. On
dresse dans son cabinet un petit temple au Bienfaisance. On porte des
robes à la J. J. Rousseau 'analogues aux principes de cet auteur.' On
choisit pour coiffure 'des poufs au sentiment,' dans lesquels on place le
portrait de sa fille, de sa mère, de son serin, de son chien, tout cela garni

their literature, our ancestors in the last century when they were alone brooded over the terrors of the grave; when they were in the company of their kind, they wept profusely. At any rate, those Germans who wept over "Miss Sara Sampson" had soon a chance to weep again, for "George Barnwell" was a few days later acted by the same troupe (Stahr, i. 145). Of Diderot's further influence on Lessing—which the German critic cheerfully acknowledged—and of "Minna von Barnhelm," etc., there is no need of speaking here. It is only necessary to say that in the "Emilia Galotti" Lessing took a step further by placing the sanctity of the family in direct opposition to the caprice of a prince (as did Schiller in his "Kabale und Liebe"), and that he lifted up the whole drama by precept as well as example when he showed the Germans how great a genius was Shakspere. He did this, too, without injustice to the French tragedians.

In England, however, there was no resuscitation of the drama, but the novel flourished as it had not done before, and we must return to Richardson to see the full nature of this change. It would be easy to turn Richardson to ridicule. The enormous length of his novels may seem absurd to us, but this must have been a great charm in the days when amusing literature was in its infancy. We have seen the strong moral tendency in the writers of this age, and although Pamela taught the practical lesson that

---

des cheveux de son père ou d'un ami de cœur. . . . Toutes les fois que des amies se disent des choses sensibles, elles doivent subitement prendre une petite voix claire et trainante, se regarder tendrement en penchant la tête, et s'embrasser souvent."

See also Erich Schmidt's "Richardson, Rousseau und Goethe," p. 190; Goncourt's "La Femme au XVIIIe Siècle," p. 380; Morley's "Rousseau," ii. 31. Compare Miss Austen's "Sense and Sensibility." See, too, "A Study of Sensibility" in the *Fortnightly* for September, 1882.

virtue secured position in this world as well as in the next, Richardson in "Clarissa Harlowe" drew a picture of real, indomitable virtue. "Pamela" was enormously admired at the time. As Mr. Morley says ("Diderot," p. 256), "All England went mad with enthusiasm over the trials, the virtue, the triumph of a rustic ladies' maid," and he points out that this novel marked a social as well as a literary transition. The people, we see, were beginning to lift up their heads and to assert themselves. In France, the enthusiasm was no less intense. Voltaire, although he really introduced English literature to the French, it is true, did not feel it; but Voltaire was above all things a member of the literary class, and that class is generally very far removed from possessing keen sympathy with the people, who are sure to introduce an element that needs refining; they prefer to refine what they already have. Moreover, Voltaire's intellectual zeal made him detest the Church as a relic of barbarism, of the Middle Ages, of popular superstition: he, in fact, never cared to introduce the barbarism which would follow social reform. What he said about "Clarissa Harlowe" was this: "It is cruel for a man like me to read nine whole volumes in which you find nothing at all. I said—even if all these people were my relations and friends, I could take no interest in them. I can see nothing in the writer but a clever man who knows the curiosity of the human race, and is always promising something from volume to volume, in order to go on selling them."

In his "Lettre à d'Alembert sur les Spectacles," Richardson praises "Pamela," and makes admiring mention of "George Barnwell," which appeared in a French translation at Paris, in 1751. In a note, he says that no novel had ever appeared in any language which came near "Clarissa."

Diderot set no bounds to his praise in his celebrated

eulogy on Richardson : " O Richardson, Richardson, unique among men in my eyes, thou shalt be my favorite all my life long ! If I am hard driven by pressing need, if my friend is overtaken by want, if the mediocrity of my fortune is not enough to give my children what is necessary for their education, I will sell my books ; but thou shalt remain to me, thou shalt remain on the same shelf with Moses, Homer, Euripides, Sophocles !

" O Richardson, I make bold to say that the truest history is full of falsehoods, and that your romance is full of truths. History paints a few individuals ; you paint the human race. History sets down to its few individuals what they have neither said nor done ; whatever you have set down to man, he has both said and done. . . . No ; I say that history is often a bad novel ; and the novel as you have handled it, is good history. O painter of nature, it is you that are never false.

" You accuse Richardson of being long ! . . . Think of the details what you please, but for me they will be full of interest if they are only true, if they bring out the passions, if they display character. They are common, you say ; it is all what one sees every day. You are mistaken ; 'tis what passes every day before your eyes, and what you never see."

Dr. Johnson's criticism is worthy of note : " Why, sir, if you were to read Richardson for the story, your impatience would be so much frighted that you would hang yourself. But you must read him for the sentiment, and consider the story only as giving occasion to the sentiment." Nowadays, however, instead of laying violent hands upon ourselves, we lay them on the book, cutting out the useless matter,* and reading Richardson, if we

---

* An abridgment appeared in Philadelphia in 1798.

read him at all, only in an abridgment. What he especially lacks is the power of delineating great passion ; he
has the keenest eye in the world for sentiment and all the
machinery of social life, and in the "Clarissa" has accomplished the task of drawing a great tragedy by the accumulation of details, but his Lovelace is as impossibly
full of vices as his "Sir Charles Grandison" (did the
name have only an accidental resemblance to Addison ?)
is of virtues. The fact is that the aim of teaching morality
by direct exhortation is as destructive to novels and plays
as works of art as it is to music, sculpture, or painting.
Society is justified in demanding that lessons of wicked-
ness should not be inculcated, but it will in time leave
lessons of goodness unread, though it may express the
warmest approval of them. There is Sir Charles Grandison, for example, who was described as a model man
after Richardson had learned with horror that some people had been so far misled as to admire the vicious Lovelace. His goodness is inexhaustible, and it is much to
Richardson's credit that, after all, we do not hate this
"faultless monster whom the world ne'er saw," even after
reading the description of his virtues and their effects.
To start with, he is young, twenty six or seven years
old—although in the popular imagination of the present
time he is eternally about fifty-two, or just twice his
real age—rich, handsome : "In his aspect," writes Miss
Byron, "there is something great and noble that shows
him to be of rank. Were kings to be chosen for beauty
and majesty of person, Sir Charles Grandison would have
few competitors. I cannot quote the whole description
of his charms ; I will turn to the contemplation of a few
of his moral qualities, and what are closely connected
with them, his personal habits. He dresses to the fashion, rather richly, 'tis true, than gaudily ; but still richly :

so that he gives his fine person its full consideration. . . .
His equipage is perfectly in taste, though not so much
to the glare of taste, as if he aimed either to inspire
or shew emulation. He seldom travels without a set, and
suitable attendants ; and, which I think seems a little to
savour of singularity, his horses are not docked ; their
tails are only tied up when they are on the road. This I
took notice of when we came to town. I want, methinks,
my dear, to find some fault in his outward appearance,
were it but to make you think me impartial ; my gratitude to him, and my veneration for him notwithstanding.
But if he be of opinion that the tails of these noble
animals are not only a natural ornament, but are of real
use to defend them from the vexatious insects that in
summer are so apt to annoy them (as Jenny has just now
told me was thought to be his reason for not depriving
his cattle of a defence, which nature gave them), how far
from a dispraise is this human consideration !" etc. And
this is as near criticism of the good Sir Charles as anything in the book. Miss Byron, who is in womanly charm
all that he is in manliness, to be sure, does most of the
writing about him, and her feelings when he is concerned
are very much inclined in his favor. She is not alone in
this. Sir Charles is already half engaged to an Italian
lady, Clementina, who is only withheld by religious scruples
from marrying him. He holds a position in the novel very
much like that which General Washington holds in the
minds of good Americans who form their opinion of the
father of their country from orations and postage-stamps.
He is placid, able, gentlemanly, and very statuesque. He
is willing to marry Clementina, if fate commands, though
he is in love with Harriet, and we feel tolerably certain
that he will not languish with a broken heart whatever
happens. Why should he indeed? Consolation was more

than abundant: he has a ward, Emily, of whom Miss Byron writes (letter lxxxvi.), "I wish my godfather had not put it in my head that Emily is cherishing (perhaps unknown to herself) a flame that will devour her peace. For, to be sure, this young creature can have no hope that —yet £50,000 is a vast fortune.—But it can never buy her guardian. Do you think such a man as Sir Charles Grandison has a price?—I am sure he has not." It is needless to say that Sir Charles was proof against this new temptation. He had a snug fortune of his own. Then there was Lady Olivia, who pursued him to England—in vain. A man who is the object of so much admiration on the part of women is generally sure to be detested by men, but Sir Charles escapes this sad fate. Although he is always correcting the faults of the wicked, he does this with so much tact that they cannot withhold their respect for him. He especially opposed duelling. And when he had rescued Miss Byron from the hands of her abductor, this villain wished to get satisfaction from Sir Charles, but there was no persuading him to fight. Not that he was a coward—far from it; he had conscientious objections to the practice. He talks so reasonably that he converts his opponents to his views, which he expounds at some length, to the admiration of his hearers. "'The devil take me, Sir Hargrave,'" says one, "'if you shall not make up matters with such a noble adversary.'" The other says: "'He has won me to his side. . . . I had rather have Sir Charles Grandison for my friend than the greatest prince on earth!'" And the third: "'I had rather be Sir Charles Grandison in this one past hour, than the Great Mogul all my life.'" "And Sir Hargrave even sobbed." He has, too, great skill with the sword, so that when he was set upon by two ruffians in his own house, he disarmed them both and turned them out-of-doors. He mourns, however,

that he has been " provoked by two such men to violate
the sanctity of his own house." This is the only crime
even his morbid conscience can convict him of, and his
excuse is "that there were two of them ; and that though
I drew, yet I had the command of myself so far as only to
defend myself, when I might have done with them what I
pleased." And indeed he was doubly armed, for not only
could he disarm two antagonists at a time, but even without his sword he was secure, for he once talked one of the
wicked into a fit.

However, this unsympathetic description of the book
does not describe it as it seemed to our ancestors or indeed to us when we read it. It does no justice to the
manner in which, in spite of the exaggeration of the hero's
virtues, the life of that day is represented. What he did
was to give us realistic drawings of impossible people.
Every line in their faces is from life ; they move about
the room, open and shut doors, talk, and act apparently as
people do in real life ; their emotions are described with
the most cunning art, yet they lack the highest truth.
They do not so much follow the laws of their own character as they do Richardson's ever-present desire to serve the
highest morality. This is the artistic fault of the novels,
and the reason why they are left stranded on the dusty
shelves, for no moral excellence will long take the place
of truth. The novels carried too heavy a load of instruction, and it finally swamped them. Yet when the general
tendency of the age lay in the direction of moral teaching,
these books were enormously admired, especially when they
were almost without rivals, and their truthfulness in regard
to many matters of detail aided their influence. Through
them spoke one of the main inspirations of the time, the
new power of the middle class, and its revolt against aristocratic corruption. This tendency in literature was as

firmly connected with political tendencies, as nowadays
the drawing of pictures from still lower life is indissolu-
bly connected with the gropings of the laboring classes
for power. The fact that the social difference between
Pamela, the serving-maid, and her aristocratic master, is
broken down by means of her superior moral qualities,
shows this. Pamela remarks somewhere that the skull of
a king is like that of a poor man; that princes and beggars
must alike appear before the judgment-seat. It is not long
before the notion of equality, when it has got thus far, is
transferred from the next world to this. When she hears
that her master is to be made a peer, she says it would be
better if he were made a virtuous man. Social distinctions
begin to be threatened when remarks of this kind are made.

On the other hand, "Sir Charles Grandison" is an appeal in the direction of conservatism by showing the great
how they should live—how, if they are virtuous, their de-
pendents will be peaceable and contented. It is easy for
us to see that the solution of these difficulties may have
appeared simple to Richardson, yet his moral lessons were
thrown away, and the French Revolution came at last.
Just as now, especially in Europe, Nihilism in various
forms lies smouldering beneath the surface, and those in
authority seek their own pleasure and aggrandizement as
if the future contained no perils and the past no lessons.
In time, perhaps, the essential interdependence of all parts
of the state will be recognized; it will not be in fiction
alone that working-men will be objects of interest.

In Germany, the influence of Richardson's novels was
very great.* Gellert wrote of him ("Ueber Richardson's
Bildniss") :

> "Unsterblich ist Homer, unsterblicher bei Christen
> Der Britte Richardson."

---

* *Vide* Erich Schmidt's "Richardson, Rousseau und Goethe," p. 11.

Translations flooded the market. Gellert, too, in 1746, wrote his novel " Das Leben der schwedischen Gräfin von G. . . . " in close imitation of Richardson. Other writers followed in the same path.

Rousseau's famous novel," La Nouvelle Héloïse " (1761), is the most important of the books that drew inspiration from Richardson; and from the impetus given by the " Nouvelle Héloïse " * started much of the spirit that animated " Werther." While Richardson's influence thus spread over the Continent, in England his impossible heroes and heroines were about to succumb to a strong reaction.†

What deposed Richardson from the undivided supremacy which he held in England was the appearance of Fielding, whose characters are certainly far from idealized. Fielding, after a life of varying experience as a theatre-manager, a student, a man of fortune, and a playwright, being reduced to such a condition that, as he said, he had no choice but to be a hackney-writer or a hackney-coachman, wrote his first novel really under something like disgust with Richardson's pious devotion to respectability.

---

* Was not Rousseau indebted to the matronly Richardson for some part of his zeal in urging that mothers nurse their children ? *Vide* " Sir Charles Grandison," letter ccc. As to Rousseau's notions about the management of a household in the latter part of " La Nouvelle Héloïse," cf. " Sir Charles Grandison," letter cclxvi., and " Pamela," letter xc.

† England has often begun a movement that it has itself in good part ignored, letting it pass over to the Continent, and only fully receiving it after it has been trimmed and put into shape and has become universal property. Thus, Locke's philosophy, to some extent the family novel, and more recently Darwinism, which is held by a few able men, but has not thoroughly penetrated the universities, and is not the inspiring spirit of students to anything like the same extent as in Germany, or as in the France of the last few years.

England produces the raw material, sends it off, and imports it again made up, as the Southerners do with their cotton.

It was not ordinary literary jealousy that inspired him, but a reaction against the morbid tendencies of Richardson's novels.* If these seem to draw their inspiration from tea and toast, Fielding's have the full flavor of beer and tobacco ; and no greater contrast can be imagined than that between Sir Charles Grandison and Fielding's hearty, roystering, careless, happy - go - lucky heroes. Richardson's people seem to be crouching over a fire in a parlor ; Fielding's are forever laughing through the world, beginning, enjoying, or getting over a carouse. They are, from one point of view, brutal fellows — for Fielding lived in a coarse time, among a coarse people— but they are at least human. The adventurous picaresque stories have borne fruit here, although much of it is of a sort that we cannot admire now. Who, for instance, over the age of fourteen, can get any amusement from the account of Parson Adams's visit to Parson Trulliber ? Parson Adams is simply one of the simplest, most lovable characters in fiction, and Fielding treats him as a jocose savage would treat a captive : he rolls him in the mire, ducks him, and plays rough tricks on him in a way that would shame a schoolboy. Here is the incident with Parson Trulliber : Parson Adams determines to make him a visit ; Mr. Trulliber, who had just been feeding his pigs, "immediately slipped off his apron and clothed himself in an old night-gown, being the dress in which he always received company. His wife, who informed him of Mr. Adams's arrival, had made a small mistake ; for she had told her husband, 'she believed here was a man come for

---

* Others, too, thought Richardson inexact. *Vide* "Letters and Works of Lady Mary Wortley Montagu" (London, 1837), iii. 40, letter of Oct. 20, 1756. Compare, too, his "Sir Charles Grandison" with Mrs. Sheridan's vivid "Memoirs of Miss Sidney Bidulph," which appeared in 1761, the year of Richardson's death.

some of his hogs.' This supposition made Mr. Trulliber hasten with the utmost expedition to attend his guest. He no sooner saw Adams than, not in the least doubting the cause of his errand to be what his wife had imagined, he told him, 'he was come in very good time ; that he expected a dealer that very afternoon ;' and added, 'they were all pure and fat, and upwards of twenty score a-piece.' Adams answered, 'He believed he did not know him.' 'Yes, yes,' cried Trulliber, 'I have seen you often at fair ; why, we have dealt before now, mun, I warrant you. Yes, yes,' cries he, 'I remember thy face very well, but won't mention a word more till you have seen them, though I have never sold thee a flitch of such bacon as is now in the stye.' Upon which he laid violent hands on Adams, and dragged him into the hog-stye, which was indeed but two steps from his parlour-window. They were no sooner arrived there than he cried out, 'Do but handle them ; step in, friend ; art welcome to handle them, whether dost buy or no.' At which words, opening the gate, he pushed Adams into the pig-stye, insisting on it that he should handle them before he would talk one word with him.

"Adams, whose natural complacence was beyond any artificial, was obliged to comply before he was suffered to explain himself ; and laying hold on one of their tails, the unruly beast gave such a sudden spring, that he threw poor Adams all along in the mire. Trulliber, instead of assisting him to get up, burst into a laughter, and entering the stye, said to Adams, with some contempt, 'Why, dost not know how to handle a hog ?'" and Adams explained that he was a clergyman, and had not come to buy pigs. After breakfast, Adams explains his errand, which is to borrow fourteen shillings, and, after a really amusing scene, he withdraws as poor as he came.

This is the way Fielding describes it : "A while he [Trulliber] rolled his eyes in silence ; sometimes surveying Adams, then his wife ; then casting them on the ground ; then lifting them up to heaven. At last he burst forth in the following accents : 'Sir, I believe I know where to lay up my little treasure as well as another. I thank G—, if I am not so warm as some, I am content ; that is a blessing greater than riches ; and he to whom that is given need ask no more. To be content with little is greater than to possess the world ; which a man may possess without being so. Lay up my treasure ! What matters where a man's treasure is whose heart is in the Scripture ? there is the treasure of a Christian.' At these words the water ran from Adams's eyes ; and catching Trulliber by the hand in a rapture, 'Brother,' says he, 'heavens bless the accident by which I came to see you ! I would have walked many a mile to commune with you ; and, believe me, I will shortly pay you a second visit ; but my friends, I fancy, by this time, wonder at my stay ; so let me have the money immediately.' Trulliber then put on a stern look, and cried out, 'Thou dost not intend to rob me ?' At which the wife, bursting into tears, fell on her knees, and roared out, 'O dear sir ! for heaven's sake don't rob my master : we are but poor people.' 'Get up, for a fool as thou art, and go about thy business,' said Trulliber ; 'dost think the man will venture his life ? he is a beggar and no robber.' . . . 'But suppose I am not a clergyman, I am nevertheless thy brother ; and thou, as a Christian, much more as a clergyman, art obliged to relieve my distress.' 'Don't preach to me !' replied Trulliber : 'dost pretend to instruct me in my duty ?' 'I fack, a good story,' cries Mrs. Trulliber, 'to preach to my master.' 'Silence, woman,' cries Trulliber. 'I would have thee know, friend (addressing himself to Adams), I shall not learn my duty from such as thee. I know what charity is, better than to give to vagabonds.' . . . 'I am sorry,' answered Adams, 'that you do know what charity is, since you practise it no better : I must tell you, if you trust to your knowledge for your justification, you will find yourself deceived, though you should add faith to it, without good works.' 'Fellow,' cries Trulliber, 'dost thou speak against faith in my house ? Get out of my doors : I will no longer remain under the same roof with a witch who speaks wantonly of faith and the Scriptures.' 'Name not the Scriptures,' says Adams. 'How, not name the Scriptures ! Do you disbelieve the Scriptures ?' cries Trulliber. 'No, but you do,' answered Adams, 'if I may reason from your practice ; for their commands are so explicit, and their rewards and punishments are so immense, that it is impossible a man should stedfastly believe without obeying. Now, there is no command more express, no duty more frequently enjoined, than charity. Whoever, therefore, is void of charity, I make no scruple of pronouncing that he is no Christian.' 'I would not advise thee,' says Trulliber, ' to say that I am no Christian : I won't take it of you ; for I believe I am as good a man as thyself.' . . . His wife, seeing him clench his fist, interposed, and begged him not to fight, but to show himself a true Christian, and take the law of him. As nothing could provoke Adams to strike, but an absolute assault on himself or his friend, he smiled at the angry looks and gestures of Trulliber ; and telling him he was sorry to see such men in orders, departed without further ceremony."

Here the later scene relieves the horse-play of the first part, but the reader wearies of the perpetual practical jokes of which Adams is the object. Such a case was that where he was reminded that in ancient days it was customary to receive a philosopher in great state. Ac-

cording to the proposer of the plan, it was a favorite
method of receiving Socrates. "There was a.throne
erected, on one side of which sat a king, and on the other
a queen, with their guards and attendants ranged on both
sides ; to them was introduced an ambassador, which
part Socrates always used to perform himself; and when
he was led up to the footsteps of the throne, he addressed
himself to the monarchs in some grave speech, full of
virtue, goodness, morality, and such like. After which,
he was seated between the king and queen, and royally
entertained. This, I think, was the chief part."... Adams
said, "It was indeed a relaxation worthy of so great a
man ; and thought something resembling it should be
instituted among our great men, instead of cards and
other idle pastime, in which, he was informed, they
trifled away too much of their lives." So the plan was
carried out ; Parson Adams read his sermon, to the great
entertainment of all present, and then was invited to sit
down between their majestics. As he sat they rose, and
he sank into the tub of water that awaited him. The
king he also ducked ; then he left the house, catching a
cold, "which threw him into a fever that had like to have
cost him his life." Some of this inexhaustible boyishness
may be merely the result of Fielding's impatience with the
superfine priggishness of Richardson's novels, and in part
a precise copy of the rough life that he had himself seen.
Some, too, is to be accounted for by the model which he
chose—indeed, one may almost say, the only model that lay
before him—the picaresque novel, for it was in the manner
of "Don Quixote," as he himself avowed on his title-page,
that the novel was written. And it is to this book, or at
least to the spirit which animated it, and to others of the
same kind, as Scarron's "Roman Comique," that he was
indebted for the mock-heroic style, the caricature of the

old romances, that is to be found in both "Joseph Andrews" and "Tom Jones "—*e. g.*, "Now the rake Hesperus had called for his breeches, and, having well rubbed his drowsy eyes, prepared to dress himself for all night," etc. The perpetual beatings of Parson Adams are, too, another reminiscence of "Don Quixote." The introduction of the episode of Leonora in "Joseph Andrews" is sanctioned, it will be remembered, by the example of the picaresque novels.

Yet the resemblance to "Don Quixote" is but an external one. Fielding has none of the poetical spirit which inspired Cervantes to write one of the few greatest works of literature, a book of which it is but the smallest merit that it expelled from literature the obsolescent romance. Life has no complexity in Fielding's eyes ; it has troubles, to be sure, but they are very simple troubles, such as tormenting creditors, the next day's headache, the difficulty of finding ready money. He does not approach that more important field of the contrast between the imagination and the lessons of reality which is described allegorically in the story of the Don and his squire. Nor did Smollett do more. They both kept closely to their task of drawing life as they saw it, and whoever does this does something rare and admirable. Yet the general movement of the novel was away from them. They brought to its highest development the novel of incident, of life, and they paid no attention to the wave of sentimentality that was bedewing the eyes of half of their contemporaries. The other half undoubtedly enjoyed the rough heartiness of these writers, and we may see, in the controversy which Sterne excited, that at length public opinion was ceasing to be a unit. Literature was beginning to be divided into sets, as various influences were at work to affect men's minds. I have just mentioned Sterne, and it is interesting to notice that the first volume of his "Tristram Shandy" was written in 1759, ten years after the publication of "Tom Jones." At this time Sterne was forty-six years old. As his books show, he had dabbled in old French writers, as, indeed, had many of his contemporaries and predecessors, for a number of the light songs of Suckling, the poets of the Restoration, of Prior, etc., are translated from that language.* It was not only in Rabelais that Sterne found a precedent for his endless digressions ; other Frenchmen had followed that great model. It was a new kind of writing in England, however, and the publishers would have nothing to do with it, so that Sterne had the first two volumes printed at York, at his own expense. He swiftly found himself famous. Two hundred copies were sold in the first two days — a large number for the time, although in 1751 Fielding's "Amelia" was issued, of which Dr. Johnson said, "it was perhaps the only book of which, being printed off betimes one morning, a new edition was called for before night." But Fielding was a famous novelist, and Sterne was unknown outside of the circle of his friends. In a few months Sterne went to London to taste the sweets of popularity, and few have ever had such great success. Indeed, he was only outdone by Byron in this respect, and Byron had many other advantages—youth, beauty, and rank. Sterne was at once the rage. Salads, games of cards, race-horses, and doubtless hats, were named "Tristram Shandy." Reynolds painted the author's portrait ; Hogarth designed a frontispiece

---

* For example, " La Fleur des Chansons Amoreuses " (Rouen, *cir.* 1600 ; reprinted Brussels, 1866) contains the French originals of some of Suckling's and Dryden's songs, as well as what was probably the original of the song printed in the " Golden Treasury," " While that the sun with his beams hot."

for the book ; Warburton, Pope's friend, in January, 1760, bishop of Gloucester, recommended the novel to his brother-bishops, and Sterne found himself suddenly lifted out of obscurity and become a popular idol. Alongside of warm praise, there was much powerful opposition. Horace Walpole said : " At present, nothing is talked of, nothing admired, but what I cannot help calling a very insipid and tedious performance : it is a kind of novel, called ' The Life and Opinions of Tristram Shandy ;' the great humour of which consists in the whole narration always going backwards. I can conceive a man saying that it would be droll to write a book in that manner, but have no notion of his persevering in executing it. It makes one smile two or three times at the beginning, but in recompense makes one yawn for two hours. The characters are tolerably kept up, but the humour is forever attempted and missed." *

Goldsmith, in his " Citizen of the World," said : " There

---

* Walpole's literary judgments are curious : " I had rather have written the most absurd lines in Lee than ' Leonidas ' or the ' Seasons.' . . . There is another of these tame geniuses, a Mr. Akenside, who writes odes : in one of them he has lately published, he says, ' Light the tapers, urge the fire.' Had not you rather make gods jostle in the dark than light the candles for fear they should break their heads ?" " I have no desire to know the rest of my contemporaries, from the absurd bombast of Dr. Johnson, down to the silly Dr. Goldsmith ; though the latter changeling has had bright gleams of parts, and the former had sense till he changed it for words, and sold it for a pension."

About the " Botanic Garden," he says : " I send you the most delicious poem upon earth. If you don't know what it is all about, or why, at least you will find glorious similes about everything in the world, and I defy you to discover three bad verses in the whole stock," etc. And to Jephson, about his " Braganza :" " You seem to me to have imitated Beaumont and Fletcher, though your play is superior to all theirs. . . . You are so great a poet, Sir, that you have no occasion to labour anything but your plots," etc.

are several very dull fellows who, by a few mechanical helps, sometimes learn to become extremely brilliant and amusing, with a little dexterity in the management of the eyebrows, fingers, and nose. . . . But the writer finds it impossible to throw his winks, his shrugs, or his attitudes, upon paper. . . . As in common conversation, the best way to make the audience laugh is by first laughing yourself ; so in writing, the properest manner is to show an attempt at humour, which will pass upon most for humour in reality. To effect this, readers must be treated with the most perfect familiarity : in one page the author is to make them a low bow, and in the next to pull them by the nose ; he must talk in riddles, and then send them to bed in order to dream for the solution. He must speak of himself, and his chapters, his manner, and what he would be at, and his own importance, and his mother's importance, with the most unpitying prolixity ; and now and then testifying his contempt for all but himself, smiling without a jest, and without wit professing vivacity " (letter lii.). Richardson, who certainly was not a man of wide literary taste, thought the book execrable, and Dr. Johnson despised it. The difference of opinion among men of authority soon expressed itself in print ; pamphlets, it is said, were printed on each side, but Sterne's popularity among his friends was preserved by his perpetual wit. Warburton gave him a great deal of good advice which he did not take, and a purse of gold which he did ; but finally the bishop grew weary of his new friend, and, after passing through the stage of indifference, reached that of positive aversion, and he finally called Sterne an irrevocable scoundrel. But what did Sterne care for that ? He was given a new vicarage, which he called Shandy Hall, the name it still bears, and made over his other parishes to a curate. He had hopes of being

made a bishop, but the accession of George III. destroyed
these. He found consolation in more worldly pleasures.
" I never dined at home once since I arrived—am fourteen dinners deep engaged just now, and fear matters will
be worse with me in that point than better." And again,
after the publication of two more volumes : " One half of
the town abuse my book as bitterly as the other half cry
it up to the skies ; the best is they abuse and buy it, and
at such a rate that we are going on with a second edition
as fast as possible."

What is to be noticed is this—that the modern men
praised him, the old-fashioned condemned him. He represented a considerable part of the new spirit that was
spreading over Europe, the sensibility that was weeping
over Rousseau and preparing to weep over the young
Werther. The reaction against the long reign of reason
was wide-spread, and was naturally detested by those who
were satisfied by the old order of things. Even now,
when we have learned to be tolerant of the eccentricity
of other ages, it is hard to read with patience Sterne's discursive pages, and we can readily understand the feelings
of those who fancied that grinning through a horse-collar
was a dignified amusement by the side of composing passages like this : " Ptr—r—r—ing, twing,—twang, prut,
prut, 'tis a cursed bad fiddle ! Do you know whether my
fiddle's in tune or no ? They should be fifths.—'Tis evidently strung—tr-a-e-i-o-u—twang— The bridge is a
mile too high, and the ' sound post' absolutely down, else
—trut, prut—— Hark, 'tis not so bad a tone. Diddle,
diddle, diddle, diddle, dum——twaddle-diddle, tweedle-
diddle, twiddle-diddle, twoddle-diddle, tweedle-diddle—
prut—trut—krish—krash—krush. We have undone you,
sir, but you see he is no worse." And the book is crammed
with these tedious attempts at facetiousness, these fling-

ings of the heels into the air, the natural result of the
escape from long repression. They serve now but to
establish one undeniable truth that is too often forgotten,
that excess on one side is followed by excess on the other;
that the pendulum, if it starts from a high place on the
right side, will reach a high point on the left. The true
place will be reached in time, but the first impulse is
probably an excessive one. We see, for instance, in
French fiction of the present day a violent reaction from
the artificial methods of romanticism, a marked depart-
ure from the civilized fairy-land in which for a long time
writers have placed the scene of their books—and the new
men go just as far in the other way; they offend us by
going so far from fairy-land into the territory of foulness
that they are condemned more than is perhaps right.
They will probably be followed by men who will be more
moderate. One thing we may be sure of, the world will
not go back to the belief in the things which they have
demolished. Tastes may differ, and swing from one side to
the other, but men cannot return to old opinions. They
try to do it; they struggle to be simple, but the very
effort destroys simplicity. This, however, is a digression.
What has made "Tristram Shandy" an immortal book is
the pathos and humor with which Mr. Shandy and his
brother, Uncle Toby, are described. Here and there,
amid affectation, tediousness, and odious leering, we come
across passages that stand out like fine paintings in a large
gallery crowded with third or fourth rate work. It was
not only Sterne's restless style that enraged half his hearers, it was the attack he made on the literary principles
that governed the world. Thus (bk. i. chap. iv.): "I know
there are readers in the world, as well as many other
good people in it, who are no readers at all,—who find
themselves ill at ease, unless they are let into the whole

secret from first to last, of everything which concerns you.

"It is in pure compliance with this humour of theirs, and from a backwardness in my nature to disappoint any one soul living, that I have been so very particular already. As my life and opinions are likely to make some noise in the world, and, if I conjecture right, will take in all ranks, professions, and denominations of men whatever,—be no less read than the 'Pilgrim's Progress' itself—and, in the end, prove the very thing which Montaigne dreaded his essays should turn out, that is, a book for a parlour-window,—I find it necessary to consult every one a little to his turn; and therefore must beg pardon for going on a little further in the same way: For which cause, right glad I am, that I have begun the history of myself in the way I have done; and that I am able to go on tracing everything in it, as Horace says, *ab ovo*.

"Horace, I know, does not recommend this fashion altogether: But that gentleman is speaking only of an epic poem or a tragedy (I forget which),—besides, if it was not so, I should beg Mr. Horace's pardon; for in writing what I have set about, I shall confine myself neither to his rules, nor to any man's rules that ever lived."

And again with the dedication (bk. i. chap. xix.): "But, indeed, to speak of my father as he was;—he was certainly irresistible both in his orations and disputations; he was born an orator, Θεοδίδακτος. Persuasion hung upon his lips, and the elements of Logic and Rhetoric were so blended up in him—and, withal, he had so shrewd a guess at the weaknesses. and passions of his respondent—that nature might have stood up and said—'This man is eloquent.' In short, whether he was on the weak or the strong side of the question 'twas hazardous in either case to attack him. And yet, 'tis strange, he had never read Cicero, nor Quintilian de Oratore, nor Isocrates, nor Aristotle, nor Longinus, amongst the ancients ; nor Vossius, nor Skioppius, nor Ramus, nor Farnaby amongst the moderns ; and what is more astonishing, he had never in his whole life the least light or spark of subtilty struck into his mind, by one single lecture on Crackenthorp or Burgersdicius or any Dutch logician or commentator ;—he knew not so much as in what the difference of an argument *ad ignorantiam*, and an argument *ad hominem* consisted ; so that I well remember, when he went up along with me to enter my name at Jesus College in . . . , it was a matter of just wonder with my worthy tutor and two or three fellows of that learned society—that a man who knew not so much as the names of his tools, should be able to work after that fashion with them." Jesting of this sort must have seemed singularly irreverent to some of Sterne's contemporaries.

The book abounds with such passages (bk. iii. chap. xxiv.): "I care not what Aristotle, or Pacuvius, or Bossu, or Ricaboni say—though I never read one of them." And (bk. iii. chap. xii.): "And how did Garrick speak the soliloquy last night?—Oh, against all rule, my lord—most ungrammatically ! between the substantive and the adjective, which should agree together in number, case, and gender, he made a breach thus—stopping, as if the point wanted settling ; and betwixt the nominative case, which your lordship knows should govern the verb, he suspended his voice in the epilogue a dozen times, three seconds and three-fifths by a stop-watch, my lord, each time.—Admirable grammarian ! But in suspending his voice—was the sense suspended likewise ? Did no expression of attitude or countenance fill up the chasm ? Was the eye silent ? Did you narrowly look ?—I looked only at the stop-watch, my lord.—Excellent observer !

"And what of this new book the whole world makes such a rout about?—Oh! 'tis out of all plumb, my lord—quite an irregular thing! not one of the angles at the four corners was a right angle. I had my rule and compasses, &c., my lord, in my pocket.—Excellent critic!

"And for the epic poem your lordship bid me look at;—upon taking the length, breadth, height, and depth of it, and trying them at home upon an exact scale of Bossu, 'tis out, my lord, in every one of its dimensions.—Admirable connoisseur!

"And did you step in to look at the grand picture in your way back?—'Tis a melancholy daub, my lord; not one principle of the pyramid in any one group!—and what a price!—for there is nothing of the colouring of Titian,—the expression of Rubens,—the grace of Raphael,—the purity of Domenichino,—the *corregiescity* of Correggio,—the learning of Poussin,—the airs of Guido,—the taste of the Carachis,—or the grand contour of Angelo—grant me patience, just heaven!—Of all the cants which are canted in this canting world—though the cant of hypocrites may be the worst—the cant of criticism is the most tormenting!

"I would go fifty miles on foot, for I have not a horse worth riding on, to kiss the hand of that man whose generous heart will give up the reins of his imagination into his author's hands — be pleased he knows not why, and cares not wherefore."

Is it any wonder that half the world despised him, especially when he gave excuse for reasonable prejudice by superfluous indecorum? The outlook would have seemed black if they had for a moment supposed that this novel would ever become a classic.

The sermons, too, though they have been praised by no less an authority than Mr. Gladstone, enable us to understand how Methodism made its way in England amid the general frivolity of the Established Church. As Gray said of them, " You often see him tottering on the verge of laughter, and ready to throw his periwig in the face of the audience." Thus when he had given out his text (Ecclesiastes vii. 2, 3), "It is better to go to the house of mourning, than to go to the house of feasting," he began, "That I deny. But let us hear the wise man's reasoning upon it. 'Sorrow is better than laughter,' for a cracked-brain order of Carthusian monks, I grant; but not for men of the world." Or this: "The way the world usually judges is to sum up the good and bad against each other, deduct the lesser of these articles from the greater, and (as we do in passing other accounts) give credit to the man for what remains upon the balance." Often, too, reputations are "sent out of the world by distant hints, nodded away and cruelly winked into suspicion." Is it surprising that they were entitled the sermons of Mr. Yorick, published by Mr. Sterne? Dr. Johnson once owned that he had read them, "but," he said, "it was in a stage-coach; I should not even have deigned to have looked at them had I been at large;" and he said at another time, in Sherlock, and Tillotson, and Beveridge, "you drink the cup of salvation to the bottom; here, you have merely the froth from the surface." Certainly, when Sterne preached in Paris, to the leading unbelievers of the place, he was in more congenial company than he could have been in at home; and we are told that once he preached by invitation before the English ambassador there, and, as Stapfer says, this gave his friends, Holbach, Diderot, David Hume, Wilkes, etc., a chance to go for once in their lives into a church.

Yet Sterne's facetious remarks on religion are scarcely further removed from the great awakening that was about to pass over the religious sentiments of the English peo-

ple than were his literary innovations from the serious
change that was even then giving signs of its approach.
Yet, as we have seen, even he was helping the work; he
was breaking through the rigid chains of conventionality,
laughing at formal rules, and showing the pathetic side
of life. But, clever as his work was, it belonged essentially to the ante-revolutionary period, that curious time
when every one's attention was turned to solving by gentle measures the questions which stirred the world at the
end of the last century. Yet it is with gentleness that
such things begin, and in ridiculing the pedantry that
marked his contemporaries Sterne was doing good work.
When, in his "Sentimental Journey," he turned away from
all the statistics that made up the books of travels written
by his predecessors, and wrote not about old churches,
and views and picture-galleries, he was judging many of
the volumes which were written in the last century and
are reprinted, for that matter, with new names on the
title-page, every year of the present. Addison, for instance, visited Italy, apparently to verify the descriptions
written by the Latin poets, and Sterne was anxious to
show that what the traveller saw depended much more on
his own whims than on the geography of the place. It
was, in short, what it is defined to be by the title.

Yet we feel that Sterne was wholly unaware of the magnitude of the change that was impending. He lived at a
time when society in France and England was, so to
speak, dancing on the edge of a volcano; but few imagined what disturbances were about to break forth. But
to ask political wisdom, which was denied even to political
students, of the novelist, is going out of our way to find
fault. It is enough that Sterne has added at least one
figure to the few immortals of fiction, and to have done
this inclines one to overlook his many and obvious errors.

16

What Sterne possessed to a greater extent than any other English writer was the combination of qualities that in a Frenchman we call *l'esprit gaulois*. There is a sort of intellectual kinship between him and La Fontaine, for instance, which may to some extent explain the Englishman's popularity in France. The resemblance does not consist in what those who do not like him call his ribaldry, alone, but quite as much, or more, in his way of being serious, as in the less facetious parts of the "Sentimental Journey." Stapfer, in his excellent life of Sterne, brings out Sterne's seriousness very clearly. The John Hall Stevenson who in his worthless "Crazy Tales" tried to assume a Gallic wit and grace, showed himself merely a degraded Englishman. Sterne's sins brought violent retribution; his books he made unreadable for half the English-speaking race, and for the half that reads most. Moreover, his minor faults were easily and freely copied. Continuations of the "Sentimental Journey" abounded. Spurious "Letters to Eliza and from Eliza" were printed. Writers imitated his digressions and typographical freaks. Diderot honored him by clever imitation, and sentimentalism became one of the vices of the time. Whereas even Sterne's sentiment was often forced, that of his imitators became unbearable; he was ruined by his friends.

II. It is curious to observe a more fruitful inspiration which offered itself to novel-writers. Sterne brought to its climax one of the prevailing forces of his day, and after him we find but feeble attempts to produce the same notes. Fiction, or at least the most successful fiction, moved in a different channel. The first to lead the way being Horace Walpole, of all men, in his "Castle of Otranto." This story fills one of the conditions to be found in almost every form of writing that leaves its mark; its main merit is its novelty; it is itself commonplace and nearly unreadable.* It was an attempt to revive what was called the Gothic romance—Walpole called it a Gothic story—with such modifications as should serve to make the book read like a true narration. He said : " That great master of nature, Shakspere, was the model I copied."

We have seen how the whole movement in art and literature ever since the Renaissance had been directed against the Middle Ages ; how that period had been regarded as one of barbarism, every trace of which had to be eradicated from the human mind ; how Gothic architecture was derided, and the classic and pseudo-classic admired ; how rigidly writers followed the steady light of modern thought, which aimed to clear away superstition and to substitute reason. The work seemed at length done ; in France, religion was deposed, and even in England it was unfashionable, as we saw when we examined Sterne's shandyisms in the pulpit—yet at the very moment the work seemed accomplished men's minds returned with curiosity towards what they had just learned to reject, exactly as at the point of noon, when all is brightest, the sun, that has been climbing the heavens since dawn, begins to decline towards setting. Mr. Leslie Stephen is right when he says that thought moves in a spiral curve. Yet in literature the night that was approaching was not the one that had been left behind ; that was a dark one, this one was lit up by a perpetual full moon.

We shall soon return to studying the way in which the change gradually made its way in poetry. In fiction the

---

* The story is so silly that some have thought it was a burlesque—but a burlesque of what? There was in existence no original to laugh at. A book that is good of its kind proves the existence of a line of predecessors ; unfortunately, poor books may be written at any time, but the faults of the " Castle of Otranto " are those of a beginner. Compare it in this respect with " George Barnwell."

plunge was taken almost without any apparent sympathy
with that slow but wide-spread. movement. Walpole
sniffed at everything and everybody, and he must have
been much laughed at for his affectations. We have seen
how Pope ridiculed in his "Dunciad" the people who interested themselves in investigations of the past. They
were looked upon as would be men nowadays who should
try experiments in tattooing themselves, but Walpole was
a good deal of an antiquary. To be sure, his taste was
uncertain : Spenser he thought wretched stuff, and the
"Midsummer-Night's Dream," "forty times more nonsensical than the worst translation of any Italian opera-
books" (Horace Walpole to Bentley, Feb. 23, 1755). Although this view of Shakspere he afterwards modified a
little when, in his preface to the "Castle of Otranto" (2d
ed.), after the passage quoted, in which he said that he
had taken Shakspere for his model, he goes on : "Let
me ask if his tragedies of 'Hamlet' and 'Julius Cæsar'
would not lose a considerable share of their spirit and
wonderful beauties if the humour of the gravediggers,
the fooleries of Polonius, and the clumsy jests of the Roman citizens were omitted or vested in heroics ? Is not
the eloquence of Antony, the nobler and affectedly-un-
affected oration of Brutus, artificially exalted by the rude
bursts of nature from the mouths of their auditors ? These
touches remind one of the Grecian sculptor, who, to convey the idea of a Colossus within the dimensions of a
seal, inserted a little boy measuring his thumb. No, says
Voltaire, in his edition of 'Corneille,' this mixture of
buffoonery, and solemnity is intolerable." When Voltaire defended his criticism, Walpole swallowed his words
with great politeness, saying that when Shakspere lived
"there had not been a Voltaire both to give laws to the
stage, and to show on what good sense those laws were

founded. Your art, Sir, goes still further; for you have supported your arguments without having recourse to the best authority, your own works. It was my interest, perhaps, to defend barbarism and irregularity," etc. There could be, however, no greater waste of time than trying to find out Walpole's real opinions, for they are carefully hidden, and when found are worthless. He tried to pin himself to Shakspere's skirts, or, as he put it, " to shelter [his] own daring under the canon of the brightest genius this country, at least, has produced." He claims credit in the next line for " having created a new species of romance," and his boast was well founded.

I have said he was an antiquarian. In 1747 he bought his famous place, Strawberry Hill, which he turned into a pasteboard Gothic castle. He was said " to have outlived three sets of his own battlements," in a " little parlour hung with a stone-colour Gothic paper, and Jackson's Venetian prints," or " in the room where we always live, hung with a blue and white paper in stripes, adorned with festoons." It would be easy to laugh at Walpole's notions of the Gothic and of house-decoration; crocodile's tears could readily flow over the insincerity of the attempts at restoration—for that matter, even Sir Walter Scott had stucco and sham carving at Abbotsford as well as in his novels—yet Walpole had a room full of Holbeins and a number of genuine curiosities. What was singular was that he possessed this rare taste at all, not that he did not possess it as modified by a century of dilettanteism.* If

---

* According to Eastlake (*vide* his " Gothic Revival "), the love of Gothic architecture had never quite died out in England. See also *World*, No. 12, March, 1753 : " A few years ago, everything was Gothic; our houses, our beds, our bookcases, and our couches, were all copied from some parts or other of our old cathedrals. The Grecian architecture . . . which was taught by nature and polished by the graces, was totally neglected. . . . This,

there was the sham Gothic in his house, there was also
much in his novel, and where our grandfathers shuddered
we yawn; what kept them awake puts us to sleep. It

---

however odd it might seem, and however unworthy of the name of Taste,
was cultivated and was admired and still has its professors in different
parts of England."

Eastlake (*ut supra*, p. 52) mentions "Gothic Architecture improved by
Rules and Proportions in many Grand Designs of Columns, Doors, Windows, Chimney-pieces, Arcades, Colonades, Porticos, Umbrellos, Temples,
and Pavilions, etc., with Plans, Elevations, and Profiles; geometrically explained by B. and T. Langley" (London : 1742). He calls it a foolish
book.

The weight of evidence goes to show that whatever love of the Gothic
existed was outside of the polished circles, more of whose opinions have
reached us. Even Gray, when he went on the Continent in 1739, with
Horace Walpole, speaks of the Cathedral at Amiens as simply a "huge
Gothic building, beset on the outside with thousands of small statues,"
and of that at Sienna as "a huge pile of marble, laboured with a Gothic
niceness and delicacy in the old-fashioned way." But Defoe, in his "Tour
through Britain" (4th ed. 1748), praises Gothic architecture (*e. g.*, iii. 106):
"Another thing worthy of Notice in this Neighbourhood is the Tower and
Spire of the Church of *Laughton*, which for Delicacy and Justness of Proportion, is not excelled by any other *Gothic* Piece of the kind." See also
his account of York Cathedral, and, indeed, *passim.*

See, too, "Tom Jones" (1749). "The Gothic style of architecture could
produce nothing nobler than Mr. Allworthy's house. There was an air of
grandeur in it that struck you with awe, and rivalled the beauties of the
best Grecian architecture; and it was as commodious within as it was
venerable without. . . . Beyond this [the park] the country gradually rose
into a ridge of wild mountains, the tops of which were above the clouds."
Consequently, Sir William Chambers must have found some people ready
to receive these views: "To those usually called Gothic architects we are
indebted for the first considerable improvements in construction; there is
a lightness in their works, an art and boldness of execution to which the
ancients never arrived, and which the moderns comprehend and imitate
with difficulty. . . . One cannot refrain from wishing that the Gothic
structures were more considered, better understood, and in higher estimation than they hitherto seem to have been. Would our dilettanti, instead

is useless to be too sincere and to give the whole plot of this obsolete novel, in 1765. I shall mention but a few of the most characteristic of its qualities. Take the opening horror : the tyrant, Manfred, Prince of Otranto, is about to marry his son Conrad, a boy of fifteen, "a homely youth, sickly, and of no promising disposition," to Isabella, daughter of the Marquis of Vicenza ; the day is appointed, the guests are assembled, but Conrad is missed. An attendant is ordered to fetch him. In a moment, he "came running back, breathless, in a frantic manner, his eyes staring, and foaming at the mouth." His first words are "Oh! the helmet! the helmet!" His emotion is pardonable, for, on investigation, "what a sight for a father's eyes! he beheld his child dashed to pieces, and almost buried under an enormous helmet, a hundred times more large than any casque ever made for human being, and shaded with a proportionable quantity of black feathers." This incident was suggested to Walpole by a dream, and it is not the last time that what has seemed terrible to the dreamer has not appalled those to whom it has been told.

Besides this monstrous helmet, there is a monstrous sword, borne by one hundred gentlemen, who seemed to faint under the weight of it. More than this, the limbs of a giant haunt the castle : one man saw his foot and part of his leg in one room ; another time, one of the servants saw, or said she saw, "upon the uppermost ban-

---

of importing the gleanings of Greece, or our antiquarians, instead of publishing loose incoherent prints, encourage persons duly qualified to undertake a correct elegant publication of our own cathedrals and other buildings called Gothic, before they totally fall to ruin, it would be of real service to the arts of design, preserve the remembrance of an extraordinary style of building now sinking fast into oblivion, and at the same time publish to the world the riches of Britain in the splendour of her ancient structures" ("Treatise of Architecture," 1759, p. 128).

nister of the great stairs a hand in armour, as big, as big—I thought I should have swooned." This giant who made his appearance in serial form, in fragments like the statue that is to adorn Governor's Island in New York harbor, is not the only thing that is terrible. The statue of Alfonso takes part in the domestic strife, and when Manfred—whose bad temper, be it said by the way, is a good match for the bulk of the giant—says, " 'Frederick accepts Matilda's hand, and is content to waive his claim, unless I have no male issue'—as he spoke these words," the incredible happened — "three drops of blood fell from the nose of Alfonso's statue!" By the side of this, a portrait that descends from its frame, sighs, walks along the floor with a grave and melancholy air, and out of the door, which it shuts behind it with violence—is a mere every-day occurrence. The story is certainly ridiculous enough, and the plot, with its numerous complications, is well adapted to its setting. The heroine flees through secret passages, heroes pop out from behind the doors, strange claps of thunder are heard, which kept muttering for half a century ; and when Matilda interrupted the art-less prattle of her maid Bianca, who was talking naturally, after the manner, Walpole thought, of Shakspere's serving-people, " 'I do not wish to see you moped in a convent, as you would be if you had your will, and if my lady, your mother, who knows that a bad husband is better than no husband at all, did not hinder you—Bless me ! what noise is that? St. Nicholas forgive me ! I was but in jest.'—'It is the wind,' said Matilda, 'whistling through the battlements of the tower above ; you have heard it a thousand times,' "—when Matilda said that, she did not know it would be heard many thousand times again whist-ling about the battlements in Scott's novels and Byron's poems. And as for the moon, it has scarcely set yet.

" The lower part of the castle was hollowed into several intricate cloisters ; and it was not easy for one, under so much anxiety, to find the door that opened into the cavern. An awful silence reigned throughout those subterraneous regions, except now and then some blasts of wind that shook the doors she had passed, and which, grating on the rusty hinges, were re-echoed through that long labyrinth of darkness. Every murmur struck her with new terror." Having found the door, she entered the vault, and "it gave her a kind of momentary joy to perceive an imperfect ray of clouded moonshine gleam from the roof of the vault." In a few minutes, while she is talking with a youth who is helping her look for the lock to the hidden passage, "a ray of moonshine, streaming through a cranny of the ruin above, shone directly on the lock they sought."

A few moments before, the moon had been of service, for "Manfred rose to pursue her, when the moon, which was now up, and gleamed in at the opposite casement, presented to his sight the plumes of the fatal helmet, which rose to the height of the windows, waving backwards and forwards in a tempestuous manner, and accompanied with a hollow and a rustling sound." And later, "Gliding softly between the aisles, and guided by an imperfect gleam of moonshine that shone faintly through the illuminated windows, he stole towards the tomb of Alfonso," and slew his daughter, mistaking her for Isabella. Certainly Byron's Manfred got something more than his name from this domestic tyrant, and the poets of the romantic school were indebted for more than moonlight and roaring wind to this curious story. Here, for example, is Bianca's sketch of the hero who triumphed so long in poetry, and has now sunk to the *New York Ledger* and the covers of prune-boxes : "'But come, madam, suppose, to-morrow morning, he [your father] was to send for

16*

you to the great council chamber, and there you should
find, at his elbow, a lovely young prince, with large black
eyes, a smooth white forehead, and manly curling locks
like jet ; in short, madam, a young hero, resembling the
picture of the good Alfonso in the gallery, which you sit
and gaze at for hours together.'—' Do not speak lightly
of that picture,' interrupted Matilda, sighing : ' I know
the adoration with which I look at that picture is uncommon—but I am not in love with a coloured pannel. The
character of that virtuous prince, the veneration with
which my mother has inspired me for his memory, the
orisons which, I know not why, she has enjoined me to
pour forth at his tomb, all have concurred to persuade me
that, somehow or other, my destiny is linked with something relating to him,' " etc. Notice another novelty, where
Matilda, who, by a curious coincidence, spoke the truth
in those last words, was killed, " Frederick offered his
daughter to the new prince, which Hippolita's tenderness
for Isabella concurred to promote ; but Theodore's grief
was too fresh to admit the thought of another love ; and
it was not until after frequent discourses with Isabella of
his dear Matilda that he was persuaded he could know
no happiness but in the society of one with whom he
could for ever indulge the melancholy that had taken
possession of his soul." There had been melancholy before this, just as there had been moonlight, but enchanting gloom was now about to sweep over the world. Let
us see what other indications there were of the change in
men's feelings.

III. A complete examination of all the poets of the
last century would be immeasurably tedious, and without
going into long analyses of these writings we will examine
them simply to discover such traces as there may be of
what afterwards developed into genuine poetry. One of

the first evidences of a desire for something different from the regular couplet, which Pope had brought to such perfection, was the frequent use of blank verse. It was doubtless the edition of Milton, in 1688, that suggested this form ; or, at any rate, it confirmed them in their choice. In his edition of Spenser (London : Tonson, 1715, 3 vols.),* John Hughes wrote ("Dedication to Lord Sommers," v.) : "It was your Lordship's encouraging a beautiful edition of 'Paradise Lost' that first brought that incomparable poem to be generally known and esteemed." We have seen John Phillips's "Cyder," written, it was supposed, in the Miltonic manner, but it was also in more serious writing that this form was used. It would be rash, or at any rate unkind, to assert that Dr. Young, in his "Night

---

* Chaucer had been less neglected than Spenser, as is readily shown. Editions of Chaucer: Caxton's, 1475-6, and a second six years later, 1532, 1542, 1546, 1555, 1561, 1597, 1602; reprinted, 1687, 1721; volume containing "Prologue" and "Knight's Tale," 1737; and Tyrwhitt's, 1775-78; 2d ed. 1798.

Thomas Wilson, in his "Arte of Rhetorike" (1553), quoted by Warton, says: "The fine courtier will talk nothing but Chaucer."

Topsel's "History of Four-footed Beasts and Serpents" (1658) quotes Chaucer's description of the Franklin.

Denham, in his poem on Cowley's death, speaks of "Old Chaucer."

In the *Idler*, No. 49, "On the third day uprose the sun and Mr. Marvel."

Chaucer's "Tales," London, 1665 ; and "Troilus and Cressida" in Latin, by Fr. Kynaston, Oxon. 1635.

This attempt to revive an interest in Spenser apparently met with little success. Dr. Johnson, in his life of Hughes : "He did not much revive the curiosity of the public; for near thirty years elapsed before his edition was reprinted." The Glossary contained the following words, now sufficiently familiar : aghast, appal, atween, ay (ever), baleful, bay (bark), bedight, behest, boot, bootless, bourn (torrent), buxom (yielding), canon (a rule), cark, carol, certes, checkmate, cheer, n., chivalry, complot, cleped, con, cotes, couth, craven, credence, distraught, dole, doff, don, doughty, dreary, eftsoons, eld, elfs, elfin, embossed, ensample, eyne, forlorn, foray,

Thoughts," tried to imitate Milton in his blank verse. He had written several satires in the form that Pope used, and these are perhaps worth brief examination. Thus (sat. iii.), "Love of Fame a Universal Passion :"

> " To show the strength and infamy of pride,
> By all 'tis followed and by all deny'd,
> What numbers are there, which at once pursue
> Praise, and the glory to contemn it, too ?
> Vincenna knows self-praise betrays to shame,
> And therefore lays a strategem for fame ;
> Makes his approach in modesty's disguise,
> To win applause ; and takes it by surprise.
> ' To err,' says he, ' in small things is my fate,'
> You know your answer, ' he's exact in great.'
> ' My style,' says he, ' is rude and full of faults,'
> ' But, oh ! what sense ! what energy of thoughts !'
> That he wants Algebra he must confess ;
> ' But not a soul to give our arms success.'
> ' Ah ! That's a hit indeed,' Vincenna cries ;
> ' But who in heat of blood is ever wise ?
> I own 'twas wrong, when thousands called me back,
> To make that hopeless, ill-advis'd attack ;
> All say, 'twas madness ; nor dare I deny ;
> Sure never fool so well deserv'd to die,' " etc.

His lyric flights were less successful ; thus, in "Ocean : an Ode" (1727), he says :

---

gear, glee, guerdon, guileful, guise, hie, hight, hoar, ire, kirtle, lief, leman, levin, plight, welkin, well, v., whilom, wend, wise, n., yore. Many of the above and the following are taken from Percy's " Reliques :" ban, beshewn, blent (blended), boon, bugle (horn), churl, dank, dell, den, doublet, foregoe, glen, gloze, leech, meed, mishap, moor, peril, quean, scant, troth, tush, unctuous, unkempt, wax, v. The Glossary to Thomson's " Castle of Indolence " contains also the following, as well as some of those just quoted : bale, blazon, cates, deftly, eke, fain, lea, moil, nathless, palmer, prankt, ruth, scar, shun, smackt, sooth, thrall, ween, whenas, wot, etc. Other words in the Glossary to Percy are : astound, aureat, caytiffe, check (stop), dint, erst, and trim (exact).

" The stars are bright
  To cheer the night,
And shed, through shadows, temper'd fire ;
  And Phœbus flames
  With burnish'd beams,
Which some adore, and all admire.

  Are then the seas
  Outshone by these ?
Bright Thetis ! thou art not outshone ;
  With kinder beams,
  And softer gleams,
Thy bosom wears them as thy own.
  *   *   *   *   *
  Those clouds, whose dyes
  Adorn the skies,
That silver snow, that pearly rain ;
  Has Phœbus stole
  To grace the pole,
The plunder of th' invaded main !

  The gaudy bow,
  Whose colours glow,
Whose arch with so much skill is bent,
  To Phœbus' ray,
  Which paints so gay,
By thee the watery woof is lent," etc.

Then there was " The Last Day " (1713), a subject that
our grandfathers were fond of treating, as Dryden's lines
about it show. Young does but little better—

" Now man awakes, and from his silent bed,
  Where he has slept for ages, lifts his head ;
  Shakes off the slumber of ten thousand years,
  And on the borders of new worlds appears.
  Whate'er the bold, the rash adventure cost,
  In wide eternity I dare be lost.
  The Muse is wont in narrow bounds to sing,
  To teach the swain, or celebrate the king.
  I grasp the whole, no more to parts confined,
  I lift my voice and sing to human kind.

I sing to men and angels ; angels join,
While such the theme, their sacred songs with mine.

    *   *   *   *   *   *

Now monuments prove faithful to their trust,
And render back their long-committed dust.
Now charnels rattle; scattered limbs and all
The various bones, obsequious to the call,
Self-moved, advance ; the neck perhaps to meet
The distant head, the distant legs the feet.
Dreadful to view, see through the dusky sky
Fragments of bodies in confusion fly,
To distant regions journeying, there to claim
Deserted members and complete the frame.
The trumpet's sound each fragrant mote shall **hear,**
Or fix'd in earth, or if afloat in air,
Obey the signal wafted in the wind,
And not one sleeping atom lag behind.
   So swarming bees that on a summer's day
In airy rings and wild meanders play,
Charm'd with the brazen sound, their wanderings **end,**
And gently circling on a bough descend " (bk. ii. l. 1).

These last lines refer to the rustic habit of collecting
bees by beating a tin pan with a stick.

" How vast the concourse ! not in numbers more
   The waves that break on the resounding shore,
   The leaves that tremble in the shady grove,
   The lamps that gild the spangled vaults above."

With this passage may be compared the lines in Fielding's " Tom Thumb," beginning, " So have I seen."

He tried another measure, of which this passage must
serve as the only specimen :

" Proud Venice sits amid the waves;
   Her foot ambitious ocean laves:
Art's noblest boast! but O what wondrous odds
    'Twixt Venice and Britannia's isle !
    'Twixt mortal and immortal toil !
Britannia is a Venice built by gods."

Is it any wonder that Young took to writing blank-verse? The wonder is, perhaps, that he was read. Yet, while we cannot read him for delight, we know that he said something that our grandfathers liked to hear. What he uttered in his solemn way, no one would care to deny. He put into somewhat formal language, adorned with much of the crude ore of Romanticism, the yearning of his century for morality. That, we saw, inspired a good part of the *Spectator*, and it was the main end of the work done by most of the writers. But, with respect be it spoken, a century of preaching palls, and too often the undeniable excellence of the subject has blinded readers to faults in the execution. One thing that the poets were never tired of was the tomb. Young is forever bringing his Lorenzo to the edge of an open grave and bidding him look in.

> " The man how blest, who, sick of gaudy scenes,
> (Scenes apt to thrust between us and ourselves!)
> Is led by choice to take his favorite walk
> Beneath death's gloomy, silent, cypress shades,
> Unpierc'd by vanity's fantastic ray,
> To read his monuments, to weigh his dust,
> Visit his vaults, and dwell among the tombs!
> Lorenzo! read with me Narcissa's stone;
> (Narcissa was thy favorite) let us read
> Her moral stone! few doctors preach so well;
> Few orators so tenderly can touch
> The feeling heart. What pathos in the date!"

And this (Night ix.):

> " My solemn night-born adjuration here:
>
>   *   *   *   *   *
>
> By the long list of swift mortality,
> From Adam downward to this evening knell,
> Which midnight waves in fancy's startled eye,
> And shocks her with an hundred centuries,
> Round death's black banner throng'd in human thought!

> By thousands now resigning their last breath,
> And calling thee—wert thou so wise to hear!
> By tombs o'er tombs arising; human earth
> Ejected, to make room for—human earth;
> The monarch's terror and the sexton's trade,
> By pompous obsequies that shun the day,
> The torch funereal, and the nodding plume,
> Which makes poor man's humiliation proud;
> Boast of our ruin! triumph of our dust!
> By the damp vault that weeps o'er royal bones,
> And the pale lamp that shows the ghastly dead
> More ghastly, through the thick incumbent gloom!
> By the visits (if there are), from darker scenes,
> The gliding spectre! and the groaning grave!
> By groans and graves, and miseries that groan
> For the grave's shelter! by depending men,
> Senseless to pains of death, from pangs of guilt!
> By guilt's last audit! by yon moon in blood,
> The rocking firmament, the falling stars,
> And thunder's last discharge, great nature's knell," etc.

This is the romantic part of the long serious poems, which are rhetorical exercises in defence of morality and orthodoxy. Lorenzo is, for instance (Night ix.), told to

> " Imagine from their deep foundations torn
> The most gigantic sons of earth, the broad
> And towering Alps, all tost into the sea;
> And, light as down, or volatile as air,
> Their bulks enormous, dancing on the waves,
> In time, and measure, exquisite; while all
> The winds, in emulation of the spheres,
> Tune their sonorous instruments aloft,
> The concert swell and animate the ball.
> Would this appear amazing?"

To this question, Lorenzo, who has had to listen to over four thousand lines of declamatory blank-verse, apparently nods his head, to signify that he should feel surprised

at seeing the mountains floating on the top of the sea;
and then he is bidden to consider

> " Worlds in a far thinner element sustained,
>   And acting the same part, with greater skill,
>   More rapid movement, and for noblest ends."

He has already had immortality proved in what must
have seemed like never-ending strains (Night vii.):

> " And can ambition a fourth proof supply ?
>   It can, and stronger than the former three;
>   Though quite o'erlook'd by some reputed wise.
>
>   *   *   *   *   *
>
>   " Man must soar.
>   An obstinate activity within,
>   An insuppressive spring, will toss him up
>   In spite of fortune's load.   Not kings alone,
>   Each villager has his ambition too;
>   No Sultan prouder than his fettered slave:
>   Slaves build their little Babylons of straw,
>   Echo the proud Assyrian in their hearts,
>   And cry, ' Behold the wonders of my might !'
>   And why ?   Because immortal as their lord;
>   And souls immortal must for ever heave
>   At something great, the glitter or the gold,
>   The praise of mortals, or the praise of heaven."

This passage has the quality, the same in kind, though
less in degree, that we find in the best passages which are
familiar to us, as

> " Tired Nature's sweet restorer, balmy sleep!
>   He, like the world, his ready visit pays
>   When Fortune smiles; the wretched he forsakes;
>   Swift on his downy pinion flies from wo,
>   And lights on lids unsullied with a tear.
>   From short (as usual) and disturbed repose
>   I wake: how happy they who wake no more !
>   Yet that were vain, if dreams infest the grave."

What impresses us throughout is the rhetorical quality

of the verse, and this seems to come directly from the imitation of Latin poetry, where we find abundant declamation. As Mr. Sellar says, in "The Roman Poets of the Republic," p. 8, "They betray the want of dramatic genius in other fields of literature, especially in epic and idyllic poetry, and in philosophical dialogues. Their poets give utterance to vehemence of passion, or heroism of sentiment, either directly from their own hearts and convictions, or in great rhetorical passages, attributed to the imaginary personages of the story—to Ariadne or Dido, to Turnus or Mezentius. But this utterance of passion and sentiment is not often united in them with a vivid delineation of the complex characters of men." This example, however, did but give encouragement to the prevailing tendency ; at least, it is not Rome alone that is to be blamed for all the heavy didactic poetry of the last century, even if we ascribe many faults to the direct imitation of those models. We have already seen how urgent was the yearning for moral teaching, and we find other poets inspired by the same gloom. Blair's "Grave" (published 1743, written before 1731) shows by its title what were the chief pleasures to be got from the poetical literature of the time. While the very subject was awe-inspiring, passages like the following are doubtless what perhaps as much as any rewarded the reader :

> " See yonder hallowed fane ! the pious work
> Of names once famed, now dubious or forgot,
> And buried midst the wreck of things which were:
> There lie interred the more illustrious dead.
> The wind is up: hark ! how it howls ! methinks
> Till now I never heard a sound so dreary !
> Doors creak, and windows clap, and night's foul bird,
> Rock'd in the spire, screams loud : the gloomy aisles,
> Black-plastered, and hung round with shreds of 'scutcheons,
> And tattered coats-of-arms, send back the sound,

Laden with heavier airs, from the low vaults,
The mansions of the dead. Roused from their slumbers,
In grim array the grisly spectres rise,
Grin horrible, and obstinately sullen,
Pass, and repass, hushed as the foot of night.
Again the screech-owl shrieks—ungracious sound!
I'll hear no more—it makes one's blood run chill."

We perceive that both Blair and Young had read Shakspere and Milton, and that they both imitated certain
qualities of the older blank-verse. They turned from the
couplet, just as it seemed to have been firmly fixed, and
received from those older writers the torch of real—as
distinguished from reasonable—poetry. The light burned
dim, and, as we have seen, blue ; the main use of the new
verse was the promotion of orthodox religious views. It
was the dramatic—can one say the melodramatic ?—view
of the grave as an inspirer of pleasing gloom that was
preparing readers for the romantic outbreak. At this
period, the properties of the poet were but few : the tomb,
an occasional raven or screech-owl, and the pale moon,
with skeletons and grinning ghosts. It was on this dark
assemblage of horrors that he depended for his most
thrilling effects. All these seemed to belong to the teacher
of morality ; they enforced his lessons with irrefutable arguments. One might as well try to drive away a ghost
with fire-arms as with ill-timed frivolity, and frivolity was
the companion of this morbid gloom ; frivolity and coarseness, for it would be hard to find a time in modern history when there was less appreciation of beauty in the
world than then. Even the poets had yet to learn to enjoy natural scenery, and what the life of the time was we
may see in Fielding's and Smollett's novel, and in the grim
horrors of Hogarth's plates. For a further proof of the
connection between the fine arts and the life of the time,

consider these memorable designs, with their moral teaching. Hogarth is celebrated as the great *English* artist; his unceasing morality and realism are what give him that fame. Every one who writes about him speaks of his useful lessons of morality, and it was the necessity of teaching morality that had so disastrous an effect on the poetry of the last century. At least, this was part of the trouble, and a great part. Even now writers maintain that the poet's first duty is to enforce moral lessons, and any one who questions this is supposed to urge teaching immorality. There is still a certain novelty in the affirmation that art is not didactic, although for nearly a hundred years Goethe's words have been slowly influencing writers and readers. What brought him to it was the inevitable reaction from the exaggerated preaching of the last century, when imagination was dead and its ghost haunted the churchyard. Even Gray's " Elegy " has its scene there, you will remember. Even Boyse, the dissolute and shirtless poet, whom I have mentioned as a frivolous person, wrote verses that would have done credit to a bishop. It was doubtless with a keen eye on his market, and not from an· overflowing heart, that he composed his long poem on Deity :

> " Hence triumphs truth beyond objection clear ·
> (Let unbelief attend and shrink with fear!)
> That what for ever was—must surely be
> Beyond commencement, and from period free," etc.

A paraphrase of the third chapter of Job, and a few sets of verses on the death of his friends and relatives, are among the further contributions of this wretched rake to the literature of his country. The influence must have been 'strong that made even him a contributor to Dr. Watts's "Horæ Lyricæ." We have seen how the need of decency impressed itself on the public after the excesses of the writers of the Restoration, and Dr. Watts himself is another witness to this fact. In the Preface to his poems, written in 1709, he says: "Thus almost in vain have the throne and the pulpit cried reformation; while the stage and licentious poems have waged open war with the pious design of Church and State" (Anderson's "Poets," ix. 296); and he goes on to show the poetical wealth of the Old Testament in order to disprove the assumption "that poetry and vice are naturally akin." It was not strange that this opinion was held, for, he says, "many, of the writers of the first rank, in this our age of national Christians, have, to their eternal shame, surpassed the vilest of the Gentiles. . . . The vices have been painted like so many goddesses, the charms of wit have been added to debauchery." It was Dr. Watts's aim to write poetry in the service of religion, and he had many rivals and aids. Society was reacting from the excesses of frivolous writers.

IV. Closely connected with these moral reformers were the didactic poets. We need not linger long over their well-meant but tedious productions. John Phillips's "Cyder," with its pseudo-Miltonic versification, seems to have been the favorite model. Take Grainger's "Sugar-Cane," for example (1764), iii. 455:

> " False Gallia's sons, that hoe the ocean-isles,
> Mix with their sugar loads of worthless sand,
> Fraudful, their weight of sugar to increase. .
> Far be such guile from Britain's honest swains.
> Such arts, awhile, the unwary may surprise,
> And benefit the impostor; but, ere long,
> The skilful buyer will the fraud detect,
> And, with abhorrence, reprobate the name."

Or take this:

> " Be thrifty, planter, e'en thy skimmings save:
> For, planter, know, the refuse of the cane

Serves needful purposes.   Are barbecues
The cates thou lovest?   What like rich skimmings feed
The grunting, bristly kind?   Your labouring mules
They soon invigorate," etc.

Then there is Dr. Armstrong's "Art of Preserving
Health" (1744), in which we are taught to

"Fly, if you can, these violent extremes
Of air: the wholesome is nor moist nor dry.
But as the power of choosing is deny'd
To half mankind, a further task ensues;
How best to mitigate these fell extremes,
How breathe, unhurt, the withering element,
Or hazy atmosphere. . . .

*   *   *   *   *

If the raw and oozy heaven offend,
Correct the soil, and dry the sources up
Of watery exhalation: wide and deep
Conduct your trenches thro' the quaking bog.

*   *   *   *   *

. . . and let your table smoke
With solid roast or baked; or what the herds
Of tamer beasts supply," etc.

I add an extract from Dyer's "Fleece" (1757):

"See the bold emigrants of Accadie,
And Massachusett, happy in those arts
That join the politics of trade and war,
Bearing the palm in either: they appear
Better exemplars; and that hardy crew,
Who, on the frozen beach of Newfoundland,
Hang their white fish amid the parching winds:
The kindly fleece, in webs of Duffield woof,
Their limbs, benumb'd, enfolds with cheerly warmth,
And frieze of Cambria, worn by those who seek
Thro' gulfs and dales of Hudson's winding bay,
The beaver's fur, tho' oft they seek in vain,
While winter's frosty rigor checks approach,
E'en in the fiftieth latitude."

Must it not have seemed as if Pegasus would never

clap his wings again, when he had been thus harnessed in domestic service and had to bear such heavy burdens? Yet the poets followed the instincts of their time in devoting themselves to the celebration of the duties and charms of civilization. May it not be that their work is not wholly lost, and that they may yet deserve our gratitude by serving as a warning for those who would follow the advice of outsiders and make poetry an advertisement of science? The arguments that are brought up now to urge poets to celebrate scientific discoveries were used in the last century in behalf of the glories of civilization and the laws of morality. What the result was, I have tried to show; it is certainly of a kind to discourage writing to order. Yet evidently this way of writing came as a natural result of what had gone before, the especial form it took being based on the didactic poetry of Greece and Rome, with, probably, blank-verse to serve as a concession to those who demanded something congenial. The same phenomenon, *mutatis mutandis*, had taken place in Italy. Hesiod's " Works and Days " and Vergil's " Georgics " found modern followers—the Vergil especially—as a matter of course. Indeed, the first Italian imitation was by Rucellai, the author of the " Rosmunda," who was most eager in copying Roman literature.* His "Api " (published 1539) was almost a continuation of the fourth " Georgic." Then there was Alamanni's " Coltivazione," a few years later. These were imitated by French writers (*vide* Ginguéné's " Hist. Litt. de l'Italie," vol. ix. chap. i.), and it was under similar inspiration that the English didactic poets wrote. The peculiar religious tone, and the funereal flavor, are peculiarly English, and it is to

---

* We should always bear in mind the enormous weight of the precedent of Roman imitation of Greek literature.

them, doubtless, that their reputation for the spleen, etc.,
is mainly due. Young's "Night Thoughts," for instance,
was put into French and Italian; Phillips's "Cyder," as
we saw, into Italian, etc.* Yet some of the men who
wrote the dreariest of these poems at times gave proof of
a finer poetical sense. There is much truth in at least the
first part of what Dr. Johnson said of Dyer, that although
he, " whose mind was not unpoetical, has done his utmost,
by interesting his reader in our native commodity, by in-
terspersing rural imagery and incidental digressions, by
clothing small images in great words, and by all the
writer's arts of delusion, the meanness naturally adhering,
and the irreverence habitually annexed to trade and manu-
facture, sink him under insuperable oppression; and the
disgust which blank-verse, encumbering and encumbered,
superadds to an unpleasing subject, soon repels the reader,
however willing to be pleased." We see here Dr. Johnson's detestation of blank-verse; and the question of the
relative excellence of that and of the couplet was a burning one in the last century. Doubtless blank-verse was a
reaction against the couplet. It was the first sign of a
protest against that rigid form, just as in Milton's hands
it was the last measure in which a poet of heroic proportions spoke to the world. Yet the instrument he commanded the puny bardlings of the last century could not
handle; his dignity was mimicked by a feeble rumble, as
if the secret of his art consisted in placing adjectives as
far from their nouns as possible, and in transposing the
intervening words. Yet they felt the charm of his verse;
that was something, and they maintained their side with

---

* *Vide* Symonds, "Renaissance in Italy," v. 236–7.

In France, among other didactic poems, L. Racine's " La Religion, La
Grâce;" Lemierre's " La Peinture;" Boucher's " Le Mois;" and the writings
of Delille and St. Lambert.

obstinacy in the face of violent opposition. The main objection to them is as well stated in these lines by Robert Lloyd, as by any one :

> "Some Milton-mad (an affectation
> Glean'd up from college-education *)
> Approve no verse, but that which flows
> In epithetic measur'd prose,
> With trim expressions daily drest,
> Stol'n, misapplied, and not confest,
> And call it writing in the style
> Of that great HOMER of our isle.
> *Whilom, what time, eftsoons* and *erst,*
> (So prose is oftentimes beverst)
> Sprinkled with quaint, fantastic phrase,
> Uncouth to ears of modern days,
> Make up the metre which they call,
> Blank, classic blank, their all in all."

Yet Lloyd had imitated Spenser, in a poem called "The Progress of Envy" (1751), in which he had defended both Spenser and Milton. Evidently the current was running with some force by the middle of the century. Dr. Johnson evidently thought so (*vide Rambler*, No. 121). "There are, I think, two schemes of writing, on which the laborious wits of the present time employ their faculties. . . . The other is the imitation of Spenser, which, by the influence of some men of learning and genius, seems likely to gain upon the age, and therefore deserves to be more attentively considered. . . . To imitate the fictions and sentiments of Spenser can incur no reproach," but not so with his diction and stanza. The imitations are carelessly done. "Perhaps, however, the style of Spenser might by long labour be justly copied ; but life is surely given us for

---

* Many of the university men were leaders in this movement ; notably the Wartons.

17

higher purposes than to gather what our ancestors have wisely thrown away, and to learn what is of no value, but because it has been forgotten."*

V. Yet the only man whose blank-verse is, even in passages, impressive is James Thomson, whose "Seasons" is still a classic. Even Johnson acknowledged this, for he says, "His is one of the works in which blank-verse seems properly used. Thomson's wide expansion of general views, and his enumeration of circumstantial varieties, would have been obstructed and embarrassed by the frequent intersection of the sense, which are the necessary effects of rhyme." Curiously enough, Pope helped Thomson with suggestions, and, more than that, with lines from his own pen. Here is an instance ("Chambers's Cyclopædia of Eng. Lit." ii. 13). Thomson had written :

> " Thoughtless of beauty, she was beauty's self,
> Recluse among the woods ; if city dames
> Will deign their faith : and thus she went, compelled
> By strong necessity, with as serene
> And pleased a look as Patience e'er put on,
> To glean Palemon's fields."

---

* Cumberland, in his "Memoirs," throws much light on the taste of his time. Thus [Am. ed.], p. 64 : "I well remember, when I was newly come to college, with what avidity I read the Greek tragedians, and with what reverence I swallowed the absurdities of their chorus, and was bigoted to their cold characters and frigid unities;" p. 66 : "I had no books of my own, and unfortunately got engaged with Spenser's 'Faery Queen ;' in imitation of which I began to string nonsensical stanzas to the same rhyming kind of measure. Though I trust I should not have surrendered myself for any length of time to the jingling strain of obsolete versification, yet I am indebted to my mother for the seasonable contempt she threw upon my imitations. I felt the force of her reproof and laid the 'Faery Queen' upon the shelf." This was when he was a student at Trinity College, Cambridge. His mother had read Shakspere with him in his boyhood.

For those lines Pope substituted these :

" Thoughtless of beauty, she was beauty's self,
Recluse among the close-embowering woods,
As in the hollow breast of Apennine,
Beneath the shelter of encircling hills
A myrtle rises, far from human eyes,
And breathes its balmy fragrance o'er the wild;
So flourished blooming, and unseen by all,
The sweet Lavinia ; till at length compelled
By strong necessity's supreme command,
With smiling patience in her looks, she went
To glean Palemon's fields."

Probably few on reading these lines would ever guess that Pope wrote them, so relentlessly was he borne away by the greater forces that carry us all on. When a regiment of soldiers is passing by, with a band of music at its head, all marching with one uniform swing, peaceful citizens straighten their backs and find themselves instinctively keeping step with the moving mass ; in the same way are poets inspired by the influences around them. We have seen how Addison, who was distinctively a man of this age, misplaced in the beginning of the last century, occasionally fell from the ranks and lost step as he praised ballads ; but he was promptly hustled back into line by his pompous contemporaries. So here we have Pope as he might have been in more truly poetical times. When he was making up his mind what path to follow, his guides—and with great intelligence—told him that correctness was lacking in English poetry, and he became a correct writer. Thomson wearied of the correctness, and, for another thing, he inherited with his Scotch blood a love of nature which we find in almost all the poets of that country, even in the most artificial times. In the present day, patriotic Scotchmen take a great deal of credit to themselves for this immunity which some of

their ancestors enjoyed from the epidemic artificial opinions. Yet may not we who are not Scotchmen be bold
enough to say this exemption is due to some extent to
their geographical position, and not wholly to their lofti-
er natures, and that they bought it at the cost of much
savageness? It was doubtless well worth the purchase-
money. Not only did the peasants keep alive the gift
of song, but many of the educated people continued to
admire and to imitate the older writers. Collections of
Scotch songs and ballads were published very early in
the last century,* and, more than this, even those who

---

* Watson's "Choice Collection of Comic and Serious Scots Poems"
(3 vols., 1706–9–11) was the first. Thus, "The Publisher to the Reader"
says: "As the frequency of Publishing Collections of Miscellaneous Poems
in our Neighbouring Kingdoms and States, may, in a great measure, justify
an Undertaking of this kind with us; so 'tis hoped, that this being the
first of its Nature which has been published in our own Native Scots Dialect, the Candid Reader may be the more easily induced, through the Consideration thereof, to give some Charitable Grains of Allowance, if the
Performance come not up to such a Point of Exactness as may please an
over nice Palate."

In England there had appeared Dryden's "Miscellany Poems" (1684–
1708). "A Collection of Old Ballads" appeared in 1723, and in 1726 and
1738. Watson's Collection inspired Allan Ramsay to compile his "Evergreen, Scots Poems wrote by the Ingenious before 1600" (1724), and his
"Tea Table Miscellany" the same year, which speedily ran through twelve
editions. The "Tea Table Miscellany" contained "All in the Downs the
Fleet was moored," "If she be not fair for me," Mallet's "William and
Margaret," etc. In short, it is very much such a collection as would be
made now. It was followed by "A New Miscellany of Scots Songs"
(1727), and, in 1769, Herd's "Ancient and Modern Scottish Songs, Heroic
Ballads," etc. This was four years after the publication of Percy's "Reliques."

It scarcely need be said that collections of admired poems were not new.
They were familiar in England and France; these volumes are important as
showing the new direction in which modern taste was turning, towards the

bowed before the fashionable idols at other times followed their own bent in writing in simpler forms. Thus, Allan Ramsay, who wrote a few now forgotten poems of the usual kind, stepped into fame with his "Gentle Shepherd" (1725), which, though it now reads like a conventional drama, seemed like a breath of fresh air to those who first read it. All the wits of the time admired it, and justly. We have seen that the pastoral poetry of the time was perhaps the most artificial of all the kinds of poetical composition then practised. The satirical poems were natural; Pope's, at least, are the talk of a witty man, and hence essentially as genuine as the talk of peasants. The pastorals, however, were as artificial as paper flowers, and these threefold dilutions of classicism were thrown into the shade by this play, which contains many true touches, and some pretty passages, although the device by which the hero and heroine are found not to be peasants at all, but very much finer people, shows us how even writers who desire to begin a reform have, like every one else, to climb up-hill a step at a time. In Gombault's "Endymion" the poor shepherd is found to be of very noble family, and is hence able to marry the rich shepherdess. In Vauquelin de la Fresnaie's "Idillie," No. 48, the rustic Sylvin learns that he is some one else, with the same result. Even now novel-writers are not

---

past. Simultaneously in France, it is curious to notice, there appeared the first signs of interest in the earlier writers. In 1723 came out Coustelier's collection containing the works of poets before Marot, and in 1731 Lenglet-Dufresnoy's edition of Marot, while what Sainte-Beuve calls the *réaction chevaleresque* dates from the reprinting of the "Petit Jehan de Saintré" (1724), and of "Gérard de Nevers" (1725). Tressan's adaptations of the old romances furthered the same taste. In 1742 appeared an edition of the poems of Thibaut de Champagne, etc. For a fuller list, see Sainte-Beuve's "Tableau de la Poésie Française au XVIᵉ Siècle," p. 482 et seq.

tired of this very old device. Ramsay was quite capable of repeating the sounds he heard about him. Thus :

> " Ye shepherds and nymphs that adorn the gay plain,
> Approach from your sports, and attend to my strain;
> Amongst all your number a lover so true,
> Was ne'er so undone, with such bliss in his view.
> Was ever a nymph so hard-hearted as mine ?
> She knows me sincere, and she sees how I pine," etc.

This, of course, is but trifling—the small-talk of poetry —which is never of the nature of an affidavit. He wrote odes, and various versions and translations, but all that lives are his " Gentle Shepherd," and a few songs written in imitation of the ancient Scottish manner—*e. g.*, " The Braes of Yarrow "—

> " Busk ye, busk ye, my bonny, bonny bride,
> Busk ye, busk ye, my winsome marrow !"

In England the poets could not so readily turn to still living popular treasures of poetry. The change had to be made by choosing other models to copy. It was a *literary* change—that is to say, writers made themselves over with an eye to imitating other poets, rather than with the simple desire of painting nature. And, as I have so often said, it was Milton and Spenser who were admired and copied.* Thomson wrote his " Castle of Indolence " in the Spenserian stanza, and this novelty was followed by many now forgotten bards.

One of the greatest poems of the last century was Gray's " Elegy in a Country Churchyard " (1749). Man's mortality, as we have seen, was a favorite subject of his contemporaries and predecessors ; but Gray does not try to show the horror of the generally recognized fact. He rather sets before us the pathos of an obscure life and

---

* *Vide* L. Stephen's " History of English Thought," ii. 359.

untimely death ; and life is, one may say, a poet's first
subject. Often, too, it is more profoundly pathetic than
any death. Young's prolonged declamation about the
tomb makes us sad, to be sure, but only by its unrelenting
persistence, while Gray's immortal elegy is full of real
melancholy, which is not despair, but thoughtfulness. It
may be doubted whether any other poem in the English
language has been so frequently imitated.* No one of
the copies, however, comes anywhere near the original.
Gray has other claims upon our admiration, for he was
one of the first of writers to treat a mountain with
proper respect. It will be remembered that earlier in
the century mountains were the scorn of mankind. Gray
was almost the first to mention their grandeur. Thus,
writing to his mother from Lyons, Oct. 13, 1739, he
says : "It is a fortnight since we set out hence upon a little excursion to Geneva. We took the longest road, which
lies through Savoy, on purpose to see a famous monastery,
called the Grande Chartreuse, and had no reason to think
our time lost. . . . From thence (Echelles) we proceeded on

---

* Falconer, Thomas Warton, James Graeme, William Whitehead, John
Scott, Henry Headley, Sir John Henry Moore, Robert Lovell, are but a few
of the numberless poets who imitated it. "It spread," Mr. Mason says,
"at first on account of the affecting and pensive cast of the subject, just
like Hervey's 'Meditations on the Tombs.' Soon after its publication I
remember sitting with Mr. Gray in his college apartment. He expressed
to me his surprise at the rapidity of its sale. I replied :

'Sunt lacrymæ rerum, et mentem mortalia tangunt.'

He paused awhile, and, taking his pen, wrote the line on a printed copy
of it lying on his table. 'This,' said he, 'shall be its future motto.' 'Pity,'
said I, 'that Dr. Young's "Night Thoughts" have preoccupied it.' 'So,'
replied he, 'indeed it is.'" The resemblance between the two men was
not confined to their admiration for that one line. Yet the difference between them was greater : one was a rhetorician, the other a poet. Each
delivered the depressing message of the age in his own way.

horses who are used to the way, to the mountain of the Chartreuse. It is six miles to the top; the road runs winding up it, commonly not six feet broad; on one hand is the rock, with woods of pine trees hanging overhead; on the other a monstrous precipice, almost perpendicular, at the bottom of which rolls a torrent, that, sometimes tumbling among the fragments of stone that have fallen from on high, and sometimes precipitating itself down vast descents with a noise like thunder, which is still made greater from the echo of the mountains on each side, concurs to form one of the most solemn, the most romantic, and the most astonishing scenes I ever beheld. Add to this the strange views made by the crags and cliffs on the other hand, the cascades that in many places throw themselves from the very summit down into the vale and river below, and many other particulars impossible to describe, you will conclude we had no occasion to repent our pains."

Even then Gray at times used the language of his day. Thus, Nov. 7, 1739 : "The winter was so far advanced as in great measure to spoil the beauty of the prospect; however, there was still somewhat fine remaining amidst the savageness and horror of the place."

And Dec. 19 of the same year, he speaks of the Apennines as "not so horrid as the Alps, though pretty near as high." *Horrid*, of course, as with Addison and others, had not its present common meaning of *odious*, but rather that of *awful*.

His warmest utterance is this, Nov. 16, 1739 : "I own I have not as yet met anywhere those grand and simple works of art that are to amaze one, and whose sight one is to be better for; but those of nature have astonished me beyond expression. In our little journey up to the Grande Chartreuse, I do not remember to have gone ten paces without an exclamation that there was no restraining : not a precipice, not a torrent, not a cliff, but is pregnant with religion and poetry."

Gray here tasted emotions which were scarcely to be shared with any one for many years. He was, in this respect, nearly half a century in advance of most of his contemporaries.*

---

* See Gray's correspondence with Rev. Norton Nicholls and Dr. Wharton, in 1769, concerning the English lakes, which he was among the first to visit, and his "Tour in the Lakes." There was by this time general interest in the beauties of the landscapes. William Gilpin's "Observations and Artistical Remarks on the Picturesque Beauty of Various Parts of England, Wales, and Scotland," began to appear; the remarks on the Lake country in 1789, though "written about fifteen years before they were published. They were at first thrown together, warm from the subject, each evening, after the scene of the day had been presented" (*vide* preface). It was the MS. of Gilpin's "Tour down the Wye" which Gray annotated shortly before his death.

We have seen that Defoe's "Tour through Britain" showed the writer's fondness for Gothic architecture. Mountains he enjoyed less. Thus, iii. 258 (4th ed. 1748): "I now entered *Westmoreland*, a county eminent only for being the wildest, most barren, and frightful of any that I have passed over in England or in Wales. . . . It must be owned, however, that here are some very pleasant manufacturing Towns, and consequently populous;" yet from Lonsdale "we have a very fine Prospect of the Mountains at a vast Distance and of the beautiful Course of the River Lone, in a Valley far beneath us." Earlier, however, "As these hills were lofty, so they had an aspect of Terror. Here were no rich pleasant valleys between them, as among the Alps; no Lead Mines and Veins of rich Ore, as in the Peak; no Coal-pits, as in the Hills about Halifax, but all barren and wild, and of no Use either to Man or Beast." Of the "Winander Mere" he says, merely, it "is famous for producing the char-fish. . . . It is a curious Fish, and, as a Dainty, is polled and sent far and near by way of Present."

In the "Beauties of England and Wales," xv. pt. 2, p. 26, under Westmoreland, "We find, indeed, a writer of considerable taste describing his visit to Winandermere, in 1748, with that glow of language which such scenes are calculated to suggest to persons living in cities or campaign

As Mr. Arnold has shown, Gray was a victim to the age
in which he lived. We every day see men ruined by some
fatal defect of character, by some overmastering vice, but

---

countries. 'We came,' says he, 'upon a high promontory, that gave us a
full view of the bright lake, which, spreading itself under us, in the midst
of the mountains, presented one of the most glorious appearances that
ever struck the eye of the traveller with transport."

Vide, also, Dr. Dalton's "Descriptive Poem : Addressed to Two Ladies
on their Return from Viewing the Mines near Whitehaven," in Pearch's
"Collection" (succeeding Dodsley's), vol. i. This poem was written in
1755. After praising the beauty of the lake, the author says:

> "Supreme of mountains, Skiddaw, hail !
> To whom all Britain sinks a vale !
> Lo, his imperial brow I see
> From foul usurping vapours free !
> 'Twere glorious now his side to climb,
> Boldly to scale his top sublime," etc.

Page 52, in the notes, see the enthusiasm of "the late ingenious Dr.
Brown," in a letter to a friend. "On the opposite shore, you will find
rocks and cliffs of stupendous height hanging broken over the lake in
horrible grandeur." The "Description of the Neighbourhood of Keswick"
was published in 1767; Hutchinson's "Excursion to the Lakes," in 1774;
West's Guide, in 1778.

Cumberland, in his "Memoirs" (Am. ed.), p. 195, speaking of a journey
to the lakes of Cumberland with the Earl of Warwick, says, "He took
with him Mr. Smith, well known to the public for his elegant designs after
nature in Switzerland, Italy, and elsewhere."

A few German writers mention Haller's poem, "die Alpen," as a turning-
point in the popular taste for mountains, but this is exaggeration (*vide*
Adolf Frey's "Alb. von Haller," p. 174). Haller held the utilitarian ideas
of his day and generation about mountains—thus:

> "Wo nichts, was nöthig, fehlt, und nur was nutzet, blüht.
> Der Berge wachsend Eis, der Felsen steiler Wand
> Sind selbst zum nützen da, und tränken das Geland."
>
> —"Poems," p. 44.

This note has already swollen beyond all measure, or it would be well to
quote passages from Rousseau's "Nouvelle Héloïse," which fairly threw
the mountains open to the world. *Vide,* also, Petrarch's account of his

we are less disposed to acknowledge the irresistible influence of an uncongenial time. Every age appears with a certain set of moulds into which it is necessary that those should fit who are to attain success, and those who fail to accommodate themselves to these conditions are thrown out. They may perform some work which their contemporaries will spurn, but which another generation may admire; yet we shall always have to regret their incompleteness, their tragic loneliness.

If all the world is a stage, a good many people are cast into the wrong parts, and Gray was a melancholy example of this uncongeniality. He was continually groping for a subject; and the whole endeavor of his life was to find something more truly poetical than the display of wit and reason. Goldsmith's remarks, already quoted, show this, and you will notice the dexterity with which he taunts those who take "pains to involve [the language] into pristine barbarity." The remote past was tabooed, and the obvious horrors of the tomb were chanted with cloying monotony, while the elegiac beauty of Gray's short poem was almost the single valuable contribution to poetry for many years.* The only other prominent example was Collins's beautiful odes (1746), which have that rare touch of classic beauty which is precision without pedantry, beauty without exaggeration, simplicity without commonness. They had no following, however, in their own time.

---

ascent of Mt. Ventoux, "De Rebus Familiaribus," lib. iv. ep. 1. See *Quarterly Review*, July, 1882.

* Gray is often mentioned as the first of English poets to return to old Norse themes (thus Gosse, "Gray," English Men of Letters Series, p. 163). But see Dryden's "Miscellany Poems," vi. 387 (ed. 1716), for a translation from the Hervarer Saga. This collection contains numerous old songs and ballads, and selections from Ben Jonson and Donne

CHAPTER IX.

I. I have already spoken of Goldsmith's taunts about those who formed the new school, and he frequently expressed very genuine impatience with his contemporaries. Sometimes he seems to have written as if Dr. Johnson were looking over his shoulder, and there is an air of solemnity and authority about him which can scarcely have been natural. Yet his position on the conservative side in the literary controversies made him assume the tone of a teacher, and his own work is full of the influences of his time. It is not surprising that he was vexed with the somewhat formless utterances of his fellow-bards, for in his hands the measure which had already been employed by so many poets acquired new grace. The "Traveller" (1765) leaves us cold, although there are good lines here and there—for we no longer seek " to find that happiest spot below," nor could we rest satisfied with the lingering optimism which persuaded Goldsmith that,

> " perhaps, if countries we compare,
> And estimate the blessings which they share,
> Though patriots flatter, still shall wisdom fiud
> An equal portion dealt to all mankind;
> As different good, by art or nature given,
> To different nations make their blessings even."

And that,

> " every state to one lov'd blessing prone,
> Conforms and models life to that alone.
> Each to the favorite happiness attends,
> And spurns the plain that aims at other ends;

> Till carried to excess in each domain,
> This favorite good begets peculiar pain."

We seem to be remote from the new spirit of poetry as we read this rhymed thesis with which the simple-hearted, childlike, merry young Irishman made his appearance as a poet. In order to be esteemed he suppressed all naturalness and simplicity, and posed for a philosopher, with a full command of rhetorical devices. The "Deserted Village" (1769), four years later, sounds another note. The poem has delighted nearly all its readers, for with exactness of form, and a form, too, generally associated in our minds with artificiality, it has pathos, simplicity, love of nature, and little touches that no one can be wholly insensible to. Indeed, it is a most fortunate thing for us that the heroic verse, which has been so unjustly decried, contains a poem so full of the very beauties which are often hastily denied it.

It also bears marks of the influence of his romantic contemporaries—*e. g.:*

> "Through torrid tracts with fainting steps they go,
> *Where wild Altama murmurs to their woe."*

And,

> "Farewell, and O! where'er thy voice be tried,
> *On Torno's cliffs, or Pambamarca's side."*

Yet, while the poem is full of the sentimentality which was making its appearance in literature, it is amusing to see how wholly unconscious Goldsmith's reason was of the changes in men's thoughts and feelings. An appeal to his inquiry into "The Present State of Polite Learning" (1759) may be hardly fair, because an appeal to a poet's arguments in support of his views is tolerably certain to be misleading; but here we have Goldsmith's views expressed very clearly. "Rousseau, of Geneva;" he says, "a professed man-hater; or, more properly speaking, a philosopher enraged with one half of mankind, because they unavoidably make the other half unhappy. Such sentiments are generally the result of much good nature and little experience." But more striking than this is the following; he is speaking of the writers of France, who, he says, "have also of late fallen into a method of considering every part of art and science as arising from simple principles. The success of Montesquieu, and one or two more, has induced all the subordinate ranks of genius into vicious imitation. To this end they turn to our view that side of the subject which contributes to support their hypothesis, while the objections are generally passed over in silence. Thus one universal system rises from a partial representation of the question, a whole is concluded from a part, a book appears entirely new, and the fancy-built fabric is styled for a short time very ingenious. In this manner we have seen, of late, almost every subject in morals, natural history, economy, and commerce treated ; subjects naturally proceeding on many principles, and some even opposite to each other, are all taught to proceed along the line of systematic simplicity, and continue, like other agreeable falsehoods, extremely pleasing till they are detected."

I quote this long passage, not for the purpose of casting scorn on poor Goldsmith's hack-work — for to condemn him for faulty philosophy would be scarcely wiser than condemning Montesquieu for his bad poems—but to show the average conservative view of Goldsmith's time regarding the one great step which science was then making towards simplification. Let us not exult too loudly : it is still possible to find mixed companies in which there are people who shudder if they hear *Darwinism* mentioned, and who have prejudices against the word *evolution*. Let us call it *growth*, and no one will be pained ; it was this notion of growth that he found fault with for being too simple. Yet no one reads Goldsmith for his views on any subject. They were as little a part of him as was his wig, and like that article they bore marks of conventionality. In his "Vicar of Wakefield," for instance, there is no faintest trace of the pompousness that lay heavy on the conservative part of his generation. Goldsmith is as simple, as winning, as delightful as a child, and his book is consequently one of the master-pieces of English literature. The fact that it described the life of a humble family, with ordinary incidents, and especially that it described the Vicar's career in a prison, excited some opposition. The book was looked upon as "low" by the fashionable critics.* Nowhere, perhaps, did it have more influence than on the Continent, and especially in Germany. How much Goethe was moved by it when, four years later, Herder read him the German translation, we may see in his "Wahrheit und Dichtung," bk. x. Yet, while the story remains unrivalled, we may notice that it belongs in many respects to the period in which it was written. In execution it is a model for all time; in plan and aim it belongs to its own day. Its idyllic tone was essentially that which we frequently observe in literature before the French Revolution. There are the mutterings of that storm, too, in the denunciations of the rich which are to be found in the

---

* Goldsmith himself said in the preface: "In this age of opulence and refinement whom can such a character please? Such as are fond of high life will turn with disdain from the simplicity of his country fireside," etc.

Mr. Wm. Black, in his "Goldsmith" (English Men of Letters Series), says, "Mme. Riccoboni, to whom Burke had sent the book, wrote to Garrick, "Le plaidoyer en faveur des voleurs, des petits larrons, des gens de mauvaises mœurs, est fort éloigné de me plaire.' "

novel, and the appeal for sounder conduct (*vide* chapters xix. and xxvii.).

Notice, too, the literary taste of the day (chap. ix.): "The two ladies threw my girls quite into the shade; for they would talk of nothing but high life and high-lived company; with other fashionable topics, such as pictures, taste, Shakspeare, and the musical glasses." And (chap. xviii.), "As I was pretty much unacquainted with the present state of the stage, I demanded who were the present theatrical writers in vogue, who were the Drydens and Otways of the day—'I fancy, sir,' cried the player, 'few of our modern dramatists would think themselves much honoured by being compared to the writers you mention. Dryden and Rowe's manner, sir, are quite out of fashion; our taste has gone back a whole century; Fletcher, Ben Jonson, and all the plays of Shakspeare, are the only things that go down!' 'How,' cried I, 'is it possible the present age can be pleased with that antiquated dialect, that obsolete humour, those overcharged characters, which abound in the works you mention?' 'Sir,' returned my companion, 'the public think nothing about dialect, or humour, or character; for that is none of their business, they only go to be amused, and find themselves happy when they can enjoy a pantomime, under the sanction of Jonson's or Shakspeare's name.' 'So then, I suppose,' cried I, 'that our modern dramatists are rather imitators of Shakspeare than of nature.' 'To say the truth,' returned my companion, 'I don't know that they imitate anything at all; nor indeed does the public require it of them: it is not the composition of the piece, but the number of starts and attitudes that may be introduced into it, that starts applause.'"

This Shaksperian revival, which was furthered as much by Garrick as by any one man, did but little in the way

of bringing valuable additions to the dramatic literature
of England, but it shows that the interest in the neglected past was spreading further and further. We have seen
that there was an edition of Spenser in 1715, followed
by another thirty years later. About the middle of the
century, Hawkins reprinted several old plays. Johnson
himself brought out his edition of Shakspere in 1765.
And in the *Adventurer* we find Warton freely discussing
the works of the Elizabethan poets. The essays of V.
Knox (1777) contain touching allusions to the changes in
men's tastes, echoes of Dr. Johnson's style and opinion.
Thus (No. xv.): "There are several books very popular
in the present age, among the youthful and the inexperienced, which have a sweetness that palls on the taste, and
a grandeur that swells to a bloated turgidity. Such are
the writings of some modern Germans. 'The Death of
Abel,'* is generally read, and preferred by many to all
the productions of Greece, Rome, and England. The
success of this work has given rise to others on the same
plan, inferior to this in its real merits, and labouring under the same fault of redundant decoration. What others
may feel, I know not; but I would no more be obliged
to read the works of Gesner repeatedly, than to make a
frequent meal on the honey-comb." Again (No. xlvii.),
"The antiquarian spirit, which was once confined to inquiries concerning the manners, the buildings, the records,
and the coins of the ages that preceded us, has now extended itself to those poetical compositions which were
popular among our forefathers, but which have gradually
sunk into oblivion through the decay of language, and
the prevalence of a correct and polished taste. Books
printed in the black letter are sought for with the same

* Numerous editions in England, one with Stothard's plates; and many
in France.

avidity with which the English antiquary peruses a mon-
umental inscription, or treasures up a Saxon piece of
money. The popular ballad, composed by some illiterate
minstrel, and which has been handed down by tradition
for several centuries, is rescued from the hands of the
vulgar, to obtain a place in the collection of the man of
taste. Verses, which a few years past were thought
worthy the attention of children only, or of the lowest
and rudest orders, are now admired for that artless simplicity, which once obtained the name of coarseness and
vulgarity. . . . Every lover of poetry is pleased with the
judicious selections of Percy, though he gives himself
little concern about dates. . . . The more antiquarian
taste in poetry, or the admiration of *bad* poetry merely
because it is ancient, is certainly absurd. It is more difficult to discover the meaning of many of our old poets,
disguised as it is in an obsolete and uncouth phraseology,
than to read an elegant Greek or Latin author. Such
study is, indeed, not unfrequently like raking in a dunghill
for pearls, and gaining the labour only for one's pains.

"Our earlier poets, many of whose names are deservedly
forgotten, seem to have thought that rhyme was poetry ;
and even this constituent grace they applied with extreme negligence. It was, however, good enough for its
readers ; . . . it has had its day, and the antiquary must
not despise us, if we cannot pursue it with patience. He
who delights in all such reading as is never read, may de-
rive some pleasure from the singularity of his taste ; but
he ought still to respect the judgment of mankind, which
has consigned to oblivion the works he admires. While
he pores unmolested on Chaucer, Gower, Lydgate, and
Occleve, let him not censure our obstinacy in adhering to
Homer, Virgil, Milton, and Pope.

"In perusing the antiquated pages of our English bards,

we sometimes find a passage which has comparative merit, and which shines with the greater lustre, because it is surrounded with deformity. . . . It is true, that those old ballads, which are in the mouths of peasants on both sides the Tweed, have something in them irresistibly captivating. Vulgar, coarse, inelegant, they yet touch the heart. . . . Addison first gained them the notice of scholars, by his praises of 'Chevy Chase,'" etc. The whole essay is worthy of attention.

Knox, No. cxxix., also says: "I think it is not difficult to perceive, that the admirers of English poetry are divided into two parties. The objects of their love are, perhaps, of equal beauty, though they greatly differ in their air, their dress, the turn of their features, and their complexion. On one side are the lovers and imitators of Spenser and Milton ; and on the other, those of Dryden, Boileau, and Pope." In the same paper Knox regrets that blank-verse was the object of "an unreasonable prejudice," and that Dr. Johnson should have treated "the illustrious Gray with singular harshness, in a work which contains very candid accounts of a Sprat and a Yalden, a Duke and a Broome." Thus it is evident that the condition of things was pretty well understood at the time. Indeed, we should naturally expect that it must have been so, just as we know that the lightning never flashes in a clear sky. The clouds gather with greater or less celerity, and with more or less remote muttering ; it is this distant foreboding that we are now studying.

Another excellent proof that a change was impending is the unanimity of the conservative people in asserting that a change would be dangerous if it were not fortunately impossible. This state of mind found expression in the writings and utterances of Dr. Johnson. Inasmuch as his wit made his sayings memorable, he is now often

looked upon as a mere creature of prejudice ; and often
we take for a simple expression of personal whim what
was simply the best statement of the thought of his time—
not, of course, of all the thought, but of what we may call
the conservative thought of his time. He led his contemporaries, but, to make a homely comparison, he led it as
the foremost of the flock—foremost, to be sure, yet one
of the flock. There is scarcely one of his views which
has not been riddled by later opinion. All that he held
dearest has been destroyed, and the process began even
before he seemed to have made irrevocably fast the laws
of literature. Thus (Boswell, July 9, 1763), "I mentioned
to him that Dr. Adam Smith, in his lectures upon composition, when I studied under him in the College of Glasgow,
had maintained the same opinion strenuously, and I repeated some of his arguments. — JOHNSON: 'Sir, I was
once in company with Smith, and we did not take to each
other ; but had I known that he loved rhyme as much as
you tell me he does, I should have HUGGED him.'" He
spoke with intelligence about Thomson, saying : "His is
one of the works in which blank verse seems properly
used. . . . His description of extended scenes and general
effects bring before us the whole magnificence of nature,
whether pleasing or dreadful. The gaiety of Spring, the
splendour of Summer, the tranquillity of Autumn, and the
horror of Winter, take in their turns possession of the
mind. The poet leads us through the appearances of
things as they are successively varied by the vicissitudes
of the year, and imparts to us so much of their enthusiasm,
that our thoughts expand with his imagery and kindle
with his sentiments. . . . His diction is in the highest degree florid and luxuriant, such as may be said to be to his
images and thoughts 'both their lustre and their shade;'
such as invests them with splendour, through which, per-

haps, they are not always easily discerned. It is too exuberant, and sometimes may be charged with filling the ear more than the mind." In his preface to his edition of Shakspere (1765), Dr. Johnson puts away the notion of the unities into the lumber-chamber, nearly thirty years after he had written his play, in which he had closely observed them.* Yet about Milton he could write strangely. We feel here that we are listening to a man with whom it is impossible to sympathize, and one who is moved by prejudice. It is not hard to find sufficient ground for his prejudice, from what we have seen of the way in which Milton was regarded by those of Johnson's contemporaries whom he despised, and whom he lashed over Milton's back. Even more violent was his onslaught on the reviving interest in ballad literature and on Ossian:

"Mr. James Macpherson,—I received your foolish and impudent letter. Any violence offered to me I shall do my best to repel, and what I cannot do for myself, the law shall do for me. I hope I shall never be deterred from detecting what I think a cheat by the menaces of a ruffian. What would you have me retract? I thought your book an imposture; I think it an imposture still. For this opinion I have given my reasons to the public, which I here dare you to refute. Your rage I defy. Your abilities, since your 'Homer,'† are not so formidable; and

---

* So that even before Lessing he drove out the unities; but by this time they had no such real existence in England as they had on the Continent. Lillo and his followers had slain them. Johnson wrote about Shakspere, however, in the old-fashioned way when he blamed him for omitting "opportunities of instructing or delighting," and for making "no just distribution of good or evil."

† A translation of Homer into English prose (2 vols. 4to., 1773; 2d ed. the same year). This was an attempt to work over Homer in the rhythm and style of Ossian. The book was generally derided.

what I hear of your morals inclines me to pay regard not to what you shall say, but to what you shall prove. You may print this if you will." So he wrote, and "he provided himself with a weapon both of the defensive and offensive kind. It was an oak-plant of a tremendous size ; a plant, I say, and not a shoot or branch, for it had a root, which being trimmed to the size of a large orange, became the head of it. Its height was upward of six feet, and from about an inch in diameter at the lower end, increased to near three ; this he kept in his bedchamber, so near the chair in which he constantly sat as to be within reach." This stick, which overshadows the one which Ambrose Philips hung up at Buttons's to beat Pope with, was as powerless against Ossian as rods are when used in the way of disseminating a love of literature ; and Ossian, as we shall shortly notice, swept over continental Europe like a fog from the northern seas.

In fact, as Hettner says, Dr. Johnson's roots ran back to the time of Queen Anne ; he inherited the opinions of that time, and he lived long enough to see in a flourishing condition many opinions that were distinctly opposed to the earlier well-established principles. Thus, besides his immortally unread tragedy, he wrote his essays after the model of the *Spectator*, and in the *Rambler* gave the English people many curious sermons. Remember, however, that in so doing he took the only method known of reaching the public ; he was not trying to make himself over into a Queen Anne writer in the deliberate way in which people now build Queen Anne houses. Let us take the *Rambler*, and see Dr. Johnson laying down the law for our ancestors in the middle of the last century. As Mr. Leslie Stephen puts it : "With Shakespeare, or Sir Thomas Browne, or Jeremy Taylor, or Milton, man is contemplated in his relations to the universe ; he is in presence

of eternity and infinity; life is a brief dream; we are
ephemeral actors in a vast drama; heaven and hell are
behind the veil of phenomena; at every step our friends
vanish into the vast abyss of ever-present mystery. To
all such thoughts the writers of the eighteenth century
seemed to close their eyes as resolutely as possible. They
do not, like Sir Thomas Browne, delight to lose themselves
in an Oh! Altitudo! or to snatch a solemn joy from the
giddiness which follows a steady gaze into the infinite.
The greatest men among them, a Swift or a Johnson,
have indeed a sense—perhaps a really stronger sense than
Browne or Taylor—of the pettiness of our lives and the
narrow limits of our knowledge. No great man could
ever be without it. But the awe of the infinite and the
unseen does not induce them to brood over the mysterious,
and find utterance for bewildered musings on the inscru-
table enigma.

"It is felt only in a certain habitual sadness which
clouds their whole tone of thought. They turn their
backs on the infinite, and abandon the effort at a solution.
Their eyes are fixed on the world around them, and they
regard as foolish and presumptuous any one who dares to
contemplate the great darkness. The expression of this
sentiment in literature is a marked disposition to turn
aside from pure speculation, combined with a deep interest in moral and social laws. The absence of any deeper
speculative ground makes the immediate practical questions of life all the more interesting. We know not what
we are, nor whither we are going, nor whence we come;
but we can, by the help of common sense, discover a sufficient share of moral maxims for our guidance in life, and
we can analyze human passions, and discover what are the
moving forces of society, without going back to first principles. Knowledge of human nature, as it actually pre-

sented itself in the shifting scene before them, and a vivid appreciation of the importance of the moral law, are the staple of the best literature of the time. As ethical speculation was prominent in the philosophy, the enforcement of ethical principles is the task of those who were inclined to despise philosophy. When a creed is dying, the importance of preserving the moral law naturally becomes a pressing consideration with all strong natures " (English Thought," ii. 370, 371).

This intelligent statement does not cover all the ground, because, for one thing, the causes which lead to the differences between two different periods of civilization are enormously complex, and it is hard, if not actually impossible, for any one observer to see them all. Yet the decay of faith, and the consequent need of enforcing moral teaching, do not fully explain the alteration in men's minds ; enthusiasm died out, because, from its very nature, it cannot last long, and the task that lay before the people of the last century was the establishment of civilization, and this was a practical question. The Renaissance was of the nature of the conquest of unknown lands, and its work was done with the fire and enthusiasm that conquest requires ; in the last century, these newly conquered regions had to be brought under the municipal law, and this is a process in which enthusiasm is apt to languish.

Where Addison spoke with grace and lightness, Johnson spoke with pomp and elaboration, and with a certain despairing melancholy ; but the main effort of the two men was the same. We do not nowadays read the *Rambler* with delight ; in fact, we do not read it at all. What we enjoy in the *Spectator* is not its moral lessons, which were dear to those for whom they were written. We enjoy the eternally delightful humour with which Addison sketched certain characters, but Johnson's humour is less easy. "Criticism," he tells us (*Rambler*, No. 16),

" . . . was the eldest daughter of Labour and of Truth; she was, at her birth, committed to the care of Justice, and brought up by her in the Palace of Wisdom. Being soon distinguished by the celestials, for her uncommon qualities, she was appointed the Governess of Fancy, and empowered to beat time to the chorus of the Muses, when they sung before the throne of Jupiter."

No. 74: "He that gives himself up to his own fancy, and converses with none but such as he hires to lull him on the down of absolute authority, to soothe him with obsequiousness, and regale him with flattery, soon grows too slothful for the labour of contest, too tender for the asperity of contradiction, and too delicate for the coarseness of truth; a little opposition offends, a little restraint enrages, and a little difficulty perplexes him," etc.

No. 126: "Sir,—As you propose to extend your regard to the minuteness of decency, as well as to the dignity of science, I cannot forbear to lay before you a mode of persecution by which I have been exiled to taverns and coffee-houses, and deterred from entering the doors of my friends.

"Among the ladies who please themselves with splendid furniture, or elegant entertainment, it is a practice very common to ask every guest how he likes the carved work of the cornice, or the figures of the tapestry; the china at the table, or the plate on the sideboard; and on all occasions to inquire his opinion of their judgment and their choice. Melania has laid her new watch in the window nineteen times, that she may desire me to look upon it. Calista has an art of dropping her snuff-box by drawing out her handkerchief that when I pick it up I may admire it; and Fulgentia has conducted me by mistake into the wrong room, at every visit I have paid since her picture was put into a new frame."

Certainly Dr. Johnson is not always associated in our minds with this airy satire of social foibles, and it must be acknowledged that much of the *Rambler* is but a cold imitation of the graceful lightness of much of the *Spectator*. No greater tribute could be paid to Addison and Steele than the fact that Dr. Johnson, in order to reach the public, had to follow, heavily shod as he was with all the learning and conservative prejudice of the eighteenth century, in their light footsteps. He maintains their most firmly rooted opinions with great vigor. His own method reads like a petrifaction of their forms of expression. In No. 32 we are told, or at least our ancestors were told, that "to oppose the devastations of Famine, who scattered the ground everywhere with carcasses, Labour came down upon earth." In No. 38, that "whosoever shall look heedfully upon those who are eminent for their riches, will not think their condition such that he should hazard his quiet, and much less his virtue to obtain it." In No. 41, that "we owe to memory not only the increase of our knowledge, and our progress in rational inquiries, but many other intellectual pleasures." It is not necessary to quote the harrowing tale, in No. 73, which contains this useful lesson: "Let no man from this time suffer his felicity to depend on the death of his aunt." It should be said in justice, however, that this phrase is more than half ironical. Johnson's views on literature, as expressed in the *Rambler*, were far more rigid than those of his great predecessors. We have seen with what contempt he spoke of those who cared for antique poetry. Addison was continually getting out of the pulpit to praise something which his taste told him was good. Johnson, on the other hand, brought all his wit and learning to crush every attempt at novelty. Science, too, fared no better at his hands than did romantic poetry. Thus in the *Rambler*, No. 24: "When a man employs himself upon remote and unnecessary subjects, and wastes his life upon questions which cannot be resolved, and of which the solution would conduce very little to the advancement of happiness; when he lavishes his hours in calculating the weight of the terraqueous globe, or in adjusting successive systems of worlds beyond the reach of the telescope; he may be very properly recalled from his excursions by this precept [know thyself], and reminded that there is a nearer being with which it is his duty to be more acquainted, and from which his attention has been withheld by studies, to which he has no other motive than vanity or curiosity." Thereupon he proceeds to draw the character of a scientific man whom he brands with the name of Gelidus. This worthless person displays the harm wrought by science, by being " insensible to every spectacle of distress and unmoved by the loudest call of social nature." It is, perhaps, worthy of a moment's notice that the objection nowadays to men like the unhappy Gelidus is, that they are, if anything, too unpractical, and are prone to exhibit a sentimental sympathy with the sufferings of others.

Johnson also lacked sympathy with collectors, as he showed in No. 82, which contains an imaginary confession of one of them : " I now turned my thoughts to exotics and antiquities. Having been always a lover of geography, I determined to collect the maps drawn in rude and barbarous times, before any regular surveys, or just observations." " I allowed my tenants to pay their rents in butterflies, till I had exhausted the papilionaceous tribes. I then directed them to the pursuit of other animals, and obtained by this easy method, most of the grubs and insects, which land, air, or water, can supply. I have three species of earthworms not known to the naturalists, have discovered a new ephemera, and can show four wasps that were taken torpid in their native quarters." One tenant brought him only "two horse-flies and those of little more than the common size ; and I was upon the brink of seizing for arrears, when his good fortune threw a white mole in his way, for which he was not only forgiven but rewarded." He collected marbles from remote regions, curiosities, a fur cap of the Czar and a boot of Charles of

Sweden. For the sake of the Harleian collection "I mortgaged my land, and purchased thirty medals, which I could never find before;" and now he is ruined. The mere catalogue of his motley tastes seems to show the inaccuracy of the portrait, which may well be a caricature of Horace Walpole.

And again in No. 177, Hirsutus collects books in black-letter; Ferratus, copper coins; "Cantilenus turned all his thoughts upon old ballads, for he considered them as the genuine records of the national tastes. He offered to show me a copy of the 'Children in the Wood,' which he firmly believed to be of the first edition, and by the help of which the text might be freed from corruptions, if this age of barbarity had any claim to such favours from him." Johnson's sole consolation is that these people were capable of nothing better, and were at least kept out of active mischief.*

Let us remember, however, that in its day the *Rambler* was far from popular. Its circulation was rather less than five hundred copies; it was only after Johnson had become famous that they were much read. Ten editions that were published in his lifetime made up for the earlier neglect of the essays.†

---

* Johnson's feeling about research was the common property of his day, and not mere personal whim. Compare the "Dissertation concerning the Æra of Ossian:" "Inquiries into the antiquities of nations afford more pleasure than any real advantage to mankind. . . . It is then [in a well-ordered community] historians begin to write, and public transactions to be worthy remembrance."

And see Dr. Hugh Blair's remark, in his "Critical Dissertation on the Poems of Ossian:" "History, when it treats of remote and dark ages, is seldom very instructive. The beginnings of society in every country are involved in fabulous confusion; and though they were not, they would furnish few events worth recording." See, too, *Tatler*, No. 216.

† Cumberland, "Memoirs" (Am. ed.), p. 183, says: "His Ramblers are in everybody's hands, about them opinions vary."

It is scarcely fair to exhume Johnson's "Irene" to show his respect for the models of his day. There is but one opinion possible about the tragedy; that was formed a century ago, and it is one of the few that have not been revised, but it is not generally known, perhaps, how very poor the play really is. For instance:

> " *Leon.* Awake, Demetrius, from this dismal dream,
> Sink not beneath imaginary sorrows;
> Call to your aid your courage, and your wisdom;
> Think on the sudden change of human scenes,
> Think on the various accidents of war;
> Think on the mighty power of awful virtue;
> Think on that Providence that guards the good."

And, in the next scene:

> " Has silence pressed her seal upon his lips?
> Does adamantine faith invest his heart?
> Will he not bend beneath a tyrant's frown?
> Will he not melt before ambition's fire?
> Will he not soften in a friend's embrace
> Or flow dissolving in a woman's tears."

Similar three and four barrelled sentences are to be found in almost every scene.

The "Rasselas" is, in form, an amplification of the Oriental apologues in the *Spectator*, but it is as complete a "criticism of life" as one will find in any English work of the time. Johnson's preface to his Shakspere, although, as we have seen, not untinged with antique notions, was of service to letters. His "Lives of the Poets" must have had, on the other hand, a bad influence. His unsympathetic treatment of Gray and his lack of appreciation of Milton doubtless affected a vast number of readers. It would be unfair to load his shoulders with all the bigotry with which the English nation long regarded much of the work of foreigners; he but gave expression to widespread prejudices. Yet his wit and his authority must have strengthened very much the raw English prejudice against the great French writers of the last century. "For anything I can see, all foreigners are fools," was one of his remarks. The opinion he expressed to Boswell about Rousseau and Voltaire will occur to every one. He told Stockdale that Voltaire and D'Alembert were *child-ish* authors.

In looking at Johnson's whole value, we pardon these eccentric utterances, and it is by no means a complete description of him to say of him nothing more than that he encouraged philistinism, any more than it would be to say that he was hot-tempered, but the discussion of his many better-known qualities falls outside of our present purpose. With all his faults, he is one of the best-loved men in the history of letters, and this is due, not to his writings, but to the faithful record which Boswell made of the evenings when the great man folded his legs and had his talk out. He could have little thought that posterity would yawn over his moral writings, sniff at his witty criticisms, and coolly respect but a small part of his poetry, leaving the rest unread. Once, it will be remembered, when some one regretted that he had not given his attention to law, in which case he would doubtless have risen to be Lord High Chancellor, Johnson impatiently turned the conversation, evidently filled with regret that he had frittered his life away with so little to show for it. But what is the ephemeral reputation of a Lord High Chancellor, which scarcely outlasts that of an actor and soon becomes a mere vague rumor, with that which Johnson now holds throughout the English-speaking world? We may say English-speaking, because people of other nations repay the contempt he felt for their grandfathers, and are far from understanding why we like him.

Dr. Johnson's reputation, then, is due to Boswell's book. His reputation as a wit, instead of being simply a tradition, surviving, like Dryden's, on a meagre handful of anecdotes, and kept alive, like that of most good talkers, by having all the old stories of centuries fathered on him alone—instead of that, I say, we hear him as he lived and spoke. What makes Boswell's "Life" so valuable is that he did not iron all the eccentricities out of Johnson, that he did not file and polish him into a faultless and bloodless hero, as photographers nowadays burnish from our portraits all the lines which time and experience have marked upon our face.* Hannah More "besought his [Boswell's] tenderness for our virtuous and most revered departed friend, and begged he would mitigate some of his asperities. He said, roughly, 'He would not cut off his claws, nor make a tiger a cat to please anybody.'"

Boswell's reward for his honesty will not surprise thoughtful people. Inasmuch as he put down instances of his own folly and of the rebuffs he drew from Johnson, it has been the fashion to decry him for a simpleton; but few sensible men, however, have given so much pleasure to an ungrateful world. He really opens the door for us and lets us overhear Johnson expressing in his talk all the opposition that conservatives felt against the modern spirit that was then rising on every hand. There were many innovators; for society had become very complex, and there were countless influences at work preparing for the second Renaissance, the Romantic movement.

We have seen in what way much of the new spirit grew,

---

* Perhaps as marked an instance of the conventional treatment is the authorized life of Day, the author of "Sandford and Merton." His life, as we may see in Miss Edgeworth's memoirs of her father, was a whirl of eccentricity, but in the authorized memoir he is as unreal and pallid as a bust with a toga around its neck.

and how the impending political revolution was antici-
pated in literature by the deposition of crowned heads
from their pre-eminence and the exaltation of the citizen.
We have seen the awakening of an interest in the past;
this continued, and was one of the most productive of the
many influences at work. This need not surprise us; the
key of the so-called classical method was the imitation of
poets of acknowledged merit. Horace, Seneca, Vergil, had
been copied and recopied. Gottsched and Bodmer agreed
in urging imitation as the one secret of success; they differed only in the poets they suggested for models. With
time there had grown up a new love for the forgotten
past, and once-neglected poets now began to be regarded
as authorities. We have seen how echoes of Milton re-
verberated through the whole century, and any one who
turns over the collections of verse of that period will find
numberless attempts to reproduce Spenser's stanza. Beat-
tie only followed what was already a fashion when he
adopted that form for his curious refutation of infidelity
in the "Minstrel." The new interest in Shakspere was
part of the same movement.*

---

* Lord Lansdowne made over the "Merchant of Venice" (1701) with
music; Otway, "Romeo and Juliet" into "Caius Marius;" Gildon, "Measure for Measure;" Cibber, "Richard the Third," 1700; Dennis, "Merry
Wives," 1702; Leveridge, "Midsummer-Night's Dream," 1716; Dennis,
"Coriolanus" 1721; Charles Johnson, "As You Like It," 1723; Duke
of Buckingham, "Julius Cæsar" into two plays, 1722; Worsdale, "Taming of the Shrew," 1736; J. Miller, "Much Ado About Nothing," 1737;
Cibber, "King John," 1744; Lampe, "Midsummer-Night's Dream" into
a sort of operetta, 1745.

Garrick, though abused by Lamb for falseness to Shakspere, did much
in the way of restoring the original text. The story runs that when Garrick was acting Macbeth according to the original text, Quin asked him
where he got all that fine language. It is to be remembered that Steele
did not quote the original text in the *Tatler*, and we should consider how

II. A wholly new voice was heard in Ossian (1762), the effect of which was, however, more distinctly marked on the Continent than in England.* The authenticity of these poems is still a matter of grave doubt. At the best, they were versions of meagre relics, composed in the rhetorical language that marks much of the tumid blank verse of the last century, with imitations of the Old Testament and of certain old Irish and Scotch poems. Macpherson's curious dependence on his contemporaries, which he exhibited in almost every line, probably endeared him to his first readers. The very vagueness of his descriptions of nature seemed like vivid accuracy to those who were but just beginning to enjoy the sight of scenery; now, on the other hand, it is but an additional proof of Macpherson's forgery.† But, such as they were—and just what they were still remains uncertain—they had a success which was incontestable. They were put into German, and were often reprinted in that country in their English dress. They were translated into French and into Italian, and were much admired by Napoleon,‡ among others; and versions appeared in Spanish, Polish, and Dutch.

---

seldom we nowadays, more than one hundred years since Garrick's prime, see the plays without great alteration.

* As Taine says, Macpherson "collected fragments of legends, plastered over the whole an abundance of eloquence and rhetoric, and created a Celtic Homer, Ossian, who, with Oscar, Malvina, and his whole troop, made the tour of Europe, and, about 1830, ended by furnishing baptismal names for French grisettes and *perruquiers.*"—"English Lit.," ii. 220.

† "Poor moaning, monotonous Macpherson," as Carlyle called him in his review of Taylor's "German Poetry."—"Essays," ii. 443.

‡ Have not his proclamations, addresses to his troops, etc., an Ossianic sound? He also liked "Werther." Goethe said to Henry Crabbe Robinson ("Diary," ii. 106), "It was the contrast with his own nature. He loved soft and melancholy music. Werther was among his books at St. Helena." But is not this statement too modest? Napoleon liked "Wer-

In England they from the first met violent opposition.
Dr. Johnson, who detested them because they were Scotch,
as well as because they were animated by all that he most
despised in the new literature, was their bitterest opponent.
Iis view of them may be gathered from the letter quoted
above. The Scotch, however, rose like a man in their behalf. An ardent patriotism sufficed to convince them that
Macpherson was a mere translator of their old epics, and
no charlatan. Dr. Blair, for instance, undertook to show
by copious arguments that Ossian was a Scotch Homer,
and how, by virtue of his genius, he had complied with
every one of Aristotle's laws :

"The duration of the action in Fingal, is much shorter
than in the Iliad or Æneid, but sure there may be shorter
as well as longer heroic poems ; and if the authority of
Aristotle be also required for this, he says expressly, that
the epic composition is indefinite as to the time of its
duration. Accordingly the action of the Iliad lasts only
forty-seven days, whilst that of the Æneid is continued
for more than a year." And, on the next page, " Homer's
art in magnifying the character of Achilles has been universally admired. Ossian certainly shows no less art in ag-
grandizing Fingal." "The story which is the foundation
of the Iliad is in itself as simple as that of Fingal," etc.

Yet Johnson's opposition to the poems was effective at
home, although it had no influence abroad, where the readers expected roughness in a twofold translation. What
the influence of the book was we may see in the second
part of Goethe's "Werther" (1774), in Klopstock, and in
many of Goethe's early odes ; and Chateaubriand has told

---

ther" because it came out when he was young. Napoleon, it must be remembered, once came near committing suicide. *Vide* also "Eckermann,"
iii. 28 (Jan. 2, 1824).

us how he was delighted by the fictitious bard. Germany especially was moved by the Ossianic spirit. That country was then awakening to the consciousness of its powers, and the vague, formless grandeur of Ossian came like a sea-breeze to expel the sultry, close air of the artificial literature that had pretended to exist for so long a time. The inspiration, you will notice, came to the Continent from England. Lillo, Richardson, Sterne, Goldsmith, Ossian, each in his own way served as model for French and German writers; Rousseau was directly inspired by Richardson, and it was from Rousseau and Ossian that Goethe drew strength for writing his "Werther," a book that swept over Europe like a meteor.

We of the present day, one of whose favorite affectations is the love of sincerity, are apt to look with a good deal of contempt on the worship of Ossian, and to sneer at our ancestors for finding any delight in his tumid pages. It may be questioned, however, whether our painstaking resuscitations of the dead, with their easily pierced veneering of local color, are actually much better than the vague grandeur and sham heroics of the famous bard. At any rate, whether the poem was really great or really pretty, it is our duty in the first place to understand why it was liked, as it undeniably was, and to do this we must remember the growing intolerance of antiquated and artificial forms. As Mr. Stephen puts it ("English Thought," ii. 447), "its crude attempts to represent a social state when great men stalked through the world in haughty superiority to the narrow conventions of modern life, were congenial to men growing weary of an effete formalism. Men had been talking under their breath, and in a mincing dialect, so long that they were easily gratified, and easily imposed upon, by an affectation of vigorous and natural sentiment." Then, too, the science of criticism, which is really not fault-finding, but precise description, was in its tenderest infancy, and men had few rules for the guidance of their belief.

III. The general interest in the past, together with the incompetence of the public to determine what was genuine, opened a tempting path before literary adventurers, and Chatterton (1752–70), with his Rowley poems (written between 1767 and 1770, and published 1777), prepared a controversy that was nearly as hot as that over the authenticity of Ossian. I have not time or space for the full discussion of Chatterton's poems; they may be found described at some length and praised with great fervor by Mr. Theodore Watts in the third volume of Ward's "English Poets." All that can be said in praise of Chatterton is said there, as well as some things that cannot be accepted without hesitation. To assert that the use of proper names, like gems, for purposes of decoration, was copied by Coleridge in his "Kubla Khan" from Chatterton, who invented it, seems rash. We have found the same tendency in the imitators of Milton, in Thomson, and in Goldsmith. It is used with a different purpose by the various poets, because each has his own special message to utter, and utters it in his own way.

Then, too, Chatterton's forgeries form scarcely "a puzzling chapter of literary history." It was, so to speak, Chatterton's only way of being romantic; he was interested in the past of the Middle Ages, and imitated it, as hosts of poets have done since, and the most natural way for him was under an assumed personality; this, too, was his only way of getting readers. If he had sent out his imitations as avowed imitations, he would have been laughed at—but there was some interest in old poems; they were curious and interesting for the people of that polished age, who would have derided taking them for

models. The old poems were at that time simply interesting curiosities, which no one thought of copying. Every one was eager to exhume relics, but with no intention of putting them to any use. Keats, it should be
said in answer to Mr. Watts, did not so much imitate
Chatterton as he did those who inspired the earlier
poet.*

At this time, as we have said, the taste of the public
was very uncritical. Dr. Percy, when he published his
famous "Reliques of Ancient English Poetry," in 1765,
felt impelled to work them over to suit modern ears, so
that a new and unamended edition had to be supplied
about fifteen years ago, shorn of Percy's attempted improvements.† Scott, too, in his "Minstrelsy of the Scot- ·

---

* It is curious to notice a similar occurrence in French literature. In
1803, a M. de Surville, who, by the way, had fought among our French
allies in the Revolutionary war, published a volume of poems alleged to
have been written in the fifteenth century by an ancestress of his, Clotilde de Surville. The poems of this Gallic Rowley he professed to have
discovered in an old chest, but the originals were said to have been destroyed in the Revolution. Criticism found itself between two apparent
impossibilities—one that Clotilde had written the poems in the fifteenth
century, the other that M. de Surville had written them in the eighteenth.
For a long time, the forgery escaped detection. Even in Longfellow's
"Poets and Poetry of Europe" (1845), p. 441, we find them mentioned and
the best one translated, although with a strong hint of their ungenuine-
ness. In fact, this had already been conclusively proved in France; more
careful study of the old language had made the deception clear, in the
same way that Rowley had been detected. The process was more difficult,
because the execution was more careful in the French poems. *Vide*
Sainte-Beuve, "Tableau de la Poésie Française an XVIᵉ Siècle," p. 475
et seq.

† Ritson objected to Percy's inaccuracy, and what was his reward? Sir
E. E. Brydges wrote of him (*vide* Allibone, *sub* "Ritson"): "Mr. Joseph
Ritson, unilluminated by a particle of taste or fancy, and remarkable only
for the unnecessary drudgery with which he dedicated his life to one of
the humblest departments of literary antiquities, and for the bitter inso-

tish Border" (1802–3), mangled some of the old ballads, not from a preference for bad work, but in order to please the public. The readers of that time wanted omissions supplied, roughnesses trimmed away, and everything polished, just as now we prefer tinkered hymns. Exactness, like all the virtues, is a plant of slow growth.

Percy's "Reliques" is commonly mentioned as the turning-point in the taste of the last century, but it was quite as much the result, as the cause, of the renewed interest in old ballads. Percy did more completely what had been done feebly before. Still, it is well to bear in mind the date of the publication, 1765, as a mnemonic point, for this was by far the most important of the collections. A copy of the book fell into the hands of Bürger

---

lence of foul abuse with which he communicated his dull acquisitions to the public."

Scott (*loc. cit.*) said: "A man of acute observation, profound research, and great labour, these valuable attributes were unhappily combined with an eager irritability of temper, which induced him to treat antiquarian trifles with the same seriousness which men of the world reserve for matters of importance."

In 1803, the same year that Scott's "Border Minstrelsy" was completed, then appeared Oehlenschläger's collection of "Volkslieder;" these, too, had been improved after the usual fashion.

Allan Ramsay had offended in the same way. He published, in 1716, "Christ's Kirk on the Green" (attributed to James I. of Scotland), and afterwards added a first, and then a second, canto of his own composition. In the "Tea-table Miscellany" and "Evergreen" "he abridged, he varied, modernized, and superadded."

We need not go so far for instances. Many of the best-known hymns are tinkered, and the process has been going on for many years. *Vide* Sir Roundell Palmer, "The Book of Praise," Preface, and *Nation*, iii. 65. The main thing desired in a hymn is religious fervour; textual accuracy is a secondary matter. In the same way, Ramsay, Percy, and Scott wanted to arouse an interest in the past, for which precision was pedantry.

(1748–94), who translated many of the ballads into German, and was inspired by it to write his own "Lenore." *
This ballad ran through Europe with the speed of its knightly hero, and it was in 1795 that a lady in Edinburgh showed it, in William Taylor's translation, to Scott, who imitated it in his "William and Helen," which he published along with his "Wild Huntsman," and was soon followed by his version of "Goetz von Berlichingen," 1799. It would be fair to say that Percy's "Reliques" had more influence in Germany than in England. Bürger and his fellow-poets of the *Hainbund*, who were all young men with a confused hatred of tyrants and great affection for the full moon, took to writing more ballads after the old pattern, as illustrated by Percy's "Reliques," and explained by Herder, and soon Herder established the new lines in which German thought was destined to run, substituting the intelligent study of the past for the faithful following of academic rules. Fully to describe Herder's work would take us too far from our subject. He was the guiding-spirit of the new movement which placed Germany in literature abreast of the richest countries of Europe, and in science ahead of any. And to describe him it would be necessary to point out at length the enormous influence which Rousseau had on thought at the end of the last century. He was one of the men

---

* Written in 1773, and published in 1774 in the Göttingen *Musenalmanach* (*vide* Döring: G. A. Bürger, "Ein biog. Denkmal").

The "Lenore" had been translated by Sir J. T. Stanley, who published his translation in 1786. It was "a paraphrase, not to say a new poem; the original being 'altered and added to,' to square it with 'the cause of religion and morality'" (*vide* Gilchrist's "Blake," i. 138).

Henry James Pye, poet-laureate in 1790, also translated the "Lenore," as did the Hon. William Robert Spencer, in the same year, 1796; this last-mentioned translation was illustrated by Spencer's aunt, Lady Diana Beauclerc.

who did most to depose reason and to set up emotion in its place, a change which began in England.

IV. The history of German literature until nearly the end of the last century is almost a reproduction, in miniature to be sure, of what we have seen in England. We have noticed certain points of likeness in the intellectual growth of England, France, and Italy. Gradually, as modern thought spread into Germany, similar results followed there. Thus, Martin Opitz (1597–1639), a man endowed with but little original genius, opened the way for a new development of German literature by announcing the necessity of following the methods of the classical writers, especially those of Rome. Yet he urged his fellow-countrymen to use their own language; and in his tastes, for he admired Seneca and Ovid, as well as in the tendency of his instructions, he belongs to those men who announced the rules of classicism which they barely understood. He was intellectually the companion of Malherbe in France, and of the early formal writers, between Waller and Dryden, in England.* To be sure, he admired Ronsard and Du Bellay among French writers, and allowed his name to be used on the title-page of a translation of Sidney's "Arcadia ;" but his own work was cool and restrained.

What is called the second Silesian school, of which Hofmannswaldau (1618–79) and Lohenstein (1635–83) were the leading representatives, corresponds to the reign of the brief-lived *précieux* in France, and that of the so-called metaphysical poets in England. We have seen some of Cowley's conceits ; Germany was not left behind. Thus, Hofmannswaldau wrote :

---

* *Vide* Hettner, " Literaturgeschichte das XVIII^ten Jahrhundert," III. i. 180, and " Koberstein," ii. 46 et seq.

" Was ist doch insgemein ein Freund in dieser Welt ?

Ein Spiegel, der vergrösst und fälschlich schöner macht,

Ein Pfennig, der nicht Strich und nicht Gewichte hält,

Ein Wesen, so aus Zorn und bittrer Galle lachet,

Ein Strauchstein, dessen Glantz, uns Schande und Schaden bringt,

Ein Dolch, der schimmernd ist, und uns zu Hertzen dringt,

Ein Heilbrunn, etc.

Ein goldgestickter Strang, etc.

Ein Honigwurm, etc.

Ein weisses Henneney, das Drachen hat gebohren,

Ein falscher Crocodil, der weinend uns zerreist,

Ein Sirenen-Weib, ein Safft, ein Giftbaum, ein Apfell von Damasc, ein
überzuckert Gifft, ein Pfeiffer in das Garn, ein göldner Urtels-Tisch,
ein Zeug," etc.

There seems no reason for his ever stopping.

Canitz (1654–99) headed a reaction in favor of so-
berer methods ; he inclined towards Opitz rather than
towards his lush successors, but he derived most of his
inspiration from the later Frenchmen, especially from Boileau. Johann von Besser (1654–1729) belonged to the
same more modern school. He lived long enough to be a
friend of Gottsched, who was the most formidable foe of
anything like indifference to the rigid rules of French
classicism. It is curious to notice how Canitz, Besser,
and Gottsched imitated in their play the real work that
was going on in France and England. Biedermann * gives
some most amusing instances of their unprofitable zeal :

"Besser, on the death of his wife, composed ' on the
day of her funeral' an elegy nine pages long, which,
however, even Gottsched declared was unnatural and
void of poetic truth. To this he added two other poems,
in the name of his children, one of which was inscribed
thus : 'This was written to his dear mamma, on his sick
bed and in his seventh year by her most obedient and

---

* " Deutschland im XVIII^{ten} Jahrhundert," II. i. 448, note.

only son.' The other, 'A lament for the untimely loss of her dear mamma by her orphaned two-year-old daughter.' The seven-year-old boy is represented as writing thus :

"Man sprach, sie hätte mir ein Schwesterlein geboren ;
Ist leider das Geburt, wo sie versterben muss ?'

[They said she had brought forth a little sister for me, but is it birth, when she must die ? O, dearest mamma ! what has your son lost ! But what has papa lost by this sad blow ! I lie sick, so sore is my grief, and she who should console me is the prey of death,' etc.] Moreover, Besser asked his friends for additional eulogies, and so appeared a stately 'memorial for the late Mrs. Besser, *née* Kühlewein.' He also composed an elegy on the death of the wife of Canitz. At the very beginning he wanted to express the thought that she had never grieved her husband except by dying, but he could not put it in such a way as would satisfy him, try as he would ; hence he communicated his perplexity to the disconsolate widower. Canitz set to work at once, in friendly rivalry, and wrote some lines that seemed to him very fair, but he suppressed them because at last Besser was able to write something which seemed better.

" In Weichmann's ' Poesie·der Niedersachsen,' vol. ii. p. 249, are printed four elegies on the death of a son of the poet Brockes, and the heart-broken father replies in verse, using the same rhymes. Mosheim, who was an abbot, on the death of his wife wrote to Gottsched that, having lost so worthy and amiable a spouse, he felt it to be his duty to give the world a testimonial of his deep grief ; but, as he was no poet, would not Gottsched write an elegy in his name ; and to make it easier he sent him a description of the departed lady. Gottsched at once composed an elegy, for which Mosheim sent a modest honorarium.

The widower expressed his satisfaction with the poem, but, he said, 'I shall have to add a few lines, for, as a teacher of spiritual truth, I must really say something about patience and trust in God.'"

For instances of incredible provincialism the reader must consult the various German authorities referred to by Biedermann. If, however, the faults of pseudo-classicism were magnified in Germany, the awakening, when it came, was such as not even the most hopeful could have dared to expect. It is to be remembered, too, that the inspiration reached Germany from the outside. Such mediocrity, and worse than mediocrity, as we have seen, was powerless even to beget a healthy reaction. It was mainly from England that the great change came, and with one bound Germany sprang into line with the oldest civilizations of Europe. It is no wonder that Germans are fond of studying the history of their own literature. Few countries have had so dramatic an experience. Although the ballads were an important indication of the new literary fervor in Germany, they were not the only one. In 1774 Goethe's "Werther" had appeared, and it was not long before the novel became known in England. Scott says in the preface to his translation of "Goetz von Berlichingen," that "it is by the elegant author of the Sorrows of Werther," of which a translation had appeared in 1779, followed by another in 1786.* The prejudice against the alleged immorality and atheism of the Germans was very great; the language was not commonly known—it held very much the same position that the Russian does

---

* There were three French translations before the Revolution—the first, from which the first English one was taken, in 1775. After the Revolution the book became better known, and nine new translations appeared between 1792 and 1809 (*vide* J. W. Appell, "Werther und seine Zeit," and "Goethe-Jahrbuch," iii. 27).

now ; it had not become an essential part of every educated person's education. The sentimentality of the Germans was much derided by the Tories. They were looked upon as destructive and dangerous radicals, philosophical socialists, and free-lovers. Coleridge, for instance, was much attacked for his praise of this people, and even Lamb was lugged in for reproof, although it was simply as a friend of Coleridge that he was held up to general execration. He himself knew very little about German literature, and was frequently ridiculing Coleridge's admiration of it. He speaks of "Faust," in a letter to him, as follows, Aug. 26, 1814 : "I have been reading Madame Staël on Germany ; an impudent, clever woman. But if 'Faust' be no better than her abstract of it, I counsel thee to let it alone. How canst thou translate the language of cat-monkeys?* Fie on such fantasies !" ("Works," i. 160). And, earlier, Aug. 6, 1800, he tells Coleridge that he has sent him, " with one or two small German books," " that drama in which got-fader performs " (i. 115). Again (ii. 114), in a letter to Patmore asking about his dog Dash, he says : " What I scratch out is a German quotation from Lessing, on the bite of rabid animals ; but I remember you don't read German. But Mrs. P—— may, so I wish I had let it stay. The meaning in English is—'Avoid to approach an animal suspected of madness, as you would avoid fire or a precipice,' which I think is a sensible observation. The Germans are certainly profounder than we." This is certainly not the language of an adorer of

---

* Lamb refers to her " De l'Allemagne," pt. ii. ch. xxiii. : " On croit découvrir, en écoutant le langage comique de ces chats-singes, quelles seroient les idées des animaux s'ils pouvoient les exprimer, quelle image grossière et ridicule ils se feroient de la nature et de l'homme."

The scene in the " Hexenküche " is meant, in which appear Kater and Kätzin.

German literature.* Another important influence at work to restrain the English from excessive enthusiasm for foreign literature was the general horror of the French principles, which greatly strengthened the English conservatism at the time of the French Revolution and later. Moreover, the very movement towards the study of their old literature confirmed the patriotism of most of the nations of Europe, and encouraged them against the enforced cosmopolitanism which Napoleon's armies were carrying everywhere. What was thought of the German radicalism, and of the plays and stories of that people in the last ten years of the eighteenth century, may be seen in many quarters; among others, in the very amusing *Anti-Jacobin Review,*† to which Canning and John Hook-

---

* Henry Crabbe Robinson ("Diary," ii. 109): "Charles Lamb, though he always affected contempt for Goethe, yet was manifestly pleased that his name was known to him." Goethe thought that Lamb had written a sonnet on his own name. Lamb even wrote a "ballad from the German" ("Works," iv. 32):

"The clouds are blackening, the storm is threatening."

† *Place aux dames.* The excellent Hannah More wrote (as quoted in Carlyle's "Essays," ii. 416): "Those ladies who take the lead in society are loudly called upon to act as guardians of the public taste as well as of the public virtue. They are called upon, therefore, to oppose with the whole weight of their influence, the irruption of those swarms of Publications now daily issuing from the banks of the Danube, which, like their ravaging predecessors of the darker ages, though with far other and more fatal arms, are overrunning civilized society. Those readers whose purer taste has been formed on the correct models of the old classic school, see with indignation and astonishment the Huns and Vandals once more overpowering the Greeks and Romans. They behold our minds, with a retrograde but rapid motion, hurried back to the reign of Chaos and old Night, by distorted and unprincipled compositions, which, in spite of strong flashes of genius, unite the taste of the Goths with the morals of Bagshot." "The newspapers announce that Schiller's tragedy of the 'Robbers,' which

ham Frere were prominent contributors. Coleridge and Southey are there spoken of in a way that makes one doubt whether poets are really as sensitive as they are sometimes said to be. The play called "The Rivals, or the Double Arrangement" (1798), is a most unjust although amusing parody of the German plays of the time, Goethe, Schiller, and Kotzebue being impartially derided. It was really not until time had shown the needlessness of the panic about Germany that the literature of that country again received anything like the attention it deserved. It was Carlyle who, more than any other one man, in his review articles now published in his Essays, directed the attention of the English people to what they had long neglected. These reviews appeared about 1830, contemporaneous with the similar work of Stapfer and Ampère in France, and since then German has been studied with ever-increasing vigor.

V. I have said that the excitement over the French Revolution had the effect of strengthening the national consciousness of the different countries of Europe, and the new literature aided this. Instead of a cosmopolitan literature which should spread over Europe like the fashion of wearing wigs, the discovery of the old ballads, of the early ante-classical plays and poems, brought before the

---

inflamed the young nobility of Germany to enlist themselves into a band of highwaymen to rob in the forests of Bohemia, is now acting in England by persons of quality."—" Strictures on the Modern System of Female Education," 1799.

The *Anti-Jacobin* was equally timorous, though with less excuse. Hannah More detested the *Anti-Jacobin;* *vide* letter in "Life," p. 169, in which she says, Sept. 11, 1800, "It is spreading more mischief over the land than almost any other book, because it is doing it under the mask of loyalty."

These views may be compared with the less timorous but equally inexact remarks of La Harpe in his notice of "Werther."

public very strongly the notion of national models and forgotten enthusiasms.*

The first effect, as well as the most lasting one, of the return to the past was a most inspiring one. Its most noteworthy representative was Burns. What a change we have here! And yet it is to be remembered that for a long time there had been fermenting the principles—so far as principles ferment—that influenced him. Throughout the eighteenth century there had been numberless song-writers in Scotland ; as Mr. Minto says, in his notice of the Scotch minor song-writers (Ward,"English Poets," iii. 486), "Peers, members of the Supreme Court of Law, diplomatists, lairds, clergymen, schoolmasters, men of science, farmers, gardeners, compositors, pedlers—all were trying their hands at patching old songs and making new songs." Allan Ramsay had made his collections, but Mr. Minto is right in saying that very little of real worth was produced by the writers of that school. The sources were poisoned by continual awe of the better-known literature of England, then in a most flourishing condition ; but, as this grew pompous and empty, the truer inspiration proved more powerful, and a large number of excellent Scotch songs were written in the last century, before the time of Burns. He was the final product of a long-continued tendency in one direction, and not a miraculous phenomenon. He had his roots deep in the past. There had been many versifiers mastering different measures, which reached Burns in a state of completeness; these men made a small but eager public familiar with countless references and

---

* One instance of the growth of national feeling at this time is the revival, in an artificial form, of the Highland dress. A somewhat similar perversion of patriotism that we see in Germany is the fervent respect which some writers show for the mediæval text. The Roman letters are regarded by them as effeminate foreign luxuries.

illusions; they introduced a number of subjects, which he, with his genius, was able to treat with greater beauty, giving them the final touch that makes poetry immortal.

We have Burns's own testimony that he busily studied the old ballads* and songs of Scotland, which had never died out of the familiar knowledge of the people. If he had not told us this, it might have been readily conjectured by observation of the metres of his poems, when he spoke, or, rather, sang words that tended to sweep away all the chill, didactic moralizing that had so long made up the body of English verse.

> "Through busiest street and loneliest glen
> Are felt the flashes of his pen;
> He rules 'mid winter snows, and when
> Bees fill their hives;
> Deep in the general heart of men
> His power survives."

Thus Wordsworth wrote in one of Burns's favorite measures, one, it may be said, that he found in common use among Scotch song-writers.† At another time Words-

---

* "In my infant and boyish days I owed much to an old woman who resided in the family, remarkable for her ignorance, credulity, and superstition. She had, I suppose, the largest collection in the country of tales and songs concerning devils, ghosts, fairies, brownies, witches, warlocks," etc. "The earliest composition that I recollect taking pleasure in was the 'Vision of Mirza,' Addison's hymn, 'How are thy servants blest, O Lord,' in Mason's 'Select Collection of English Songs.'" This may have been the book he refers to as "my *vade mecum*." "I pored over them driving my cart, or walking to labour, song by song, verse by verse; carefully noting the true, tender, or sublime from affectation and fustian" (letter to Dr. Moore, Aug. 2, 1787).

† *Vide* Watson's Collection, pt. i. p. 32, "The Life and Death of the Piper of Kilbarchan;" and "William Lithgow, Writer in Edinburgh, His Epitaph," pt. ii. p. 67:

worth, who was by no means lavish with praise of other poets, wrote of Burns :

> " Whose light I hailed when first it shone,
>   And showed my youth,
> How verse may build a princely throne
>   On humble truth."

The formal literature of Scotland before Burns was peculiarly stilted ; but the poet turned his back on that exaggerated artificiality, and went back to the people, whose influence began to be felt in literature and in politics as never before. Now was the time that we find fully stated one of the truths which it had been long learning from many teachers—namely, that man *qua* man is an object of interest and sympathy. In other words, what is a platitude in literature and conversation, and still a surprise to us when we became aware of it in life— the notion, that is, that all men are brothers—was by him plainly asserted ; asserted, we must remember, not discovered ; the century had done that. The great democratic truth to which we all bow with great civility, but seldom take home with us, so that possibly it may some day enter the house without invitation, was reached with great difficulty. We have seen its slow attainment in the history of fading literary tenets and of revolutionary conceptions of literary propriety, just as, possibly, the impending struggle in Europe between authority and freedom is foreshadowed in certain forms of more recent literature, as in realism, for instance.

> " His wife was also (as all are) Bad.
> She sold away all that he had,
> Which broke his heart and made it sad
>   And cold as lead ;
> Yet he was ay an honest Lad
>   But now he's Dead."

19

This notion of what is called the brotherhood of man—a phrase that is offensive to our ears from its being so much mouthed by demagogues—is not necessarily at variance with what we noticed of the growth of national feeling ; for that is but one step towards the comprehension of the higher truth. What formed the common basis of both movements, or, rather, made them practically one thing, was, first, the perception of an identity of interests, and so of emotions, and then, as a matter of course, sympathy quickly followed. It would be unwise to give all the credit of this to literature, for literature, while it teaches, is but the expression of opinions already formed. Doubtless, widening commerce did much towards opening the way for a change, but literature aided the great movement. The infinitely reasonable being who, for instance, fired his imagination with Akenside's description of its pleasures, was far removed from wide interests or from general sympathy with mankind. That was growing up in out-of-the-way corners, not in the great highway which was adorned with the stuccoed monuments that are now crumbling. In those the Reason was worshipped ; the adoration of the emotions had a touch of heresy about it. Reason was the state church ; only dissenters worshipped the emotions.*

We have already seen numerous instances of this extension of sympathy, and other evidence is readily to be had, and notably in Thomson. Thus, in his "Summer" (l. 961 et seq.) :

---

* It would be extremely interesting, if space permitted, to point out how Methodism, which arose simultaneously with the great romantic movement—*i. e.*, the revival of emotional feeling—was the religious expression of the same general movement. Ritualism would then be another development of romanticism.

"Breathed hot
From all the boundless furnace of the sky
And the wide glittering waste of burning sand,
A suffocating Wind the pilgrim smites
With instant death.   Patient of thirst and toil,
Son of the desert, e'en the camel feels,
Shot through his withered heart, the fiery blast.
Or from the black-red ether, bursting broad,
Sallies the sudden Whirlwind.   Straight the sands,
Commoved around, in gathering eddies play;
Nearer and nearer still they darkening come;
Till, with the general all-involving storm
Swept up, the whole continuous Wilds arise;
And by their noon-day fount dejected thrown,
Or sunk at night in sad disastrous sleep,
Beneath descending hills, the Caravan .
Is buried deep.   In Cairo's crowded streets
The impatient merchant, wondering, waits in vain.
And Mecca saddens at the long delay."

This passage shows us how commerce was widening the interests of the English ; and the interest in the poor is indicated by these lines ("Winter," l. 322 et seq.):

"Ah! little think the gay licentious Proud,
Whom pleasure, power, and affluence surround ;
They who their thoughtless hours in giddy mirth,
And wanton, often cruel, riot waste ;
Ah! little think they, while they dance along,
How many feel, this very moment, Death,
And all the sad variety of pain.
        *   *   *   *   *
        "How many bleed,
By shameful variance betwixt man and man.
How many pine in Want, and dungeon-glooms ;
Shut from the common air and common use
Of their own limbs.   How many drink the cup
Of baleful grief, or eat the bitter bread
Of Misery.   Sore pierced by wintry winds,

> How many shrink into the sordid but
> Of cheerless poverty.
>
> *   *   *   *   *
>
> And how can I forget the generous band,
> Who, touched with human woe, redressive searched
> Into the horrors of the gloomy jail—
> Unpitied and unheard, when Misery moans ;
> When Sickness pines ; when Thirst and Hunger burns,
> And poor Misfortune feels the lash of Vice ?"

In the same book he describes the shepherd dying in the snow ; the descent of the wolves,

> " By wintry famine roused, from all the tract
> Of horrid mountains which the shining Alps,
> And wavy Apennines and Pyrenees,
> Branch out stupendous into distant lands ;"

the Grisons, overwhelmed with avalanches (l. 414, etc.); and (l. 800, etc.) the Russian exile. Although the descriptions are too often academic and marked by the false Arcadianism of the time, they were all new appearances in English literature, and what Thomson stated with a good deal of rhetorical flourish was also uttered in their own way by other poets. Shenstone's "Schoolmistress," which Shenstone tried to save from criticism by pretending that he meant the poem for a caricature, Goldsmith's "Deserted Village," and Gray's "Elegy" deal with the condition of the poor. And the ballads which began to be written at about the same time naturally took hold of new and simpler subjects, which were simply treated.

It may be justly urged that some of these poets were more concerned for the picturesqueness of what they described than animated by any great zeal for the welfare of their kind, but that does not affect their claims to be the first discoverers of this new and fertile region; and, moreover, it is only a proof that they were better writers than philanthropists; and the world requires, before all things, of poets that they should be able to put well whatever they may have to say. Nothing is ever put as well as it can be until it is expressed by some one who is mastered by an overwhelming need to utter that above all things in the world. Such a person is more likely to take the current forms of his day, and say his say in them. New models are often chosen by men whose first desire is for novelty.

If Thomson was cold, and possibly indifferent, the accusation cannot be brought against Cowper, the English fellow-worker with Burns. He, to be sure, did not spring from the soil like the Scotch singer; he was rather the product of a combination of literary culture and delicate susceptibility to nature and simplicity. One main difference between him and his contemporaries, to which Hettner calls attention, is this—that, while they copied other poets, he copied nature. They drew their inspiration from Milton, or Spenser, or Pope; he drew his from the simple life he led and the things he saw about him. He was the first of the modern English poets to describe nature directly, as he saw it, instead of doing it by culling adjectives and phrases from others' books.

I will not quote corroboratory passages; waning space forbids this; but I will refer the reader to the descriptions in the "Winter Morning Walk," the "Garden," the "Winter Evening," and the "Timepiece," for examples. Cowper's poetry will not win hosts of admirers; no societies will be formed for the purpose of reading papers on his verses and expounding his meaning; but the reader who may be interested in other things than the pomp and clatter of contemporary poetry will be rewarded by occasional tender, simple passages. He will detect many attractive qualities in the poems, but he is tolerably sure not to be swept off his feet by enthusiasm. This is generally the fate of a reformer, of the first man who writes under a new impulse. He is like the guide-post where roads divide ; he points the way which others are able to make more attractive, and is soon forgotten. We overlook Cowper's simple record of nature while we are under the influence of Wordsworth's mightier verse, and we grow impatient of his philosophy when we see how much further later poets carried the notion of the brotherhood of man which he was one of the first authoritatively to utter.

Cowper's poems appeared in 1782 and 1783. Ten years later Wordsworth gave the world his "Evening Walk" and "Descriptive Sketches," in which we find much more distinctly the traces of the eighteenth century than any indications of what was to make the nineteenth memorable. Wordsworth had not yet caught up with his own time. He was still in leading-strings,* and these poems abound with reminiscences of Goldsmith's sonorous lines. Even such men as Michael Bruce (1746–67) and John Logan (1748–88), though evidently the product of their own day, had their faces more directly turned towards the day that was dawning. Wordsworth was doubtless rendered harsh in his judgment of the eighteenth century by the recollection of some of the unprofitable enthusiasms of his youth, which inspired such lines as these, which echo Goldsmith and Thomson :

> "To hear the roar
> That stuns the tremulous cliffs of high Lodore;"

and these :

> "Fair scenes, erewhile, I taught, a happy child,
> The echo of your rocks my carol wild;

---

* *Vide* Mr. J. R. Lowell's article on Wordsworth in "Among my Books," 2d series.

Then did no ebb of cheerfulness demand
Sad tides of joy from melancholy's hand.
In youth's wild eye the livelong day was bright,
The sun at morning, and the stars at night,
Alike when first the vales the bittern fills,
Or the first woodcocks roamed the hills.
In thoughtless gaiety I coursed the plain,
And hope itself was all I knew of pain ;
For then, e'en then the little heart would beat
At times while young Content forsook her seat,
And wild Impatience, pointing upward, showed,
Where, tipped with gold, the mountain summits glowed."

In such lines as these we are back in the calm of the
eighteenth century :

"Even here Content has fixed her smiling reign
With Independence, child of high Disdain."

"Plunge with the Russ embrown'd by Terror's breath."

"Bare steeps, where Desolation stalks, afraid."

Yet before the century had reached its end by the almanac, he was speaking with his own voice, for the "Lyrical Ballads" were published in 1798. The discussion of
that book, however, falls outside of our present limits.
In them there spoke the spirit of a new age, which the
greater part of the previous hundred years had been preparing ; for the centuries, like the magazines, always appear in advance of their date.

VI. It is sometimes urged against this way of regarding literature, that it tends to lower our admiration of
genius by showing that this lacks what we may call its
dæmonic quality, and is itself subject to the control of
law. It is demanded of us that we regard genius as something absolutely inexplicable, as a miraculous quality that
occasionally flashes over the amazed world as a comet
does over the midnight sky, more brilliant than the mo-

notonous stars and apparently following its own free will. Yet, while the genesis of comets is obscure, their paths are all marked out beforehand; and from them they cannot swerve save in obedience to law. Genius is no less wonderful for being modified by circumstances; only when these are favorable does it attain its highest development. A man must have hearers before he will say his best. When we are talking to ourselves we speak below our breath; only when we are addressing some one else do we use our full voice. The man who is sure of an audience derives from that feeling the delight that a speaker knows when he stands before an eager multitude. Without that he is dumb. Doubtless the orations that Demosthenes uttered on the sea-shore were inferior to those with which he fired the Athenians against Philip. The man who bows to his time may waste his strength in uncongenial and inferior work, as did Addison when he ceased to be natural and wrote his " Cato." The writer who defies his time is fortunate if he is merely eccentric : it cannot be simply a coincidence that Collins and Blake, the most rarely poetical minds of the last century, were mad. Gray gave up trying to reach deaf ears, and consoled himself with study.

Yet the opposition to regarding the laws by which genius is limited lies deep. We cannot bear to think that the intellect is subject to law, like the dull stone. We cannot endure the thought that while our bodies are limited in power, as in size, our minds are not superior to restraints and shackles; yet all history goes to show the existence of the control of the mind by heredity and circumstances, whether these inspire assent or contradiction. In time, doubtless, the extent of these influences will be settled with greater definiteness than is now possible when even their existence is widely doubted.

Genius is no less dæmonic than it ever was. Science does not destroy the inexplicable—it merely pushes it back a little; it widens the horizon, but it cannot widen it infinitely. We discover some of the things that control genius, but not its whole secret. We see that great writers are distinguished from madmen by the coherence of what they say with what has been said before. This they may contradict, but yet their words are inspired by it. Briefly, literature is a vast conversation; it strays over a large number of subjects, discussing, affirming or denying, pointing out an unsuspected application or an unanswerable argument, always affected by what has gone before, just as in talk a witticism, a profound or pathetic remark springs from something already said or done. This fact, that there is no parthenogenesis in intellectual life, should not be looked upon as degrading the man who utters the witty, profound, or pathetic remark, for it certainly does not.

In the fine arts we see the same laws. We discover the beginning of painting, we trace its early growth in Italy, and its swift rise. We see the influence of a master on his pupil, as of Perugino on Raphael. We notice its decay, as in the artificial painting of the last century, the sentimental painting coinciding with the sentimental novel and play, and pre-Raphaelitism in this century contemporaneous with the neo-romantic movement and realism nowadays in pictures and novels. Yet we do not feel that we are unjust to painters when we point out their dependence on their predecessors and contemporaries, either by way of agreement or divergence; to some, however, this way of looking at writers savors of irreverence.

One main reason of this is doubtless the feeling—derived, with some justification, from the time when literature was the artificial creation of scholars—that literature is something apart from human life. The divergence, if it exists, is fatal to literature, which is nothing but the utterance of the human race on the subjects that attract its attention. Every generation comes face to face with the old problems of life, with grief, joy, death, as well as with the new ones that every century brings ; and it says its say, it puts on record what impresses it, what fills its thoughts, what it hopes, and what it fears, and whether it prefers to stand up against fate or to yield without a struggle, whether to do its duty or to hide its face in the sand. This utterance is what is called literature, just as art is an expression of the same emotions by other means.

Looked at in this way, the study of literature becomes something more than a means of gratifying æsthetic tastes ; it throws light on history, which records men's actions ; indeed, it becomes a part of history.

INDEX.

THE END.

PUBLIC & PRIVATE LIBRARIES,

PUBLISHED BY HARPER & BROTHERS, NEW YORK.

☞ *For a full List of Books suitable for Libraries published by* HARPER & BROTHERS, *see* HARPER'S CATALOGUE, *which may be had gratuitously on application to the publishers personally, or by letter enclosing Nine Cents in Postage stamps.*

☞ HARPER & BROTHERS *will send their publications by mail, postage prepaid, on receipt of the price.*

MACAULAY'S ENGLAND. The History of England from the Accession of James II. By THOMAS BABINGTON MACAULAY. New Edition, from new Electrotype Plates. 8vo, Cloth, with Paper Labels, Uncut Edges and Gilt Tops, 5 vols. in a Box, $10 00 per set. Sold only in Sets. Cheap Edition, 5 vols. in a Box, 12mo, Cloth, $2 50; Sheep, $3 75.

MACAULAY'S MISCELLANEOUS WORKS. The Miscellaneous Works of Lord Macaulay. From New Electrotype Plates. In Five Volumes. 8vo, Cloth, with Paper Labels, Uncut Edges and Gilt Tops, in a Box, $10 00. Sold only in Sets.

HUME'S ENGLAND. The History of England, from the Invasion of Julius Cæsar to the Abdication of James II., 1688. By DAVID HUME. New and Elegant Library Edition, from new Electrotype Plates. 6 vols. in a Box, 8vo, Cloth, with Paper Labels, Uncut Edges and Gilt Tops, $12 00. Sold only in Sets. Popular Edition, 6 vols. in a Box, 12mo, Cloth, $3 00; Sheep, $4 50.

GIBBON'S ROME. The History of the Decline and Fall of the Roman Empire. By EDWARD GIBBON. With Notes by Dean MILMAN, M. GUIZOT, and Dr. WILLIAM SMITH. New Edition, from new Electrotype Plates. 6 vols., 8vo, Cloth, with Paper Labels, Uncut Edges and Gilt Tops, $12 00. Sold only in Sets. Popular Edition, 6 vols. in a Box, 12mo, Cloth, $3 00; Sheep, $4 50.

GEDDES'S JOHN DE WITT. History of the Administration of John De Witt, Grand Pensionary of Holland. By JAMES GEDDES. Vol. I.—1623–1654. With a Portrait. 8vo, Cloth, $2 50.

HILDRETH'S UNITED STATES. History of the United States. FIRST SERIES: From the Discovery of the Continent to the Organization of the Government under the Federal Constitution. SECOND SERIES: From the Adoption of the Federal Constitution to the End of the Sixteenth Congress. By RICHARD HILDRETH. Popular Edition, 6 vols. in a Box, 8vo, Cloth, with Paper Labels, Uncut Edges and Gilt Tops, $12 00. Sold only in Sets.

MOTLEY'S DUTCH REPUBLIC. The Rise of the Dutch Republic. A History. By JOHN LOTHROP MOTLEY, LL.D., D.C.L. With a Portrait of William of Orange. Cheap Edition, 3 vols. in a Box, 8vo, Cloth, with Paper Labels, Uncut Edges and Gilt Tops, $6 00. Sold only in Sets. Original Library Edition, 3 vols., 8vo, Cloth, $10 50; Sheep, $12 00; Half Calf, $17 25.

MOTLEY'S UNITED NETHERLANDS. History of the United Netherlands: from the Death of William the Silent to the Twelve Years' Truce—1584–1609. With a full View of the English-Dutch Struggle against Spain, and of the Origin and Destruction of the Spanish Armada. By JOHN LOTHROP MOTLEY, LL.D., D.C.L. Portraits. Cheap Edition, 4 vols. in a Box, 8vo, Cloth, with Paper Labels, Uncut Edges and Gilt Tops, $8 00. Sold only in Sets. Original Library Edition, 4 volumes, 8vo, Cloth, $14 00; Sheep, $16 00; Half Calf, $23 00.

MOTLEY'S JOHN OF BARNEVELD. The Life and Death of John of Barneveld, Advocate of Holland: with a View of the Primary Causes and Movements of "The Thirty Years' War." By JOHN LOTHROP MOTLEY, LL.D., D.C.L. Illustrated. Cheap Edition, 2 vols. in a Box, 8vo, Cloth, with Paper Labels, Uncut Edges and Gilt Tops, $4 00. Sold only in Sets. Original Library Edition, 2 vols., 8vo, Cloth, $7 00; Sheep, $8 00; Half Calf, $11 50.

GOLDSMITH'S WORKS. The Works of Oliver Goldsmith. Edited by PETER CUNNINGHAM, F.S.A. From new Electrotype Plates. 4 vols., 8vo, Cloth, Paper Labels, Uncut Edges and Gilt Tops, $8 00. Uniform with the New Library Editions of Macaulay, Hume, Gibbon, Motley, and Hildreth.

HUDSON'S HISTORY OF JOURNALISM. Journalism in the United States, from 1690 to 1872. By FREDERIC HUDSON. 8vo, Cloth, $5 00; Half Calf, $7 25.

SYMONDS'S SKETCHES AND STUDIES IN SOUTHERN EUROPE. By JOHN ADDINGTON SYMONDS. In Two Volumes. Post 8vo, Cloth, $4 00.

SYMONDS'S GREEK POETS. Studies of the Greek Poets. By JOHN ADDINGTON SYMONDS. 2 vols., Square 16mo, Cloth, $3 50.

TREVELYAN'S LIFE OF MACAULAY. The Life and Letters of Lord Macaulay. By his Nephew, G. OTTO TREVELYAN, M.P. With Portrait on Steel. Complete in 2 vols., 8vo, Cloth, Uncut Edges and Gilt Tops, $5 00; Sheep, $6 00; Half Calf, $9 50. Popular Edition, two vols. in one, 12mo, Cloth, $1 75.

TREVELYAN'S LIFE OF FOX. The Early History of Charles James Fox. By GEORGE OTTO TREVELYAN. 8vo, Cloth, Uncut Edges and Gilt Tops, $2 50; 4to, Paper, 20 cents.

MÜLLER'S POLITICAL HISTORY OF RECENT TIMES. Political History of Recent Times (1816–1875). With Special Reference to Germany. By WILLIAM MÜLLER. Revised and Enlarged by the Author. Translated, with an Appendix covering the Period from 1876 to 1881, by the Rev. JOHN P. PETERS, Ph.D. 12mo, Cloth, $3 00.

LOSSING'S CYCLOPÆDIA OF UNITED STATES HISTORY. Popular Cyclopædia of United States History. From the Aboriginal Period to 1876. By B. J. LOSSING, LL.D. Illustrated by 2 Steel Portraits and over 1000 Engravings. 2 vols., Royal 8vo, Cloth, $12 00. (*Sold by Subscription only.*)

LOSSING'S FIELD-BOOK OF THE REVOLUTION. Pictorial Field-Book of the Revolution; or, Illustrations by Pen and Pencil of the History, Biography, Scenery, Relics, and Traditions of the War for Independence. By BENSON J. LOSSING. 2 vols., 8vo, Cloth, $14 00; Sheep or Roan, $15 00; Half Calf, $18 00.

LOSSING'S FIELD-BOOK OF THE WAR OF 1812. Pictorial Field-Book of the War of 1812; or, Illustrations by Pen and Pencil of the History, Biography, Scenery, Relics, and Traditions of the last War for American Independence. By BENSON J. LOSSING. With several hundred Engravings on Wood by Lossing and Barritt, chiefly from Original Sketches by the Author. 1088 pages, 8vo, Cloth, $7 00; Sheep, $8 50; Roan, $9 00; Half Calf, $10 00.

PARTON'S CARICATURE.   Caricature and Other Comic Art, in All Times and Many Lands. By JAMES PARTON. 203 Illustrations. 8vo, Cloth, Uncut Edges and Gilt Tops, $5 00; Half Calf, $7 25.

MAHAFFY'S GREEK LITERATURE.   A History of Classical Greek Literature. By J. P. MAHAFFY. 2 vols., 12mo, Cloth, $4 00; Half Calf, $7 50.

DU CHAILLU'S LAND OF THE MIDNIGHT SUN.   Summer and Winter Journeys in Sweden, Norway, and Lapland, and Northern Finland. By PAUL B. DU CHAILLU. Illustrated. 2 vols., 8vo, Cloth, $7 50.

DU CHAILLU'S EQUATORIAL AFRICA.   Explorations and Adventures in Equatorial Africa: with Accounts of the Manners and Customs of the People, and of the Chase of the Gorilla, Crocodile, Leopard, Elephant, Hippopotamus, and other Animals. By P. B. DU CHAILLU. Illustrated. 8vo, Cloth, $5 00; Sheep, $5 50; Half Calf, $7 25.

DU CHAILLU'S ASHANGO LAND.   A Journey to Ashango Land, and Further Penetration into Equatorial Africa. By P. B. DU CHAILLU. Illustrated. 8vo, Cloth, $5 00; Sheep, $5 50; Half Calf, $7 25.

DEXTER'S CONGREGATIONALISM.   The Congregationalism of the Last Three Hundred Years, as Seen in its Literature: with Special Reference to certain Recondite, Neglected, or Disputed Passages. With a Bibliographical Appendix. By H. M. DEXTER.   Large 8vo, Cloth, $6 00.

STANLEY'S THROUGH THE DARK CONTINENT.   Through the Dark Continent; or, The Sources of the Nile, Around the Great Lakes of Equatorial Africa, and Down the Livingstone River to the Atlantic Ocean. 149 Illustrations and 10 Maps. By H. M. STANLEY. 2 vols., 8vo, Cloth, $10 00; Sheep, $12 00; Half Morocco, $15 00.

BARTLETT'S FROM EGYPT TO PALESTINE.   From Egypt to Palestine: Through Sinai, the Wilderness, and the South Country. Observations of a Journey made with Special Reference to the History of the Israelites. By S. C. BARTLETT, D.D., LL.D. With Maps and Illustrations. 8vo, Cloth, $3 50.

FORSTER'S LIFE OF DEAN SWIFT. The Early Life of Jonathan Swift (1667–1711). By JOHN FORSTER. With Portrait. 8vo, Cloth, Uncut Edges and Gilt Tops, $2 50.

GREEN'S ENGLISH PEOPLE. History of the English People. By JOHN RICHARD GREEN, M.A. Four Volumes. 8vo, Cloth, $2 50 per volume.

GREEN'S MAKING OF ENGLAND. The Making of England. By J. R. GREEN, LL.D. 8vo, Cloth, $2 50.

SHORT'S NORTH AMERICANS OF ANTIQUITY. The North Americans of Antiquity. Their Origin, Migrations, and Type of Civilization Considered. By JOHN T. SHORT. Illustrated. 8vo, Cloth, $3 00.

SQUIER'S PERU. Peru: Incidents of Travel and Exploration in the Land of the Incas. By E. GEORGE SQUIER, M.A., F.S.A., late U. S. Commissioner to Peru. With Illustrations. 8vo, Cloth, $5 00.

BENJAMIN'S CONTEMPORARY ART. Contemporary Art in Europe. By S. G. W. BENJAMIN. Illustrated. 8vo, Cloth, $3 50.

BENJAMIN'S ART IN AMERICA. Art in America. By S. G. W. BENJAMIN. Illustrated. 8vo, Cloth, $4 00.

REBER'S HISTORY OF ANCIENT ART. History of Ancient Art. By Dr. FRANZ VON REBER. Revised by the Author. Translated and Augmented by Joseph Thacher Clarke. With 310 Illustrations and a Glossary of Technical Terms. 8vo, Cloth, $3 50.

ADAMS'S MANUAL OF HISTORICAL LITERATURE. A Manual of Historical Literature. Comprising Brief Descriptions of the Most Important Histories in English, French, and German. By Professor C. K. ADAMS. 8vo, Cloth, $2 50.

KINGLAKE'S CRIMEAN WAR. The Invasion of the Crimea: its Origin, and an Account of its Progress down to the Death of Lord Raglan. By ALEXANDER WILLIAM KINGLAKE. With Maps and Plans. Four Volumes now ready. 12mo, Cloth, $2 00 per vol.

MAURY'S PHYSICAL GEOGRAPHY OF THE SEA. The Physical Geography of the Sea, and its Meteorology. By M. F. MAURY, LL.D. 8vo, Cloth, $4 00.

ENGLISH MEN OF LETTERS. Edited by JOHN MORLEY. The following volumes are now ready. Others will follow : JOHNSON. By L. Stephen.—GIBBON. By J. C. Morison.— SCOTT. By R. H. Hutton.—SHELLEY. By J. A. Symonds.— GOLDSMITH. By W. Black.—HUME. By Professor Huxley. —DEFOE. By W. Minto.—BURNS. By Principal Shairp.— SPENSER. By R. W. Church. —THACKERAY. By A. Trollope.—BURKE. By J. Morley.—MILTON. By M. Pattison.— SOUTHEY. By E. Dowden. —CHAUCER. By A. W. Ward.— BUNYAN. By J. A. Froude.—COWPER. By G. Smith.—POPE. By L. Stephen. —BYRON. By J. Nichols. —LOCKE. By T. Fowler.—WORDSWORTH. By F. W. H. Myers.—HAWTHORNE. By Henry James, Jr.—DRYDEN. By G. Saintsbury.—LANDOR. By S. Colvin.—DE QUINCEY. By D. Masson.—LAMB. By A. Ainger.—BENTLEY. By R. C. Jebb.—DICKENS. By A. W. Ward.—GRAY. By E. W. Gosse.—SWIFT. By L. Stephen.— STERNE. By H. D. Traill. —MACAULAY. By J. C. Morison. 12mo, Cloth, 75 cents per volume.

HALLAM'S LITERATURE. Introduction to the Literature of Europe during the Fifteenth, Sixteenth, and Seventeenth Centuries. By HENRY HALLAM. 2 vols., 8vo, Cloth, $4 00; Sheep, $5 00.

HALLAM'S MIDDLE AGES. View of the State of Europe during the Middle Ages. By H. HALLAM. 8vo, Cloth, $2 00; Sheep, $2 50.

HALLAM'S CONSTITUTIONAL HISTORY OF ENGLAND. The Constitutional History of England, from the Accession of Henry VII. to the Death of George II. By HENRY HALLAM. 8vo, Cloth, $2 00; Sheep, $2 50.

NEWCOMB'S ASTRONOMY. Popular Astronomy. By SIMON NEWCOMB, LL.D. With One Hundred and Twelve Engravings, and five Maps of the Stars. 8vo, Cloth, $2 50: School Edition, 12mo, Cloth, $1 30.

PRIME'S POTTERY AND PORCELAIN. Pottery and Porcelain of All Times and Nations. With Tables of Factory and Artists' Marks, for the Use of Collectors. By WILLIAM C. PRIME, LL.D. Illustrated. 8vo, Cloth, Uncut Edges and Gilt Tops, $7 00; Half Calf, $9 25. (In a Box.)

LIVINGSTONE'S SOUTH AFRICA. Missionary Travels and Researches in South Africa: including a Sketch of Sixteen Years' Residence in the Interior of Africa, and a Journey from the Cape of Good Hope to Loanda, on the West Coast; thence across the Continent, down the River Zambesi, to the Eastern Ocean. By DAVID LIVINGSTONE, LL.D., D.C.L. With Portrait, Maps, and Illustrations. 8vo, Cloth, $4 50; Sheep, $5 00; Half Calf, $6 75.

LIVINGSTONE'S ZAMBESI. Narrative of an Expedition to the Zambesi and its Tributaries, and of the Discovery of the Lakes Shirwa and Nyassa, 1858–1864. By DAVID and CHARLES LIVINGSTONE. Illustrated. 8vo, Cloth, $5 00; Sheep, $5 50; Half Calf, $7 25.

LIVINGSTONE'S LAST JOURNALS. The Last Journals of David Livingstone, in Central Africa, from 1865 to his Death. Continued by a Narrative of his Last Moments and Sufferings, obtained from his Faithful Servants Chuma and Susi. By HORACE WALLER, F.R.G.S. With Portrait, Maps, and Illustrations. 8vo, Cloth, $5 00; Sheep, $5 50; Half Calf, $7 25. Cheap Popular Edition, 8vo, Cloth, with Map and Illustrations, $2 50.

BLAIKIE'S LIFE OF DAVID LIVINGSTONE. Dr. Livingstone: Memoir of his Personal Life, from his Unpublished Journals and Correspondence. By W. G. BLAIKIE, D.D., LL.D. With Portrait and Map. 8vo, Cloth, $2 25.

NORDHOFF'S COMMUNISTIC SOCIETIES OF THE UNITED STATES. The Communistic Societies of the United States, from Personal Visit and Observation; including Detailed Accounts of the Economists, Zoarites, Shakers, the Amana, Oneida, Bethel, Aurora, Icarian, and other existing Societies. With Particulars of their Religious Creeds and Practices, their Social Theories and Life, Numbers, Industries, and Present Condition. By CHARLES NORDHOFF. Illustrations. 8vo, Cloth, $4 00.

NORDHOFF'S CALIFORNIA. California: for Health, Pleasure, and Residence. A Book for Travellers and Settlers. New Edition, thoroughly revised. By CHARLES NORDHOFF. With Maps and Illustrations. 8vo, Cloth, $2 00.

GROTE'S HISTORY OF GREECE. 12 vols., 12mo, Cloth, $18 00; Sheep, $22 80; Half Calf, $39 00.

SHAKSPEARE. The Dramatic Works of Shakspeare. With Corrections and Notes. Engravings. 6 vols., 12mo, Cloth, $9 00.   2 vols., 8vo, Cloth, $4 00; Sheep, $5 00. In one vol., 8vo, Sheep, $4 00.

BAKER'S ISMAILÏA. Ismailïa: a Narrative of the Expedition to Central Africa for the Suppression of the Slave-trade, organized by Ismail, Khedive of Egypt. By Sir SAMUEL WHITE BAKER, Pasha, F.R.S., F.R.G.S. With Maps, Portraits, and Illustrations. 8vo, Cloth, $5 00; Half Calf, $7 25.

GRIFFIS'S JAPAN. The Mikado's Empire: Book I. History of Japan, from 660 B.C. to 1872 A.D. Book II. Personal Experiences, Observations, and Studies in Japan, 1870-1874. By W. E. GRIFFIS. Copiously Illustrated. 8vo, Cloth, $4 00.; Half Calf, $6 25.

SMILES'S HISTORY OF THE HUGUENOTS. The Huguenots: their Settlements, Churches, and Industries in England and Ireland. By SAMUEL SMILES. With an Appendix relating to the Huguenots in America. Crown 8vo, Cloth, $2 00.

SMILES'S HUGUENOTS AFTER THE REVOCATION. The Huguenots in France after the Revocation of the Edict of Nantes; with a Visit to the Country of the Vaudois. By SAMUEL SMILES. Crown 8vo, Cloth, $2 00.

SMILES'S LIFE OF THE STEPHENSONS. The Life of George Stephenson, and of his Son, Robert Stephenson; comprising, also, a History of the Invention and Introduction of the Railway Locomotive. By SAMUEL SMILES. Illustrated. 8vo, Cloth, $3 00.

RAWLINSON'S MANUAL OF ANCIENT HISTORY. A Manual of Ancient History, from the Earliest Times to the Fall of the Western Empire. Comprising the History of Chaldæa, Assyria, Media, Babylonia, Lydia, Phœnicia, Syria, Judæa, Egypt, Carthage, Persia, Greece, Macedonia, Parthia, and Rome. By GEORGE RAWLINSON, M.A. 12mo, Cloth, $1 25.

SCHWEINFURTH'S HEART OF AFRICA. The Heart of Africa. Three Years' Travels and Adventures in the Unexplored Regions of the Centre of Africa—from 1868 to 1871. By Dr. GEORG SCHWEINFURTH. Translated by ELLEN E. FREWER. With an Introduction by W. WINWOOD READE. Illustrated. 2 vols., 8vo, Cloth, $8 00.

SCHLIEMANN'S ILIOS.   Ilios, the City and Country of the
Trojans.   A Narrative of the Most Recent Discoveries and Researches made on the Plain of Troy.   By Dr. HENRY SCHLIE-
MANN.   Maps, Plans, and Illustrations.   Imperial 8vo, Illuminated Cloth, $12 00; Half Morocco, $15 00.

ALISON'S HISTORY OF EUROPE.   FIRST SERIES: From
the Commencement of the French Revolution, in 1789, to the
Restoration of the Bourbons in 1815.   [In addition to the
Notes on Chapter LXXVI., which correct the errors of the
original work concerning the United States, a copious Analyti-
cal Index has been appended to this American Edition.]   SEC-
OND SERIES: From the Fall of Napoleon, in 1815, to the Accession of Louis Napoleon, in 1852.   8 vols., 8vo, Cloth, $16 00;
Sheep, $20 00; Half Calf, $34 00.

NORTON'S STUDIES OF CHURCH-BUILDING.   Historical
Studies of Church-Building in the Middle Ages.   Venice,
Siena, Florence.   By CHARLES ELIOT NORTON.   8vo, Cloth,
$3 00.

BOSWELL'S JOHNSON.   The Life of Samuel Johnson, LL.D.,
including a Journal of a Tour to the Hebrides.   By JAMES
BOSWELL.   Edited by J. W. CROKER, LL.D., F.R.S.   With a
Portrait of Boswell.   2 vols., 8vo, Cloth, $4 00; Sheep, $5 00;
Half Calf, $8 50.

ADDISON'S COMPLETE WORKS.   The Works of Joseph
Addison, embracing the whole of the *Spectator*.   3 vols., 8vo,
Cloth, $6 00; Sheep, $7 50; Half Calf, $12 75.

OUTLINES OF ANCIENT HISTORY.   From the Earliest
Times to the Fall of the Western Roman Empire, A.D. 476.
Embracing the Egyptians, Chaldæans, Assyrians, Babylonians,
Hebrews, Phœnicians, Medes, Persians, Greeks, and Romans.
Designed for Private Reading and as a Manual of Instruction.
By P. V. N. MYERS, A.M., President of Farmers' College,
Ohio.   12mo, Cloth, $1 75.

JOHNSON'S COMPLETE WORKS.   The Works of Samuel
Johnson, LL.D.   With an Essay on his Life and Genius, by
A. MURPHY.   2 vols., 8vo, Cloth, $4 00; Sheep, $5 00; Half
Calf, $8 50.

THE VOYAGE OF THE "CHALLENGER." The Atlantic: an Account of the General Results of the Voyage during 1873, and the Early Part of 1876. By Sir WYVILLE THOMSON, K.C.B., F.R.S. Illustrated. 2 vols., 8vo, Cloth, $12 00.

BLUNT'S BEDOUIN TRIBES OF THE EUPHRATES. Bedouin Tribes of the Euphrates. By LADY ANNE BLUNT. Edited, with a Preface and some Account of the Arabs and their Horses, by W. S. B. Map and Sketches by the Author. 8vo, Cloth, $2 50.

BROUGHAM'S AUTOBIOGRAPHY. Life and Times of Henry, Lord Brougham. Written by Himself. 3 vols., 12mo, Cloth, $6 00.

THOMPSON'S PAPACY AND THE CIVIL POWER. The Papacy and the Civil Power. By the Hon. R. W. THOMPSON. Crown 8vo, Cloth, $3 00.

ENGLISH CORRESPONDENCE. Four Centuries of English Letters. Selections from the Correspondence of One Hundred and Fifty Writers from the Period of the Paston Letters to the Present Day. Edited by W. BAPTISTE SCOONES. 12mo, Cloth, $2 00.

THE POETS AND POETRY OF SCOTLAND: From the Earliest to the Present Time. Comprising Characteristic Selections from the Works of the more Noteworthy Scottish Poets, with Biographical and Critical Notices. By JAMES GRANT WILSON. With Portraits on Steel. 2 vols., 8vo, Cloth, $10 00; Sheep, $12 00; Half Calf, $14 50; Full Morocco, $18 00.

THE STUDENT'S SERIES. Maps and Illustrations, 12mo, Cloth.

FRANCE.—GIBBON.—GREECE.—ROME (by LIDDELL).—OLD TESTAMENT HISTORY.—NEW TESTAMENT HISTORY.—STRICKLAND'S QUEENS OF ENGLAND (Abridged).—ANCIENT HISTORY OF THE EAST.—HALLAM'S MIDDLE AGES.—HALLAM'S CONSTITUTIONAL HISTORY OF ENGLAND. — LYELL'S ELEMENTS OF GEOLOGY. — MERIVALE'S GENERAL HISTORY OF ROME.—COX'S GENERAL HISTORY OF GREECE.—CLASSICAL DICTIONARY. $1 25 per volume.

LEWIS'S HISTORY OF GERMANY. — ECCLESIASTICAL HISTORY.—HUME'S ENGLAND. $1 50 per volume.

BOURNE'S LOCKE. The Life of John Locke. By H. R. Fox Bourne. 2 vols., 8vo, Cloth, Uncut Edges and Gilt Tops, $5 00.

SKEAT'S ETYMOLOGICAL DICTIONARY. A Concise Etymological Dictionary of the English Language. By the Rev. Walter W. Skeats, M.A. 12mo, Cloth, $1 25. *Uniform with " The Student's Series."*

DARWIN'S VOYAGE OF A NATURALIST. Voyage of a Naturalist. Journal of Researches into the Natural History and Geology of the Countries Visited during the Voyage of H.M.S. *Beagle* round the World. By Charles Darwin. 2 vols., 12mo, Cloth, $2 00.

CAMERON'S ACROSS AFRICA. Across Africa. By Verney Lovett Cameron. Map and Illustrations. 8vo, Cloth, $5 00.

BARTH'S NORTH AND CENTRAL AFRICA. Travels and Discoveries in North and Central Africa: being a Journal of an Expedition undertaken under the Auspices of H.B.M.'s Government, in the Years 1849–1855. By Henry Barth, Ph.D., D.C.L. Illustrated. 3 vols., 8vo, Cloth, $12 00 ; Sheep, $13 50 ; Half Calf, $18 75.

THOMSON'S SOUTHERN PALESTINE AND JERUSALEM. Southern Palestine and Jerusalem. Biblical Illustrations drawn from the Manners and Customs, the Scenes and Scenery, of the Holy Land. By W. M. Thomson, D.D. 140 Illustrations and Maps. Square 8vo, Cloth, $6 00 ; Sheep, $7 00 ; Half Morocco, $8 50 ; Full Morocco, Gilt Edges, $10 00.

THOMSON'S CENTRAL PALESTINE AND PHŒNICIA. Central Palestine and Phœnicia. Biblical Illustrations drawn from the Manners and Customs, the Scenes and Scenery, of the Holy Land. By W. M. Thomson, D.D. 130 Illustrations and Maps. 8vo, Cloth, $6 00 ; Sheep, $7 00 ; Half Morocco, $8 50.

CYCLOPÆDIA OF BRITISH AND AMERICAN POETRY. Edited by Epes Sargent. Royal 8vo, Illuminated Cloth, Colored Edges, $4 50.

NICHOLS'S ART EDUCATION. Art Education applied to Industry. By G. W. Nichols. Illustrated. 8vo, Cloth, $4 00 ; Half Calf, $6 25.

CARLYLE'S FREDERICK THE GREAT. History of Friedrich II., called Frederick the Great. By THOMAS CARLYLE. Portraits, Maps, Plans, etc. 6 vols., 12mo, Cloth, $7 50; Sheep, $9 90; Half Calf, $18 00.

CARLYLE'S FRENCH REVOLUTION. The French Revolution: a History. By THOMAS CARLYLE. 2 vols., 12mo, Cloth, $2 50; Sheep, $3 30; Half Calf, $6 00.

CARLYLE'S OLIVER CROMWELL. Oliver Cromwell's Letters and Speeches, including the Supplement to the First Edition. With Elucidations. By THOMAS CARLYLE. 2 vols., 12mo, Cloth, $2 50; Sheep, $3 30; Half Calf, $6 00.

BULWER'S HORACE. The Odes and Epodes of Horace. A Metrical Translation into English. With Introduction and Commentaries. By LORD LYTTON. With Latin Text from the Editions of Orelli, Macleane, and Yonge. 12mo, Cloth, $1 75.

BULWER'S KING ARTHUR. King Arthur. A Poem. By LORD LYTTON. 12mo, Cloth, $1 75.

BULWER'S MISCELLANEOUS PROSE WORKS. The Miscellaneous Prose Works of Lord Lytton. 2 vols., 12mo, Cloth, $3 50. Also, in uniform style, *Caxtoniana.* 12mo, Cloth, $1 75.

EATON'S CIVIL SERVICE. Civil Service in Great Britain. A History of Abuses and Reforms, and their Bearing upon American Politics. By DORMAN B. EATON. 8vo, Cloth, $2 50.

DAVIS'S CARTHAGE. Carthage and her Remains : being an Account of the Excavations and Researches on the Site of the Phœnician Metropolis in Africa and other Adjacent Places. By Dr. N. DAVIS. Illustrated. 8vo, Cloth, $4 00; Half Calf, $6 25.

TROLLOPE'S CICERO. Life of Cicero. By ANTHONY TROLLOPE. 2 vols., 12mo, Cloth, $3 00.

PERRY'S HISTORY OF THE CHURCH OF ENGLAND. A History of the English Church, from the Accession of Henry VIII. to the Silencing of Convocation. By G. G. PERRY, M.A. With a Sketch of the History of the Protestant Episcopal Church in the United States, by J. A. SPENCER, S.T.D. Crown 8vo, Cloth, $2 50.

ABBOTT'S HISTORY OF THE FRENCH REVOLUTION.
The French Revolution of 1789, as Viewed in the Light of
Republican Institutions. By JOHN S. C. ABBOTT. Illustrated.
8vo, Cloth, $5 00; Sheep, $5 50; Half Calf, $7 25.

ABBOTT'S NAPOLEON. The History of Napoleon Bonaparte.
By JOHN S. C. ABBOTT. Maps, Illustrations, and Portraits. 2
vols., 8vo, Cloth, $10 00; Sheep, $11 00; Half Calf, $14 50.

ABBOTT'S NAPOLEON AT ST. HELENA. Napoleon at St.
Helena; or, Anecdotes and Conversations of the Emperor during the Years of his Captivity. Collected from the Memorials
of Las Casas, O'Meara, Montholon, Antommarchi, and others.
By J. S. C. ABBOTT. Illustrated. 8vo, Cloth, $5 00; Sheep,
$5 50; Half Calf, $7 25.

ABBOTT'S FREDERICK THE GREAT. The History of Frederick the Second, called Frederick the Great. By JOHN S. C.
ABBOTT. Illustrated. 8vo, Cloth, $5 00; Half Calf, $7 25.

DRAPER'S CIVIL WAR. History of the American Civil War.
By JOHN W. DRAPER, M.D., LL.D. 3 vols., 8vo, Cloth, Bev-
elled Edges, $10 50; Sheep, $12 00; Half Calf, $17 25.

**DRAPER'S INTELLECTUAL DEVELOPMENT OF EU-
ROPE.** A History of the Intellectual Development of Europe.
By JOHN W. DRAPER, M.D., LL.D. New Edition, Revised. 2
vols., 12mo, Cloth, $3 00; Half Calf, $6 50.

DRAPER'S AMERICAN CIVIL POLICY. Thoughts on the
Future Civil Policy of America. By JOHN W. DRAPER, M.D.,
LL.D. Crown 8vo, Cloth, $2 00; Half Morocco, $3 75.

McCARTHY'S HISTORY OF ENGLAND. A History of Our
Own Times, from the Accession of Queen Victoria to the Gen-
eral Election of 1880. By JUSTIN McCARTHY. 2 vols., 12mo,
Cloth, $2 50.

ABBOTT'S DICTIONARY OF RELIGIOUS KNOWLEDGE.
A Dictionary of Religious Knowledge, for Popular and Professional Use; comprising full Information on Biblical, Theological, and Ecclesiastical Subjects. With nearly 1000 Maps and
Illustrations. Edited by LYMAN ABBOTT, with the Co-operation
of T. J. CONANT, D.D. Royal 8vo, Cloth, $6 00; Sheep, $7 00;
Half Morocco, $8 50.

M'CLINTOCK & STRONG'S CYCLOPÆDIA. Cyclopædia of Biblical, Theological, and Ecclesiastical Literature. Prepared by the Rev. JOHN M'CLINTOCK, D.D., and JAMES STRONG, S.T.D. Complete in 10 vols. Royal 8vo. Price per vol., Cloth, $5 00; Sheep, $6 00; Half Morocco, $8 00. (*Sold by Subscription only.*)

MOHAMMED AND MOHAMMEDANISM: Lectures Delivered at the Royal Institution of Great Britain in February and March, 1874. By R. BOSWORTH SMITH, M.A. With an Appendix containing Emanuel Deutsch's Article on "Islam." 12mo, Cloth, $1 50.

MOSHEIM'S ECCLESIASTICAL HISTORY, Ancient and Modern; in which the Rise, Progress, and Variation of Church Power are Considered in their Connection with the State of Learning and Philosophy, and the Political History of Europe during that Period. Translated, with Notes, etc., by A. MACLAINE, D.D. Continued to 1826, by C. COOTE, LL.D. 2 vols., 8vo, Cloth, $4 00; Sheep, $5 00.

HARPER'S NEW CLASSICAL LIBRARY. Literal Translations.
The following volumes are ready. 12mo, Cloth, $1 00 each: CÆSAR.—VIRGIL.—SALLUST.—HORACE.—CICERO'S ORATIONS. —CICERO'S OFFICES, etc.—CICERO ON ORATORY AND ORATORS.—TACITUS (2 vols.).—TERENCE.—SOPHOCLES.—JUVENAL.—XENOPHON.—HOMER'S ILIAD.—HOMER'S ODYSSEY. —HERODOTUS.—DEMOSTHENES (2 vols.).—THUCYDIDES.— ÆSCHYLUS.—EURIPIDES (2 vols.).—LIVY (2 vols.).—PLATO [Select Dialogues].

VINCENT'S LAND OF THE WHITE ELEPHANT. The Land of the White Elephant: Travels, Adventures, and Discoveries in Burma, Siam, Cambodia, and Cochin-China. By FRANK VINCENT, Jr. Illustrated. Third Edition. Crown 8vo, Cloth, $3 50.

RECLUS'S EARTH. The Earth: a Descriptive History of the Phenomena of the Life of the Globe. By ÉLISÉE RECLUS. Profusely Illustrated. 8vo, Cloth, $5 00.

RECLUS'S OCEAN. The Ocean, Atmosphere, and Life. Being the Second Series of a Descriptive History of the Life of the Globe. By ÉLISÉE RECLUS. Profusely Illustrated. 8vo, Cloth, $6 00.

www.ingramcontent.com/pod-product-compliance
Lightning Source LLC
Chambersburg PA
CBHW052339110726
47901CB00005B/1287